# CONFESSION

# NANCY PICKARD

# *CONFESSION*

*A Jenny Cain Mystery*

**POCKET BOOKS**

New York   London   Toronto   Sydney   Tokyo   Singapore

POCKET BOOKS, a division of Simon & Schuster Inc.
1230 Avenue of the Americas, New York, NY 10020

Library of Congress Cataloging-in-Publication Number: 93-87794

ISBN: 0-671-78261-4

First Pocket Books hardcover printing August 1994

10  9  8  7  6  5  4  3  2  1

POCKET and colophon are registered trademarks of
Simon & Schuster Inc.

Printed in the U.S.A.

This novel is dedicated to Meredith Bernstein, my agent and friend from the first word.

I confess my heartfelt appreciation to Loretta Loftus, M.D., and to my "readers," including Sally, Janice, Julie, Trish, Carolyn, and Kay. I confess to being passionately grateful to my editor, Linda Marrow; to my son for being so understanding about life with a writer-mom; and to Richard.

# CONFESSION

# 1

I STILL HAVE FANTASIES ABOUT THE DAY WHEN FATE came riding up to our house like "The Highwayman" in the old poem: *"Riding, riding, riding, up to the old inn door . . ."*

Only in this case, on this particular Sunday in that specific August, it wasn't an inn that he came riding up to, and he wasn't a man yet, and I wasn't an innkeeper's black-haired daughter. It was our home, and he was just a boy, and I was a policeman's wife.

Even so, the refrain is inescapable: *". . . the highwayman came riding . . ."*

In some of my fantasies of that day I get a chance to cheat fate: I get to spy fate as it speeds down the highway toward us as determinedly as a meteor slamming toward earth. I get time to glimpse it in the dayscape, to puzzle, half amused, only half paying attention—"What can this unexpected, rapid, unfamiliar phenomenon be?"—and then to register both thrill and horror as I slowly recognize it as something aberrant from another space and time. I get time to react melodramatically with alarm, to widen my eyes and to gasp, to drop everything and to run and slam the door in fate's face, and to yell, "No, you can't come in!" As if I could stop a meteor from falling or deflect it from its path; a million people meditating all at once could do it, maybe, or one really effective yogi, but not me, not on that day, not with all I didn't know then. It unnerves and intrigues me, this particular fantasy does, because it suggests that maybe I still don't understand the far-reaching eon-changing power and consequence of meteors—those dinosaur-killing, fate-dealing messengers of absolute change. It hints that I wish that my husband and I could go back to the time before everything shape-shifted, an ignoble wish.

And we can't; it was already too late for that, many years ago.

In the fantasies, I see myself as I was that day, watering houseplants. Tending. Mothering. (Everything in this word is, I'm convinced, symbolic, a lot of it's ironic, but not everything is real, and that's the saving grace.) Caring. Feeling happy and light-hearted in my serious way. Absorbed in not looking up to notice what's going on around me, which doesn't at all keep it from happening. The heat of late-afternoon summer sunshine is pouring in the west windows of our cabin/home because we hate to turn on the air-conditioning until the temperature gets unbearable; we're always trying to convince ourselves that we feel a cool watery breeze off the Atlantic Ocean, which is only a few hundred yards away, down a steep and rocky hillside to the east of our front door. From that door, a gravel drive circles out into a dirt road that winds through a tunnel of tall, old overgrown evergreen and locust trees to the state highway, which in turn leads to a short stretch of interstate, which quickly cuts back toward the ocean and then toward our hometown, which is Port Frederick, Mass.

So it's hot in the house in my fantasies and as it really was that day. I'm moving slowly, languidly, like a goldfish swimming at the surface of a warm pool. Like the fish, I feel gold all over, in the sunlight, yellow hair, summer tan, yellow shorts. I feel molten, melted, lazy, I feel like lying down and taking a nap and then waking up and making warm slow love to my husband. In my fantasy I think of putting down my watering can—it's baby blue, plastic, with a long thin spout like an anteater's nose, a piece of tough, touchable reality—and of going to find my husband, of wisping my fingers over the skin of his bare tanned shoulders, of touching my lips to the sweet skein of sunlightened brown hair below his neck bones. In one version of my fantasies, I do that, and we go upstairs to our bedroom to make love and so we don't even hear the doorbell ring. We're busy. Fate gets discouraged, changes its mind, goes away forever.

I have very real-seeming fantasies.

It still smells like breakfast bacon in the house on that particular Sunday in August in reality and in my imagination; the heat has caught that greasy rich smell in its humid fist and has refused to let it go even hours later into the day. Into this moist, hot scene the doorbell rings, annoying me as if it were a sudden fly in my face, making me want to bat it away, to shoo away whatever pest it is who is intruding on our August idyll. I look up and when I do my hand jerks, causing a little cascade of water to slosh out of the can and to drench a spot the size of a man's palm print on the rag rug at my bare feet. My toes get wet. That, at least, feels good.

"Damn," I exclaim.

The *damn*'s partly for the spill and partly because I don't want visitors. It's been a lovely, quiet, communing sort of Sunday. My husband and I have slept late. We've read snippets of newspapers to each other—the *Port Frederick Times*, the *Boston Globe*, and the *New York Times*. We've emptied two pots of coffee, abandoned our breakfast mess on the counters and the table in the kitchen, piddled about, mending this, watering that, making jokes, touching, smiling, kissing as we pass in the halls, the bedroom, the living room, the kitchen, moving slowly. It's just us, just as it has always been since we met, then moved in together, and then finally married. No dog, no cat, no parakeet. Only the two of us, still young enough to have children, but also still arguing about the necessity, the probability, the wisdom of it. He wants; I don't. I waver; he presses. I capitulate; he changes his mind, because he doesn't believe I really want to. He wants; I don't again. The upshot being: We haven't. And so we remain two, very two, blending, merging, weaving our separate egos into a strand of long, long twine, the kind whose threads are so inextricably connected you cannot easily pick them apart, not even with your fingernails or even by sticking a pin between them and trying to lift them apart from each other. He remains exceedingly who he is: Geoffrey Bushfield, thirty-nine years old (but soon to be impressively older), police lieutenant, native of our town. I remain absolutely who I am: Jennifer Lynn Cain, thirty-six years old (on that day), do-gooder, optimist, native. But who we are is altered by the presence of the other, our molecules rearranged to accommodate each other's DNA, so that it feels as if I form one-half of that strand and he is the other, twisting upward, tighter, closer, as if we could adhere so fast to one another there would be no room for error, for surprise, for fate. We were Siamese twins, he claimed, separated at birth. We were attached by Velcro, I said, and I pointed to an imaginary strip of the fastener at my side or his. Increasingly, in his absence, I felt an ache at my side, where the tiny plastic hooks in the Velcro reached for connection with him.

"Damn," I repeat, and then I call out, "Can you get that?"

No answer. Where is he? Out back? Oh, right, he's in the basement.

The rug will absorb the spilled water, so I don't hurry to clean it up but simply set down the can on the floor, thinking, *This is not a good idea, I am going to forget it's there and trip over it, or Geof will.* But there's somebody at the door, damn it all, and I don't want to carry the can back to the kitchen.

Ring. Again. In my fantasies, the second ring of the doorbell takes on personality, intent. It's aggressive. RING. It's demanding. ANSWER ME! It makes my heart beat unaccountably hard and fast, it causes me to pick up the speed with which my bare feet walk to respond to it. It makes me tuck my braless, sleeveless, scoop-neck T-shirt into my shorts and to tug with my hands at my hems to pull them down into modesty. It makes me alert, like a rabbit in our front yard where neighbors' dogs and strays come nosing around.

I approach the front door.

I stare. Stop. I have a chance to comprehend that our lives will never from this moment ever be the same again, like getting an opportunity to say good-bye to someone you love just before she dies. There's even time in this fantasy for me to take a deep breath and to pause for a bittersweet moment to savor the slow revolving of our histories to this instant. And then I pivot and face the back of the house.

*"Honey?"* I yell in my fantasy. *"Fate's here!"*

It was male, fate was, and looked about sixteen or seventeen years old. It wore black and white running shoes; white socks; blue jeans; a long-sleeved, button-down white dress shirt with the sleeves rolled up at the elbows and no T-shirt underneath; and a black baseball cap with a Star Trek logo above its bill. It looked rumpled, fate did, and sweaty, but basically clean, as if it had bathed recently and then had thrown on any old clothes that happened to be lying around on the floor of its bathroom. They looked clean, too, just unironed. But then, does fate iron? It's more likely, I think, that fate irons things out or throws irons in the fire or removes ones irons from the fire or tosses iron-y about like confetti. Confetti. Now that makes me think of parties. Celebrations. Welcomings. Farewells. Fate's irony, a strand of confetti: We could, I guess, call this astonishing happening on that day a birthday party, but not Geof's, even though his fortieth was only a few weeks away, and not mine. No, we'd have to call it fate's belated birthday—the fate who arrived in a wrinkled white shirt that looked as if his father had passed it down to him when it no longer looked good enough to wear to work, or maybe his mother had lifted it out of the ironing basket and had given it to him. Irony basket? Fate had acne, did I mention that? And didn't you always just expect that of fate? There was an interesting face beneath the spots, I thought as I looked at him, but at the moment at which fate rang our doorbell it was still a face only a mother could love, which was a problem for the boy on our doorstep.

# 2

"YES? HELLO?"

I stood inside the screen door, staring up at the kid who stood on the opposite side of it staring in at me. There was a motorcycle parked in our gravel drive, an ancient and battered-looking black one that resembled a wasp: with a thorax so bleached out by the sun that it seemed tie-dyed, silver handlebars with black grips like a wasp's bent legs, and a long silver stinger of a tailpipe. I didn't recall hearing it buzz up to our house.

Behind the boy and the bike, the day was bright enough to hurt my eyes; it made the inside air feel newly cool, like a shadow directly under the branches of a leafy tree on a very hot day.

The kid's baseball cap, the one with the Star Trek logo, was pulled low on his forehead, so I couldn't see his eyes, only his long straight nose and his mouth with its lower lip that was fuller than the top one and the acne that was splattered as if an angry painter had flipped his brush at the kid's face.

"I'm here to see Lieutenant Geoffrey Bushfield."

He pronounced it correctly: Jeffrey. It was always a problem,

Geof's name, because most people couldn't pronounce it when they saw it written, and he was always having to spell it for strangers. Blame it on Geof's mother, I always told people: She had an English aunt, pretensions, and no idea her firstborn would be a cop.

The visitor lifted his chin, and now I could look up into his eyes. They were hazel, more golden than either brown or green. He was staring at the interior of our house with a look of intense curiosity. That stare and his announcement, stated in a don't-give-me-any-shit kind of hard voice, raised the hair on my fore-arms as if I'd stepped under an air-conditioning vent. The day seemed to darken for a moment, and I wondered if a cloud really had passed over the sun or if the pupils of my eyes had briefly contracted in response to his words. I felt my neck muscles cord, my jaw tighten, my diaphragm contract defensively, as if to ward off a blow through the screen in the door. My lips shrank back from their tentative smile of Sunday welcome. I lived with a former homicide detective, and you just never knew.

"Please," the boy said in a more courteous tone.

I relaxed a little.

He had a mature-sounding baritone voice with a familiar tim-bre, and I wondered where I had heard it before.

"Whom shall I say . . . ?"

The kid's gaze shifted away from me, and the right side of his mouth lifted in a secretive-looking half smile, as if he found my question bitterly amusing.

"The lieutenant went to school with my parents."

"Oh?" I said.

I looked at the latch that hooked the screen door to the house. Locked. When I did that, I saw that he was holding a large book that looked like a scrapbook. It was pink as a prom dress, stuffed with clippings whose edges stuck out like petticoats. I looked back up at him. It was clear that he didn't want to give me his name.

"I'll get him," I said.

I thought he nodded, but it was hard to tell in the glare of the sun.

Sweat coated the backs of my knees and trickles of it ran down inside my T-shirt as I moved back into the house and pushed through our swinging door into the kitchen. I saw that our back door was wide open. I walked over to it quickly and closed and locked it. Then I leaned down into the basement stairwell and called softly, "Geof! Can you come up? There's a boy here to see you!"

In a moment he appeared at the bottom of the steps.

*"Who's* here?"

He looked surprised and hot and annoyed, although not with me. We didn't get drop-in visitors very often out where we lived, which was one of the reasons we'd bought the place. Our dirt and gravel roads made visitors fret about their tires and paint jobs, and we were nearly inaccessible in snow. It wasn't only that we liked the privacy and solitude but also that Geof-the-cop felt anonymous and unreachable thirty miles outside of town.

"It's a kid," I said, looking down fondly at the half-naked man at the bottom of the stairs, at the curly graying brown hair on his head and chest, his beefy shoulders, his long, muscular legs, and his big bare feet on the cool cement floor. Just seeing him there in all his solid, aggressive maleness made me feel better, safer, more secure. He was wearing his favorite summer weekend attire: a pair of old red boxer swim trunks. "A teenager. He's got a motorcycle."

"I didn't hear it."

I hadn't either, and that bothered me. How and why did the kid approach us so silently? Had he walked the bike up to our front door? Didn't he want us to hear him coming?

"What the hell's he want with me?"

"I don't know," I said with an exaggerated patience that made him smile. "Maybe he wants to mow our yard. Maybe he's the new kid on the paper route. He says you went to school with his parents."

"Yeah?" He placed one hand on the railing, one foot on the first step. I felt an urgency to get him moving, to overcome his reluctance to come upstairs and go to the door. It looked like the same reluctance I'd felt when the doorbell rang first. "So who are *they?*"

"I don't *know.*"

I felt like calling 911. Maybe I'd get a cop faster that way.

"How the hell did he find us anyway?"

"Geof! I don't know! Will you please get up here!"

He heard my tone, took a better look at my face, and then bounded up the stairs two at a time. "Is there a problem? Why didn't you tell me to get my ass in gear?"

"I thought I did."

Our sweaty bodies touched as he moved past me, heading for the refrigerator, where he kept a gun on top, below the cabinets.

"Is there some problem with this kid?"

"I don't know. I can't tell. There's just something weird . . ."

In a deliberately light tone, he said as he reached up, "So he looks like a serial killer?"

"Sure." I played along, watching him remove his .38 from the shadows over the refrigerator. He also lifted a little .22 from out of the dusty darkness and showed it to me to remind me it was there if I needed it. "He's here to confess to you." I watched him check both guns for ammunition, and then lay the .22 back on top of the fridge and stick the larger gun down in the right pocket of his swim trunks where its handle stuck out in plain sight.

"Maybe it's somebody I put in jail."

"Uh-huh." I lifted one of his T-shirts, a white one, off the back of a kitchen chair where he'd left it, handed it to him, and watched him pull it over his head. "That could be. Or maybe you put his father in prison, and now the kid's going to rape and torture me before he kills you in revenge."

"Hah." He tugged the bottom of the shirt over the bulge and handle of the .38. In a Humphrey Bogart drawl, he said, "Tell me, sweetheart, did you have this strange sense of humor *before* you met me?" He patted his pocket, smiled at me, a half-cocked grin that reminded me of the boy at our front door. "So, who's this kid really?"

I shrugged. "He looks familiar, so maybe his folks did go to school with you."

My husband placed the palm of his right hand against my jaw and my left cheek, briefly cradling my face. His skin felt hot and damp on mine, like a facecloth in a steam room, and I leaned into its comfort. "That could be half the town," he said. "Everybody's folks went to school with us."

9

"Yeah."

Geof and I had been four years apart at Port Frederick High School. He was the older of us, I liked to remind him, but not necessarily the more mature.

He started for the swinging door. "You stay."

"Yes, Lieutenant."

His smile flashed, a great full smile that cracked his stern face into equal parts mischief and wit.

"This looks like a very serious boy," I warned him.

"No joke?" he said, and with those words, he disappeared through the swinging door into the hallway that led to our visitor at our front door. It was the last time I would ever see Geof in just that way; I didn't know it then, but forever after that moment, my husband was never going to be the same again nor was our marriage. Ever since then, when I've come to a crossroads in my life, I think of that last sight of his smooth, tanned back and of a swinging door. I see it swaying, making that little creaking sound on its hinges, that ruffling sound where the edge rubs the doorsill after you've gone through, when the door's still settling back into place.

We'd kept the kid waiting a long time. I wondered if he had been patient enough to stick around. I stood still and listened. The front screen door slammed softly shut. And then there was a quiet rumble of male voices moving from the vicinity of our front door into our living room. I relaxed a little. If Geof had invited the boy into our home, there was no threat. Nothing to worry about this time. I turned away from the door and started to stack the Sunday newspapers in the recycling bin. A Schubert quintet was playing softly on the boom box we kept in the kitchen; the music and chores harmonized to soothe my fears away.

# 3

 Soon I had slipped happily back into the day, unlocking and reopening the kitchen door, moving in and out of the house.

Our back door led to a walkway of plain cement rectangles stuck in the dirt and grass. There was nothing manicured about our property; we let it go wild as much as possible, allowing the leaves to fall and stick, mowing only enough to keep the bugs down, coexisting contentedly with dandelions and crabgrass. Our first year, Geof planted azaleas by the front door and I stuck in flowering ground cover wherever a bare spot called to me. He had his tomato plants out by the garage and I'd scattered enough wildflower seed to germinate a small meadow. So our property was, by and large, a wild garden of surprises. We never knew what sweet little delight might pop up right at our feet to dazzle us. It could be blue cornflowers one month and black-eyed Susans the next, even carnations, or precious little wild roses with yellow hearts and snowy petals with a blush of pink. We had floral bounty to fill our fields of vision, as well as our vases, from early spring daffodils to late fall bittersweet. We were heady with honeysuckle in the summertime, and when the

11

iris bloomed—too briefly!—in the spring, it seemed I spent half my days with my nose stuck down their sweet fragrant throats. The house in the middle of all this natural beauty was timber and stone, with a real honest-to-God slate roof and a couple of chimneys. Our niece and nephew called it the Hansel and Gretel cottage, and when we moved in, it truly did seem to me like a fairy tale come true, where Geof and I had a fighting chance to live happily ever after.

So involved in my chores was I that I nearly jumped out of my skin ten minutes later when he called, *"Jenny!"*

I nearly dropped the half gallon of milk I was holding up in the refrigerator as I sponged a shelf. They'd been so quiet, the teenager and the cop, and I'd been puttering so happily that I'd nearly forgotten they were there.

In the manner of spouses everywhere, I yelled back, *"What?"*

And received no reply.

I closed the refrigerator door, straightened my shirt, and hurried in the direction of Geof's voice. Somebody who didn't know him wouldn't have detected anything untoward in that single word: *Jenny.* It would only have been the raised voice of a husband requesting the attention of his wife in another room. Dear? Would you come in here? But I thought I heard something else in its timbre, I thought I sensed a tension and an urgency, even a plea. An unspoken message hung in the bacon-scented air between the back of the house and the front, and that word was *HELP!* And not just any "help" either, not come'ere and help me make the bed or help me hold this string while I tie it or help me empty the trash, but HELP ME, JENNY! As in, Help me, I don't know how to handle this, I need you, please come quick!

I didn't even think of grabbing the .22.

It wasn't that kind of help. It wasn't physical terror calling to me, it was simply, as Geof himself explained it later, "Oh, Christ, Jenny, come in here quick, I don't know what to do! I'm in over my head, I need you . . ."

So I went on the trot, slowing as I neared them. I stopped in the double-wide doorway between the hall and the living room and stared in. Through the open windows I heard a bird chirp heavily as if it were complaining about the heat. The boy sat with his back to me on one of our two facing sofas, big old comfy things where we could sprawl out together or alone. He didn't turn around at the sound of my bare feet padding on the hardwood floors, so I couldn't see his face. I saw Geof's well enough, though. He was leaning forward, toward the boy and me, with his forearms on his thighs and his hands clasped together between his knees. His face looked the way it appears in emergencies like homicides or car wrecks: frozen, stoic, but the eyes alert; it's a sort of show-no-emotion facial reflex that hides his furiously operating thoughts and complex feelings he doesn't wish to reveal at that moment. He tended to wear that face home with him from work during tough cases or particularly brutal ones, and it always took awhile for him to melt into expressiveness again. I'd also seen that look on the day, a few years before, when I'd started bleeding at the start of a miscarriage. I had called to him—much as he had just beckoned me—to come help me up from where I sat crying on the bathroom floor. It was only at that moment that I'd known I was pregnant, and it had felt strangely thrilling to think it was so and that now it was over. I'd had an odd thought that was also a fragment of a line from a T. S. Eliot poem: *"well now that's done, and I'm glad it's over."* I'd felt sad, which surprised me, and also frightened. Later, I felt only relieved, so much relief and so strongly that I could not confess it to Geof for fear of hurting his feelings.

He waved me toward him and patted the cushion next to him. When I took that seat, our sweaty thighs stuck together. I looked across at the boy. He was separated from us by a gulf of five feet and a large square coffee table littered with books and magazines. Geof touched my knee with the palm of his left hand and left a glisten of sweat on my skin.

"Jenny, this is David Mayer."

He pronounced it like Bayer, as in aspirin, or slayer.

"Hello," I said, feeling foolish.

Silence unfolded around us like cards laid down, and I wondered, *What game is this, and who holds aces?*

"You gonna tell her?" the kid said to Geof. And then, with cold scorn, "Or you gonna make her guess?"

I suddenly really didn't like this kid, this David Mayer.

What seemed at the time to be irrelevant thoughts flitted through my mind. In retrospect, they seem pretty damned relevant. They were thoughts almost without words, more like feelings, about what a pretty, comfortable home Geof and I had created together. Our furniture didn't match, at least not in theory, but it fit together perfectly in practice. We'd used my favorite clear, bright colors—yellows, oranges, reds—and mixed them with his favorite deep brown wood tones, so the house had an autumnal atmosphere all year long, kind of crisp and cheerful and cozy all at once. There were always books and magazines littering the rooms like scattered leaves, and often a week's worth of newspapers trailing from the kitchen to our bedroom upstairs into the bathrooms down to the living room and finally into recycling. And books, so many books it looked as if a convention of librarians had dropped by with armloads and joyously tossed it all up into the air and dumped everything, leaving us to sort through the detritus on our deliciously erratic quest for wisdom. From just where I sat on the couch I saw Geof's *Smithsonian* and *Science* magazines tumbled in with my own professional journals that kept me informed about the world of trusts, foundations, and not-for-profit agencies. There was one of the couple or so novels I was reading more or less at the same time and pages from the *Wall Street Journal*, which I felt I had to read. Everywhere there were objects to catch our eyes; snag our brains; stimulate an idea, a conversation, a thought, an argument. There were yellow floor-length draperies that we hardly ever closed, because we achieved our privacy from our isolation and from the branches of the huge old fir trees outside our windows. There were bookcases and coffee tables and end tables and crooked lamps, an appearance of having lived there for centuries—or at least since Gutenberg invented his press—but that was misleading, since we'd only been in the cottage for a few years. It only felt like forever. All this I noticed half consciously. It was almost as if I had a sense that I wasn't ever going to see it again quite like this; I was observing it, lovingly, longingly, like a woman going off to prison or like one who's been given a month to live. It made my heart swell, this loving mess of a living room, and I felt a rush of totally irrational anger directed at our smart-mouthed young visitor: *Leave us alone!*

He, the boy, the stranger, sat in the middle of the opposite couch as if he'd taken it over. He didn't slouch, not as I expected of teenagers. Rather, he had his spine pressed hard against the back of the couch with his feet flat on the floor, his legs slightly apart, his big hands resting on top of the incongruous pink scrapbook in his lap. He didn't fidget. His expression was unreadable except when it expressed patronizing contempt for Geof and a sort of hostile curiosity toward me. Now, looking back, I'd say his face was frozen with purpose and fear, that he was paralyzed with the intensity of his refusal to surrender to us any revelation of his true feelings.

"You and I went to school with David's parents," Geof said in an excessively polite tone of voice. My curiosity stirred. He sighed, shifted in his seat, then placed his left arm on the back of the couch behind me. It felt like a protective gesture. "They were in my class. Judy Baker. Ron Mayer." Geof looked at me searchingly, and finally my heat-soaked brain grasped hold of the horrifying truth, and I blurted out, "Oh, God!"

I felt my expression soften as I looked over at the boy again, but I also saw his jaw tighten and his eyes narrow at the sight of my sympathy, and so I struggled to conceal it. The previous winter, this boy's father had killed his invalid wife and then himself. Murder/suicide. Port Frederick's first as far as anybody knew. An odd and modest record but our own. They'd left one child: this one. No wonder he looked and sounded familiar: His family's photographs had been plastered all over our local newspapers for days, and our local TV and radio stations had played, repeatedly and chillingly, the 911 phone call that this boy's father had made—to announce that he'd just killed his wife and was about to do the same thing to himself.

"I'm so sorry about your parents, David."

His gaze slid away from my face to a spot near some woodwork.

I turned to Geof, silently asking, *Now what?*

He cleared his throat. "Show her the scrapbook, David." His voice came out hard, authoritarian, coplike, and I saw the kid's

15

hands draw up into fists on top of the pink book. But he said, "Yeah," and got up and walked around the coffee table to thrust the book at me. As I put it on my lap, he returned to his seat quickly, as if he couldn't stand to be any closer to us than he had to, for any longer than he had to.

"You'd like me to look at this?" I asked Geof. "Is that it?"

He withdrew his arm from around me and said, "That's it." Then he turned his face away from both of us and stared at the window. I thought he was looking at the blue jays that were poking around David Mayer's motorcycle.

"What kind of bike is that?" he inquired, proving me wrong.

"1978 BMW 1,000. I bought it." Said aggressively, that last part.

"Like it?"

"Yeah."

I said, "Didn't you used to have a motorcycle, Geof?" I hadn't opened the scrapbook yet.

He turned, frowning, to me as if to say, *"Why in the world did you ask me that?"* But he nodded and said, "I've been thinking about getting one."

That was news to me.

Suddenly I thought of the .38 stuck down in his pants, and I was struck by the surreality of this scene: secretly armed cop in red swim trunks, puzzled wife with pink scrapbook in lap, tense teenager with mysterious agenda, ghosts of his dead parents hanging about in the heat, Mozart in the kitchen, blue jays screaming in the yard. What's wrong with this picture? There was a languorous, heavy feeling in the air because of the heat. But there was also a crackling, an electric-blue voltage, like high-tension lines snapping at each other across a ditch on a sultry day that threatened storms.

I opened the scrapbook and gasped aloud.

There, on the first page, blown up in grainy black and white photography, was my Geof. Somebody's Geof. It was his senior high school photograph, greatly enlarged. It showed him as I remembered him from back then, with hair to his shoulders, a stubborn straight line of a mouth, clear skin, and amused, hard, cynical eyes. He looked like a tough, wild, scary kid who was good-looking enough to be dangerous to imaginations of nice girls like me. I was a freshman then. Judy Baker and Ron Mayer would have been seniors, too. I glanced up at the actual teenager in our living room, then back down at the photo of Geof. Funny, did they all look alike, these teenage boys? It was oddly still in the room, as the air usually is before tornadoes or hurricanes, as if the house was holding its breath, or maybe the two males were.

"What's this all about?" I asked them but got no response.

I turned the pages one by one. Geof was the featured attraction on all of them. There he was on the football team, a short-lived career if there ever was one. There were newspaper advertisements for Bushware, Inc., his family's dynastic hardware company, which he had chosen to abandon in favor of becoming a policeman. There were clippings and photos of his parents in the local society pages; more than once, coincidentally, they were shown in group shots that included my own parents, before my mom got sick. There were articles about the Bushfield family's relocation to upstate New York after Geof graduated from high school. There was Geof listed as a new police cadet, then a photo of his installation, along with notices of every promotion, even stories about crimes he helped to solve—or not—and every little quote he'd ever given to a newspaper reporter. There were photos of his weddings—all three of them, which meant I finally came across my own mug grinning up at me. Of course, there being clippings about his weddings, there were Geof's two divorce notices as well. Then there were even clippings about my own exploits. Toward that point in the scrapbook, things were not pasted in, they weren't even neatly scissored but looked as if they'd been torn out of the newspapers and then stuffed into the scrapbook. The last thing in the book was a copy of an editorial that concerned my resignation as director of the Port Frederick Civic Foundation. In the ragged margin, somebody had penciled in the word *wife*.

Too weird!

I left the book open there, and I stared over at David Mayer, then at Geof.

"So what's this all about?"

*So what's this round, red thing? asked Eve.*

17

"My mother saved all that," David said.

Geof caught my hand in his and held it. "Jenny, he says he's my son."

An invisible hand shoved my chest, pushing me backward into the couch, making it hard for me to breathe or speak. *Oh, no!* I thought. *No no no . . .*

"No!" The boy yelled it for me, springing to his feet and to vehement life. His eyes—hazel like Geof's—flashed a message of indignation and insult. "My *dad* was my father! You're incidental, asshole, you're not related to me at all, you're Newtonian, that's all, you're just a biological accident, you're just the stupid cause of an effect. My *dad* was my father! You're *nothing* to me."

He was visibly trembling and, by then, so was I.

Through his hand that still held onto mine, I could almost feel Geof absorb the attack, like a sponge taking water. He was known to snap at me now and then or occasionally at the cops who worked under him, and he could yell as loud as anybody, but he also knew how to contain it, how to accept the other person's anger and hold it within him until he figured out what to do with it. This was one of those times when he wasn't going to fight back, not yet.

I, on the other hand, wanted to hit the kid.

My sympathy for him dried up shockingly fast in the hot surge of protectiveness I felt for my husband. I wanted to shelter Geof from this boy's accusations and hatred. I was taken by surprise at the intensity of my resentment, my fear, and my protectiveness.

Like an angry child, I blurted, "Says who?"

Geof gently squeezed my hand to restrain me.

"He can take a blood test," the kid shot back. "I've done mine. He can do it, too. Prove he's not!"

"How do you *know*?" I insisted.

He turned my way again that half smile of bitter amusement I'd seen at the front door, and he said in a singsong, mimicking a toddler, "Because my mommy told me so."

"When? What did she say?"

"I'll get the blood test," Geof interrupted me. "Don't worry." I couldn't tell if he was saying that to the kid or to me.

*Don't worry?!* I stared at my husband and realized, *My God! He's excited, he hopes it's true, he's delighted!* I felt utterly confused: How could he take this boy's word just like that? It didn't have to be true! She could have lied, and this scrapbook could be the product of a schoolgirl obsession that never died . . .

"Why now?" I asked coldly.

Geof looked at me, and I glimpsed his desire in his eyes.

"Why is he coming to us now?" I repeated with cold precision for Geof's benefit to try to wake him up. I felt rigid with suspicion and frantic with Geof's lack of it. Was he just going to swallow a "son" whole simply because he'd always wanted one?

He faced the kid. "Because Judy wanted me to know? Is that why?"

*Because you want money from us, is that it?* I thought.

"No! Hell, no!" David Mayer stepped away from the couch so quickly that he bumped against it. He came closer to Geof as if he wanted to loom over him but didn't quite dare it. "It was my mom's secret, and *I'd* rather you never knew the truth! I'm only here for one reason, and that's because you owe me, cop!" And suddenly the boy was a hardened and fully grown man, his voice low and coarse and so threatening it made the hair on my neck rise again and a shudder passed across my shoulders. "I've come to collect your debt, that's the only reason I'm here."

*Ah yes,* I thought. *I was right. He wants money.*

And still Geof absorbed the boy's attack, holding the boy's anger and gently containing his own emotions as if he cherished everything that was happening to us in that room. I wanted to shake him!

"What do you want from me, David?"

*By his first name, so intimate, so accepting!*

The kid leaned forward on the balls of his feet and stabbed his right forefinger at Geof. "You said . . . the cops said . . . my dad killed my mom. And then he's supposed to have shot himself. And it's all a fucking lie. My dad wouldn't do that!"

"It wasn't even Geof's case," I protested.

It was true that at one time, back when Geof and I first got together, he would have been involved with any case like that. But he was a homicide detective then, one of only a few on the force, and it was his job to investigate any suspicious death in

Port Frederick. Things were different now. For one thing, he'd been promoted. And for another, our "town" had become a small city, thanks to a boom period of new business and population growth, all of which brought more crime, which therefore required a larger police force. He wasn't the only lieutenant by any means, and now there were many cases that he only heard about, like any other citizen.

But again, Geof squeezed my hand, infuriating me, preventing me from defending him, and I saw that I was so wrong: *This was going to be much, much more costly than money could ever be.*

"David, do you have new evidence . . . ?"

"Shut up, cop! I don't have to tell you fucking anything! Here's all you need to know from me: My dad didn't do that! No way! I want you to fucking prove it! You pay up! You prove they didn't die that way." The boy choked over those words, he began to cry, but he fought the tears, wiping them furiously away from his face by hitting his own cheeks with the backs of his hands.

I watched him coldly, feeling a detached kind of sympathy that I might feel for any stranger that I read about in a newspaper. It was too bad his parents were dead; it was tragic how they died, and how sad for a boy to be left alone like this. But it didn't have anything to do with us. There was a swelling of warmth in my chest, a hint of a deeper feeling of compassion that wanted to break through, but I fought it back, I didn't want it, I wanted to stay cool, evaluative. If Geof wasn't going to defend himself against this craziness, then one of us had to defend *us.*

Raging over us, David Mayer choked out the words: "You prove they didn't die like that! You clear my *father's* name!"

He practically spat the word *father* at Geof.

"Well, David, if your father didn't do it . . ."

"My father *didn't* do it!"

"And you don't think your mother—"

"Are you *kidding*?"

"Then who—"

"You tell me, cop!"

"All right, David, I'll try."

I stared at my husband. "Just like that?"

"Don't give me your fucking *try*!" The kid's voice was rising

20

again, filling our living room with violent noise, shoving all the peace and quiet out of our home. I tried to pull away from Geof, I wanted to jump to my feet to confront the boy. Somebody had to stand up to this kid. But my husband held me down on the couch with both of his arms while the boy yelled at him, and I fumed. "Just do it, cop! You owe me! You pay up!"

And still, Geof absorbed it all.

"If I'm going to do this for you, there are questions . . ."

"Forget it!" The kid looked as mulish as he sounded.

"What do you mean?" For the first time, I heard a spark of indignation in Geof's voice. "David, if I'm going to reopen the case, I'll have to ask you—"

"Not me, you don't have to ask me anything, cop. I got no answers for you. Somebody else has all the answers, and that's your job. Not mine." The kid was holding something, which he tossed to Geof: keys tied together on a string.

"What are these for?" Geof cupped them in his hands.

"They're for 3582 King Terrace." The kid spoke with sarcasm so deep his voice couldn't contain it and shook with it. "Home sweet home. You go there, you see for yourself. Don't come asking me how to do your job. Listen, man, my dad taught me when somebody goes in debt, they don't keep going back to the person they owe money to, they don't keep asking him how they're supposed to pay it back. That's your job to figure out."

And suddenly, he was leaving, turning on his heel, turning away from us, heading for the hallway and the front door, moving out of our lives as abruptly as he'd entered them.

"Wait!" Geof stood up, called out. "David, wait—"

But he didn't, wouldn't, and even as Geof stepped around the table as if to follow and detain him, the kid broke and ran. I watched him disappear out of the living room, heard his feet hitting the hardwood in our front hall, heard the screen door open and slam shut, listened to the sound of feet running across gravel, an engine revving up, his motorcycle roaring out of the drive. He didn't care if we heard him leaving; it was only his approach that he'd hidden from us.

From the doorway, Geof looked back at me.

"Jesus!" he exclaimed.

21

"Is that a prayer?"

He smiled slightly, and I glimpsed it again, his excitement, and with his next words, he proved me right. "When he first told me, Jenny, I was so astonished! And I wanted to say, 'No kidding, really? That's incredible, let me look at you! You're my *son*? This is fascinating! Tell me all about you, I want to get to know you! Come on in here!' But I couldn't, it was so obvious he hated my guts, I couldn't show him how I felt right then."

"And how do you feel right now?"

"It's amazing!" But he either heard something in my voice or saw it in my face, and suddenly he changed course. "What do you think about it, Jenny?"

"I think I could kill you."

He looked surprised, hurt. It appeared that he didn't feel he had to absorb *my* anger in the same way that he'd taken whatever the kid dished out to him.

"Why in the world do you feel that way?"

"*Why?*"

"Well, yes. This isn't your problem."

"Oh, sure," I said bitterly. "Right. Geof, I don't remember you dating Judy Baker. When did you? Well, obviously you did about seventeen years and nine months ago, but when *was* that exactly?"

He looked embarrassed. "Well, I didn't exactly."

"You mean you just screwed her, was that it?"

"Well, once. I think, just the once. Yeah."

"A one-night *stand*?" My voice rose. "This is the result of a one-night stand?"

"Jenny, that's the way she was, don't you remember?"

"She?" I shot back. "I guess that's also the way *you* were."

"All right, But it was different for guys—"

"It is not dif—"

"And even if it was only a one-night stand, that doesn't make him any less my son—"

"Your son? Just like that? You accept it—"

"Yes, I do! I think that scrapbook's pretty damned convincing. And if Judy said so, if she actually told the boy, then I can believe it. Why can't you? Why in the world would she lie about it—"

22

"There could be a thousand reasons!"

"Why don't you want to believe this?"

I stared at him, knowing he'd caught me out. I *didn't* want to believe a word of it. I knew why, too, but I couldn't tell him, not right then, because I didn't know how to put it so that it wouldn't sound selfish, so that it wouldn't cast me in an unflattering light, so that it wouldn't make him turn away from me.

"It isn't your problem," he repeated more gently this time.

*How can you be so naive?* I thought, feeling frantic again. *Don't you know this is going to change our lives, don't you realize that?*

When I didn't answer, he held up the keys in his right hand.

"Want to go take a look?" he asked me nicely.

"Now?" I said not so nicely. "Oh hell, sure, why not?"

When I went back into the dining room to find my sandals where I'd left them, I forgot about the blue watering pitcher that I'd left on the floor, and I stumbled against it and knocked it over. At the same time, I heard him on the phone in the kitchen, talking to Lee Meredith, who was a young sergeant, one of Geof's protégés in the Port Frederick Police Department. I heard Geof apologize for disturbing her Sunday with her family, I heard him confirm that she had assisted on the Mayer homicide/suicide, I heard him ask her to refresh his memory about the case, I heard him tell her the truth about why he was asking and to keep it confidential, I heard him ask her to come over to our house tomorrow night and to bring her files with her, I heard him thank her, and then I heard him hang up the phone.

He appeared in the doorway in front of me.

"Sergeant Meredith says everything pointed to murder/suicide," he told me. "She says it was an easy case, open/shut, and she doesn't think I'll find any evidence to refute that."

"Then why try? Don't you trust your own people?"

"Oh, come on, we make mistakes."

"What if you have to tell him it's no mistake?"

"Then I'll tell him." He shrugged. "Maybe it'll help him to accept the truth. And maybe in the process, I'll get to know him." He turned away from me, and soon I heard him bounding up the stairs to the second floor as if he were feeling a burst of adrenaline.

I stared down at my feet. All of the water left in the pitcher had spilled onto the rag rug and seeped over onto the hardwood floor.

"Damn," I said softly, despairingly.

*Damn, damn, damn you!*

# 4

THE DREGS OF THE DAY SMELLED LIKE BAKED GRASS and honeysuckle.

It took us two hours to leave the house, because it had come to me as I was standing in my bare feet in the puddle of water on the dining room floor that I must refuse to be rushed. And so I insisted that we clean up around the house and that we both shower and change clothes and even that we fix and consume sandwiches before we left. Geof went along with it all without saying much; he mostly walked around with a hypnotized look on his face, as if somebody had cast a spell on him. I didn't attempt to break it. The tuna fish on wheat bread that we ate for supper sat like wood chips in my mouth, but I forced it down so I wouldn't get hungry and cranky in addition to already being worried, angry, ashamed of myself, disappointed and depressed. We sat across from each other at the kitchen table, chewing, swallowing, and I thought, *Where did the happiness go?* Then I looked at his face, so bemused, so stunned looking, and I amended that to, *Where did my happiness go?* From the looks of him, Geof still had his.

Because of all of that delay, twilight was already weaving a

25

sticky violet web around us as we climbed into the Jeep for the ride into town to 3582 King Terrace. It was Geof's new car, a snappy, khaki-colored number with a tan top. In fact, we both had new vehicles although for different reasons. His rationale was strictly practical, he claimed: four-wheel drive, tow hitch, able to ford broad streams in a single bound. He nearly hadn't bought it because of how it would sound: Geof's Jeep. "Too goddamn cute," he'd groused, and he did take some ribbing from the other cops, not to mention the robbers: Bushfield's Bush Wagon was one of the milder nicknames, along with Yeof's Yuppie Yeep and Geof's Go-Cart. After he pulled a couple of them out of ditches last winter, what they said was "Thank you." I had other reasons for buying my new car, none of them practical, and I didn't make any excuses about it either.

We sat clean and neat in our fresh shorts and T-shirts side-by-side separated only by the gearshift and his car phone and an emotional abyss the size of the ocean to the east of us.

"Can we talk about it now?" he said.

I plucked my shoulder harness safety belt like a cello string and thought about switching on the radio instead of answering his question. The Jeep was a noisy ride, especially with the top off. I thought about pretending that I hadn't heard him. The radio would make it even harder to converse.

"Their deaths, you mean?"

"Well, yes, but I really meant . . . David."

I knew what he meant all right. I plucked my seat belt one more time and then decided to quit being childish. It was beginning to look as if he already had one teenager; he didn't need me acting like one, too. "Yes," I said, sighed, and stared out the gaping "window" beside me, the open space that exposed the passenger to the elements from head to toe. Rocks pinged against the Jeep's belly, and leaves brushed my bare arm. I worried vaguely about scratches to my skin and the car's.

"You first," I said.

"Only if you promise to tell me why you're so upset."

I thought that was a stupid thing to say, but I didn't say so.

"Oh, I will . . . as soon as I figure it out. You'll be the second to know."

He smiled over at me in an understanding sort of way, so I felt I owed it to him to capitulate a little more.

"I'm deflating you, I know that, and I'm sorry about it." It seemed like a nice thing to say, conciliatory, decent, even if I didn't mean it. "You probably wish I were as astonished and excited and fascinated by this boy as you are, and instead, I'm being a bitch."

"You're not," he said loyally.

I appreciated the effort.

"We don't even know you're his father, Geof."

"You're right."

He could be conciliatory, too, even when he didn't mean it.

"So talk," I said as he turned right out of our private road onto the two-lane blacktop highway that would take us into Port Frederick, detouring around a dead raccoon on the shoulder of the road. To avoid looking at that, I glanced out the mirror on my side of the car and saw something that made me jerk as if somebody had forced a cattle prod to my side: a black motorcycle was pulling out of the trees at the side of the highway. I stared at the mirror as the rider waited until one car passed him, and then he roared out onto the highway behind it, following us.

"Do you see him!"

"Oh, yes."

"What are you going to do?"

"Nothing. He's got a right to be on the road, same as we do."

"But he's been waiting for us! He's following us!"

"Let's talk about his mother—"

"But, Geof—!"

"He's not hiding, Jenny. He wants us to notice him. So now we've seen him, so now we just keep driving on into town. Come on. Relax. We were going to talk, remember? And I was going to start first. Judy Baker Mayer. I just barely remember her, isn't that lousy? But the thing is, she was easy. It's a rotten thing to say, and I'm a son of a bitch to say it, but that was her reputation and she damn well earned it."

*Easy?* I thought, trying to lean back and relax, trying to listen and concentrate, trying to keep my eyes on the motorcycle rider in my sideview mirror. *What a laugh! This is hard.*

27

"They were a couple forever," Geof was saying, his illegitimate, hateful, vengeful teenage son riding one car behind us with some mysterious intent in his strange little mind. "They started going together when they were in junior high school, and he was always crazy about her. Blind crazy. Judy cheated on him from the time she was, I'll swear, thirteen. Well, maybe fourteen. Everybody knew it, and everybody knew that Ron didn't know it, and it was like this big joke with all of us."

*Ha*, I thought, staring at the boy. *Ha, ha.*

"It doesn't sound so funny now," Geof admitted. He was driving easily, his left fingers guiding the steering wheel at the bottom, his right fingers loosely on the gearshift knob. He looked like a man who hadn't a concern in the world beyond shifting into third gear to make the sharp turns in the highway. He glanced into his rearview and sideview mirrors frequently, but he would have anyway on this road.

My vision was glued to my side mirror.

*Aren't teenagers just a riot,* I thought, remembering how it had been. Even as a lowly freshman, I had heard about Judy Baker, because we'd idolized the upper-class boys and girls and we'd gossiped about them as if they were movie stars. If Judy Baker *had* been a movie star, we'd have said she was the one who got the part by sleeping with the casting director. I didn't remember Ron Mayer well enough to know what part we'd have assigned to him: maybe the Ashley Wilkes role in *Gone with the Wind*, only stouter and less cultivated but that same kind of nice, boring, devoted husband role. It was difficult to picture Judy as Scarlett. Geof as Rhett Butler was easier to imagine.

"She wasn't very cute," Geof said, echoing my own unworthy thoughts. "And she wasn't popular, at least not with the other girls, and she sure as hell wasn't very smart. But she was going steady with Ron, and everybody liked Ron. He was just this nice guy, decent looking, real practical, I think he was good at math, and I remember he built neat stuff in shop—"

"Neat stuff?" I had to smile at that.

Geof seemed eager to return my smile. "I'm regressing. Next thing, I'll be saying groovy. So here was Ron, he played football, never got in any kind of trouble, sort of hung out on the fringe of the popular crowd, and he dragged Judy in with him, and then she slept with everybody and his brother."

"Maybe he knew."

Geof's eyebrows arched in surprise. "Christ. Maybe he did. Wouldn't that be something? No, I don't believe it. He was a simple kind of guy. I don't mean stupid, I just mean . . . simple, not complicated, not layered, not devious. He'd never have been able to look us in the eye and slap us on the back if he'd known a thing like that. And she always said that he didn't know."

"Judy told you that?"

"And other guys."

"How many, do you think?"

"How many boys are there on a football team?"

"Geof! You're serious?"

"No." He laughed a little. "I don't know how many."

"One, at least." I glanced at him.

He seemed to be looking for a hint of humor in my eyes, seemed to find it, and when he did, he grinned shamefacedly. "Yeah, at least one. But I can also think of a few friends of mine."

"Yeah, well, boys lie."

He shrugged. "I didn't. Look, Jenny, things look different now, on this side of the women's movement, but back in those days, you'd have thought I was a model of restraint, because for all those years we were in school together, I hadn't screwed her yet." He glanced at me again. "And it wasn't for lack of opportunity. She was after me from the time we were eighth-graders—"

"What a compliment," I said sarcastically.

"Ah, Jenny."

He raised his right hand from his gearshift knob and turned it over, palm up, like a dog presenting its stomach to be scratched. I grasped it, squeezed once, and released it.

"Anyway, she didn't let up until we finally did it."

"The deed."

"The deed, indeed."

"The Wild Thing."

"It was a classic. Back of my car, can you believe that? On somebody's side street. Wham, bam. I hope at least I said thank you, ma'am. I don't remember much about it except that we were probably high, must have been a party going on at some-body's house, and I think maybe I walked out to my car, and there she was, and I guess I had more hormones than self-re-straint, and . . . there it was."

"Geof." The math of the situation had just sunk in on me. "If David is seventeen, and you're forty, you had to be . . . Wha? . . . forty minus seventeen plus nine months . . . twenty-two? Not exactly an innocent boy."

"I think I was actually closer to twenty-one at the time, but yeah, okay, that's how old we all were, and there wasn't a whole lot of innocence going around. Those were still the wild days." He glanced at me. "You know that. You were there. Before AIDS. Some of us had already been to college. But we still got together for parties, you know how it is during semester breaks, summer, Christmas. It was one of those times when it happened."

"How'd you feel about it?"

"Then?" He shook his head. "I forgot about it, that's how I felt. I don't know, I probably felt guilty because of Ron and be-cause I'd kept away from her all those years, and it seemed kind of weak to cave in like that. But I've got to tell you the truth, Jenny, I was a horny young bastard, like everybody else, and I probably didn't have what you would call a crisis of conscience over it. I was probably half proud of it. Sorry."

"No birth control?"

"I guess not." He laughed, but then he looked in the side mirror, saw the boy, and got a hit of instant reality. "This is too fucking weird, Jenny. Talking about this, seeing him back there. My life has turned into the Twilight Zone."

*Our lives.*

The "zone" we were actually nearing was a commercial one of fast-food restaurants and strip malls on the edge of town.

A second car, a Toyota, came between us and our teenage tracker. He weaved out and passed it, then squeezed back in behind the Pontiac that was right behind us.

"I told you, he's not much good at undercover surveillance, is he?"

"He's not hiding," Geof said tersely. "He wants us to know he's there. When I used to have to tail cars, the only time I followed within sight of them was when I was so pissed at them that I didn't care if they saw me or I was trying to provoke them.''

"So is he angry or provocative?''

"Maybe he'll show us.''

"Great,'' I muttered and slunk down in my seat.

For the next couple of miles, we drove in silence, and I gazed at the scenery to avoid staring obsessively at the side mirror. There wasn't much to see that I hadn't already observed hundreds of times before, starting clear back in my childhood. Geof and I both had seen it all grow and change. For a couple of centuries, the ones when we didn't live here, Port Frederick was a fishing village, long on hard work and short on charm. It was only in the last half of this century that it developed into a full-fledged place on the map. To the natives, even the old-line wealthy ones, it was Poor Fred, but now there was also a Rich Fred—Nouveau Riche Fred, according to the snobs—with malls, a fancy new harbor, suburban developments, all contributing to the feeling I sometimes got of being a visitor to my own hometown. Our destination was in part of Rich Fred, where the streets had names like Sovereign, Prince, Gloucester, and Duke of York. When those streets signs went up, some people opined as to how maybe the Tories had won the war after all.

Nearer town, I said, "Did you ever?''

"What?''

"Use birth control.''

"Hell, no. I was practically still a teenage boy, Jenny—emotionally, I probably still was a teenager—and it was back then.'' We reached the first stop sign on our route, and he braked. We waited for drivers at the other three corners to go first. Suddenly, as we sat there, as the motorcycle idled behind us, Geof slammed his right palm against the steering wheel, and he exclaimed, "Goddamn!''

I jumped in my seat, whirled to look behind me. *"What?"*

"My God, Jenny! How could I have had a child, a son, and not know it? Shouldn't I have known it at least at some intuitive level? Shouldn't I have had a gut feeling about it? Didn't it even occur to me to count backward nine months when Judy had her

31

baby? Everybody knew she was pregnant, that's why she and Ron got married before his college graduation. I don't think Judy ever did go to college. Hell, what did I do? I just screwed her and walked away, that's what. You're right to ask, What did I feel? Did I feel anything? For her? About that night? Didn't it even cross my mind that she could get pregnant? It's driving me crazy, Jenny. I don't understand how something so important, something so *attached* to me, could happen and I wouldn't have a clue about it."

The car behind us honked, urging us through the intersection.

Geof waved to thank the driver, to apologize.

"You want to know the truth?" he said as he let out the clutch, stepped on the gas, changed gears. "It gives me the creeps! Not David, I don't mean him. I mean *her*, Judy, knowing it all this time. And that scrapbook! Hell, it's spooky. Don't you think it's spooky?"

I nodded and glanced in the mirror again: *Yes, indeed.*

"She knew!" Geof repeated. "Judy knew, and Ron didn't, and their son didn't, and I sure didn't. But she had this knowledge, this incredible secret she kept from all three of us."

When he said three, I thought he meant himself, Ron Mayer, and me. Then I realized he meant only the two men and the boy.

*Four of us*, I thought. *Don't forget me.*

We were approaching the entrance to Royal Estates, where King Terrace was. All those years they'd lived there, I thought as Geof put on his left-turn indicator, maybe we'd all stopped at the four-way intersection at the same time without recognizing one another. Or maybe Judy *had* recognized us—that was an unpleasant thought—maybe she'd pulled out in front of me sometime when I was driving into town and she was leaving her subdivision, and maybe she'd known who I was: Geof Bushfield's wife. And all the times that we were driving by here, there was a little boy growing up at 3582 King Terrace . . .

When we turned into the entrance to the subdivision, the car behind us drove on past and so did the motorcycle behind it.

"He's gone," I said and breathed more easily in the muggy twilight atmosphere of Royal Estates. "Geof, if she had such a crush on you, why didn't she go after *you* to marry her?"

"Maybe I disappointed her."

"In the sack? Fat chance." I could be loyal, too.

"Thank you, but it wasn't the sack, it was a back seat, and I doubt I was the most considerate and tender lover she ever had." He sounded sad when he spoke again. "I wonder if she had any of those."

"Maybe Ron," I said shortly, and then I rendered a harsh judgment: "Anyway, you wouldn't have wanted to know she was pregnant."

"I'm afraid you're right."

He turned onto King Terrace, which was a lane of two-story homes all built on variations of modern Colonial: They were all two stories high, finished in clapboard siding, with all the right additions—long porches, columns, painted shutters on their windows, brass hardware, electric "gaslights," bicycles in their circle driveways, and lawns that were chemically lush and green. There was another section of Port Frederick that looked much like that, too, but it came by its Colonial appearance authentically, because its houses really had been around for a couple of hundred years. This subdivision was modeled on that older, more established part of town, and if I had my dates right, this had all gone up about fifteen to twenty years ago. It was actually quite attractive in a Stepford kind of way, now that the trees had grown tall and once you got past the unfortunate street names. It suddenly came back to me that the Ron Mayer I'd read about in the newspaper had been a home builder; I wondered if he'd had a hand in this suburb.

"I wouldn't have wanted to know, but I think I resent it anyway."

"What?"

He'd been talking; I hadn't been listening.

"Isn't that bizarre, Jenny? I'm relieved, and I'm damned glad she didn't put me through it, but I still resent it! I'm nuts. And that scrapbook! I know I keep harping on it, but it gives me the fucking willies. It's like something out of a Stephen King novel, you know?" Suddenly, he laughed. "I'm confused, Jenny. Can you tell?"

I stopped searching for house numbers and looked at him.

He pulled over to the side of the road and stopped the car to finish saying his piece: "This may sound crazy, but I feel—Jesus, this is going to sound stupid and egomaniacal—but I feel violated. Can you believe that? What a laugh. I take advantage of her when she was probably high or drunk, plus I screw over her boyfriend who was always a decent guy to me, I get her pregnant, they raise my kid, and I'm the one who claims he feels violated!" He seemed bewildered, embarrassed, . . . and excited. His gaze shifted so that he was looking over my shoulder. "This is the house."

I turned around in my seat and saw one of the Colonials, painted blue-gray with dark blue trim. It didn't look like a house that would have a battered old BMW motorcycle parked in its driveway.

"Women's groups ought to take me out and lynch me."

"Possibly," I said, but I turned around again, and this time I put my hand on top of his, which was resting on the telephone he'd had installed when he bought the Jeep. He drove a city car with a police band radio for work; this car was for play, but he'd put in the phone to "be a good boy, and keep in touch with the station" if they needed him. Or if I did. It never rang unless it was the dispatcher or me calling him, because he wouldn't give out the number to anybody else. He seemed to resent it as an intrusion on his personal space/time, as the physicists say, so I hardly ever dialed him on it, but it comforted me to know he could call for help if he ever needed to.

"It's not that I blame her," he continued. "I don't. Do you believe that?"

"Sure," I said and tried smiling at him.

"Okay." He switched off the engine. I heard a lawn mower down the block and a radio playing rock and roll music. It was quite a ways away, but I thought it was Jimi Hendrix. I was sweating, and my legs were stuck to the car seat, and I wanted to get out and walk around for a while. "It's your turn to talk now."

I felt my heart shift into third gear.

"No. We're here. Let's do this first."

"He's back," Geof said quietly.

Sure enough, when I turned my head slowly to look down the

34

street, there was a battered black motorcycle idling at the curb, its driver sitting astride it, looking our way.

Geof turned the key in the ignition and the car started again.

"What are you doing?" I asked him.

Instead of answering me, he pulled away from the curb and did a slow U-turn, heading us back in the direction from which we'd come.

"I don't like being lured," he said.

"But we're *here!*"

"Which is exactly where he wants us to be." He drove back out of the entrance to the subdivision, then he looked over and smiled at me with a cocky half grin like the one I'd seen on his ... son's ... face earlier that afternoon. "I can be provocative, too."

"Oh, for heaven's sake!" I flung myself back in my seat.

"I can also be careful," he added with a glance in his rearview mirror. "If I'm the bait, I want to know more about what it is he's trying to catch with me. Before I go in that house, I'll review the case against his father."

"What does he *really* want?" I murmured for the wind to hear. But Geof heard me, and he replied, "A psychologist might say that he wants to displace his anger and grief onto me. Think how pissed *you'd* be if you were seventeen years old and your parents killed themselves and abandoned you. You might want to take it out on somebody."

"I was nineteen."

"What?" And then he made the association: When I was nineteen, my mother was as good as dead—comatose in a psychiatric hospital—and my father ran away from home with his lover, the same woman who was now my stepmother and who had indeed been the surrogate object for some of my unhappiness.

"It took me about fifteen years to realize how mad I was at my parents," I reminded Geof. "And when I realized it, I could have killed them." That was hyperbole, of course. I meant it only figuratively.

"You see?" he said. "That's what I mean."

On the ride home, I looked repeatedly in the mirror, but I

didn't glimpse any more motorcycle-riding teenagers in black jeans and white shirts.

We didn't say much after that; he'd already depleted his supply of words, and I wasn't ready to talk yet. When we got home, we both dragged around through the rest of the evening like exhausted, overheated hound dogs, and when we went to sleep—early for us—we curled up together like pups in a manger.

Geof made one more stab at trying to get me to talk to him.

"Your turn?" he mumbled, his nose touching mine on my pillow.

"Tomorrow," I lied and kissed the bridge of his nose.

He was satisfied with that, too easily satisfied, I thought.

We slept with the windows open, not knowing it was the last night we'd feel secure enough in our house to do that.

# 5

By morning, he seemed to have forgotten that we'd only had a monologue, not a dialogue, the day before. I encouraged his amnesia by bustling about and smiling a lot when we got out of bed, as if it were a normal Monday following an average Sunday.

But at breakfast, I asked, "Is it a secret?"

"Which?"

*Give me a break!* I thought, but I hid my sarcasm behind my cup of coffee. "That you might have a son. Ron and Judy. David. What happened. You know." I lowered my gaze to the kitchen table and pushed a crumb around on my white plastic placemat with my right forefinger.

There was no breeze coming through our screens; the air was suddenly as still inside the kitchen as it was outside. I listened to the birds chorusing; the song they were singing was, "It's too darned hot."

I looked up at Geof: He was caught in a still moment, paused in the tying of a plaid tie that he had put on over a navy blue shirt, which he wore with gray trousers and black loafers. Then he moved and spoke, his voice easy, casual. "David didn't ask us to keep it quiet, did he?"

"I don't know what he told you."

"Nothing you didn't hear, too."

"Oh."

The lieutenant looked great, I thought, certainly better than I thought I did in my bare feet, underpants, floppy T-shirt, and barely brushed hair. The past weeks had been full of luxuriously pleasurable days for me, because I was enjoying being temporarily unemployed—I was especially enjoying it in the mornings, Monday mornings most of all. I'd left my long-time job as director of the Port Frederick Civic Foundation, and I was walking, not running, toward future employment. Fortunate enough to remain financially secure in the meantime, I had been honoring that privilege by using it to take my time, skipping stones along the way, pausing to lie down in summer grass, splashing my feet in sweet pools of idleness.

"Do *we* want to keep it quiet?" I asked him.

"Why would we? Are we hiding something?" He shot the knot the rest of the way up to his collar and gave me an intimate, knowing glance. "Who do you want to tell, Jenny?"

"I'm having lunch with 'the girls' today."

"I don't give a damn who knows."

That sounded a shade defensive to me. I watched him lift his coffee mug, take the last sips from it, and set it down again. It was a brown ceramic one that he'd picked up at a garage sale, and it said in blue script that wound around it, "If I knew then what I know now, I'd know more now." I stared at it for a moment, recognizing the irony of that particular mug in this particular moment. *If we had known seventeen years ago, what we knew now . . .*

"What will the wise women say about me?" he asked, interrupting my reverie on his coffee mug. "You can tell me their verdict at dinner tonight. Am I guilty? Not guilty? Definitely not innocent." He laughed. "How will they judge me?"

Automatically, I said, "It's not their right to judge you."

"Yeah, well, they don't often exercise their right to remain silent."

I had to smile at that: It was so true. My friends Ginger, Mary, Marsha, and Sabrina had opinions. Oh, my, did they ever have opinions. They had advice. They had lots to say about any conceivable topic, and they did not hesitate to say any of it.

Geof leaned over to give me a quick kiss, then a longer one.

"Don't forget that Lee is coming over tonight," he said on his way out the kitchen door. On the other side, he looked back in and spoke to me through the screen. "See you tonight. I love you."

*Sergeant Meredith. With the files on the Mayer Case.* Oh, yes, I remembered.

"Love you, too."

His response, a moment later, was unexpected: *"Goddammit!"*

I was so startled that I slopped coffee onto my toast. I threw a paper napkin onto the mess and ran to the screen door. "What happened, Geof?"

"Don't come out here!" He was bending over something on one of the cement blocks in the path that led from the house to the garage. "There's a dead possum out here. Shit, what a mess." He looked back up at me. "Don't worry about it. I'll take care of it."

I followed his advice and didn't go out to view the corpse. Living in the countryside, we'd grown accustomed to dead creatures as part of the way of life, so to speak. I spared a moment of sympathy for the possum—which was not easy, as they had never struck me as being one of creation's more adorable ideas—and padded barefoot to a window to stare eastward toward the ocean and the rising sun. I leaned on the windowsill and stared at the landscape I knew so well only to discover that it looked different to me than it ever had before. It didn't look merely like a new day had dawned while we had slept. Instead, it felt as if a whole new world had come up with the sun that August morning: I had the unsettling feeling that all of my familiar landmarks had shifted in the night, as if the Washington Monument had inexplicably moved over a quarter of an inch, and Teddy Roosevelt had opened his mouth on Mount Rushmore, and Niagara Falls was now cascading onto the American side of the river.

I heard the thud of one of our heavy plastic trash bin lids.

Another thought, not very profound, crept in: Maybe I'd get Geof a copy of *Dr. Spock* for a fortieth birthday gift.

"Very funny," I said to myself.

Lazily, I turned away from the east view back toward the kitchen dishes. I had lots of time to get them washed. Being unemployed had its advantages. When I worked for the foundation, it was my generally pleasant task to distribute money to deserving (we hoped) causes. Now, with time to spare, I was launching a dream that still wasn't much more substantial than wispy clouds in the wide blue sky of my imagination. I wanted to start my own foundation with my own money and some of my friends'. That much, I knew. A foundation unlike any other, that much I knew, too. No "old boy's" network. No stifling traditions of old-fashioned charity. Nothing to rein in our imaginations, nothing to stop us except our own timidity or the IRS. And that's why my wise women met once a week for lunch, for they were to be the revolutionary core of my board of directors. Once a week, we met to figure out what else we needed to know, to do, to become . . .

I heard Geof start the Jeep and back out of the garage, I watched him drive away, and I waved good-bye, although he couldn't see it.

Three hours later, I walked out to my own car.

I raised the automatic door on the garage, and there it was . . . My baby. My new red Miata convertible. I'd traded in my good gray Honda Accord for this snappy little piece of pleasure. Hot damn!

But halfway to Port Frederick, with my hair streaming out in a ponytail behind me, my little engine purring, and the sun beating down on my immaculate hood, I noticed something that hadn't come with the car.

"What's that awful smell?" I said, conversing with the wind.

A skunk by the side of the road? Decaying vegetation in a ditch?

It stayed with me as I drove, growing stronger as the sun rose higher and the morning got hotter, until finally I thought I'd be sick to my stomach if I didn't get rid of it. Finally I had to admit that it was probably coming from the front end of my car. Maybe, I thought, a stiff breeze will blow it away . . .

That was all the excuse I needed to step harder on the gas pedal.

"You've got a dead mouse under the hood, Jenny." The owner of my favorite Amoco station wiped his hands on a red towel and made a face at me. "At least I think it used to be a mouse. Hard to tell once it's got ground up by the engine, it's just hair, skin, and bloody chunks."

I made a face back at him. Great, I thought. First, Geof's dead possum, now this. Poor little guy. "It's a real pain out where we live, Joe. Little furry things like to build nests in cars and eat things like wiring. Frankly, I was hoping they'd boycott foreign cars."

"Want to see?" He laughed at the expression on my face. "No? Okay. Pull it on up to the hose, Jenny, and we'll wash it out for you. Good thing you came in soon, hot as it is today you'd have the smell of cooked mouse in your car for weeks. It's damn hard to get an odor like that out once it gets into the upholstery and the carpet and everything. Not the sort of smell you want in your nice new car. How's it runnin', anyway?"

Ten minutes later, the Miata smelled fresher.

"Reckon it was Mickey Mouse?"

"You're a wicked man, Joe."

He laughed and carefully lowered my hood. "Mighta been Minnie, though."

I got back behind my wheel. A faint odor lingered, but maybe it was only in my nostrils, not in the car. I said, "Or maybe Mighty Mouse will no longer be able to Save the Day."

Joe gave me a reproachful look. "Now you've gone too far, Jenny. Mighty Mouse was always my favorite."

I waved my thanks and roared off toward lunch.

Ordinarily, my buddies would have convened for lunch at the Buoy, which is our local historical pub. But this foursome included Mary Eberhardt, the mayor of Port Frederick, and Mary swore—well, no, I take that back, Mary never swore, Mary vowed, she predicted, she declared—that she would get irate phone calls from Southern Baptists if she was seen "carrying on" in a tavern. To which another of our group, Sabrina Johnson, always protested—no, Sabrina wouldn't merely protest, *she'd* swear—"Well, what the hell are they doing up north if they're Southern Baptists?" The fact that the mayor was wed to a prominent minister also carried some weight in our choice of eating establishments. And so, we'd settled on the dining room of the local Holiday Inn, a sly choice, we thought, as the locals didn't frequent it. And so the mayor wouldn't get castigated by her constituents, the psychiatrist among us wouldn't run into her clients, the social worker wouldn't encounter any of her unemployed, and the philanthropist and I wouldn't know anybody either. It was anonymity we craved, in part so that we could gossip and cackle to our hearts' content and also because we had revolutionary plans afoot. Just for starters, in *my* foundation, there would be no glass ceiling to keep any woman, anybody, from rising to the top. Maybe we'd have no ceilings at all, nor any walls, just fresh air, fresh thinking. I got jazzed all over again just thinking about it, about them.

I drove faster toward the hotel, steering confidently.

This foundation of mine—of ours—was going to happen.

I sped the Miata into a shady parking spot and left the top down, hoping the interior would finish airing out while I was inside. Before I went in, I glared up into the branches of the tree above my car and spoke sternly to any birds who might be contemplating the prospect of dirtying my finish or my upholstery.

"Don't even think about it," I warned them.

# 6

THANKS TO THE DEAD RODENT, I WAS LATE FOR lunch.

When I walked into the coffee shop, my wise women were already seated at our regular booth, a semicircular one in a far corner. Out of all the women I knew, I'd picked them to head my foundation because they were intelligent, caring, daring women who, among them, knew just about everybody, every need, and every source of money in and around Port Frederick. What they didn't know much about, though, was foundations, and so we were still at our very beginnings, which so far had consisted mainly of me educating them, my dear, eager pupils.

On either side of me in the restaurant, as I walked toward my pals, there were strangers in short sleeves and shorts, all of them looking like tourists; happily, I didn't recognize a single face. There were chef's salads to the right of me, club sandwiches to the left, french fries all around, and many glasses of half-melted ice in sodas or weak tea. The price for our privacy was bland food.

My long promenade up the center of the dining room gave me a chance to observe my friends as I approached them. On the far left end of the red upholstered booth was Ginger Culverson, known to the rest of us as Moneybags. She was the only one, besides me, who was bringing the resources of her own trust fund to the foundation we were creating. She was thirty-four years old, short, with pale skin and blue eyes and frizzy reddish brown hair, a lovable round face and matching chubby body. Ginger also possessed a nice round sum of three million dollars that she'd inherited from her father a few years earlier. Ginger didn't work at much of anything except fixing her house up and figuring out ways to give away bits and pieces of her inheritance, so she was dressed casually, like me, in shorts, a T-shirt, and sandals. To look at her, you'd never have guessed she was loaded. We all thought she was adorable—earthy and sweet and generous, maybe to a fault—but unfortunately, Ginger didn't see herself that way and neither had many men in her lifetime. Their loss, in our opinion.

To Ginger Culverson's left was Mary Eberhardt, known to us as Madam Mayor or simply the Madam, an appellation she tried desperately to discourage us from using in public. Mary was late fortyish, a tall, slim, black woman with short gray hair, who was given to dressing in prim dresses or suits, with low heels and small hats. Today it was a dotted swiss navy blue dress with white heels and—I guessed without ever seeing it—a matching white purse at her side. Mary had a certain rah-rah cheerleader quality that we tried strenuously, and totally without success, to squash.

In the middle sat Sabrina Johnson, our brown beauty, thirty-eight years old, tall as the model and college basketball player she used to be, with her hair dyed to a shiny black and slicked back into a tight bun and dressed all in a shade of caramel that came so close to matching her skin color that from a distance she looked as if she had come shockingly naked to the coffee shop of the Holiday Inn. Ivory earrings the size of my fists dangled from her lobes. She was a social worker with a slam-dunk wit. We called her Slick.

Finally, on the right, there was Marsha Sandy, our resident psychiatrist and my best friend from forever. Marsha was my age, my height, but darker, calmer, quieter, more voluptuous and luscious looking, with big brown eyes that could hypnotize men and patients and a full head of thick dark brown hair. We called her Doc, none too originally, except for Sabrina who called her Shrink so that she could logically refer to Marsha's patients as "the shrunken heads," much to Marsha's resigned bemusement. "So how are the shrunken heads?" Sabrina would ask each week that we met for lunch. And Marsha would smile, shake her head, sigh, and plead, "Show a little respect, will you, Slick?"

I'd rather not divulge the nickname they chose for me.

As I drew near to their booth, I saw Sabrina turn and whisper something in Mary Eberhardt's ear, then I saw Mary look up at me and smile.

"I love you guys," I said as I slid in beside Ginger on the end.

"See?" Sabrina said to Mary. "I told you."

The Madam looked at me and laughed.

"What?" I demanded.

Sabrina grinned. "I told Mary you were going to say something like that." Marsha started to laugh, too, and I heard Ginger snicker beside me. "I said, Look, Mary, Jenny's having a Hallmark card attack. She's looking at the four of us, and she's thinking how utterly bee-oo-tee-ful we all are and how incredibly wonderful we are, and isn't she lucky to have us as her friends, and, I said, she's going to say something mushy as soon as she sits down."

Mary reached over Ginger to pat my hand. "We love you, too."

"Thank you, Mary," I said with a show of wounded dignity. "And screw you, Slick."

She laughed harder than any of them at that, but then she jabbed me again. "Did you drive up in your little blue roadster, Nancy?"

Oh, hell, now I have to admit it. That was it, my nickname. They'd taken to calling me Nancy Drew, Girl Detective, ever since I bought the Miata.

"It's red, dammit," I said.

They were laughing harder by then. A waitress had appeared at my side and was patiently waiting for an opportunity to get a word in edgewise. Mary gently chided me in the funny, stilted phrasing of those long-ago novels: "Now, Nancy, what would your father, Mr. Drew, think of such language?"

"Where *are* Ned and Mr. Drew?" inquired Ginger, playing along.

"I had to leave them at home!" I propped my menu in front of my face to hide my own laughter and to review the luncheon possibilities. "My father, Mr. Drew, has to work, you know!" I looked up at the patient waitress who was smiling down on us. "A BLT on whole wheat toast, please, and iced tea. Thank you."

She nodded, wrote that down, grinned at us, and departed.

"You're late," Marsha observed from the other end of the table. "We've already ordered and we've already made our weekly report on our private lives, and we refuse to repeat a word of it for people who don't arrive on time. It's your turn. So vat's new mit you?"

"Ned has an illegitimate son," I said, lowering the menu.

They laughed uproariously at the very idea of Nancy Drew's boyfriend being a father.

"Just the one?" Ginger said kiddingly.

"And he's seventeen years old," I continued, trying to smile at them. "And he dropped in on us without any warning yesterday afternoon to announce his existence. And he's the product of a one-night stand between, uh, Ned and a girl named Judy Baker that he went to high school with."

Mary, Ginger, and Sabrina were still laughing, but Marsha's brown eyes were losing their twinkle. She, who knew me far better than the others and might have recognized the name Judy Baker, was beginning to look alarmed.

"And Ned never knew the kid even existed until yesterday," I continued. "And the kid's name is David. David Mayer. And he's the child whose parents were the murder/suicide here in town last spring. Only the man who died, Ron Mayer, wasn't David's real father, Geof was. And now David wants Geof to know that while he really can't stand the sight of him and he never wants to lay eyes on him again, he would appreciate it if Geof . . . Ned, I mean . . . could manage to prove that Ron Mayer didn't really kill Judy Mayer and then kill himself."

There was now a shocked silence in the booth, but it exploded into pandemonium in about three seconds flat.

"Oh, my God!" Ginger grabbed my left hand and held on to it.

Sabrina let out a low whistle. "Well, geez. Don't you have any *exciting* news? Is this dull stuff the best you can manage?"

"Oh, my dear." Mary reached over and patted my hand, which Ginger was still holding. "Oh, my dear!"

Marsha smiled at me and leaned back against the upholstery. "This is going to be good, isn't it?" I looked at her in shocked surprise at first, and then I began to laugh kind of helplessly, and she started to laugh, too, while the other three looked at us as if we'd gone nuts. "Yes," I admitted, "that's one way of looking at it, Marsh, I guess you say this is going to be good."

"I remember Judy Baker Mayer," she told me, and suddenly it was only me and my best friend, alone in the booth.

"Yeah, we all went to the same high school."

"No, I mean later, just a few years ago, in fact."

"Why? Was she a patient of yours, Marsh?"

"No, I was a client of hers. Judy had a telephone answering service that she operated from her home, and I hired her to take my calls for a couple of years."

The waitress arrived with the other women's lunches and began passing them out. I talked to Marsha around the waitress's weaving arms as the others got their orders all straightened out and started to eat. We had an understanding that you ate when your food arrived, good manners notwithstanding, because Sabrina, Mary, and Marsha all had jobs they had to get back to on time.

"Why no longer than a couple of years?"

Marsha grabbed the salt and pepper shakers and liberally applied the seasonings to her chef's salad in a vain attempt to bring out some flavor. "Let's just say that Judy didn't quite grasp the concept of confidentiality."

"What's that supposed to mean?"

Marsha made an apologetic, comical face at me. "It's confidential." But when nobody else was looking at her she mouthed a word to me. "Later." I relaxed, knowing she'd tell me when no one else could overhear her.

"I knew her, too." We all shifted our attention from Marsha the psychiatrist to Sabrina the social worker. I saw that she'd ordered a taco salad. I could have told her it would taste like

47

crumbled cheeseburger, but there wasn't any reason to spoil it for her ahead of time. Maybe suspecting as much, Sabrina poured red sauce over it. I could have told her that would only make it taste like crumbled cheeseburger drowned in catsup. She explained, "During her second marriage, I mean. They hit some rough spots and she came to us for assistance. When I heard her husband killed her, I assumed it was the second one, he was just the type! Then I realized she had remarried the first one. The woman had a hell of a talent for picking the wrong men." Sabrina, suddenly aware of what that implied, glanced at me and grinned slyly. "Oops."

"Those salads taste like crumbled cheeseburger in catsup," I said in revenge and made a face at her. "What second marriage? To whom?"

"I don't remember the schmuck's name." Sabrina took a bite and grimaced at the taste of it. "Damn. You're right."

"Why was he a schmuck?" Marsha asked.

Sabrina laughed the bitter laugh of a woman who also had little talent for picking men. "Why are they all schmucks?"

"I knew *him*," Ginger interrupted, and now we turned toward her. Her sweet round face turned a little pink at the sudden attention.

"The schmuck?" Marsha asked.

"No, Ron Mayer, I knew him." Ginger picked at her pasta salad with her fork, turning over the spiral noodles as if she were looking for worms underneath them. "His family's company did the remodeling job on my house, remember?"

"No," I said.

"Yeah, you do. Mayer Construction."

"I didn't pay any attention to who was doing the job."

"That's because you've never done a major remodeling, or you would have paid attention, because I was always raving about how good they were." She popped some pasta into her mouth and didn't seem offended by its obvious blandness. "Ron was in charge of the company overall, he's the one who started it, but the grandfather did the supervising on the job, the grandmother kept the books—I didn't see much of her—the other four brothers did the actual labor, along with the daughters-in-law and a

48

couple of grandkids, the older boys. They were kind of strange people, I thought, real religious—"

Mary said mildly, "That doesn't make them bad people."

Sabrina retorted, "Doesn't make them good people either."

Mary smiled. "You've got me there, Slick."

Ginger continued, "I mean I felt like I couldn't even cuss when they were around—"

"Damn!" said Sabrina. "Even Mary lets us cuss!"

"I can't even stop my own husband," Mary protested. "How could I ever stop you?"

"—and they're expensive as hell, but they were absolutely reliable and they did great work, and he was nice."

"I hate nice," Sabrina said.

"Yes, that's your problem," Marsha told her.

"You're telling me?" Sabrina asked her.

"You don't accept the fact that you're a nice person, Sabrina," Marsha continued, "so you project your own better qualities onto men who aren't really that nice, and then you blame them when they disappoint you by not being who they never were to begin with."

"What bullshit," Sabrina said, looking annoyed.

"Yeah, but it's free bullshit." Marsha smiled at her. "I charge other people seventy-five dollars an hour for the same load of crap."

"Ladies!" pleaded the mayor as she glanced around the dining room.

"Strange?" I said to Ginger. "How were they strange?"

"I knew both of them," Mary Eberhardt interjected hurriedly as if she wanted to change our language more than our subject.

As my glance shifted from Ginger to Mary, I thought of how I'd heard some men complain that when women got together in groups we all talked at the same time. Of course we did, it was like jazz, everybody jumped in on pitch, in rhythm, and everybody had a good time. Sitting there with them, comfortably watching and listening to them, I postulated a theory for my own entertainment: If men tended to take center stage or to monologue, and God knows they did, then maybe we tended to wander on and off stage and to "dialogue." I would have tried that

49

theory out on my friends, but it would have jerked the conversation "out of tune" at that moment.

"Oh, well, hell," Sabrina said dismissively, jokingly. "You know *every*body, Madam, and if you don't know them, Hardy does."

Sabrina was referring to Mary's husband, the Reverend Dr. Hardy Eberhardt, preacher at the First Church of the Risen Christ, the major black congregation in town.

Mary's mouth lifted in a smile, but I could see the compassion in her eyes for the Mayer tragedy. "Only through church events. But I can't say I really *knew* them."

I whined, "Am I the only one who *didn't* know them?"

"God, Jenny," Sabrina said, "you're so competitive!"

I laughed, waiting for her to expand the joke.

Sure enough, Sabrina looked to her left at Marsha and then she nodded at me. "Can you believe it? We bring our tales of boyfriends and husbands and bosses and employees and politics and children and money and religion to lunch. But Ms. Cain, here, she's got to up the ante. Murder. Suicide. Bastard sons. Damn." Sabrina leaned back in the booth and crossed her slender arms over her stomach. "Who do you think you are, Cain—Toni Morrison? You just have to top us, don't you?"

I feigned astonishment. "*I'm* competitive? Who's jealous?"

"Jenny?" The mayor looked thoughtful. "This news of yours, is it going to hurt my reelection chances to say I know you from now on?"

We all burst out laughing at that. That was one of the reasons we loved Mary, just when you thought she was all goody-two-shoes, she'd spring some bit of cynicism on us. I smiled at her as the waitress set my bacon, lettuce, and tomato sandwich down in front of me. I saw they'd put it on white bread instead of whole wheat but decided not to make a fuss about it. "Hasn't it always, Mary?"

She reached over Ginger to squeeze my hand again. "Sweetheart, tell us all about it. Is it really true? How do you feel about it? Are you upset? How is Geof taking it? What's the boy like? How's he doing now, with his parents gone? Why does he think

50

they didn't die as everybody thinks they did? What's going to happen?"

"From the beginning," Marsha commanded.

"Well, yesterday afternoon . . ."

When I finished talking, they'd finished eating.

Mary said, "Is there anything we can do to help?" She was asking on behalf of all of them, that was obvious from the nodding of heads around the table.

"I don't know." I threw it back at them. "Is there?"

"I'll check with some of her other answering service clients," Marsha said.

"I'll review my files on them," Sabrina offered.

"I'll talk to Hardy about it," Mary said.

That left us all looking at Ginger, though I don't suppose that any of us meant to put her on the spot like that. She shrugged, looking helpless and a little pink again. "I'll . . . think about it."

"You're wonderful," I said gratefully to all of them.

"Yeah, yeah." Sabrina reached toward the middle of the table for her check, which the waitress had long since delivered. "Listen, I'm sorry, but I got to get back to work. No way I can tell my welfare moms that I'm late because I was havin' lunch with my rich white friends."

Mary nudged her. "Who you callin' rich?"

"But we haven't talked business yet," I protested.

"Honey . . ." Sabrina waved her check at me as she pushed Marsha out of the booth so she could leave. "I only have one lunch hour a day and it ain't long enough for *both* your soap operas *and* your business! But I'll be thinking about you . . . and Geof." That was accompanied by a sardonic snort as she stood on the other side of the table, and Marsha resumed her own seat. "Men!"

Mary defended him: "He was still practically a boy, Sabrina."

"Father of the man," Sabrina retorted.

"Father of the boy," I muttered. "And he wasn't any boy himself; he was plenty old enough to know better. Hey," I spoke up quickly, forestalling their critique of my husband's history, "while you're thinking about him, think about the fact that he's turning forty soon. Got any ideas about what I should do?"

51

"Shoot him?" suggested Marsha.

"Castrate him?" suggested Sabrina.

"Divorce him?" suggested Ginger.

"You guys!" I protested, laughing. "I thought you liked him!"

"We do like him." Sabrina made an impatient face at her watch as she looked at it. "But our first loyalty is to our pal Jenny, not to him. Frankly, my dear, drop-in children were not part of the bargain when you married the man, least not as I've heard you say. Especially *complicated* children, kids with murdered mothers and suicidal fathers. And don't think I'm making light of this, because I'm not. I'm sure that poor child needs help, but I don't know that you should necessarily have to be the one to give it. Or maybe you have to grin and bear it, like a good little wife, but we don't. We're pissed on your behalf. Except Mary, Mary never gets pissed—"

"Who says I'm grinning and bearing it?"

"I get riled up," Mary said with dignity.

Sabrina said, "Yeah, me too. I think this could screw up your life, Jenny."

My blood ran a bit cold at that bald statement of my exact fears.

"Well, but Sabrina," Ginger suddenly said, "he didn't mean to."

"What?" Sabrina stepped backward and splayed her right hand to her chest in mock surprise. "Somebody only recently invent condoms? They didn't have them back in the dark ages when Geof went to college?"

"Did you use them?" I challenged her.

"Never got the chance," she shot back. "I was too tall and too mouthy. Nobody wanted me."

That silenced the rest of us for a second. The thought of nobody desiring Sabrina Johnson was unthinkable. Then we adjusted to the probable truth of her assertion. The conversation carried on.

"I *have* to leave!" Sabrina finally made good on her word, but she couldn't resist calling over her shoulder, "Don't you dare say anything interesting while I'm gone!"

And then she was gone.

"Quick," I said. "Business."

"I've been thinking," Mary said, "that we ought to leave it to your old foundation to handle all the traditional charities in town. Let's not compete with them at all, Jenny; let's fund the sorts of things they can't fund."

"Or won't," I said, remembering the fights I'd had with my hidebound board of old men trustees at the Port Frederick Civic Foundation.

"The other day, I was standing in the grocery store," Ginger said, "staring at Paul Newman's Spaghetti Sauce, and I thought, Why do we have to depend on trust funds and traditional investments as our source of income for this thing? Why can't we also earn some of the money with some kind of business, like his spaghetti sauce?"

"Ginger!" I nearly hugged her; this was the kind of freewheeling, inventive thinking I dreamed of, and I didn't want to discourage any of it—no matter how unlikely—yet. "Yes, maybe we could . . . can . . . clams." I laughed out loud, thinking of the clam-canning business my family ran for three generations and how it had been destroyed by certain people in Port Frederick, and what sweet revenge it might be to reopen a small version of the old Cain canning company, only this time, all the money might go to charity . . .

I stopped that fantasy before it ran away with me.

"I've been thinking," Marsha said, "of how difficult it used to be for women's shelters to get money, even from foundations. Remember the bad old days, when nobody funded women's issues? Well, what I'm wondering is . . . what is the 'women's shelter' of today? Let's find out which issues are getting rejected by all of the conventional funding sources, and let's be the first ones to help them out."

"Yes," I said. "Yes!"

Our meeting ended in a flurry of check paying and good-bye hugging and cheek pecking. At the cashier's counter, I ran into Roy Leland, one of my old bosses at my old job, a long-time trustee of the Port Frederick Civic Foundation. So much for anonymity; it appeared that other locals also sought it now and then at the Holiday Inn.

"You girls having lunch?" Roy asked me cordially.

*Will you old boys never learn?* I thought crabbily. *Did I accomplish nothing, exert no lasting influence, in all those years of working for you?* With one thoughtless word, Roy had renewed my great pleasure in unemployment.

"Sure are, Roy."

I beamed a sincere smile at him and hurried after my friends. I didn't want Roy getting any more curious than that; the old boys weren't going to like this new foundation idea of mine. I had already anticipated their reactions: "The money pool's not big enough in this town for two foundations, Jennifer." "You'll take money away from our worthy causes, undermine our years of good work, Jennifer." "Nobody wants to fund the kind of things you do, Jennifer." "You'll split this town apart, Jennifer." In other words, their probable attitude could be summed up by the sheriff's code of the Old West: "This town ain't big enough fer both of us." I knew from long, painful experience that the old guys knew only competition. They would never really believe that I didn't intend to compete with them or fight with them, so I wasn't going to waste my energy trying to disarm them, especially not so early in the game.

My game, this time, not theirs. Their betrayals were many, but they were part of my childhood; they were the past. Now my friends were the grown-ups, the new generation of influence in Port Frederick.

I caught up with one of those younger power brokers—Mary Eberhardt—in the lobby. She tucked an arm through mine and pulled me back a bit so that the two of us were tagging behind Ginger and Marsha.

"Jenny, forgive me, but I just have to say this to you." Mary spoke so softly I had to lean toward her to hear. "Call me a minister's wife, but I still have to. Maybe I'm just feeling sympathy for the boy, but I can't help but think that there's an angel at work in this situation you're facing. Now don't look at me like that! After all these years, I guess I'm an expert on zoning boards and angels! Where there are problems, there are angels hovering about just waiting for us to ask them to help us transform our suffering into blessings. I'm not being religious, I'm telling you the truth as I have experienced it. Even on the city council." She smiled warmly at me. "And I'm not being trendy either. I'll have you know I was talking to angels long before they got fashionable." Her smile widened, and she squeezed my arm tighter. "So maybe you don't believe in angels, that's all right, they don't care. They're not like Tinkerbell, you know, they don't depend on your faith in order to exist. A lot of people didn't believe the earth was round either, but that didn't make it any flatter. So you just keep an ear open for the flutter of wings, Jenny, that's all I'm suggesting to you. There's a richness being offered to you and Geof and the boy. It's a wonderful opportunity for all of you, I just know it is."

This was more optimism than even I could take at the moment.

"I think you mean we're going to be knee-deep in rich and fragrant fertilizer, Mary."

"You know I don't mean that at all."

I smiled back at her, but I felt annoyed all the same.

"Listen, dear." She tugged me close enough to sniff the mint in her mouth. I was being lobbied by an expert politician. "A child. Two deaths. A father. And you, now you're kind of a stepmother."

"Oh, God, Mary!" I said in not-so-mock dismay.

She laughed and gave my arm another quick, affectionate squeeze before releasing me. "Look for the richness, Jenny. You have a treasure of experience and emotion just waiting for all of you, and that's where the angels are sitting, right on top of that treasure."

"Do I have to take it in experience and emotion?" I whined at her. "Can't I just take it in commodities options instead?" I sighed. "How would *you* feel, Mary, if a kid walked up to your door one Sunday and announced he was Hardy's illegitimate son?"

"You forget, I'm a minister's wife: I believe in virgin births."

I was still laughing at that as she strutted off to her humble, mayoral, ministerial black sedan with her white purse slung over one shoulder.

*Angels!* I thought as I walked to my car. *Good grief.* The kid had looked more like the devil to me.

The Miata smelled worse for sitting in the sun, and there were several fresh black and white spots on my windshield. Thrown into a sudden ill humor by Mary's exasperating lecture and by my old boss's infuriating condescension and by the sacrilege to my car, I glared up into the tree branches and snarled at the birds. "Fly over my house and you're chicken fingers!"

# 7

THAT EVENING, GEOF SEEMED TO FIND THE STORY OF my dead mouse far more titillating than I had at the time. He kept pressing me with questions about it.

"Did you look at it, Jenny?"

"Are you kidding?"

We were in the kitchen, it was still very light outside, even at seven o'clock, and I was chopping garlic on the built-in cutting board next to our oven.

"I smelled it," I told him, "that was enough."

"Are you sure it wasn't there earlier, like yesterday?"

"I would have known, Geof, I mean, consider the heat . . ."

He held a fistful of fettuccine noodles upright above the water boiling in a large pot. He released the pasta and they spread apart in the pot like pickup sticks, distributing themselves evenly for boiling. I used the flat side of a paring knife to slide little bits of garlic into my left hand and I dumped that load in with the mushrooms, tomatoes, black olives, capers, chili peppers, and anchovies that were frying in olive oil and vermouth. I pulled another clove of garlic toward me and began chopping; we operated on the assumption that there is no such thing as too much garlic. Besides, it was helping to finally clear my nose of cooked mouse. Meanwhile, Geof opened the refrigerator in his perpetual search for unlikely leftovers to add to our impromptu pasta repast. Lately, we two noncooks had taken to collaborating a few times a week in the kitchen; I attributed it to the fact that I had more time and energy since I'd quit the foundation, but he said we were just sick of eating out.

Other people probably would have said it was hot in the kitchen that early evening, but we'd grown accustomed to turning off the AC, opening all the windows, turning on the overhead fans, and wearing as few clothes as possible. For me, that meant a halter top and shorts and bare feet and my hair pulled high off my neck, and for him it meant his trusty red swimming trunks, period. I would have gone without a shirt myself, but I was leery of splattering hot oil.

"Can we talk about something besides dead mouse?" I pleaded. "It's ruining my appetite."

He was quiet for a moment, watching the pasta boil.

"So what did the girls say about me at lunch?"

"You are not their favorite poster boy this week."

*"Moi?"*

It was okay that he called them girls, because I called his friends boys. Postfeminist, that's what we were, which entitled him to say anything, because I was confident of his sensitivity to the layers of meaning in a single word, its history of hurt. Between us, powerful words like *girl* could be said humorously, like a rueful joke between old warriors. In the same trusting way, he could even open car doors for me, which I accepted as acts of gallant sweetness and not of dominance, and he could walk next to the curb "to protect me from the horses." We turned such acts into choreography, with me dancing under his arm and both of us laughing.

He smiled a little as he handed me a jar of Parmesan cheese, then feigned surprise and dismay. "What did I do?"

"You got a girl pregnant. Knocked her up. Left her with a kid. Landed me with the kid years later. That's how they see it."

"I thought they were my friends, too." He picked up a fork

and began separating the strands of fettuccine in the pot, and I thought I heard an undercurrent of actual unhappiness in his voice. "How come we've suddenly got a gender dividing line here? Did you tell them I didn't even know she was pregnant?"

"Well, as Sabrina said—"

"Yeah, it would be her."

"—hadn't anybody invented rubbers back then?"

He put the fork down, folded his arms across his bare chest, and looked at me. "Okay, so I was a typical teenage boy."

"And she was a typical easy lay?"

"Oh, boy, I can see where this is going. Don't you think those were slightly different times back then?"

"Not from what I read in the papers these days, no. Boys are still looking for easy girls and easy girls are still looking for love and they're still getting pregnant or pelvic inflammatory disease or herpes. No, except for AIDS, I don't think it's very different now."

"Oh, I see how it is! How it always is. All the guy's fault, right? So your friends think I was irresponsible and they think that now you're going to have to pay half the price of it, is that what they think? What about her responsibilities? Is it fair just to blame me? If I recall, Judy was extremely there at the time, so wasn't she also responsible for doing something about birth control? Or for telling me no?"

I made a hissing sound between my teeth.

"Dammit, Jenny, that's just the trouble with women!"

"Oh, now it's not just one teenage girl twenty years ago, it's 'women'?"

"You don't want to take responsibility for yourselves."

I put down the spoon I was using to stir with, and I crossed my arms over my chest and I looked at him. "I beg your pardon?"

"You claim you want independence, but you think all that means is your own condo and your own money and your own car and a job. What you still don't want or even understand is real autonomy. I'm not talking about you personally, Jenny, so don't explode at me, all right? I'm speaking of women in general who don't want to grow up. Deep down, they still want to grab some man who'll go to work for them, so they can quit and stay home if they want to, so they don't ever have to be totally responsible for themselves."

"Been giving this a lot of thought, have you?"

"Yes, why not?"

"Well, tell me this, how did we jump from one teenage girl named Judy Baker Mayer to women not wanting autonomy? Did I miss something in your lecture? It seems to me that we zoomed from the specific to the universal in just under ten seconds from a standing start. So what you're saying is, you're pissed because I'm staying home while you keep working—"

"What? I am not saying any—"

"I'd do the same for you, you know."

"Jenny, I didn't—"

"Your pasta's getting overcooked."

"What? Oh, shit!" He quickly used his fork to lift out a strand of the fettuccine and tested its doneness by throwing the strand up to the ceiling to see if it stuck. If it did, or so the theory went, it wasn't done yet.

The strand fell onto my left foot.

"Can't you just *taste* it?" I complained, bending to pick it up.

We put our dinner together quickly so it wouldn't get cold, piling our plates high and adding buttered bread and green salads and glasses of wine and water, all without speaking to each other until we sat down and spread our napkins on our laps. The ringing of our portable phone beside my elbow provided a bridge back into conversation for us.

"Mutt or Geof?" inquired the voice of my best friend, the shrink, Marsha Sandy.

"Mutt." To Geof, I mouthed, "It's Marsha." He mouthed back, "Hello." To her, I said, "We're eating. Geof says hello. Do you mind if I chew in your ear?"

"Geof wants to chew in my ear?"

I laughed and glanced at him. He cocked an inquisitive eyebrow.

"Jenny," Marsha said, "I want to tell you what I couldn't say at lunch about Judy Baker Mayer. Do you want to call me back?"

"No, I can chew and listen at the same time."

"I always knew you were a bright girl. Judy wasn't one of my patients, you understand, that's why I'm free to blab. God, if anybody had told me that being a shrink means you never get to gossip, I might have gone to air traffic control school instead of medical school. Okay, the thing about Judy is that I originally found her telephone answering service through a doctor I know. He said she was always polite to his patients, she was extremely reliable, he liked her service better than any other in town even though she wasn't a real company, she was just one woman answering the phone.''

"What'd she do about taking night calls?''

"She took them. All of them. She was simply amazing, Jenny. I don't know when she ever got a decent night's sleep. In fact, I had the impression that she had terrible insomnia—''

"Sure, phone ringing all the time.''

"Very funny, Jenny. Anyway, I think she watched TV most of the day and half of the night, and I know she sat propped up in a reclining chair with her phone and her notepads beside her. Maybe she slept there or dozed between calls. There wouldn't usually be many, you know, and some nights there might not be any. I imagine she had a couple of phone lines. She was expensive, but she gave us better service than any of the other services do. She was great, like an old-fashioned central telephone exchange operator, you know? She got to know us and our clients and their problems and our schedules, and that made her a wonderful judge of what was a true emergency and what wasn't. She knew when to call me at three in the morning and when to let it ride at least until the sun came up.''

"That's kind of amazing, Marsha. So *autonomous* of her.''

I made a face at my husband, who had glanced up from his eating when he heard me emphasize the word.

"Yes, I was sorry I had to leave her.''

"Okay, I'll bite . . . Why did you?''

"She told the name of one of my patients to one of her other clients.''

"Oh, dear. How'd you find that out?''

"I ran into this guy—her other client, who isn't a doctor, just a businessman—at a meeting or a cocktail party or something, and he said, 'Hey, I heard ol' Jimmy Joe has flipped out.' ''

"Oh, dear."

"Yes, *I* flipped out when I heard that. Not only that, but she also gossiped to him about how poor Jimmy Joe was nearly suicidal one night and how he was going to hang himself from a beam in his parents' garage and how he called her and said if she didn't get me on the line, he'd do it with the phone cord."

"You had to fire her."

"Damn right I did."

"And this is to tell me . . . ?"

"Only what I know about her."

"I think I'm missing a conclusion here, Marsha."

"That's because you really *can't* chew and think at the same time. Jenny, the point is that Judy Baker Mayer knew a hell of a lot of sensitive things about a hell of lot of people in Port Frederick. At least once, she gossiped about what she knew. I don't know if she did it more than once, but common sense suggests she may have. I don't know if she ever used her knowledge for any purpose besides gossip. I don't even know if what I'm telling you is important or not."

"No, no, Marsha, that's not what you say if you want to be a police informer. You're supposed to tell me that your information will break this case wide open, and you want your money as soon as it does."

"I'll try to remember that next time."

We bid each other a good evening and hung up.

Naturally, Geof was staring at me by then.

"Your girlfriend was a tattletale." I related Marsha's story to him. When I finished talking, he said, "If you don't want any more pasta, I'll eat the rest of it."

"No comment?" I said.

"She wasn't my girlfriend." He got up from the table with an empty plate in his hand and returned with a full one. "You're not jealous, are you?"

"What could be more intimate than making a baby?"

He looked at me, started to say something, stopped, then finally came out and said it: "I've tried to tell you that."

"The voice of experience."

"Oh, please."

"Yeah, and when our intimate moment was done, we'd have several billion more moments of raising a child ahead of us. And I've tried to tell you *that*."

"Call Sabrina," he said. "Ask about the bologna."

"The what?"

"Judy's second husband." He smiled. "The one who was sandwiched between two slices of Ron."

He had a knack for tickling my sense of humor just in time.

"I love you, Geoffrey."

"I know, Jennifer."

I was smiling as I dialed Sabrina Johnson's home phone number. When I greeted her voice, she said, "So, tell me, has Geof changed his mind about getting an abortion?"

"It's a little late for that, Sabrina, like about seventeen years and nine months too late."

"What's she saying?" Geof asked.

"Geof wants to know what you asked, Sabrina."

"Go ahead and tell him."

He frowned when I did.

"What'd he say?"

"Never mind. Tell me about Judy's other husband, Sabrina."

"You're no fun. Okay. Dennis Clemmons, that's his name. I looked up the case files like I told you I would, and that triggered a few memories. I have this fuzzy memory that she was scared of him, I think it was a real strong impression I had at the time. She saw me to find out if she could get Aid to Families with Dependent Children for her son and Social Security for her own disability and unemployment benefits for Clemmons. At first I couldn't find her because of the different last name. But then, there she was."

"Why the aid for dependent children? Ron Mayer must have been paying child support, wouldn't you think?"

"There's no record of it in my files, Jenny. In fact, what I want to tell you is that she lied like hell to me. Until I read it in the paper last winter, I never knew she'd been married before. She never mentioned a first husband, she never mentioned child support or alimony or a divorce settlement or anything else she might have been getting. We'd have discovered all that, eventually, if she'd stuck around, but she didn't. She came in a few times for information, and she got as far as filling out some applications, but then she asked me to hold on to them for a while. That's where they've been all this time—in my file cabinet, pending."

"Ever clean out your files, Slick?"

"In whose free time, Cain?"

"Okay, I know, I'm sorry."

"The thing is, Judy Clemmons—that's who she was when I saw her—she let me think the kid belonged to the man she was married to at the time—"

"Dennis Clemmons."

"Right. She called him Denny."

"What was his story?"

"Nonunion laborer. Unemployed a lot."

"Why do you say she was scared of him?"

"Because she was applying for all that welfare behind his back."

"She said that, Sabrina?"

"I just know I could never get her to get him to cooperate." She paused, and when she spoke again, I thought I heard a grin in her voice. "Although now that I think about it, I guess I understand why."

"So? Why?"

"Because in order to get aid for dependent children, we have to have a paternity test proving the man the woman claims is the father really is the father. I guess now we know why she didn't want him to take *that* test, don't we?"

I groaned while Sabrina hooted with laughter in my ear.

"I thought she was afraid to ask him to help her, like it would offend his pride or something, a lot of men are like that. Little did I know . . ." I heard another throaty chuckle. "By the way, I have an address . . ." She said it in a way that was meant to tantalize me, but her next words revealed who had the curiosity. "The address when she was married to Dennis Clemmons. Maybe he still lives there. Maybe you should come pick me up at noon tomorrow, and we'll go drive by on my lunch hour and see what it looks like . . ."

I glanced over at my lieutenant husband, but he had picked up his plate and mine and left the table and now he was busy at the sink.

"Sure, why not?" I said. "Anything else, Slick?"

"Adoption," she said.

"What? Dennis Clemmons adopted David?"

By that time, Geof was pouring powder into the dishwasher. But now he straightened up and stared back at me.

"No!" Sabrina was laughing. "*You* could adopt the kid out to somebody else. Or maybe a foster home?"

I said warningly, "Sabrina!"

Geof demanded, "What'd she say?"

"Sabrina said that Judy inquired about public assistance when she was married to Dennis Clemmons, but that she lied about a lot of things, like not reporting her previous marriage or any alimony or child support and claiming that Clemmons was David's father. Sabrina also said she'd like to be a sort of foster mother to David."

"I did not!" she screeched in my ear.

"She did?" Geof looked baffled but pleased as he turned away to finish his work. "Really?"

"Basketball?" I said to her as if she'd asked me a question. "Sure, I think that playing basketball with him is a great idea, Sabrina, you being a former collegiate all-star and all, and you could take him to a movie once a month, go bowling, whatever you like."

"Like hell." She was laughing again.

"Better thee than me," I said softly so Geof couldn't hear me over the racket of the dishwasher starting up. "See ya, Slick." I hung up. To my husband, I said in a voice that carried quite well over the noise of the dishes rattling in the machine, "Well, it seems your girlfriend was a liar, too."

Immediately, I regretted my hard humor.

Geof looked as if I'd slipped a small, thin knife between his ribs, and he was trying hard not to let me see how much it scared him, how much it hurt. I knew what he was thinking: *If she'd lied twice about David's paternity—first saying the father was Ron, then claiming it was Dennis Clemmons—she might have lied about it really being Geof. If she had no scruples about divulging confidential information, if she'd slept around like a cat during high school, and if she'd tried to cheat the welfare system, then the adult Judy Baker Mayer might have been a pathological liar at best, an entirely unethical woman at her worst.* By now, after twenty-four hours of allowing himself to entertain the possibility, Geof really wanted this "child" to be his. It was written all over his face. At that moment of recognizing the depth of his desire, I felt a sharp quick stab of fear in my own heart as well. Part of the fear was for me in case it was all true and we were really going to have that difficult, spooky boy in our lives. But part of my fear was for him in case it wasn't true.

Not looking at me, his voice as calm as if he weren't concerned about anything more than the fact that Sergeant Lee Meredith was due to show up with the case files in a few minutes, he said, "How about some ice cream?"

# 8

THE NIGHT FINALLY LIVED UP TO ITS NAME AND DARK-ened, but that lowered the air temperature only infinitesimally. The air was so heavy inside the house and out that you'd have thought a storm was coming; the weather reports said it wasn't. An upper air stream had stalled, that was all, trapping summer indefinitely down on the baking ground in Massachusetts.

"Come on, Fall," I urged as I stood on our front stoop, staring at the headlights coming toward me. "Change things."

"What?" called Geoffrey from inside. "Is Lee here?"

"Just driving up," I called back in to him, "like a breath of fresh air."

"Good." Suddenly he was behind me, pressing close for an instant, wrapping my hot body in his arms, but briefly. "We could goddamn well use some."

With a face like a cherub and a body like a wrestler, Lee Meredith was a walking paradox: Geof claimed that sweet round face, with its halo of soft brown hair, could wring a tearful confession out of a killer, while her fireplug arms and legs could disable a man twice her size. She was twenty-nine years old, five foot eight inches tall, and the first female sergeant in Port Frederick history.

"Hey," I greeted her in our living room. "How you doin', Sarge?"

She grinned back at me. "Hi, Mom."

I turned toward Geof. "Who invited her?"

Behind me, she laughed, while Geof just shook his head at us.

"I guess you know about everything," I deadpanned to her.

Her smile broadened to include her so-called superior officer, the lieutenant. "Must have been a C-section, Jenny? It's a hell of a late-term delivery."

"The episiotomy was a bitch," I said.

"You two!" Geof looked uncharacteristically helpless. Lee and I snickered at each other and at him. "Get in here!" He faked a blustering swagger. "Both of you! Dammit!" We faked obedience and, still snickering behind his back, followed him into the dining room, which he and I had cleared so the sergeant could lay out her files for us. Lee brought into our house an aroma of the pipe tobacco that her husband, Charlie, smoked, and it intertwined comfortably with our own lingering garlic. We were all in shorts and T-shirts, but the dining room was the hottest room in our house, having no cross-ventilation, so I'd brought in a floor fan, which I now turned on, aiming it at our legs under the table, so the breeze wouldn't ruffle her papers. Lee's outfit, a starkly plain tank-top T-shirt atop equally plain tan cotton shorts, displayed the fact that she was sweating lightly—and the powerful quads and biceps that helped her compete successfully on police martial arts teams.

I took a seat at one end of the table, Lee and Geof sat opposite one another.

She dumped two bulky files with a thud on the tabletop and then released the contents from the rubber bands that bound them.

"This was a clear case," she said firmly as she sat down.

She started right in, working rapidly, efficiently, pointing to papers with her powerful, stubby fingers, their nails filed into short, clean mounds. ("Keep an edge on 'em," she had once advised me, "for good defensive weapons.")

"Here's my sketch of the crime scene, Lieutenant. Here's the report of the first uniform on the scene. Here's my initial report. Lab reports. And here's everything that came after, right up to the time we closed it." She grabbed a neatly paper-clipped pile. "I clipped these newspaper articles, too. Not everybody does, but I think they should, because sometimes reporters talk to people we don't, and sometimes they print stuff we don't know about." She nodded toward Geof, then grinned at me. "Those are quotes. I'm brownnosing."

He pulled at the nose and smiled slightly.

"I'm trying to show I can do it the way he taught me to do it," she joked with me. "You never know, he might make chief someday, and I want to stay in good with him." She grinned at him. "Dad."

"Yeah," he said dryly, "that's the way, all right."

But Lee was irrepressible. She arched her eyebrows in a comical way, then pointed at all the forms littering our table. "So, it's all here, like you requested, Geof. What I suggest, if you don't mind my suggesting something in your esteemed presence, is that we take the time right now for both of you to read whatever you want to—I'm assuming you want to, Jen?"

I nodded. "Yep."

"Great, and you can ask me anything, and we'll talk about it."

Geof took the laboratory reports, while I went for her sketch of the crime scene. Her pencil strokes were thick and bold, and although her artistry would never hang on anyone's wall, the sketch was clear enough for its single purpose.

"Living room?" I said.

"Between the living room and the dining room," she corrected me.

"Judy's body was found in this chair you've drawn here?"

"Right." Lee's voice was encouraging, as if I were a recruit she was training. "The chair had been pulled in from the dining room and placed in the doorway between the two rooms, facing the living room. It was one of the dining room chairs."

"And this is his body on the floor at her feet."

"Yes."

69

"Geof, are we bothering you by talking out loud like this?" I asked him. "Can you concentrate while Lee and I are talking?"

He didn't even look up.

"Geof?" I smiled at Lee. "I guess we're not bothering him."

"He's used to a heck of a lot more commotion than we're making, Jenny. The lieutenant has amazing powers of concentration."

I knew that—in ways that his fellow and sister cops down at the station would never know—and I kicked him under the table to remind him.

"Darn right," he muttered without looking up.

"Is there anything else I should notice here, Lee?" I asked her.

"I don't know. Tell me what you see."

"Just four walls and the furniture you've drawn here. As you said, her chair is in the middle of the doorway. The rest of the furniture around the walls of the living room includes, let's see, two couches, a couple of arm chairs, a TV, two coffee tables, four end tables. Lot of furniture. Sort of a strange arrangement, all pushed up against the walls like that? Not exactly a cozy conversational grouping, was it?"

"Plenty of room for a wheelchair to get around in though."

Geof and I both looked up. I spoke first: "Judy was in a wheelchair?"

"Parkinson's," Geof told me. To Lee, he said, "She was really that much of an invalid?"

"She was that much of an invalid, yes . . ."

Lee left the rest of the sentence hanging.

I reached for a stack of color photographs, eight-by-tens that showed every inch of the crime scene. The officer who took them had stood in the front doorway and snapped overlapping shots of the rooms, and then he or she had walked to the opposite wall and shot overlapping pictures from there. There was a log in which the picture taker had noted the time of each shot, the brand and speed of film, the F-stop, and the subject of each photograph.

My stomach rolled, and I drew in my breath.

What had until that moment been only outlines and x's on Lee's sketch now turned into detailed, graphic, bloody reality.

70

Now I could see that the chair in which Judy had died was a dark brown ladderback with no arm rests. I could see that she was wearing a white long-sleeved pullover blouse when she died and a full white skirt with an elasticized waistband and no belt. It looked like clothing that might be easy for a disabled woman to pull on and off. She was soaked in blood. She was slumped over to her right, as if the force of the bullet had shoved her there, pinioning her against the chair with her head hanging over the back, turned slightly to the right.

"She was shot twice," Lee offered. "Left temple. Heart."

Geof interjected, reporting on what he was reading: "The first bullet sliced through her cerebral cortex, massive damage, exit wound consistent with her husband kneeling on the floor at her feet, holding the gun to her temple, looking up. The second was dead center in her heart. It says he was covered with her blood as well as with his own, but her blood was smeared on him, as if he had embraced her after he shot her."

On hearing that Ron had hugged Judy after he killed her, Lee and Geof and I glanced at one another, each of us appearing to bite back the comments on the tips of our tongues. I tried to think about it charitably: *Okay, maybe he loved her, maybe she begged him to do it, maybe it broke his heart, maybe it was like that.*

"Kneeling at her feet?" I said, but then it burst out of me. "What crap! Who do these men think they are? They kill themselves and take the little woman out with them, like they think she couldn't possibly live happily without them. You ever hear about *women* doing that?"

"Hell, no." Lee agreed. "They want to get *away* from the son of a bitch, they don't want to take the bastard *with* them when they go!"

She and I both laughed, but Geof said, "It wasn't like that, ladies, it was the other way around. The note he left said she was the one who wanted to die, and he was the one who thought he couldn't live without her."

"He *said* so," I argued. "But maybe it was all getting too hard for *him* to take care of her and to watch her suffering, maybe that was 'their' problem. Maybe she could have stood it a good while longer if he hadn't wimped out on her."

"Wimped out?" Geof smiled.

"There are other choices," I said.

"Even so," Lee pointed out, "it's still murder/suicide."

"What about him?" I asked to change the subject, to calm myself down a little. They were pros at this, I was the emotional, indignant amateur. "How many shots?"

"The same. Two shots, both to the chest."

"Could a person really do that to himself?"

"Oh, sure. You'd be surprised."

I suppressed the wow I felt like saying and merely shook my head to show my amazement: what determination to shoot one-self twice in the chest. The man had definitely wanted to die. "He shot her from close range?"

"Yes, he held the gun right up to her."

His body—Ron's—lay at her feet, on his right side with his head touching the toes of her brown loafers that looked too big for her. She was a short woman and plump. *Boobs*, I thought meanly, *Judy Baker always had boobs*. He was stocky, like the ex-high school football player he was. Her left hand had fallen to her lap, palm up, and her right arm dangled to the side of the chair, as if she were reaching down for him.

"She looks like somebody slapped her," I said, "the way her head's thrown back." Her face was invisible behind a coating of blood that had also sprayed her hair, which was a dark ash blond. I examined the picture of the body of Ron Mayer. He was face down, and he was wearing a brown business suit, business shoes. *Taking care of business*, I thought. "The way he's dressed . . . it's an odd way to dress to die."

"What is?" Geof held out a hand for the photo I was examining, and I passed it to him.

"A business suit. He didn't even change clothes."

"How would you dress to die?" Geof asked, then he glanced at Lee. "You want something to eat or drink, Sergeant, or a beer?"

"Thanks, no. I had a huge dinner. You couldn't tempt me to eat anything." She glanced at the stack of photos, then grinned at Geof. "Unless you kneel, Lieutenant. Maybe if you get on your knees and plead with me—"

"In your dreams," he told her.

72

"I'd get comfortable," I said.

They looked at each other, then at me.

"What are you talking about?" Geof asked me.

"How I'd dress to die. I'd get comfortable."

"You'd get naked," he said.

Lee let out a "pssh" of laughter, and Geof grinned at me.

"Sweats," I continued, rolling my eyes for Lee's benefit. "Tennis shoes. I don't know. I'll have to admit that it's something to which I've never given a lot of thought. What about you guys?"

"Naked is good," Lee concurred. "I think I'd go sit in a shower with my back propped against a corner, make it easier for people to clean me up afterward. They could just turn on the shower and spray me down."

"That's thoughtful of you," I said. "Geof?"

"My wet suit," he declared without hesitation. "I'd put on my wet suit and then I'd shoot myself through it in as many places as I could manage, so the medical examiner would have a hell of a time cutting it off me and figuring out which shot killed me. It'd be a holy mess inside the suit, she'd have to scrape it to get all the tissue. She'd cuss me every inch of the way, and I'd be looking down and laughing at her for all the times she rapped my knuckles when I missed some scrap of evidence that only a microscope could have picked up. I'd look like a whale that got harpooned."

"You'd be looking *up* at her," I corrected.

"Huh?" He thought about it, then laughed. "Oh, right."

"You married a really strange man," Lee said to me.

"This is nothing," I assured her. "What time did this crime occur?"

"Can't you tell from the photos?" Geof inquired.

"Are we getting cranky, dear? No, I can't. The living room curtains are pulled shut, so I can't tell whether there's a sun or a moon outside, there's no clock on the wall and there's no close-up of a wristwatch on either of their arms. You want to just tell me?"

"He doesn't know," Lee said, "but I do. Ron Mayer called 911 at five forty-six that afternoon to say he'd shot his wife and he was going to kill himself."

That was the dramatic and horrifying tape that everybody in town had heard all too many times on the newscasts. Some national broadcasts had even picked it up.

"The medical examiner agrees with that," Lee continued, "and she said he probably died very soon after that. In fact, he was dead when the paramedics got there at six-oh-one."

"How'd they get in?" Geof asked.

"Front door was open."

"Did you confirm that the voice on the 911 tape was his?"

"Yes, sir, two of his relatives did, his father and a brother." She shuffled through the file papers, looking for something. "He left this combination confession/suicide note. Shall I read it to you?" Upon our nods of encouragement, Lee began: "Hello."

A bubble of laughter erupted from my throat.

They both stared at me.

"I'm sorry," I said, feeling helpless. "It's just such a funny way to start a confession . . . hello. I'm sorry, Lee. Carry on."

She read: "I killed my wife. She was so sick. She begged me. I don't want to."

"Well, then, *don't* do it!" I said furiously and slapped my open palms on the tabletop. "Maybe she was unhappy because he did a *lousy* job of taking care of her, I guess that never occurred to him, maybe she would have been better off with other people taking care of her!"

"Well, she'd certainly be more alive," Geof said calmly.

Lee continued reading: "I'm going to kill myself now. Who would take care of her if I weren't here? Tell David we're sorry. We love him. I feel so sad about this. I don't want to live anymore. Good-bye. Sincerely, Ronald S. Mayer."

"Good-bye?" I said. "That's it? Not exactly the Faulkner of confession writers, was he? Hemingway maybe." I mimicked cruelly: "The woman was sick. The man was sad. They loved the boy."

Geof's mouth lifted in amusement at me. "The fish died."

"Why does this make me so *angry*?" I asked them. I thought it was only a rhetorical question, but Lee answered me anyway.

"Because she's not in it, that's why, Jenny. She's just this passive, unhappy crippled creature that he does things to. He keeps her alive, or he kills her. He's God."

"Which would seem to imply," I said ironically, "that God answers prayers if Judy really did ask Ron to kill her. What do you know about Parkinson's disease, Lee?"

"It's a degenerative disease leading to physical incapacitation. But the brain keeps working fine. It's the worst kind of nightmare. I have an aunt who has it, and she's in despair all the time and so's my uncle. Truthfully, Jenny . . . Lieutenant . . . when I heard that Judy Mayer had Parkinson's, I didn't have all that much trouble believing this. Except . . ."

For the first time that evening, Lee looked uncomfortable.

"Except?" Geof echoed impatiently.

"Well." A flush rose to her cheeks and spread until it pinkened her entire face so deeply that she looked as if she were wearing makeup, which she never did to my knowledge. "The M.E. didn't find any indication of Parkinson's in the autopsy . . ."

Both of us said, *"What?"*

In that moment, I felt a chill of something, some first hint of something awry, like the first tiny, unnerving symptom of a terrible illness.

"Now wait." She patted the heavy air with her hands, pacifying us. "It's not all that dramatic. She didn't find Parkinson's, and she didn't find any evidence of any other degenerative disease beyond the normal aging process. But she did find nerve *damage* in a couple of cervical vertebra—"

"Did you talk to Judy's physicians?" Geof interrupted.

"Yes, sir, I did. Her primary care physician said that Judy and Ron both knew the truth. She didn't have Parkinson's. What she was, was paraplegic with some other complications from the nerve damage. But Judy didn't want anybody else to know about that, because she was so embarrassed by the truth . . ."

"Which was?" Geof pressed, sounding angry, as she hesitated.

"That her second husband, a man named Dennis Clemmons, beat her up so bad one time that he caused permanent nerve damage."

I looked over at Geof and didn't doubt that he could read my mind: *She lied about David's parentage, she cheated the welfare system,*

*she divulged damaging, confidential information . . . and now this lie,*
*this whopper, not Parkinson's, but an abusive second husband.* You
could almost understand her spreading the first lie and this last
lie, but when you took them all and added them together, you
didn't know what to believe any longer about Judy Baker Mayer.

"Shit," Geof said softly and put his face in his right palm.

"She was still an invalid," Lee said insistently, looking puzzled
and worried by Geof's reaction. I, however, understood it all too
well: Was this boy his son, or wasn't he? Well, I thought, impatiently, he'd take the paternity test and find out. That would
settle it. But would it settle this investigation or his involvement
with the boy?

Lee was still talking, arguing, pressing her point with Geof.

"She was in pain, Lieutenant. She suffered. It was bad, even
if it wasn't Parkinson's. It's still the same motive for him to shoot
her and kill himself. From our point of view, it doesn't change
anything." She waited a moment, then she added nervously,
"Does it?"

"What about this Dennis Clemmons," Geof asked sharply.
"Could he have killed them?"

"No, sir. He was alibied."

"By whom?"

"Forty-five other veterans at the American Legion hall. He was
drinking beer at the hall with his war buddies that afternoon."

"What else do you know about him?"

"He has a record. Burglaries. Served some time."

"What was she doing with him?"

"I don't know."

"You don't know," he said heavily, sarcastically.

She was defensive. "It didn't seem important."

"Everything odd is important, Sergeant. Didn't you think it
was just a little fucking *odd* that a respectable middle-class matron
would divorce her respectable middle-class husband and leave
her nice home in the suburbs and take her only child with her
to go live with and marry an ex-con who beat her up?"

"He was alibied, Lieutenant! We have a confession note!"

I said, partly to distract him from being such a bastard to her,
"What about her answering service, Lee?"

"What about it?" She still sounded defensive.

I told her about Dr. Marsha Sandy's information and her implied suggestion that Judy might have made some unethical use of her answering service, but with a derisive wave of her hand, Lee dismissed the idea.

Still, Geof bored in on her. "Did you actually investigate the answering service, Sergeant?"

"No, sir."

"Because you had the note."

"Because we were sure of our conclusions, sir."

I tried again to distract him from taking out his emotions on her.

"Geof, what are you going to tell David?"

His glance shifted to me, and I saw how dark and thoughtful his eyes looked right then. "When we can find him—or he finds us again—I'm probably going to tell him that his father killed his mother. And then I'm going to tell him I'm sorry."

I heard Lee quietly release a pent-up breath.

"But first I'll clear up a few details," he said.

From the look on Lee's face, I knew she was thinking the same thing I was: *What* details?

"What details, Lieutenant?"

"You're out of this now," he said to her, not unkindly but totally ignoring her question. "You did a good job, but I want a new perspective, and that's what Jenny and I bring to it."

"What's this *we* business, white man?" I muttered.

He ignored me, too, and kept looking at her. "Call it double jeopardy, Sergeant. You've already investigated this crime once, you shouldn't have to serve the time again."

She bit her lip before saying, "Be the same verdict anyway."

"I expect so," Geof agreed easily. "But we'll poll a new jury."

"Because?" she asked carefully.

He shrugged. "Because it's on appeal."

"To a higher court," she retorted, sounding a little bitter.

"He's my son," Geof told her.

I stared at him, startled, and thought: *This isn't going to end well.* Just like that, I knew it. *Somebody is going to regret this.* And it would probably be the boy, who was never going to be satisfied to hear what he would never be willing to believe.

Then I realized that Lee was answering Geof. "You understand," she said to him, "that we also investigated the possibility that the boy did it, that David killed them. I don't have to tell you that anytime we have two dead parents and one live teenage boy, we're suspicious."

"And?" Geof said impatiently.

"He was clear."

In a tough voice, Geof said, "Maybe you didn't look hard enough."

Lee and I looked at each other, each of us seeing surprise on the other's face: *What the hell did he mean by that?* But when she asked him, the lieutenant disclaimed any particular meaning. "It wasn't an accusation," he said, still sounding impatient with her, so that a flushed, defensive look came to her face again. "Leave your files with me, Sergeant. I'll take responsibility for them." He got up from his chair. "Come on, we'll walk you to your car."

By the time Lee and I got up from the table and started following him, he was already out in the driveway and the screen door had already slammed behind him.

"I think I screwed up," Lee said to me in a low voice.

I didn't know what to say to her, whether to reassure her or not. When we got outside, he was standing on the gravel, his hands in his shorts pockets, staring up at the sliver of late summer moon overhead. The crunching of Lee's shoes and mine across the gravel sounded unnaturally loud in the overheated silence of the country night.

"Bye," she said softly to me, and she looked over at him and raised her voice to say, "Good night, Lieutenant."

He called out a courteous thank you and a good-bye.

I tried to make it up to her by seeing her off in as warm and friendly a manner as I could, and I gently closed her car door for her after she got in, and I waved her off into the night. Then I walked over and stood close to my husband.

"What's wrong?" I asked him.

The gaze he turned on me seemed at first as cold and distant as the moon above us. "What?" Then he seemed to really see me, to recognize me, as it were. He put his left arm around my shoulders and started me moving back toward the house with him.

On the second step, pushed against the back, there was a thick shadow, and when we stooped over to look, we both saw that it was another dead animal. We'd all stepped over it when we'd walked down to see Lee off.

"Squirrel," Geof said after taking a longer look than I wanted to.

"I'll get rid of this one," I told him.

He looked at me with surprise. "You will?"

I suppressed a shudder. "You got the possum this morning. It's my turn. That's only fair."

"Yeah, but you had the mouse in your car."

"But I didn't have to pick the pieces out of my engine block. I can do this, honey. No problem. I am woman, hear me roar."

"Well, thanks." He looked truly grateful. "I hate these jobs, too. I don't think there's a sex-linked trait for dealing with dead things. I hate dealing with the bodies of dead people, too. Did you know that?" He stepped over the little corpse and walked on into the house, happily murmuring, "I do love the women's movement, yessir."

I was laughing as I held my breath and squatted down to look.

It wasn't too bad, just a furry tail and part of a squirrel's leg.

I pulled a tissue out of a pocket in my shorts and gingerly picked up the pieces and walked them back to the covered trash bin, considering the unpleasant chore a small price to pay for equal rights.

"Hey, out there." I spoke to the black wilderness around me. "Die someplace else, all right? Our steps are not a morgue and my car is not a cemetery." I paused. "Got that?"

I waited until something rustled some tree branches.

"I'll take that as an affirmative," I said sternly.

It was not until I had my hand on our back doorknob that the thought came to me: Wait a minute. No squirrel tail crawls up on a front step to die. That squirrel didn't walk up on one leg. Something left it there, probably between the time Lee first arrived and when she left. But what was bringing us its trophies?

A fox, maybe, or a stray dog or cat. Great, I thought. Geof and I had evidently been selected to be the recipients of its prizes from now on.

I stepped into a dark kitchen.

"Don't turn on the light, Jenny."

Geof was leaning up against the far wall, his hands in his pockets again, waiting for me.

"You startled me," I told him, a little angry.

"Sorry. It's just that I don't want us to be visible from outside the house. Jenny, the FBI has commissioned psychological profiles to enable them to identify serial killers by the patterns of their childhood behavior. There are three signs you almost always find: As a boy—and it's almost always a male—the killer will have committed arson, he will have been a Peeping Tom, and he will have exhibited cruelty to animals by torturing or killing them."

I reached out to touch something: the sharp metal edge of the kitchen counter. "If you really think that, then why did you let me go out there in back by myself?"

"It was a mistake, I shouldn't have. I'm sorry I did. I was slow to realize he could still be here."

*He.* The awful implication hung in the darkness between us. Suddenly, impatiently, I shook it off. "Geof, honestly, I think it's just a dead squirrel!"

*And a dead possum. And a dead mouse.*

*And a teenage boy, creeping up to our front door, silently, so we didn't know he was coming.*

"I hope so."

"Anyway, where's the serial part of that?" I said it half facetiously, resisting the idea of taking this notion of his seriously.

My husband, however, wasn't joking around.

"His father and mother are dead. And now he has identified me as his father, which makes you—"

"I get it. I think it's crazy, but I get it. But Lee said he didn't do it, remember? She said they looked into it, and he didn't do it."

"And that's probably true."

"But we're not taking any chances, is that it?"

"That's it."

"All right," I said, impatiently. "Is the front door locked?"

"Yes." He said it casually, as if this were a familiar routine to us, like saying good night and kissing once before we rolled over on our sides to go to sleep, no more than that. "I've closed all the windows and locked them. I thought we could turn on the air conditioner tonight instead of leaving the windows open. It's so hot."

My mouth felt dry, and my face felt suddenly hot and tingly.

"Okay," I capitulated, feeling resentment ebb as fear began to flow. I walked over to take his hand and to follow him up our darkened stairway to our bedroom, where we moved about without any lights, finding our way to bed by the bit of moonlight that slatted through the curtains, which he closed.

But I asked him in bed, "So why did you let me throw the dead squirrel away?"

"Because I don't think it's true."

"Now you tell me."

He pulled our top sheet and our blue summer blanket up under his arms. I looked over at him lying there, and even in my pique I silently admired him: his attractive, lived-in face; his muscular shoulders and chest, now relaxed and spread out on his pillow; his long tanned arms with the dark hair on them; and his long fingers interlaced on top of the blanket. The rest of his body was outlined by the sheet and blanket. I felt a swelling, nearly an ache in my chest as I stared at him, and I remembered how sweet it felt to place my face in the crook of his neck and to breathe his smell and to kiss the curve of his skin there. I knew how that made him murmur and roll over toward me. He was looking back at me, not knowing what was going through my mind, and he said, as if he needed to hear it again, "Lee did say they cleared him of suspicion."

*But he's your son.* I noticed his contradictory behavior, noticed that now I apparently was willing to believe the "fact" of his parentage, too. His son. My . . . what?

Our problem.

"I'm not used to the air conditioner," I complained, turning my face away from him. "It'll wake me up."

He rolled toward me, taking me in his arms, kissing my hair, refusing to release me until he felt me relax, until I'd kissed him back, a real kiss, with real love behind it.

"Are you sorry you married me?" he murmured.

"Every other day," I retorted and kissed him again.

But I was right about the air conditioner: Whenever the fan shut off, I came suddenly awake to a silent room, aware that something was gone, something was missing. I lay listening to the soft slough of the summer wind outside our closed windows, the tree limbs rubbing against one another, the birds shifting sleepily on their branches, the squirrels shuddering in their nests, the barn owls and the foxes moving stealthily as they stared into the darkness of the woods around us to see what small living things might make the mistake of moving carelessly. I imagined I overheard the ocean withdrawing its tide from our shore, changing its mind, removing itself from us, taking itself to safer, deeper, more comfortable waters. I wanted to go, too. I wanted to sail away on it and to take the sleeping naked man beside me on a boat with me, the two of us and the outgoing sea, drifting further and further away from our home. Each time, when I came awake and before I slipped back to sleep again, I was aware of his skin, the warmth, the smoothness, the roughness and hairiness, the moisture and the heat and the pressure of it, which I could feel even inches away from me, and I wanted more of it: more skin, more touching and stroking and pressing and embracing, more, more.

Once, he woke, too, and he asked, when he felt my insistent caresses, "Now?"

And I said, even though it was three-thirty in the morning, "Yes, now, please."

# 9

AT NOONTIME OF THE NEXT DAY, MY FRIEND SABRINA Johnson came running out of the building where she was a state social worker to meet me. Her braided black hair was flying in a long pigtail behind her, and there was a wide grin on her face. I—not feeling much like smiling and moving considerably more slowly in the sticky weather—got out of the Miata to greet her.

"Want to drive it, Slick?"

"Hot damn!" she exclaimed and ran around the car to trade places with me. She slid behind the wheel, then peered suspiciously at me over her sunglasses, which were white plastic with mirrored lenses. Below them, her mouth was a tangerine, round and full and looking juicy. "Why do I rate this?"

"Because you're giving up your lunch hour for me."

"What would I get if I gave up dinner?" She whooped with laughter as she nudged the gearshift into first and pressed in on the clutch. Her scent, a men's cologne, filled the front seat. She was wearing a short black cotton skirt, a plain black T with a round neck and short sleeves, and flat black sandals. She didn't have on any earrings today. When she worked the car's pedals, her skirt hiked up on her long, thin athlete's legs. "You got any other errands I can do for you, Jenny? You just let me know, listen, I'll get your groceries, run to the bank . . ."

"Baby-sit," I yelled over the roar of her acceleration.

"Are you kidding?" She took the corner of Third Avenue and Wisconsin like Janet Guthrie at the Indy 500. "You couldn't get me to do that for a Porsche. No car is worth *that* much!"

"You sure this is the place?" I asked her.

We were parked across the street from 500 SE Bennett, the old address Sabrina had from her files. "Better be," she said, " 'cause it didn't occur to me to do the obvious thing and look him up in this year's phone book."

"You think Judy lived here?" I asked doubtfully.

"That's what she told me."

"God. Do you think it looked this bad then?"

"Places like this never look any better."

We gazed at the house across the street in mutual appalled silence.

It was big, three stories of dingy old gray clapboard set like a rotten tooth in a nearly empty mouth: This was a decimated block, with empty lots and blowing litter. It faced north and must have been cold as a sailor's nose on an icy winter's night. On this day, with the temperatures in the upper nineties, we heard the laboring of air conditioners in windows. The idea of Judy Baker Mayer—or any woman—bringing a child here to live with her utterly depressed me.

"Why?" I said.

"Why what?"

"Why would she marry him, live here, bring David here?"

"Love," said Sabrina in a cynical voice.

"You think it's a boarding house?"

"For an independent woman, you sure ask a lot of questions."

"I'm trying to avoid going over there."

Sabrina laughed and opened her door. "Thought so. Think we ought to put the top up on this thing and lock it?"

"Now *you're* doing it." I got out on my side and looked over at her. "No, convertible tops are too much of a temptation to slash. This way, anybody can see there's nothing to steal. Did you forget to wear earrings today?"

"I left them at somebody's house this morning." Sabrina joined me on the street side of the car on the one-way road, making an obvious point of avoiding my eyes. "I've been a supervisor too long," she said. "I should be making more house calls. I forget that tickle in your stomach that you get when you've got to go up and ring a doorbell in a tough part of town where you don't know what's on the other side of the door and who's going to be opening it."

Alarmed, I said, "We're not planning on calling on him!"

She looked at me, surprised. "We're not?"

"No, Sabrina, we're just . . . looking."

"Damn," she said, "I thought we were going to play cop."

"You really do think I'm Nancy Drew."

"Sometimes." She grinned as she leaned lightly against my car frame and folded her arms across her chest and crossed one leg over the other. "So what are we trying to see?"

"Whatever's there. Whose house, Sabrina?"

She looked up at the yellow-blue sky. "Whose house what?"

"You know what. The earrings this morning."

"Might have a new man," she said, still gazing skyward. There were no clouds, not even any little stray puffs, no hope of rain to cool things off.

"Hey."

"Then again, I might not." Now she looked at me, and I saw in the expression in her eyes: one-night stand. Port Frederick was a very small and limited town for a woman like Sabrina. If it were the sky and men were clouds, Sabrina was in a long drought. I knew better than to ask her if she'd been careful with this new man; she'd snap my head off for asking. "You got anything against me sauntering over and looking at the names on the mailbox?"

"I suppose not."

When she started walking, I moved with her. She looked over at me in surprise again. "We get cloned, and I missed it?"

I kept pace with her long stride. "I am not a chickenshit."

"Never said you were." She smiled. "You're just a middle-class white girl in a bad neighborhood, that's all."

"Upper class."

"That right?"

"Hell, yes."

We both laughed, because we both knew how utterly low rent my family could act at times, and we also both knew that Sabrina had attended Boston College on a basketball scholarship only because she deserved it and not because her folks couldn't afford to send her, both of them being physicians retired from army practice. Slick had lived all over the world, from Polynesia to Fort Bragg, North Carolina, which was why she had settled down here and never traveled anywhere anymore. When we had once accused her of being overly sophisticated, she had told us sharply, "Sophistication is nothin' more than the ability to look cool at a cocktail party, and you want to know how I learned how to do that? By standing on ten different playgrounds at ten different schools in eight years from the time I was four till the time I was twelve pretending I didn't care if nobody paid any attention to me. Yeah, I'm sophisticated, all right."

"How old was David when they lived here?" I asked her.

"He was ten when she applied for assistance."

I thought about a ten-year-old, accustomed to a nice house, a good school, a bedroom probably decorated to suit him, and I thought about him leaving all that—not to mention his father— to move in here.

"How long did Judy stay with this man?"

"I don't know, Jenny."

"Did she tell you he had a record?"

"No, one of many things she did not say. What was he in for?"

"Burglary, I think."

By that time we were standing by the curb on the other side of the street, nearest the house. Under our shoes, the asphalt was so hot it made me feel as if we were propped on a cookie sheet, baking at 350 degrees. I was beginning to feel brown and crispy around my edges. I thought of what else Sergeant Meredith had said the night before.

"He beat her, Sabrina, did you know that?"

"No, but I'm not surprised."

"That's what put her in the chair."

Sabrina whistled her dismay.

"I wonder if he beat David, too," I said.

"That wouldn't surprise me either."

"Shit," I said, feeling depressed.

"How you talk," she said in mock disapproval, but then she put an arm around my shoulders and patted me. "It's kind of nice to see you get upset about it. I see so much of it, I get kind of inured to it."

"How you talk," I said, and Sabrina took her arm away and laughed.

"Maybe with our foundation . . ." I let her fill in the blanks.

"Yeah. Maybe we can." Suddenly she raised a long arm and pointed with a long, crimson fingernail. "Hey! Lookit that! I thought those were steps going up the side of the house!"

There was a wide appendage with railings that was attached like a stairwell to the west side of the building going up from the yard to the second floor. Now we were close enough to see that it wasn't stairs at all, but instead a cleverly constructed ramp. Even as we stared at it, the grating noise of a sliding door drew our attention up to the second floor. We watched the front edge of a wheelchair and the front half of a seated body appear in a wide doorway that exited onto the top of the ramp, and then we watched as the rest of him rolled onto a small landing. He reached behind him to slide his door closed and we watched, rather fascinated, as he made his way down, zigzagging from landing to landing, to the ground. First he rolled down a gentle slope to a second landing, where he made a forty-five-degree turn that led him down a second slope to a third landing where he made another turn onto a third slope, a fourth landing, a fourth slope and then he was on the ground on an ordinary cement pathway. It was ingenious, for somebody who didn't have an elevator, but I wondered how he got back up again.

He rolled directly toward us.

Sabrina stepped up onto the curb and then to the sidewalk, so she was right in his path. I hung back, a little worried about what she might be up to. When the man in the wheelchair was within earshot, Sabrina called out to him, "How come you don't just live on the first floor?"

"Can't get the bastard who lives there to move out."

"How do you get back up that ramp?"

He stopped his chair, then put his hand on top of a box on one arm of the chair and jiggled something on the box. The chair moved forward a couple of inches and then backward. In the bored, exasperated voice of a man who had been asked that question many times before, he said to her, "I can work this chair manually or by electric. Going down, I roll it myself, going up, I use the switch."

"I've never seen anything like that." She meant the ramp, whose inclines were articulated gently enough to allow for just the sort of movement he'd described. "And I've seen a lot of handicapped access in my time. Where'd you get the idea?" She was walking toward him, looking friendly and interested and long-legged and gorgeous. I thought she could surely make a lame man walk, possibly even raise the dead, which, in this town, might be somewhat easier than finding a decent date. "Did you design it yourself? Who built it for you?"

I remained standing where I was, thinking, *Sabrina, you're over-doing it!* And what *was* she doing anyway? She walked a circle around his chair, making sounds as if she admired it as well as the ramp. But the man was looking resentful, intruded upon, not at all flattered by the attention of the black goddess in the short black skirt, much less the ambulatory white girl a few feet away. He looked about fifty years old, and he had a puffy, red-veined face with a sulky, martyred-looking mouth and mean little eyes. He was dressed in old jeans and a gray, wrinkled T-shirt with one of my least favorite epithets lettered on it: "You're ugly and your mother dresses you funny." His shoulders and the arms that protruded from the short-sleeved T looked enormously strong. Black running shoes and a black baseball cap with a Western Auto logo completed his ensemble.

Sabrina chattered on, the very essence of flirty, feather-headed, girlish charm, the very antithesis of who she was: "Was it very expensive, or did you get some sort of government assistance, or did insurance pay for it?" She stopped in front of him and gave him a toothy smile. "It's none of my business, I know, but . . . do you think it's really worth all the trouble instead of just finding a place to live on the first floor or someplace with an elevator?"

"It ain't my idea. Some friends built it for me. I didn't pay for it, they did. And do you think I'd live in this shithole if I had the money to move someplace else?"

She regarded him calmly. "I wouldn't know about that."

"You wouldn't know about shit," he said and rolled away from us.

But Sabrina wouldn't let it go. "What happened to you? 'Nam?"

"Fuck you," he yelled and kept rolling.

She turned my way, posing. "Think I have a career in the diplomatic corps?"

"Hey," I said, walking up to her and laughing so that only she could hear me, "just because a man's disabled, that don't make him adorable. Why did you do that to him?"

"Did you notice what was printed on the back of his chair?"

"No."

"Property of D.C."

"That was *him*?" I was flabbergasted. "*That* repulsive creature was Dennis Clemmons?" I stared suspiciously at her. "How'd you know that?"

"I didn't, I was working up to asking him if Clemmons still lives here when I saw the back of his chair."

I looked up at the ratty old house, then at the man rolling away, and then at Sabrina. "I guess he's not a burglar any more. Tell me one more time why you think she married him?"

"Love?" Sabrina said again, but this time she also sounded doubtful.

"You didn't tell me he was disabled, too."

"That's 'cause she didn't tell *me*." Sabrina turned on the flat heel of her right sandal, and I had to trot to keep up with her as she recrossed the street to my car. "Damn stupid woman. He was probably getting Social Security or V.A. payments, and they were hiding it from me so she could get more benefits. She should have told me the truth. I might have gotten her more help, not less."

"I'm finding this all very confusing," I confessed. "Judy was supposed to have Parkinson's, but she didn't, she had injuries because that man beat her up. And he was supposed to be able-bodied, but he isn't, because . . . we don't know why. I'm confused, Sabrina."

She patted my arm. "That's because you're personally involved, Jenny. It's very simple. She was a liar and he's a thug. There's nothing confusing about that, is there?" She arched her eyebrows at me. "So now, let's see . . . first the kid, then"—she gestured toward the man in the wheelchair that was now a block away from us—"him. How do you like your new family so far, Jenny?"

I gave her a sour look. "I guess you don't want to drive back."

Sabrina held up her hands, palms out, in surrender.

"Sorry," she said, grinning in high good humor.

I relinquished the keys to her.

"I'm good at this!" she bragged as she got back behind the wheel. "Maybe I should go into detecting . . ."

"Just follow the clues back to your office, please." A few blocks later, I said, "Sabrina, I've been thinking about names for this foundation we're putting together. What would you think of calling it the Hercules Foundation? For strength, for endurance, for—"

"For another man, you want to name another damn foundation for another damn man? Especially when it's a foundation we particularly want to be sensitive to the needs of women?"

"Oh. Well, he was into labor . . ."

"Very funny."

"Okay, scratch Hercules."

"Yeah, scratch Hercules and all you'll find underneath is another damn man."

I glanced over at her, at the set of her jaw, at the stiffness of her posture and the jerkiness of her movement as she shifted gears, and I realized I had ruined her good mood. I did a little inductive reasoning of my own and detected that Sabrina didn't have a very good time on her date last night.

As we traded places again, I asked her: "Why aren't you surprised to hear that he beat her up?"

"Because he looks like the type."

"What does that type look like, Sabrina?"

"Like Dennis Clemmons," she yelled back to me over her shoulder as she ran back into work.

I got back into my driver's seat and then sat in the sun a moment thinking: It must be something about the martyred look, that air of being so aggressively aggrieved at the world, those mean little eyes. Hardly scientific. I remembered a married cop that Sabrina had played around with a few years before; he'd been a wife beater, too. So maybe what Sabrina "recognized" was something dangerously familiar: the perverse, magnetic pull of an attraction to violence. Maybe Sabrina had a bit of it. It certainly looked as if Judy Baker Mayer Clemmons Mayer had succumbed to that pull at least three times in her life: once to the husband who permanently injured her and twice to the one who killed her.

*"What about her attraction to Geof?"* a little voice asked me.

"Yeah, well," I said out loud, "cops may be attracted to guns and violence, but they can work it out in a healthy way." Some of them. Maybe.

At breakfast, Geof had asked me if I'd drive by Port Frederick High School that day to see if David was in attendance. We didn't know where he was living, so Geof just wanted to know if he could locate the kid whenever he wanted to fairly easily. It seemed a safe enough little errand for me to run for him in the middle of the day.

So, next, I went looking for David Mayer.

And I wondered in regard to the violence: like fathers, like son?

# 10

THIS LAST MONDAY IN AUGUST, A WEEK BEFORE Labor Day, also marked the first day of public school in Port Frederick. I cruised the high school parking lot looking for the old black BMW motorcycle. In the years since Geof and I and the Mayers had attended, it had changed for the better—if your priorities were an air-conditioned gymnasium and soccer fields to accompany the football field. But now there were also computers in every classroom and girls teams on the new soccer fields, and there'd been peaceful desegregation without busing, not such a difficult task when there's only about a three percent minority population in an entire metropolitan area. All that aside, Port Frederick High was still just a big block of a red brick building where the town's most active hormones hung out during the weekdays for nine months a year.

I found the motorcycle parked off by itself under one of the four gargantuan Norwegian spruce trees that formed an imposing line streetside. When I was David's age, they'd been less than half as tall as they were now. Their long needles and tapering tan-colored cones still littered the ground as they had in my day when my girlfriends and I had gathered the cones in our skirts one year to take home and work into Christmas wreaths. I wasn't good at crafts; my wreaths had looked like dead foliage drooping from a bent hanger. Another of those quirky little nodules of memory came back to me every time I drove past those trees: a high school biology teacher telling us there was a kind of Norwegian spruce that was used to make violin sound boxes. Who cares? I'd thought then. Now, I thought: Isn't that interesting? I wondered what it was about Norwegian spruces, specifically, that made them good for resonating sweet sounds. Ah, if only I'd had the intellectual curiosity then that I had now, but back then I was mostly curious about boys.

Like the boy David, of whom I was also curious, I chose to park under a tree, but the one I selected was a cedar of Lebanon on private property, a few feet down a side street, where I could park with the top down, facing the school, and still keep an eye on the motorcycle. A cedar branch extended its long, green-sleeved arm into the street, offering a natural umbrella of shade for my small car. I had my laptop computer and some loose files with me, so I didn't care how long I had to wait for school to let out. When a person wants to establish her own charitable foundation, a person has to fill out enough forms to keep the IRS happy for a lifetime.

The first school bell rang at one-twenty, the last bell at one-thirty. School still let out early the first day.

I had a sudden, startling memory of what it had been like to sit in those hot classrooms in late August, early September. Boys with their legs sprawled wide under their desks, their elbows taking up most of the aisle space. Girls with their chins in their hands, their other hands holding pencils, doodling on the cover of the steno pads they used to take classroom notes. All of us drooping, barely awake, now and then exchanging glances, arching our eyebrows at each other as the teacher droned at the front of the room. White chalk words on the blackboard up front. All the windows open, but nothing moving in the stifling air inside where we were. A smell of bubblegum as somebody surreptitiously unwrapped a piece. The feeling of a scar in the wood of my desk, under my fingertips. The sense of the presence of the

93

cute boy one row back to my left. The sweat at all of the places on my body where my clothes were binding me. All of life feeling as if it were on hold waiting for the bell to ring . . .

I quickly stashed my files away under my dash where they wouldn't get blown, then started the car in readiness for following David when he came out. I didn't spot him until he reached the bike. What a gangly, unattractive kid he looked from a distance—not the child most likely to be selected from a lineup of potential stepchildren, that was for sure. He had on another white, long-sleeved shirt—or maybe it was the same one—and jeans that hung loose at his thin hips, a blue backpack, the black tennis shoes, and the Star Trek cap over his bush of long, curly brown hair. He took off the cap and stuck it in his backpack, which he attached to the bike with elastic cords, then he unhooked a black helmet from the handlebars and put it on along with a pair of clear plastic goggles.

The other kids were flowing out of the school and flowing to their cars and the sidewalks like long lazy drops of water separating from a meandering stream, but David moved as if he was in a hurry to get away from there—kicking up the stand on the bike, swinging a leg over, revving up, and starting to move out, weaving between the cars whose owners were slower to get going. I was glad I'd already started my car, and now I rapidly put it in gear, released the brake, and edged to the corner, watching him. He bumped over a curb, a sidewalk, another curb, and then he was noisily careering off down the street toward downtown.

I bypassed the traffic starting to emerge from the school parking lot by turning left into a private circle drive and then exiting it from the other side, ahead of the teens in their cars. With a quiet roar, I sped ahead of them. From behind, I heard a young male voice yelling at me: "Yo, baby!" I smiled to myself. Seen from behind, with my blond ponytail streaming out and dressed so casually, I probably looked his age. What a shock and disappointment he'd get if he drove up beside me, ready to throw me a line, and I looked over at him and smiled, and he discovered that I was old enough to be his mother.

As for the boy whose stepmother I might be, he had slowed

to a sedate pace. Now, away from the school, he was a surprisingly careful driver. I'd expected him to be a wild male teenage driver, to speed, to race through yellow lights and the beginnings of red ones, to be one of those cocky, impatient, angry boys who tailgate, who dart between lanes, who curse and honk. But no: He drove the speed limit. He looked both ways several times before entering any intersection, he always signaled when he changed lanes, giving the drivers behind him plenty of time to notice his blinking light and upraised arm. He didn't tailgate. He didn't thread the lanes or slither between two cars at a stoplight. You'd almost have thought he was guiding me. Now I began to see the logic of why a kid might go around dressed in a man's dress shirt on a hot day: It made good, light, protective clothing on a motorcycle, shielding him both from the sun and the pavement in case he landed on it. Even his reckless exit from the high school parking lot made a certain kind of sense: He was a teenager, after all, and maybe he needed to show off for his peers. Or thumb his nose at them.

"Do you have peers?" I muttered to the kid three cars ahead of me. "How about friends? Got any of those?"

I thought back over his hasty exit from school: He hadn't stopped to talk to anybody, no high fives, no shouted jibes, no greetings or farewells. Just jump on your bike and gun it. I didn't know what that was like, being solitary in high school, because it hadn't been that way for me. I'd been lucky, there'd been friends, and it was a rare afternoon that I went home alone.

"What's it like to be you?" I asked his curved white back. "A kid like you?"

Geof wouldn't know either. Granted, he'd been a hellion, a rebel, even a juvie in his bad old days, but he was never alone either. Even juvies have friends, they telephone each other, they ride in cars together, they hang out, even as cheerleaders and football players do. Geof would never have joined up with a real gang—he was too much of an iconoclast even then for that—but he'd been popular in his own weird way, just as I had been in my goody-two-shoes way.

We weren't like the kid driving ahead of me.

"What the hell do you know about it?" I demanded of myself

as he signaled for a left turn and I followed him slowly onto Central Avenue. "For all you know, he's got a whole team of pals waiting for him at the harbor, and they're all going sailing this afternoon, and his worst problem is trying to find time alone to do his homework."

No. That wasn't this kid's worst problem.

We were heading straight downtown, not to the fixed-up touristy part, but to the old rundown part where working fishermen still lived in boarding houses, the fishermen without families. It was the same neighborhood where I'd gone with Sabrina earlier that day, and when David stopped, it was on 15th Street, only three blocks west of where his former stepfather, Dennis Clemmons, still lived and a universe away from the nice suburban home where he'd resided with his parents.

He drove his bike up over the curb in front of an old clapboard boarding house with a sign out front advertising rooms to let: TV, private baths. I quickly parked at the opposite curb, far down the street, keeping my engine running, my foot on the clutch. But when he turned off his own engine, got off his bike, and propped it on its stand, I shut down my car. I watched him lope up the front walk and use a key to open the front door. He wasn't gone long. Just as I was considering whether to sit there a while longer or to go on my way, he came running back out again, but he'd changed clothes while he was inside. Now he wore the same shoes but cheap-looking black trousers, a short-sleeved white shirt with an insignia on it, and a black baseball cap with an insignia on it, too. Not the Star Trek cap, but it was familiar; in fact, the whole outfit looked like something I'd seen before, although not on him. He looked like a dork in it, a dweeb, a whatever insulting word his peers would have used to describe what we used to call a nerd. He hopped back on the bike, backed it over the curb before starting it, turned his cap around so the bill hung down his neck, snapped his helmet on, and started off again.

I followed him a mile and a half through light afternoon traffic to a McDonald's restaurant. He parked at the back door and went in that way.

So now I knew where I'd seen that uniform before, and I knew where he lived, which didn't look like any relatives' house, and I knew that he worked and where, which suggested he wasn't living off any inheritance or an allowance from his relatives either.

"And why is that?" I asked the back door of McDonald's.

He'd left his backpack on the bike.

I pulled my car closer to the back door of the restaurant, and engine idling, I looked it all over: I thought he'd said the bike was a 750, which meant it was a good-sized one, and it looked it up close. It would take a person of some strength to hold it upright when it wasn't running and long legs to feel comfortable sitting on it. Again, it reminded me of a wasp because of the way it looked and because of the intimidating buzz it made going down a road at any speed. Motorcycles made people stare in interest or alarm, like stinging insects did; they made people angry, annoyed, or frightened or drew their envy and fascination. Not a neutral machine.

Why had he left his backpack out here, unprotected, unsecured except for a bungee cord that tied it down behind the black vinyl seat? The pack was mostly dark blue, but close up, I saw that the flap that came down over the top was forest green, and it was fastened only by a black cord looped over a barrel-shaped button. There were a couple of zippers on it, and it looked heavy and bulgy, as if it had school books in it. I fantasized about getting out of my car, going over to the bike, touching the backpack, and then opening it.

A sound from inside the restaurant made me look up. The kid was standing there, holding the door open, staring at me as I examined his bike.

I held his gaze, trying to show no more surprise than he was.

"I've never been on one of these," I said, talking kind of loud over the noise in the parking lot and the sound of my own car and my own heart pounding. I resented the fact that this kid had the capability of making me feel ill at ease in my own body, my own personality, my own home and hometown. Who was he, this pimply stranger, to have that kind of power over me, us, our lives?

"Wait a minute," he said and disappeared into the restaurant.

97

When he appeared only a couple of minutes later, he had somebody with him, a girl in a uniform just like his. She ran over to a white multispeed bike—as in bicycle—and unlocked a matching white helmet from it, which she handed to David before she ran back into the restaurant. They didn't exchange any words; he didn't even say thanks.

"You can wear this," he said to me.

*Oh, shit,* I thought, *push has come to shove.* He was offering me a ride on his motorcycle.

I thrust myself out of my car and took the flimsy-feeling helmet he handed me and eased it down on my head and fumbled the strap into place under my chin. "Is this legal?" I asked him, pointing to my head, which all of a sudden felt extraordinarily fragile to me.

"No, but it'll get us past a cop."

That didn't seem to me to be the point of a motorcycle helmet, but I decided to let it pass and to take my chances. People rode on motorcycles every day without getting their skulls squashed like cantaloupes, didn't they? And he'd seemed to be a careful driver. Maybe I'd survive without being paralyzed for the rest of my life.

"Wear your sunglasses," he instructed. "They'll protect your eyes."

I stuck the arms of my sunglasses between the inside of the helmet and my head, and they wedged there a little painfully over my ears.

"You can leave work?" I asked.

"Screw 'em. They're looking for an excuse."

"But I don't want to get you fired."

"It's not your problem."

He got on, turned a small key in an ignition, and twisted his right handlebar. The bike's engine revved up louder than my heart. "Put your foot here," he said, pointing to a small silver bar in back of his left foot. "Watch out for the exhaust, or you'll get burned. Get on behind me."

Awkwardly, I did, and once seated, I didn't know what to do with my hands. He answered that for me by starting up with a jerk, so that first I jolted backward and then was yanked forward again by gravity, and my arms instinctively went around his waist. He was bones and muscle, no extra flesh at all. It felt strange to be so intimately connected to this kid, this stranger, with my sweaty chest pressed up against his sweaty back and my bare arms around his midriff. We roared off down Frederick Boulevard, and I wondered how in the world I could have gotten the impression he was a cautious driver. He weaved between cars, skidded around corners, squealed to stops at lights, until I just had to give in to the fear and put the left side of my face against his sweaty back and close my eyes and pray it wasn't my day to die. Closing my eyes all the way wasn't a good idea, however; it made me feel vertiginous and vulnerable, as if I were sitting in space going a million miles an hour through an asteroid field where I felt as if I were going to collide with something hard and fatal at any moment. I squinted through my sunglasses, but the world was a blur going by. Maybe one of Geof's uniformed officers would time us or spot my illegal helmet, pull us over, make me deplane from this rocket. One could only hope.

When I opened my eyes fully again, we were almost out of the city.

"Where are we going?" I shouted in his right ear.

"I can hear you," he said over his shoulder in an almost normal voice. "You don't have to yell. It hurts my ears."

"Where are we going?" I repeated more quietly. I thought about telling him that I had to get back soon, but then I realized I was beginning to enjoy the ride, now that we were out of traffic. I loosened my grip on his waist and leaned back and sat more upright, putting my fingers lightly on his belt for security but allowing a few inches of space between our bodies.

"I'm just taking you for a ride," he said.

"I've got to get back," I objected.

His response was to rev the bike to a faster speed.

I was already scared; there didn't seem to me to be much point in getting any more frightened. But this time, I kept my eyes open.

# 11

 Geof used his own lunch break that day to get a paternity test.

"Will it be essay," I had said as we were getting dressed that morning, "or multiple choice?"

"Neither," he had retorted just before he had stepped into the shower. "A paternity test is where they tie you to the bed with sheets and beat you until you scream, 'Yes! He's my kid, yes, I admit it, he's my kid!' "

Personally, I thought he still looked eager to make that confession.

"No, really . . ." I stood in the steam in the bathroom and raised my voice over the pouring water. "Is it still a blood test, or do they do some kind of DNA test these days?"

"What?" he called out.

I had already put on my shorts and T-shirt for the day, but now I shed them and stepped behind the shower curtain with him.

"Well, hi," he said, water streaming over his grin.

"So is it a blood test or DNA?"

He grabbed my left arm and turned it over to expose the inside of my elbow, which he stroked with the bar of soap he was holding. "What they will do is suck a couple of vials of my precious bodily fluids out of here, and they will check my blood type and some obscure red blood antigens and they'll do what they call HLA typing, which detects proteins that are present in my lymphocytes, whatever the hell those are."

"Will they check your carbohydrates, too?"

He laughed. "No, my carburetor."

I took the soap away from him and started soaping him down.

"Um. Lower."

"So what will all of that tell them?"

"It'll determine whether David and I share the same blood type, for one thing, but as I understand it, the deciding factor is the HLA typing. If I'm the one, David will have half of those little proteins from his mother and the other half from me. If he doesn't have any from me, then he won't have to buy me a Father's Day gift next spring."

I looked into his eyes and smiled a little. "And are you counting on a bottle of cologne?"

He smiled back at me. "I guess I am, kind of."

I gave him a wet kiss, patted his tush, and got out of the shower before I made the mistake of saying what I was thinking: *So what are these little dead trophies that you were so concerned about last night, Geof? Mother's Day gifts?*

The house was cold from having the air conditioner on all night, but neither of us had made a move to turn it off and to open the windows again.

That was the morning, a peaceful start to a day that was about to become one of the strangest of Geof's life.

Taking the blood test was weird enough, of course.

But after leaving the clinic that noon, feeling keyed up, anxious, and curious, Geof—I found out later—went looking for David's relatives, starting with his grandparents, the Ronald Mayer Seniors.

He drove out to the home of Ron's parents in the old rich part of town, the one on which the suburb where Ron and Judy had lived was modeled. In this, the original one, when you described a house as Colonial, you literally meant that it was built around the time King George was on the throne, and when you said a house was Federalist, you meant it had stood since John Quincy Adams wrote the papers of the same name.

I grew up near that neighborhood; so did Geof, but that didn't mean we knew everybody who lived there. I didn't know any of the Mayers, for instance, and Geof had only known the oldest boy, Ron. Geof sometimes accused me of talking about Port Frederick as if it were still a cozy little fishing village when the truth had always been that while there were dozens, maybe even hundreds, of residents we'd known all of our lives, there were also plenty of strangers, even to a cop.

The senior Mayers' house was a huge, old rambling one set way back in the curve of a sheltered cul-de-sac, a luxurious, semicircle of shade, one of many in that part of town. Their house was sheltered, nearly hidden, by vast reaches of shrubbery and flowers that were themselves descendants of fine old roots and trees so venerable you wondered if minutemen had propped their muskets against them.

Geof parked in some gravel at the side of the house.

When he got out of his car and looked up at the house, he had a feeling he'd been there before. After a football game? At a party? Probably, although he wasn't a jock like Ron. He didn't hang around with jocks, and he didn't go to respectable parties, and his recollection of the Mayers was that they were extremely "respectable." There wouldn't have been any booze at any party of theirs, which would have eliminated Geof right away, because according to his own testimony he drank like an intake valve back then. And they certainly wouldn't have had any dope, no drugs, no necking parties, no drunken brawls, nothing that would have attracted Geof's itinerant attention. If he'd ever been in the Mayers' house, it would only have been to get kicked out, and when he had that thought, he knew: Yes, he had, indeed, been booted out that baronial front door! And it was, indeed, for arriving for a party with a beer can in his hand.

Standing in their drive, all these years later, he smiled. The house was also familiar from driving past the cul-de-sac for so many years. He didn't think any police duty had ever brought him out here. Not that those in this quiet, stately neighborhood didn't suffer—or commit—illegal acts; they did, including a homicide every quarter century or so, but Geof was sure that he'd never entered this house during any investigation while he was a homicide detective.

He recalled the family: five brothers, Ron being the oldest, but he couldn't think of the other brothers' names. They were blanks to him, as were the parents. He did have a "memory" of elegance, intimidating, forbidding elegance, and propriety, and . . . godliness. Godliness? Where in hell, he wondered, did he get that word to describe them?

"Silly bullshit," he muttered, losing patience with himself.

He walked up the gravel to the front door and rang their bell.

There were woods behind the house, cypress rising tall and dark like a living curtain that was always pulled down, hiding whatever was behind it: the next block, other houses, the neighbors. It gave him the same somber feeling he got in the tropics, where big old houses hid among the heavy foliage. Here he was, walking up to the door of an archetypal New England mansion, and yet he wouldn't have been too surprised to see a lizard dart out of the bushes in front of him or to have a green snake fall from the trees and land near his feet. He half expected to smell magnolia or to look up and glimpse a black maid shaking out a blanket from one of the bedroom windows on the second floor.

"You are fucking nuts," he said to himself.

He rang the bell again.

In a moment, the door opened to reveal an older woman.

"How do you do," she said in the exquisitely polite but frigid way that only proper New England matrons can ever really master. She was in her seventies, Geof decided, straight backed, with white hair that she wore short and straight in a bowl cut, and she stared at him with a stern, questioning expression set in softly lined skin. She was wearing a suit; Geof thought maybe it was linen, white and cool looking. She was tall; standing slightly higher than he was on the front porch she looked him in the eyes. And then he noticed her high heels. Also white. White hosiery that made him think of nurses. He looked at her left hand when she touched her neck. No fingernail polish, though

103

her short nails looked shiny and the cuticles looked immaculately neat and clean. Prominent veins traced paths like blue rivers on the backs of her hands. (Some of these details come from what Geof told me and the rest from my own later observations. Sometimes it's hard to tell where Geof's brain leaves off and my own begins.) "Yes?" she said, prompting him to state his purpose, this stranger at her door, this whoever-he-was who hadn't telephoned first and who now stood gazing at her. "What is it?"

This time he had identification to show her, rather than a beer.

"Mrs. Mayer?"

When she nodded reluctantly, he continued: "Ma'am, I'm Lieutenant Bushfield with the Port Frederick Police Department. I'm sorry to bother you, but there are a few matters, simple questions, that still need to be cleared up in regard to the deaths of your son and his wife." He paused, looking into gray eyes that had suddenly darkened with surprise and evident pain. "I'm sorry."

"That can't be so!" she protested. Geof thought he saw dread and a mist of tears in the gray eyes. "I can't believe there's anything more to say. You people told us you wouldn't bother us anymore. It was all over, months ago."

"I'd like to talk to the boy," Geof said as an opening gambit. "To David."

She held her right hand, palm up toward him. "I won't allow it."

Geof knew how to act as if the other person hadn't spoken. "Can I find him here, ma'am? Is he living with you now?"

"No, and don't expect me to tell you where he is, because I don't want that child to be bothered." Her voice held indignation, but her eyes still registered immense pain. "He's my grandson . . ."

"Yes," Geof said gently. "I know." He let the silence grow for a moment to let her see that he wasn't going to go away just because she willed him to. "If I can't speak to the boy, may I speak to you and your husband? It won't take more than a few minutes, and right now would be best if you could manage it." He was a persistent sod, my husband—he'd gotten me to marry him, he'd never given up working on me to agree to have a child, and he wasn't going to let her get off easily either, not even if she was a grieving grandmother.

She turned her head as if attentive to some sound within her house. "All right, yes, come in, we'll talk to you." For a moment she seemed confused, disoriented, and Geof felt an impulse of sympathy for her and of loathing for himself: her oldest son dead, her daughter-in-law dead, killed by that son. Yes, a grandmother would want to protect the child of that deadly union, would want to defend him against the possibility of being hurt by tactless questions from unfeeling police officers. He watched her gather herself together again, watched her appear to grow ever taller as she drew dignity from a pool deep inside herself.

She pushed open the screen door to let him in, and he followed her rigid white-clothed back into a living room.

"Mrs. Mayer," he said, "did you used to have French Provincial furniture in here?" He recalled a glimpse of white elegance.

She looked startled. "Why, yes, but that was years ago."

A man, taller than she, also white haired and straight backed and wearing a white cotton suit with a white shirt and white summer loafers with white socks, stepped into the living room through a far door. "How did you know that, Lieutenant?"

"How did you know I'm police?"

Ronald Mayer, Sr., smiled as he walked forward; Geof thought he'd seen warmer smiles on murderers. "I know who you are, Lieutenant Bushfield. I've seen your picture in the paper and your wife's. I knew your parents slightly. They are Tom and Susanne Bushfield, dear," he told his wife. "You remember. And his wife is a Cain, the daughter of Margaret and James . . ."

"Ah," she murmured and moved toward a sofa to sit down. She motioned for the men to take seats as well.

Not for the first time, Geof wondered what it would be like to live in a truly big city, like Boston, to be anonymous, to meet in your line of work *only* strangers who'd never heard of you or of any relative of yours or of your wife's. In some ways, this was easier, because sometimes the familiarity of living in his hometown established an instant rapport with a lot of people, but sometimes it was harder to keep things official when people insisted on saying things to him like, "So, how's your old man?"

"You're here to see us about . . . ?" Mr. Mayer let it hang.

It was his wife who replied in a voice barely above a whisper: "David."

"David," the grandfather said heavily, "is supposed to be living with our second eldest son, Matthew, and his wife. That was what we all agreed when Ron and Judy died." The old man said that without so much as a pause in his breathing or a stutter over his son's name or a blink of his narrowed eyes. "But my grandson has a mind of his own. He has decided to disown us all, because he doesn't like our religion, I gather. Any child who lives with us is expected to go to church, to pray, to attend to certain spiritual duties. We do not, however, chain anyone to a pew." His lips moved in an ironic smile. "David is only a few months away from being of legal age, and he's a mature boy, capable of surviving on his own. Since that appears to be what he wishes to do, we have acceded to his wishes. I don't say we like it. My wife, especially, finds this very hard. We wish he would at least call us now and then or live someplace where it would be easier for us to contact him, but he seems to want to cut us off, and we can't force the pieces back together again. Not until he's ready." He looked at Geof directly. "Now. Is there anything else you want to know about David?" There wasn't any questioning inflection at the end of that sentence, it was a statement, a challenge, as if to say, There, I have met your questions before you asked them.

But Geof was not so easily fobbed off. "What about your late daughter-in-law's family?"

The Mayers didn't respond.

"Could he be living with any of them?" Geof prodded.

"Impossible," Mr. Mayer said quickly, just as his wife was saying, "There's only his other grandmother, and she's . . ."

"Unsuitable," her husband pronounced as if finishing his wife's sentence for her. "Mrs. Baker—Annabelle Baker, Judy's mother—is a businesswoman, far too busy to take care of a teenage boy."

"Then where does he live?" Geof insisted.

"In a boarding house downtown, I'll give you the address."

"No . . ." Mrs. Mayer raised her hands as if pleading with her husband, but then surrendered, crossing her hands over her chest. Her husband glanced over at her for a long moment, then looked back at Geof. "Perhaps you think I am uncaring, but you can see that my wife is very concerned about the boy."

An interesting sentence, Geof thought, with its emphases, its omissions. He felt an urge to rattle the old man out of his arrogance. He wanted suddenly and deeply to know what words or emotions might cascade out of the woman on the couch if something were to nick the skin of her dignity. He looked for a resemblance to David in both of them and thought he found it, unfortunately, in the old man's haughtiness, the old woman's stiffness of posture. Suddenly he was thankful for the kid's heat and fury; at least David Mayer still *had* passion, nobody had successfully chained that down yet. Geof sought Mrs. Mayer's gaze and asked her, "Do you believe that your son killed Judy and then killed himself?"

It worked so well that he nearly felt ashamed of himself. It elicited an odd sound, like a grunt, from the old man and it made her suck in her breath and then to exclaim, "No! No! I never did believe it! But I'm only his mother."

"Why do you ask that now, Lieutenant?"

But her voice, which had dropped nearly to a whisper before, overrode her husband's, growing loud, bitter, even while she avoided her husband's stare. "No one in this family trusts my opinion about my children!"

"There's no reason to doubt the sad facts, Lieutenant."

Geof ignored her husband, too, and told her quietly, "Try me. Why didn't Ron do it, Mrs. Mayer?" He could see in her eyes that she appreciated the fact that he had not said, "Why do you *believe* Ron didn't do it," that instead, he was willing to consider her opinion as possible fact. Nevertheless, her gaze wavered, and she seemed suddenly much less definite, more vague and tentative than she had at any moment since she'd first opened the door to him.

"He just wouldn't," she said. "He couldn't." Her face was flushed beneath her careful makeup as if she knew how clichéd she sounded and she felt humiliated by it, as if she knew that she sounded exactly like the typical mother of a criminal as she loyally and desperately denied the demonstrable fact of her child's guilt. It sounded so lame. Geof was disappointed in her; he'd hoped for better from her, not just a mother's wishful thinking.

"My wife," said the old man, recalling Geof's attention to himself, "will always believe that." His stare seemed to defy Geof to say anything that might disturb a mother's touching trust in her dead son.

"And you, sir?"

"What about me?"

"Do you think your son did what they say?"

"They?" Mr. Mayer laughed contemptuously. "The 'they' you speak of is your own police department. 'They' are you." When Geof didn't rise to any defense, the old man said, "I believe my son was a loving husband who was under more strain than any of us will ever experience and that he finally did what he sincerely believed in his heart was the right thing to do."

Mrs. Mayer moaned, a harsh and shocking sound in that proper room. Geof had a sudden mental image of a wild creature confined to a cage. When he looked over at her, he saw only a woman whose face was held rigidly neutral and whose hands were clenched at her sides on the couch, and he wondered if he had only imagined the strange, brutal sound that could only have escaped against her will. And then he saw her knuckles: white as her hair, white as her clothes. Her face was milked of color, too, her cheeks sunken, her skin loose against her bones. David's grandmother looked bloodless, a corpse propped upright and beautifully dressed upon a couch.

He had to drag his gaze away from her.

He asked her husband one more time: "Was it, Mr. Mayer? The right thing for Ron to do?"

The old man seemed shaken, either by the question or by the visible transformation in his wife. Geof felt as if something had actually managed to provoke authentic feeling in the old son of a bitch. A flash of agony passed across Ronald Mayer, Sr.'s face, as if somebody had stabbed him, but then he said in a hard voice that hammered each word as if it were a nail in his son's coffin, "I believe in hell."

The terrible words hung in the room. Even the old man sank down a bit in his seat, his head hanging slightly as if his neck had lost the strength to hold it upright. His wife got to her feet shakily and walked slowly out of the living room, holding onto the backs of the furniture and then touching walls, doorsills, banisters, to support her way. She looked as if she had aged a hundred years since the moment when she first opened the door to Geof, and he nearly had to sit on his own hands to keep himself from rushing to her, putting his arm around her, assisting her. Her own husband didn't move, but he watched her leave. In the silence of the big house, Geof heard her quiet footsteps slowly ascending the stairs in the main hallway.

Geof stood up. "Mr. Mayer, do you have any reason to think that the deaths of your son and his wife occurred in any way that is different from the finding of murder/suicide?"

"No," the old man muttered, still gazing toward the stairway.

"Does anyone in your family doubt the finding?"

"No!" Now the proud face raised, and blue eyes glared at Geof. "Do you think we wouldn't doubt it if we could? Do you think we *want* to have a dead son, a dead brother, who committed deadly sins? Why are you asking these questions? Do *you* have doubts? For God's sake, and I mean that literally, for the sake of God who desires for his son Ronald to return to him in heaven, tell me what they are! Let my wife have some hope that our son is not the worst kind of sinner who is damned to eternal torment! For God's sake, man!"

"It is our policy," Geof prevaricated, "to take a second look at all major crimes at some time after they have been solved in order to confirm that we came to the right conclusions at the time. Hindsight gives us perspective. It can be a disturbing process, but we feel that it's necessary for effective law enforcement. I'm sorry to have upset your wife."

That last part, he meant sincerely. He didn't know where the first part came from.

He turned to leave the room, knowing his good-bye wasn't needed or wanted. But the old man's voice followed him. "You didn't answer my question. Have you been in this house before, Lieutenant?''

Geof turned around again, smiled. "Not quite." He hesitated. "I was a friend of Ron's. I came here for a party sometime."

"No, you weren't a friend of his."

"Really, Mr. Mayer?"

The old man got up, seeming to regain vigor with every movement. He barely bothered to glance at Geof as he spoke, leaving the room by the back doorway through which he had entered. "I made sure I knew all of Ron's friends. I would never have allowed him to be friends with a boy like you."

Geof was left regarding an empty room.

As he climbed back into the Jeep, he thought about me, and he wondered if I was having any luck in finding David that day.

# 12

 AT THAT MOMENT, I WAS FEELING AS IF I COULD ride on the back of that motorcycle for the rest of my life. My body swayed with the turns in the road, my hips melted into the seat, my legs loosely held the sides of the bike and my feet sat on the pedals as comfortably as the toes of a queen touching the floor of her throne. Within a few windy miles of being out on the highway leaving town, I felt as at home on that bike as a country girl riding bareback behind her friend on a horse. The thrust of the engine threw me into another world, one in which everything flew by as if it didn't matter—all decisions, deadlines, worry. Nothing existed but the warmth flowing from David's back and the heat crawling up my legs from the bike and the sun on my back. There was nothing in the world anymore except the hand of the wind caressing my cheek and lifting the hairs on my bare arms and pillowing my T-shirt out in back. There was only the smell of honeysuckle when we passed by patches at the side of the highway and oniony freshcut grass and the smell of horses in meadows and the smell of hot melting pavement under our wheels. The world came down to movement and sensation;

there was no more thinking, no emotion except exhilaration, no intuition. There was only what information came in by way of my tongue and skin and nose and eyes and ears, and all of it was good news. On the back of the bike, there was no bad news, there were no wars, no accidents, no pain or anxiety, there was only liquid happiness that roared in my ears like a constant waterfall. The sound was like a powerful surf that only came in and never ebbed. On the back of a motorcycle, I discovered a tide that was always in, full of mystery and treasure; the wind washed around my ankles just like the sea soaks the legs of a playing child. I was the child, and the grown-up on that bike was the teenage boy who rode in front of me, the kid who drove now with such panache, such sureness, such adult confidence, such a magical combination of aggression and lightness of touch upon the road. Or maybe he was driving just the same as he had in town; maybe I was the one who'd changed from a frightened passenger to an easy rider.

This is the way to die, I thought: You get on the back of a bike behind somebody else, a good driver, and you lean trustingly in to him and you close your eyes and give yourself blissfully up to the crash.

"Your father had it all wrong," I said quietly into his back, into the wind that carried my words tactfully away from the ears of the boy. You don't kill yourself and somebody you love with a gun in a stifling, unhappy house, you get on the bike, and you ask her if she wants to go with you and if she says yes, you give her a hand up onto the bike with you and you both ride hellbent for leather into a perfect night when there's a fiery moon overhead and a billion burning stars and the weather is a silky stream of warm air and cool that wraps around your shoulders like a satin shawl, and you don't wear many clothes or maybe any at all, and you run your bike up to a speed where everything is pure sensation and right at the height of it, right when you feel as if you can't absorb any more sensation through your skin or your eyes or your nose or your mouth, that's when you do it, that's when you aim for the light pole, the bridge abutment, the side of the barn. And you pass straight over from bliss to ecstasy, from heaven to heaven, and you never even remember the despair that drove you to it, and you don't miss earth for a minute.

"That's how to do it," I whispered, and the words flew back at me.

"You're crazy," I told myself next, and I laughed on the back of the bike. Who cared? Who could possibly care where we were going, for what reason, or even if there were a reason? I didn't. I just wanted to ride on the back of that bike forever. I didn't want to drive it, I never wanted to drive it, I just wanted to ride and ride.

It felt absurdly like tragedy when he began to slow down.

He pulled onto a bumpy side road, more like a dirt path gouged out of the grass by car and truck tires and bordered by tall pine trees that cast it into midday darkness. I didn't have time to start getting nervous again, because the ride lingered in my blood like a drug and because he abruptly pulled up to a barbed wire fence and stopped, allowing the bike to idle while he held it up with one of his feet on the ground.

"I spent a lot of time out here when I was a kid," he said.

Over his shoulder, I saw a bucolic scene: a two-story red wood barn, a one-story ranch house, outbuildings, a couple of calves in a pen, a few horses nibbling grass.

"Who does it belong to?" I asked him.

He didn't answer me and he didn't give me any longer to look at the view. Instead, he backed the bike back onto the road, turned it in a short radius, and took off back the way we had come to the highway. I didn't care, I wanted only to get back to that high-speed road again, and if we never made it back into town, that was all right with me.

Halfway there, he turned his head and raised his voice. "You like this?"

"Yes!" I shouted, forgetting that I didn't have to yell.

He turned his face forward again, and the road and the wind and the sun and the sound of the engine took over the universe, and soon, too soon, we had to slow down at the outskirts of Port Frederick.

David dropped me back at my car at the McDonald's restaurant.

When I tried to thank him, he shrugged and frowned and backed away from me, then hurried back in to his job. I wondered if it was still waiting for him. Once he was inside, and I felt confident that he wasn't coming out again, I sidled back up to his motorcycle. I slid my hands along the handlebars, I warmed my palms on the seat, I slipped open the backpack and reached my right hand inside and felt three books, a notebook, pencils, pens, and a plastic box, which I pulled partway out. It was a videotape, and its label said "Mom."

He was luring us, Geof had guessed.

Leading us on, manipulating us, pointing us to where he wanted us to go, seducing us . . .

I took the tape.

When I slid back behind the wheel of my beloved Miata, I felt like a changed woman. Even in the convertible, as I drove away, I felt confined, I missed the feel of the rushing air on my bare toes and the vibration of an engine on my thighs. I wanted to go faster than the law allowed in the city, and I wanted to tell Geof that if he wished to purchase a motorcycle for his fortieth birthday, it was okay with me, so long as he bought a second helmet for his passenger.

I found out that evening that while my husband was quite interested in the chance encounter that Sabrina and I had that day with Dennis Clemmons, he wasn't thrilled with my new-found enthusiasm for motorcycles.

"You went for a *ride* with him, Jenny?"

"When will you get the results of your blood test? And what do you mean their house felt familiar, Geof? Like déjà vu, you mean?"

"What if he's the one who's been leaving the dead animals around here, Jenny? Did you think about that before you just rode off with him?"

"You've probably driven by it a thousand times, that's all."

"You didn't even know if he was a safe driver, did you?"

I put my fork down and stared at him across our dinner table. "I thought that since he was a teenage boy, I could probably take it for granted that he was not a safe driver."

"And you went anyway?"

"I was wrong. He's a great driver. Smart and safe."

He didn't have a retort to that, so he ate a bite of rice and swallowed. "I haven't driven by that house a thousand times; it's on a cul-de-sac, hidden by a lot of tall trees; I wouldn't drive in there unless I had a reason. Maybe we'll go over to Ron and Judy's house tonight. You want to go?"

"Oh, heck," I said.

He stared at me.

I made a disappointed face. "I was hoping we could go shopping for motorcycles."

Geof shook his head in wonderment. "I can't believe this. If you knew how long I've been putting off telling you that I'd like to get one, you'd laugh."

I laughed and said, "Surprise."

My laughter sounded nervous, and no wonder: I was feeling queasy with anxiety. My God, I'd stolen something out of the boy's backpack. Why had that wild ride tempted me into theft? The fact that I intended to return the videotape did not redeem the act. Nor did I really accept my own excuse that if the kid wouldn't openly talk to us, we had to sneak the facts out of him. And my original feeling—that he had left it out there practically begging me to take it—seemed like a sick fantasy to me now. No, there was only one fact: I had stolen a videotape from David Mayer. No, there were actually two facts, and the second one was that I hadn't told my police lieutenant husband about the first fact yet.

"So what's your due date?" I asked him.

"My what?"

"When will you know the results of the blood test?"

"Soon, tomorrow." He looked amused. "My due date?"

"Well, don't you feel a little like an expectant father?"

"Now that you mention it, I guess I do."

I grinned at him, feigning good sportsmanship. "We could throw a baby shower for you."

As I hoped he would, he laughed at that. "Great."

*Yeah. Great.*

\*　　\*　　\*

115

"Speaking of fathers," I said as we were clearing the dishes. "What'd you find out today about David's stepfather?"

"Funny thing." Geof swabbed the stovetop with a wet dishrag. "Dennis Clemmons did serve time for burglarizing a house, just as Lee told us. It wasn't his first arrest on that charge, but it was his first conviction." He laughed as he flipped food crumbs into the sink. "The arresting officers actually caught him in the house, Jenny, stuffing silverware into a laundry bag."

"So thoughtful of crooks to get caught in the act."

"Isn't it? He has a long jacket on other charges, though, petty theft, shoplifting, it goes way back. His juvenile record's been expunged, but I talked to an old-timer who remembers a kid named Dennis Clemmons getting in trouble for everything from numbers running to delivering porno for the local slime."

I put the salt and pepper away. "He sounds charming."

"Yeah. I find myself less flattered that Judy was ever attracted to me."

I smiled to myself. "I'll bet."

Geof draped the rag over the faucet. "There's no record of the beating he gave Judy, and there's nothing in the files to tell us how he got hurt himself."

"That doesn't surprise us, does it?" I asked him. "That there's no record of what he did to her? According to her doctor, she didn't want anybody to know."

To which my husband observed, "There seem to have been a lot of things that Judy Baker didn't want anybody to know. I think maybe I'd like to talk to Annabelle Baker."

"Who?"

"Judy's mother."

"What for?"

He looked surprised. "Well, maybe she can clear up some of these questions."

"Are you kidding?" I shook my head at his naivete. "Haven't you heard that mothers are the last to know? It's true! Parents don't have a clue what their children are really like, and kids don't understand their parents either."

"We're a little cynical tonight, aren't we?"

I pointed a clean fork at him. "I'm just telling you."

He flipped off the kitchen lights and said, "Yes, ma'am," as he pushed me out of the room ahead of him. "Then why don't you talk to her for me? That way I won't take her word for anything, since she doesn't know anything about her own daughter."

I elbowed him in his stomach. Then I decided to call his bluff.

"All right," I said, suddenly turning on him in the dining room. "I'll do it. What's her number?"

He grinned. "I suppose it's in Lee's files or the phone book. You're going to call her right now?"

"Why not?" I feigned a certain insouciance, which dropped away from me the instant I actually did connect with the number in the phone book and did actually hear the voice of Judy Baker's mom on our telephone. Instantly, I thought, *What have I done? This is the mother of a woman who was murdered, I can't just barge into her life like* . . . "Uh, Mrs. Baker?"

"Yes?" It sounded chirpy, brittle, like a woman who was trying very, very hard to be cheerful for anyone who called.

"Mrs. Baker, my name's Jenny Cain, I'm so sorry to disturb you—"

"No bother, honey!" She gave a fake little laugh that twisted my heart. "Is this business or—"

"No, I . . . well, I went to school with Judy, Mrs. Baker . . . and I was just wondering if I could come over and talk to you about her . . . just kind of reminisce . . ." Invisibly to her, I shuddered at my own prevarication.

"About my Judy?" she said, sounding as if I'd taken her by surprise, and then she said kind of breathlessly, "Well, aren't you sweet?"

*No!* I thought with utter guilt. *I'm not!*

"That would be lovely to meet a friend of Judy's," she continued in that awful, bright, false cheerfulness. "But maybe not right now, I'm a little busy right now . . ."

"Oh, I didn't mean right this very—"

"Maybe some other time, maybe in a week or two—"

"Oh, yes, fine, thank you—"

"Call me again, honey . . . and come by and see me, that would be just awfully nice, but maybe not right now, maybe . . ."

"Later," I agreed.

117

Humbly, I said good night to her and hung up. Even more humbly, I turned to my husband, who had been standing by, listening, watching me. "I'm not tough enough to do what you do," I told him quite seriously. "I could never be a cop or even a reporter."

"Why? What'd she say?"

"It's too soon, Geof." I thought of her heartbreaking effort to be sweet to me. "I don't think she wants to talk about it yet." I gave him—or myself?—an encouraging smile. "But she said maybe in a week or two I could call her again."

He shrugged. "That's fine, Jenny."

"It is?"

"Sure. I might have pressed harder, but maybe I wouldn't have. It's not an active case, after all, and I might have felt just as sorry for her as you do."

I stepped into his embrace and murmured, "Good for you."

# 13

BEFORE WE LEFT FOR TOWN TO TAKE A LOOK AT RON and Judy Mayer's house—and because I was feeling guilty and paranoid—I slipped David's videotape into my purse. The only one it fit into was a huge black leather affair that looked a little odd with my shirts and T-shirt and red vinyl sandals. But I didn't want to leave the tape unprotected in the house. And I thought that if I worked up the nerve to confess to my crime, I'd better have the evidence with me. Of course, Geof immediately noticed when we got into his Jeep and I placed the ugly old thing in my lap.

"Why are you bringing that along, Jenny?"

"My purse? You never know, we might want to stop and get an ice cream cone on the way back."

"You could carry your life savings in that. I have money with me."

"I just feel like taking it, Geof, all right?"

"Okay!" He laughed a little at my testiness. "Take the whole house if you want to."

"Thank you. But this will do."

He looked at me as if he thought I was crazy, then started the

119

engine for our quiet, hot ride into town. It was going on eight o'clock by the time we arrived at the Mayers' house in Royal Acres. The sun was setting on the steamy day, but it was like a hot iron coming down on a wet shirt; the world was only getting darker, not cooler. As I climbed out of the Jeep to meet Geof on the sidewalk, I felt like surrendering, like giving up and melting into everything.

"I apologize," I said. For my earlier testiness, I meant.

"It's hot, we're all cranky."

"Nice of you to say so."

It must have been the heat, but at that moment I looked up at his face, so hard at the jaw line, so evaluative, so *gauging* around the eyes, and I wondered what it was about a person's psyche that would make her marry a cop. My own father couldn't have been less coplike. If Geof was "fuzz," then my dad was fuzzy, so maybe that was the reason, one of the reasons.

"What?" he asked intuitively.

I hedged. "I always think a house where a murder has taken place is going to look different somehow." I knew I was babbling, as guilty people are inclined to do. "I don't suppose you think so. I know it's silly, but when we drove up here, I half expected to see the crime scene ribbons still in place after all this time."

"No, I know what you mean."

"You do? An old cop like you?"

"Don't say old." His grin appeared briefly, and my guilty heart warmed to him. "Not to a man who's turning forty." He grasped my left elbow and steered me forward. "Come on. No more stalling. Let's see if there is, in fact, anything different about this house."

From the outside, it looked like all the others on the block: safe, secure, conventional, where nobody would ever raise her voice except to call the children in to dinner. I'd never have picked it as a location where a woman would die violently at the hands of a man who said he loved her.

We'd been talking over the noise of a lawnmower in the next yard.

The man who was mowing made his pivot to come back down

his lawn, and when he did, he noticed us. He released the handle of the machine, which shut down the engine. A few yards behind him, a woman in orange Bermuda shorts was clipping hedges. She had her back to us, but when his mower stopped, she looked up, too. As Geof and I ascended the front steps to the Mayer house, the man in the next yard came walking toward us, smiling tentatively, looking curious and friendly like a dog coming to sniff us out.

We stopped and waited for him to reach us. I resisted an impulse to put out the back of my hand for him to smell.

Mentally, I put him in his forties and the woman in her late fifties or early sixties. She was tanned and pudgy, with a yellow tank top over the orange shorts and gray-blond hair pulled messily up on top of her head. He was slimmer and darker and bare chested over black Bermuda shorts, with tennis shoes and white socks. He wiped the sweat off his forehead with the back of his right hand and called out before he reached us, "Hello! May I help you?"

The woman lowered her shears to stare openly at us.

In the quiet, which came as a relief, I heard a prattle of traffic on the road into town; from somewhere in the vicinity came the thump of a basketball repeatedly hitting a garage door and a woman's voice was calling, "Here, Fanny, here kitty-kitty!" The smell of fresh-cut grass and a sniffle of dust filled my nose. We hadn't had a good rain in a couple of weeks, typical for late August in Massachusetts.

"Hello!" Geof was all smiles, reaching out his hand for the man to shake. "I'm Geof. This is my wife, Jenny." Downright folksy, he was, as he dangled the Mayers' house keys in the air between him and the neighbor to assert our bona fides. "David asked us to come take a look at the house."

"David did?" The man seemed extraordinarily happy to be shaking Geof's hand and then mine; he looked unaccountably pleased to see us. "That's great!"

"Well, thank God!" The woman had tossed her shears to the lawn and come up behind the man. Now she stood with her hands on her hips, her legs apart, nodding her head at us. "It's about time!"

"What Mom means," the man said, looking a little embarrassed, "is that we can't keep this up forever, looking out for David's property the way we've been doing since his parents died. Somebody ought to help him sell it if he isn't going to live here." He smiled hopefully at us. "We've been glad to pitch in with the yard maintenance and to watch out for the property, please don't misunderstand us, we're more than happy to help David, but it's a lot of work, you know, keeping up our home"—he gestured to a dignified dowager of a Colonial in Harvard crimson and white to the immediate south—"and this one, too."

His mother muttered, "Too damn much work."

They seemed to be assuming a certain amount of knowledge on our part, a mistake we were willing to let them make. She had on cotton gardening gloves and now she pulled off the right one and stuck out that hand first to me, then to Geof. "Please excuse the grime. Will you please tell David that we don't mean to push him a moment sooner than he's ready, because God knows he's been through hell, but either he's got to take over this yard or he's got to hire somebody to do it. We've tried to be understanding, but we've been doing this all spring and summer now—keeping the lawn mowed, trimming the bushes, plucking the weeds, even taking off that damned mean graffiti—and it's getting to be too much for the two of us to handle. I hope the boy will understand and that he won't take offense, because there's certainly none intended. Will you please tell him that?"

"Other people help," the man corrected her in a gentle, chiding tone. He had a softer way about him than she did, not effete, just unusually patient and pleasant. Up close, I saw that he was younger than he'd appeared at first, probably only in his thirties, with a balding crew cut, a trim body, and a quite ordinary face, intelligent looking, but not remarkable in any way. I could have passed him a dozen times in the grocery store and never have recognized him from one time to the next as anybody I'd ever seen before. She looked twenty or thirty years older, with stronger features, a bolder manner, a louder voice. There was something straightforward and honest about her that I liked.

"Help? Not so's you'd notice, not much anymore," she re-

torted, sounding ready to argue about it with him. This had the
feel of an old quarrel, although how old could it be, because the
Mayers had been gone for only a few months? "And I, for one,
don't blame them!" she continued, wiping at her forehead with
one hand. Sweat ran down into the deep bosom of her yellow
tank top. "I'd quit doing this, too, if I didn't have such a saint
for a son." She threw him an affectionately sour look, which he
received with a small smile that wrinkled the corners of his eyes
and reddened the skin above his cheekbones.

"The boy still needs our help, Mom." He said it patiently.

"That boy's needed *help* for some time now." She glanced at
us as if to make sure we'd caught her emphasis on the word
*help*. "And before that it was his mother who needed so much
*help* and before that it was his father . . . most *help*less family I
ever met." Again, that sardonic glance at us. "And let me ask
you this, my sainted son. If you didn't help the child, who is
really no child at all, but a teenager, nearly a full-grown man
who has family of his own who ought to be doing these chores
instead of you and me, he'd have to help himself, now
wouldn't he?"

The man glanced at us, looking embarrassed again.

"Graffiti?" Geof said.

I had to hide a smile. He was a cop, sho' nuff, even if he hadn't
as yet revealed that fact to these people.

"Please don't tell David," the man said.

"Teenagers can be so *mean* sometimes," his mother said.

"Mom, we don't know it was teen—"

"Damon, for heaven's sake!" She glanced at me as if counting
on understanding from another woman. "Who else would it be?
No adult in his right mind would do anything like that! Honestly,
dear, sometimes you are so determined to see the good in people
that you don't even recognize the knife in their hand when it's
coming at you!" To Geof and me, she invited, "Come on, I'll
show you where the last of the graffiti was. But Day's right about
one thing at least—don't tell the boy. It would be terribly hurtful
to him, I'm sure."

We followed her up to the house, and there we observed that

a block of blue-gray paint, about three feet tall by five feet wide, looked fresher than the rest.

"What did it say?" I asked her.

"It was an equation," she said promptly, "written like a math problem, you know? One time what it said was, Three minus two equals one."

It took Geof and me both a second to grasp it, and then I exclaimed, "Oh, no," feeling the hurt of it. Geof's face went stoic, all in an instant.

"More than once?" he asked.

"Yes," Damon spoke up from behind us, sounding wounded on David's behalf. Unnecessarily, he translated the equation for us: "A family of three, minus both parents, equals one lonely child. Isn't that terrible? We've seen graffiti like that three or four times since they died, isn't that right, Mom?"

"What else did it say?" Geof asked.

"Oh, there's been, let's see, one plus one equals none—"

Again, I couldn't restrain an exclamation of dismay.

"Yes, it's quite cruel," Damon said in a gentle voice, and again he translated the obvious for us: "The death of one parent plus the death of one parent equals no parents. There was also two times zero equals zero, which I believe was probably supposed to mean that when you multiply two times zero parents you still don't have any parents. You're still an orphan. And there was two into two equals zero."

"Two into two equals zero?" I said, not getting it.

"We couldn't figure that one out either," his mother told me. "It's always somewhere on the house, spray painted, always in red, which is so difficult to cover over—"

"And a bit of particularly awful nastiness," he interjected.

"Yes," she agreed. "It always happens at night, of course, when nobody's watching. We've talked about posting a guard, staying up every night until we nab them, but somehow we just haven't done it—"

"The two of you?" I asked her.

"And some of the other neighbors," her son said. "The ones who've known David since he was a little boy, the ones who remember him . . . before . . ." His voice trailed off. He and his mother exchanged glances. I assumed they meant: before the boy's parents died.

"Have you reported this?" Geof asked.

"Somebody has," the man said. "I'm sure."

"Damon!" His mother was exasperated again. "Didn't you ever check?"

"Well, no, I trusted somebody would—"

"Oh, you! The somebody should have been you or me!"

As his mother probably did, I suspected this might be an instance of "everybody" thinking that "somebody" had done the job, when actually nobody ever did, like the times when the power goes off in a neighborhood and everybody assumes that "surely" all the other neighbors have called the electric company, and so they all go without lights for a while longer than necessary.

"I guess we'll take a look inside," Geof said to me as if he'd only just thought of it. And to the neighbors, he said politely, vaguely, "It's so kind of you to help out. We'll try to talk to David about it. I might need to come back and discuss it with you some other time . . ."

"Of course," Damon said. "I'm always home."

I wondered what that meant. Did he work at home?

"I'm going back to my hedges," his mother announced. "Nice of you folks to come by . . . How do you know David?"

"My husband knew David's mother quite well," I said.

Geof grasped my elbow again. I thought his touch was a bit tight this time. "I didn't catch your last names," he said.

"Montgomery," she called back over her shoulder. "I'm Sheila."

Damon Montgomery stuck with us, following us up the walk and around to the south side of the house to the back door. "Why didn't we just go in the front door?" I asked, then regretted it. Maybe there was some police reason for the fact that Geof was leading us around to the rear. But he easily covered my gaff by saying, "I wanted to check out the house all the way around."

I noticed nothing remarkable on our way. It didn't really look like a vacant house, especially when I stared in the windows and saw furniture.

"Look here," Damon Montgomery said suddenly just as Geof and I were walking single file up a wooden wheelchair ramp to a wide back stoop. We both turned and looked back down at the neighbor. "The thing of it is, I've got to warn you about something that even my mother doesn't know. It may be pretty . . . unpleasant . . . inside." He gave a little shudder even with the fading sun still pouring its heat down on us. In response, I felt the hair rise on my own neck, and goose pimples sprouted on my sweating forearms. "I don't think the place has ever been cleaned up. I mean, I don't think anybody ever sent a crew of any sort to clean up, well . . . afterward."

I felt clammy and knew my eyes had widened like an ingenue's.

"What?" Even the cop looked nonplussed.

"I haven't even told Mom," Montgomery confessed to us, "because I'm afraid she might think we ought to go in and clean it up ourselves, and frankly, I couldn't stand it. I think it would break my heart. As you may know, I was very close to Judy, she was probably my best friend, and I don't think I could stand to go in there."

I wondered why he thought we might know that, and then I remembered: Oh, right, he thinks Geof and Judy were friends. Well, that was one way of looking at their relationship, I supposed. They were, at one time, close.

"Anyway, I haven't known what to do about it, about the fact that nobody's been here to clean up. I don't have a number to call to reach David, he was supposed to go live with those awful relatives, those"—suddenly, he laughed a little wildly—"*god*awful relatives! But he didn't, so I don't know where he is. Listen here, I'm . . . sorry. I feel kind of responsible now, having this knowledge and not doing anything about it. I hope it won't be awful for you in there."

"No one's been here?" Geof still sounded unbelieving.

"I don't think so," Montgomery said. "I could be wrong."

I looked at Geof, and he glanced at me with the same thought showing in his expression that I felt in mine: *God, let's hope so*. We watched the man lope away from us. Even from the back, he looked embarrassed, dejected, kind of sad and lost.

"Do you think he knows about me?" Geof asked me as he put the key in the lock in the storm door at the back of the Mayers' house. The doorway was extra wide; like the ramp leading up to it, it was designed for wheelchair access. "He said they were best friends."

"No, he said she was his best friend."

"There's a difference?"

"Yes, it means he tells her everything, but it doesn't mean she necessarily tells him everything."

"Told."

"Yes."

"What would I do without you?"

I was tempted to ask him to find that out: He sounded perfectly calm, this was all in a day's work for him, but I was really dreading the moments to come. I knew I could back out, I could let him go in without me. In other circumstances—okay, other murders, if you will—I would have done that. I'm no cop; I don't have to do these nasty things. But this one was different, it was personal for him. I knew he could do it alone, but I didn't want him to, I didn't think he should have to.

The lock worked, turned. Geof pulled at the storm door. The handle was lower down than usual to make it easier for a woman in a chair to grasp, and when he opened it, it stayed open. It appeared to have special hinges to hold it and then to close it very slowly to give time for Judy Mayer to wheel her way into her home. When Geof unlocked the inner door and pushed it open, it moved back at the merest touch as if welcoming whoever entered there. Somebody'd put a lot of thought and consideration into easing Judy's comings and goings. There was no metal sill for her to have to bump over; the entrance from porch to kitchen was perfectly flat and smooth, from the wood right into linoleum. We found ourselves staring into a spacious kitchen where all of the counters had been lowered to wheelchair level and even the refrigerator door handle had been moved down a few inches.

I was hanging back, holding my breath.

"I guess if you're disabled," Geof commented, looking in, "it pays to marry a man in the construction trade."

"And one who loves you," I murmured tightly.

127

He glanced back at me. "You think so?"

"Looks that way to me."

I wanted to delay the moment when we entered that dreadful house where we might find God-knew-what reminders of dreadful moments. In this heat, with all the time that had passed, all that blood and tissue from two deaths by gunshot . . . I swallowed hard. So far, no horrible odor had emanated from within, and I hadn't seen anything terrible yet.

Geof touched his fingertips to my face, then smiled a little. "Are we avoiding going in there, Jenny? Do you want to stay outside while I go in there by myself?"

"Oh, no, I'm fine," I lied. "Let's go."

"You don't have to—"

"Open the door, dammit!"

He laughed, pushed open the door, and walked onto the linoleum, which was a common brown and tan pattern. He looked around for a moment, then took an ostentatiously deep breath. Then he turned and grinned at me. "When we walked around the side of the house, there weren't any flies on the insides of the windows, Jenny. *Some*body's been here to clean, whether the neighbors know it or not. I knew it would be okay for us to come in."

I released the breath I'd been holding.

"Cops are jerks," I said, stepping in behind him, and he laughed. "Why did that man tell us that if it wasn't true?"

Geof led our way out of the kitchen, down a long wide hallway toward the rest of the house. "Maybe he really didn't know. Or maybe he wanted to scare us away from here."

"Almost worked," I muttered behind him.

The house had no unpleasant odor, only a faint, sweet, woody, dusty smell that was actually rather pleasant.

"If I weren't a cop," he responded, "it would have worked. I'd have gone away and never come back."

I let him get several steps ahead of me before I whispered to his back: "It's not too late for that, dear." Just because Ron and Judy's house was clean didn't mean it was going to be pleasant.

# 14

SOMEBODY *HAD* BEEN IN TO CLEAN UP THE CRIME scene, but no amount of scrubbing could make it all go away. Deep dark stains radiated from the center of a wide doorway that separated the dining room from the living room, giving the appearance that children had tripped and spilled their glasses of grape juice on the plain beige wool carpet. It was there where Ron—presumably— had placed one of the dining chairs in which he had sat his wife and then shot her to death. A quick check of the five matching chairs around the dining room table told us which was the one, it being ruined like the carpet. The woodwork of the doorsill that arched over the spot where they died was painted a glossy version of the beige of the walls and the carpet, but its finish was defaced by dark spots that I didn't wish to examine closely.

The house was stuffy but not stifling as I'd expected.

"The air conditioner's on," I observed, surprised.

Geof walked over to a thermostat that we had passed on our way down the hall from the kitchen and examined it. "Should be cooler in here," he commented, coming back in toward me. "The thermostat's set at sixty-two degrees."

129

"Must be broken."

"Or maybe somebody only recently turned it on."

I considered that silently, then offered the opinion, "It would have to be very recent." Like, within the last couple of hours. "Why would somebody just happen to turn on the AC right before we showed up, Geof?"

"I don't know, Jenny."

There was an edge to his voice that hadn't been there before. He shifted his body enough for me to see his face then, and I noticed a tension around his mouth and eyes. Instantly, I eased up on him. Inside this disturbing house where his—alleged—son had experienced so much tragedy, Geof was emitting an edginess that was like a cloud of black spikes all around him.

"I'm going to look at the rest of the house," I said.

"Fine," he replied, his voice pitched low but tight as a string on one of those violins that my biology teacher had claimed they made out of Norwegian spruce trees. Don't pluck with me, that tone suggested.

I took the hint and wandered off through the rest of the house but not before taking a good long look at the "scene of the crime." It looked exactly like the sketches and photos that Lee had showed us, except that the chair had been moved back to its place under the table and the bodies were gone. The furniture in the living room was still lined up against the walls, as if they'd pushed it all back for dancing. Just as in Lee's sketches, the drapes in both rooms were shut, which was probably a good thing, having helped to keep the rooms cooler during this hot summer.

I found broad hallways on the first floor of the house. Widened doorways. A minimum of furniture, and most of that moved back against walls. Mostly flat vinyl flooring, few carpets, and no throw rugs in this household. Drawers and knobs placed down low, even a special bathroom off the master bedroom, with handicapped railings and a low sink, just like public access restrooms. Everything arranged for someone in a wheelchair. I'd never seen it in a private home before, and I felt sure the extent of it was unusual, that most disabled people didn't have it so good. Everywhere I looked, there was evidence of a contractor husband with carpenter brothers.

I found a wheelchair folded against a wall in the master bedroom. It was a simple contraption made of aluminum, with wide bands of black vinyl to support her rear end and her back.

Always the curious type, I pried it open and sat down in it. It was amazingly comfortable, especially at the small of my back.

I found a hand brake, released it, and then began to experiment with rolling myself around the blue and gold vinyl floor. I quickly discovered that the wheelchair was lightweight and easy to maneuver, but I was a beginner and awkward. I rolled forward, backward, turned a couple of circles. It was fun if you didn't have to be there. I began to understand children's wheelchair races in hospital hallways, wheelchair basketball, and Special Olympic events.

I rolled to what was obviously her side of the bed, where there was one of those hospital trays that's on a rolling stand that can be pushed aside. How disabled was Judy? I wondered. It didn't take a trained detective to deduce that her legs hadn't worked well if at all. But I didn't know about the rest of her.

I made my own body go limp and heavy below my waist. It actually took some concentration to do it, but finally my pelvis seemed to melt into the vinyl seat and my ankles felt weightless.

What about her arms and hands, did they still function?

I thought about the railings I'd seen in the bathroom and the knobs and drawer handles, all at her wheelchair height, and decided that she still had use of her upper body. So, trying to use only my muscles above my waist, I pushed the hospital tray off to the side.

As I did that, the wheelchair scooted backward. Oops. I located the brake again, and after rolling closer to the bed, I set it. Now then. How did she get herself up into bed? It was closer to the ground than ordinary beds, but still . . . I didn't see anything to grab onto except a dark blue bedcover, and that might only pull me onto the floor . . .

Placing the palms of my hands on the armrests of the chair, I pushed until I stood on the metal footrests, and then I just kept up the momentum until I fell face forward onto the bed. *Ouch. Damn.* My head landed on something hard. When I fished around in the covers, I discovered a television remote control box. If I were disabled and my husband left that thing lying hidden in the covers, I'd kill him.

I couldn't stop even to rub where my head hurt, because I was starting to slide backward off the covers. Quickly, I grabbed handfuls of anything I could get hold of: cover, blanket, sheets, mattress cover, mattress, and tugged and pulled until I had three-fourths of my body on the bed, which was by now, of course, completely torn up. I rolled over onto my back and used my elbows and my head to inch myself around until I lay properly, parallel to the sides of the bed. Then I could use the palms of my hands again to push myself upright until I was sitting, propped against the headboard. My T-shirt was up around my neck, I was breathing like a whale in labor, and I was dripping sweat and exhausted. But it was all worthwhile for one reason, at least: There at the side of the bed was an eight-by-ten color photograph of Judy, inscribed, "With All My Love," to her husband, and she looked gorgeous in it.

I was astonished at that sight of her. The Judy I recalled from high school had been a basically plain girl, but evidently, she'd grown into greater beauty. I picked up the photo to examine it and observed: movie-star makeup, anchor-woman hair, white fur off the shoulder, showing a lot of rouged cleavage and a tremendous smile for the camera. Ah-ha. It was one of those "glamour" photos from one of those studios that claim they can transform any woman into Lana Turner. Judy's eyes even glistened as if with real emotion for the camera. And there I had it: my idea for a very funny, very private surprise present for Geof's fortieth birthday. As he was always saying, you never knew what might turn up at a murder scene.

"What in God's name are you doing, Jenny?"

Quickly, I put the photo facedown on the bed beside me. On the back of it was the name of a studio: Illusions. I looked over at Geof, who stood in the bedroom doorway, staring at me in disbelief.

"Hi. I was just wondering what it felt like to be Judy."

He shook his head. "This is so like you, Jenny."

"I'm not going to ask you what that means. Geof, why do you suppose he shot her in a chair in a doorway? Don't you think that's a strange place to do it? Why wouldn't he just shoot her in here when she was sleeping and she wouldn't know what hit her?"

He stepped into the room. "Maybe she wanted to know."

I started to hike myself up straighter with my arms until I remembered I could use my legs. I drew them up and hooked my arms over my knees, thinking.

"Why'd you turn the VCR on?" he said.

"I didn't!" But when I looked where Geof was pointing, at a big screen set in a built-in entertainment center in the wall, I saw that there was a red light glowing on the VCR box. "Maybe I punched it by accident." I fished around in the covers for the remote control gizmo, but when I found it, I held it up so Geof could see that it wasn't one that controlled the VCR, only the TV. He was on his way over to turn off the machine when I said, "Geof, wait."

He stopped and looked back quizzically at me.

"Don't go anywhere, don't touch anything," I commanded him as I clambered out of the bed. "I have to go to the car for my purse." I left him spreading his hands in bewilderment and saying, "Now?"

It was only a few minutes later when I said, "Just don't ask me where I got this, not yet."

I pushed the videotape that I'd stolen out of David Mayer's backpack into his parents' VCR and tried to figure out how to get it to play. Geof walked up behind me, studied the machine for a few seconds, and reached over me to punch a series of buttons.

"Men," I muttered gratefully.

We heard a soft thud and then a click and a whir, and then an image appeared on the television screen.

"Jesus Christ," Geof exclaimed.

It was Judy Baker Mayer on the film, and she was seated in a chair in a doorway—some other doorway, not the one in her own dining room—and her mouth was moving and tears were falling down her face, but we couldn't hear any of it.

"Where did you get this, Jenny!"

133

"Turn it up!" I left that job to him as I raced back to the bed and sat down on the end of it. "Then come here!"

Geof fiddled with the buttons again, and suddenly a woman's thin voice filled the room, a voice filled with misery.

". . . confess," she said, caught in midsentence, "to the fact that my husband, Ronald Mayer, Jr., is not the biological father of my son David. I confess to fornication. I confess to adultery. I confess that I lied to my husband about the parentage of my son. I confess that I am a liar and a whore and a thief." Between each dreadful, condemning sentence she drew a ragged breath, which she let out in a ripple of crying that looked as if it must dreadfully hurt her throat and her chest. Tears coursed down her face, and now and then she put a hand to her cheeks to rub them, but always her eyes came back to the camera as if pulled to it by a magnet, and every terrible word was spoken directly to us who watched her. "I confess my sins to my husband and to my Lord Jesus Christ, and I accept the penance of my guilt, and I beg their forgiveness."

For long seconds, there was nothing on the screen except for the sight of her face as the camera caught her in a spasm of weeping that crumpled her face and shook her whole body. The tape ended there, being less than a minute long.

Geof replayed it and replayed it and replayed it.

"What did she mean she was a thief?" I said.

"And what sort of penance did she mean?" Geof asked.

The second time through, he pointed out a fact that I had noticed right away, which was that she was seated in a doorway that was not in her own house. There was no furniture behind her, only a white wall. We couldn't see much of the chair she was sitting in, just a rounded corner on either side of her shoulders, and it was yellow vinyl, like a kitchen chair. That time through the tape, we pointed out to one another that she was wearing the clothes she was killed in. The third time through the tape, Geof noticed that her hair appeared to be the same length, style, and color it was in the crime-scene photographs. What I didn't say to him, because it seemed cruel even to think it, was that the woman on the tape resembled the glamorous woman in the photograph beside the bed only in the way that a plain and empty canvas resembles a painted one. Finally, we both thought we heard another voice, just a hint of it, right at the end, just before the tape ended. It sounded to both of us as if the other voice said something like "good." The voice wasn't condemning or harsh; it was soft and comforting and sad, so soft, in fact, that neither of us even heard it through Judy's crying until Geof suggested that we try listening to the tape with our eyes closed to see what extraneous sounds we might pick up.

"Who is that other person?" I demanded when he finally rewound the tape for the last time and took it out of the machine. "Is it the person who was working the camera? And why, for heaven's sake why, did she tape this confession? If Ron *didn't* know those . . . facts . . . and he saw this tape for the first time, this might be the motive that would explain why he killed her. It could be the motive that finally convinces David that his father really did do it."

"Where the hell did you get this tape, Jenny?"

I said peevishly, "I just knew you'd ask that."

"Yeah, I'm a perceptive devil. I like to ask those subtle little questions that wouldn't occur to anybody else."

Like Judy before me, I confessed.

And sure enough, he looked as upset and disturbed as I'd ever seen him look. But, it turned out, that his distress wasn't directed at me. "Don't you see, Jenny? We were led to this tape. We were led to this house, where the air conditioner was thoughtfully turned on for us and the VCR was already turned on and ready to play for us. David wanted us to come here that first day we met him. David has already seen this video of his mother, don't you see? He has seen it, and he *still* thinks his father didn't kill her. He wanted us to see it, too."

I looked around at where we were, sitting on the bed of the man and woman who had died in the other room, and I thought of their son preparing this scene for us.

"I want to go home."

"Right now?"

"Right now, Geof. I want to go home."

"All right." He looked confused, but he caught me in a firm embrace, and I responded immediately by wrapping my arms

135

tightly around his waist. "You're shivering. Are you cold? What's the matter?" Then he laughed at himself. "I ask stupid questions sometimes, don't I? Don't mind me, I'm just a hardened old cop who doesn't have enough sense any more to be bothered by terrible things. I've had the top layer of feelings scraped off of me until I'm all calluses."

"No, you're not," I said, holding him tight. "I'm just a coward."

"Oh, no, you're not," he replied with feeling. "And you're right about this place: It's grim and scary and sad. Let's go home."

But on the way out, he stopped me at the doorway of one of the bedrooms. "David's," he guessed.

It was stripped bare, as if the occupant had packed all of his belongings and taken them away with him. Only the bookshelf contained clues that a child had ever lived there: encyclopedias on one shelf, used school books and a pile of notebooks on the next shelf, and a couple of small teddy bears stuffed in each corner of the top shelf, like soft forgotten bookends.

I tried arguing with him in the Jeep on the way back home.

"David couldn't have known I would look for him and follow him from school, Geof. He couldn't even have been sure that I'd take the tape just because he left it in the backpack."

"He doesn't have to plan every step," Geof argued back at me. "He only needs to be alert and imaginative and flexible enough to take advantage of the right moments. So he happened to have the tape with him—and why not, for safekeeping? Didn't you do the same thing when you felt you had to keep it with you in your purse?—and you show up, and he sees a chance, and he takes it."

"He *couldn't* know I'd steal it."

"No, but he could keep trying until he got it into our hands."

"Why not just hand it to us?"

That silenced him for a couple of miles. Finally, he said, "I think it's about control. His control over us, his control over his own life that's out of control. It's about a kid playing a deadly serious sort of game, and he's the game master, and we're the pieces he wants to move around on his board. And one of the hallmarks of a good player is preparedness from which spontaneity can spring. And the goal is to see if he can move us into place to make the final logical leap to the game's conclusion."

I absorbed that for a while before I said, "Nobody wins."

"You don't know that, Jenny. We'll see."

"Nobody wins," I insisted.

"You're just upset."

I stared at his profile. *No shit, Sherlock!*

"I'm sorry," he hastened to say next. "There I go again, saying something stupid. Of course you're upset, any normal person would be. I'm just not normal, that's all. I shouldn't have said that to you."

"It's hot," I said. "We're all cranky."

"Nice of you to say so."

*Not upset?* I thought, glancing at him. *Who are you fooling, Sherlock . . . yourself?*

At three o'clock that morning, the telephone on Geof's side of the bed rang and woke us. He grabbed it, as he always does, because he's the only one of us who gets calls commanding him out of bed in the middle of the night. But this time, he said into the receiver, "Just a moment." Then he handed it to me, speaking in such a calm voice that I was immediately alerted to trouble: "It's some doctor at Baptist Hospital."

"What?" I sat up against my pillow and grabbed the receiver from him, thinking, *My dad? No, he is in California. My sister? My brother-in-law, my niece or nephew? Please, no.*

"Who's this?" I demanded.

"Ms. Cain? I'm Dr. Stephanie Rogers, the resident on call at Port Frederick Baptist. We have a young man named David Mayer who has been in a motorcycle accident. He's not badly hurt, so don't be worried, but I'd like to admit him overnight for observation, just to be sure there are no internal injuries or concussion. The problem is, Mr. Mayer says he doesn't have any insurance and he can't pay for his treatment. He's not quite up to holding a phone against his face, so he asked me to call you. Are you his mother?"

"No," I said grimly, "I'm not his mother."

"Oh. Can you help him?"

A certain acidity crept into my tone as I replied to the doctor: "I'll have to find my checkbook first, and then I'll be right down."

"Who?" Geof asked as I handed the receiver back to him.

"Your son."

# 15

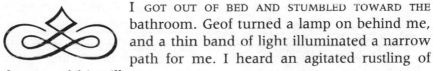

I GOT OUT OF BED AND STUMBLED TOWARD THE bathroom. Geof turned a lamp on behind me, and a thin band of light illuminated a narrow path for me. I heard an agitated rustling of sheets and his pillow.

"What about him, Jenny? Is he all right? Why did they call us?"

Spoken like a true father, I thought sourly, as I threw a T-shirt over bare skin and reached for underpants. From the bathroom, I called back into him, "They didn't call *us*. They called *me*." I told him what the doctor had said; by the time I finished talking, I was hair-combed and tooth-brushed and ready to leave the house.

"Why you? Why not me?"

Geof was sitting up naked in bed, looking completely non-plussed by this whole turn of events. It unnerved me a little to see him that way; I wasn't used to this, I was accustomed to living with a police lieutenant who remained cool under any line of fire. But not, evidently, when the "shots" were being fired by his own child. Alleged child, I reminded myself.

I shrugged, just barely holding onto my spousal forbearance. Outside the locked windows of our bedroom, the wind was blowing as if maybe we'd get some rain soon. Suddenly I craved the feeling of that wind against my face, my arms, my legs. I wanted to get out of this closed-in, locked-up house. "Maybe after this afternoon, after our motorcycle ride, he feels like he knows me better."

"No." Geof looked forlorn, or maybe it was only a lack of sleep that I thought I perceived. "He doesn't want anything to do with me. He's taunting me with the fact that he hates me." He looked up and started to get out of bed. "You don't have to do this, Jenny. This is my job. You stay here."

"As you were, Lieutenant."

"What?" He was halfway out from under the covers. "Why?"

"Geof, if we weren't both so tired, we wouldn't be coming up with these cockamamy theories about why he called me instead of you. If we were thinking straight, we'd remember that you think he's playing some kind of control game to lead us where he wants us to go. So let's play it his way for a while longer."

"A kid doesn't have a motorcycle accident on purpose!"

"Geof, we don't know what this kid would do on purpose, do we? And you're the one who said that a master game player takes his advantages wherever he finds them."

"Shit, you know I hate it when you defeat me with my own logic. All right, you win. But I'm following you in the Jeep."

"Fine," I said shortly and left the bedroom to go look for my keys.

"You're a saint, honey!" he called after me.

"Fuckin' a," I muttered.

"What?" he yelled.

"What the hey!" I hollered back at him. "I'll be downstairs."

Baptist was the smallest of the three hospitals in town, also the most expensive. That figured, I thought. I pulled into the trauma center parking lot right next to David's motorcycle a few minutes ahead of Geof. I hadn't quite waited for him to start his Jeep before I roared off in the Miata, and I'd slaughtered the speed limit coming into town. Well, hell, who was going to give

140

me a ticket—the cop in the next car? By the time I reached the outskirts of Poor Fred, my engine was running cool and happy and so was my psyche, thanks to the wind and the night and the music on my cassette player.

No longer feeling so martyred, I was now mostly curious.

Before I went inside, I examined the bike. It didn't appear to me to be damaged. I ran my fingers along some scratches, but they had the look and feel of old wounds with smooth, healed edges. I turned toward the brightly lit double doors. If he'd been in an accident and the bike wasn't hurt, then either it wasn't a very bad spill or else he'd taken all the impact and the dents on himself. The kid had his priorities, I thought caustically: save his motorcycle first, his own body second.

Or he'd faked an injury just to get me down here.

I saw him immediately, just past the nurses' station, sprawled in an orange plastic chair, holding an icebag to his left eye. The other eye was fixed on my entrance. He didn't bother to sit up straight; if anything, he only slouched further down into the bowl of the chair, his long legs sticking out in front of him as impediments to anybody trying to get by him. As I approached, I looked him over: Other than the icebag to the head, he didn't appear any more the worse for wear than his bike. His blue jeans were still intact, they weren't even fashionably torn. His white T-shirt looked wrinkled in front, but it wasn't ripped either. His motorcycle helmet, all in one piece, sat on the yellow plastic chair to his left.

I was almost glad to see him slouch; it made him look more like a real, maybe even average, teenager.

I took the red plastic chair to his right. "What's under the ice bag, David?"

He removed it long enough for me to see a swelling bump and a bruise that was threatening to take over his entire right temple, including his eye. It did look convincing, and it was damned hard to imagine somebody doing that to himself.

"Your bike has not been damaged," I said to him. "You look all right except for that shiner. What happened? Did you brake suddenly and fly off the bike onto your right eyeball?"

It was four in the morning by then, and I was shut into a

fluorescent-bright, ugly hospital lobby with a manipulative, surly kid, and I was starting to get angry again. Damn fool kid!

"I had to tell them something," he said in a low voice.

"I beg your pardon?"

He made an impatient face, directed either at the pain he was feeling or at me, possibly both. Slowly, as if it hurt, he pulled himself up in the chair, straightening out the slouch, until his back was straight. "What happened is, I had a fight with my uncle, but I couldn't very well tell the doctor that, could I? So I told them I had an accident on the bike. I told them I ran into a curb and got tossed off. They bought it, I guess."

"What about this fight?"

"What about it?"

I counted to ten, and when that wasn't enough to keep me calm, I added ten more digits. "What uncle? What was the fight about? Is he hurt, too? In other words, what happened, David?"

"You wouldn't be interested."

I looked down at my toes in my sandals and counted all ten of them. Once from the little toe on my right foot, all the way over to the little toe on my left foot, and then in reverse.

"Possibly not," I agreed. "But go ahead and start talking. I'll tell you if I get bored."

"Fuck you," he said.

"And you," I agreed, smiling pleasantly at a passing nurse. "Well?"

"Forget it."

"I'll tell you what, David. Let's start with the premise that I am not good with children." I laid a heavy emphasis on the last word as I stared at him. He flushed or maybe blushed. "So why don't you act like an adult instead?"

"Bastard grabbed me and tried to beat the shit out of me."

"The uncle did? Uncle Bastard?"

"Matt. My uncle Matthew. My father's next oldest brother."

"The one you're supposed to be living with?"

He glanced at me, and I thought I saw a pleased expression flit across his face. Now he knew we'd been following up, checking things out. Just what he wanted us to do from the look of it. *He's leading us,* Geof had said from the beginning, and now I

142

thought maybe he was right. So where was this kid taking me now?

"Yeah."

"Why did he do that, David?"

"Hell, I didn't know he was home! I just went in the house, I just wanted to pick up a few of my things. They always go to services on Monday nights, so they aren't supposed to be home. So I go in, and I'm just gathering up my own stuff, and bam! Uncle Matt grabs me from behind and starts whalin' on me."

"Did he think you were a burglar?"

"Like stepfather, like stepson, you mean?" He laughed, a brief, bitter explosion of sound that made him wince. "Ow. Damn. When's that pain pill gonna work? They told me it ought to work really fast."

"Burglar . . . ?"

"Yeah. Right. Like Uncle Matt thinks I'm Dennis or something, like he's never seen me from the back before."

"David, can you make this any easier or at least any briefer? I just want to know why your own uncle would hit you."

"Beats me."

"An appealing thought," I muttered.

"Get in line," he shot back.

"You're not going to tell me anything else, are you?"

"Can you pay for this?"

I smiled sweetly at him and cooed, as to a toddler who has asked for something from his mother, "What do you sa-ay?"

"Please!" I could have sworn there was a grin lurking at the edges of his mouth, and at that moment if he had only opened it full throttle, I would have smiled back at him. Instead, he chose to grunt. "Please, if you'll cover this, I'll pay you back."

"Oh, all right, I'll take care of it."

I went off to ransom his care. When I came back about fifteen minutes later to tell him they still wanted him to spend the night for observation and to pummel him with all of the other questions I wanted to ask him, his orange plastic chair was empty and the helmet was gone. When I raced out to the parking lot, his bike was gone, too.

The wind that had blown me into town had also disappeared,

143

but the rain that followed it had begun. It fell in big slow warm plops on the parking lot pavement, raising a smell of hot asphalt, and it fell on my bare arms and dripped down my skin, and I knew it was also starting to fall upon the leather interior of my little convertible and on boys riding motorcycles on slick streets, even boys I could have happily killed at the moment.

There was a khaki-colored Jeep sitting in a dark spot under an elm tree up on street level. Before I put the top up on my car, I ran up there to have a word with the driver. The word was *damn,* a cannon burst of outrage that was followed by a machine gun fusillade of a lot of other words of one syllable.

All he said when I stopped was, "Is your top up, Jenny?"

"Of course not," I snapped and ran back down to the parking level.

In our separate vehicles, we went back home to bed.

This time, I drove the speed limit, with Geof's headlights always visible in my rearview mirror. In our garage, he walked over to open my door for me and give me a hand out.

Instead, I handed him something else.

"What's this?"

"When I had returned to my car in the parking lot, I found this"—it was a collapsed ice bag, the one David had used in the hospital—"sitting on my driver's seat along with this note." I handed that to Geof as well.

In printed letters, it said, "I'll pay you back."

"Good," Geof said.

I grunted as I got out of my car. "Geof, that note could as easily be a threat as a promise."

When we arrived at our back door, walking from the garage in a steady rain, we had to wonder if David had already made good on his "promise": A small, torn corpse of some kind of small animal, maybe another squirrel, lay at our back door.

"I'm sorry about this, Jenny," my husband said to me.

I didn't know what to reply, so I merely gave him a quick hug.

We were so tired that we stepped over the little body, but we were not so weary that we didn't take the time to double bolt the front and back doors.

"Geof?" I said on the stairs going up.

He turned to look back down at me.

"Remember that piece of graffiti? Two into two equals zero?"

He nodded. "I didn't get that one, did you?"

"Not until just this minute. Sergeant Meredith told us that Ron used two shots to kill Judy and two to kill himself. Two into two equals zero."

It continued to be a quiet rain, with no thunder or lightning, but it kept me awake, all the same.

Finally, unable to sleep, I padded downstairs and opened Judy's pink scrapbook and read through it more carefully than I had the first time. There were so many questions I wanted to ask David about it, like, Where'd his mother keep the scrapbook? How'd she manage to hide it all these years? and How did David get his hands on it?

When all those and many other questions began to drive me crazy and to worsen my insomnia, I rummaged in our bookcases until I found Geof's high school yearbooks, and I thumbed through them, looking for him, Ron, and Judy, watching them mature from fourteen-year-olds to graduates. The girls in their senior class pictures had all gone to the same photographer who had dolled them all up in white fake fur around their shoulders. Just like Judy's "glamour" photo! There was a tag line for each boy and girl: Geof's was Wild Thing, Ron's was Most Likely to Build the World's Better Mousetrap, and Judy's was, bluntly, Most Likely.

I reread that one, hardly believing it, it was so cruel, so blatant, so clearly a double entendre, that everybody but the faculty and the parents would understand immediately and which would give the kids a good snicker. I wondered how she had explained it to Ron, how he had managed to misunderstand even that, but most of all, I wondered how she had felt when she saw it for the first time.

Had she burst into tears? Had she gone hot and then cold with humiliation or panic or anger? Was it possible that she might have laughed at it, even felt cocky about it? No, that was not possible to believe.

I hoped that she'd felt a good and healthy fury, I wished she had stormed into the yearbook staff and raised holy hell, I wished she had beaten the shit out of the faculty advisor and then sued the bastards. But I would have bet my house and my husband that what she actually had felt was pain and shame of the most mortifying teenage kind, of which there is no worse in all the world, the kind of humiliation that makes you want to run to the furthest corner of the basement of your parents' home and curl up in a corner with your head on your knees and your arms crossed over your head and never ever come out when they call you, no matter how loud and how long they yell your name, the kind that makes you want to turn to dust and blow away.

Sitting there on my couch in the middle of the night, all those years later, I felt so sorry for her that I could have wept.

"What are you doing, Jen?"

I looked up from the yearbooks and the scrapbook to see that Geof had come downstairs searching for me. He'd slipped on a brown-and-white-striped terrycloth robe, his feet were bare, and his hair was sticking up all over his head.

"So what if she was a liar?" I said angrily. "So what!"

"Huh?"

He came over to the couch, and I moved all the books so he could sit down beside me. I showed him the yearbook entry that had me so upset on Judy Baker Mayer's behalf, and that got him interested in going through all his memories, too. While he was leafing through the pages, I got up and wandered over to the bookshelves again. But the next time I came across an entry that caught my interest, it made me laugh.

Geof looked up at me. "What'd you find?"

I had an unabridged dictionary spread open on a desk, and I read from it: " 'Mother. A stringy, slimy substance formed by bacteria in vinegar or on the surface of fermenting liquids.' The second meaning is: dregs. Then we have something called *mother water*, which is defined as 'in chemical operations, a liquid residue containing water, salts in solution and impurities, remaining after crystallization.' But my personal favorite is 'motherwort, an herb of the mint family, prickly, a bitter taste . . .' "

Then I saw what came next in the definition, and instead of continuing to laugh, I began to feel chilled in our air-conditioned house with our locked doors and windows and its mutilated dead animal getting soaked in the rain on our back stoop. Slowly, I continued reading aloud to Geof. " 'In the Court of the Inquisition, a motherwort was a person who assisted in apprehending and imprisoning the accused.' "

For some reason, I didn't want to look at him at just that moment.

He let a beat pass, while we listened to the rain fall, and then he asked, "And how do you define *father?*"

"I'll look it up."

When I did, I was able once more to find some amusement and to look Geof in the eyes again. "I'll be darned. The word *father* comes right after *fathead.*"

"We already knew that," he said and smiled at me. "Aren't we exhausted by now? Can't we finally go to bed and stay there?"

*Motherwort. Prickly and bitter,* I thought as we went back upstairs to bed together some few minutes later. *Yes.* But no matter how caustically the dictionary defined *mother,* at least the rain seemed cozy to me now, like a coverlet over our home, a protective, invisible sheath that no unhappiness could penetrate, and it thrummed a comforting lullaby that soothed both of us to sleep.

# 16

WHEN THE TELEPHONE WOKE US AGAIN, THE RAIN
had already stopped and the sun was shining.
Our bedroom windows were fogged over from
the cool air inside hitting the already hot air
outside. Great, I thought when I saw those windows: The rain
didn't cool things down, it only steamed them up. The phone
rang two more times before I realized my husband wasn't in bed
to get it, so I rolled over to pick it up.

It was only six-thirty, but this time the call was for Geof,
which was a fairly normal and regular occurrence at that hour.
The Port Frederick police didn't seem to think he could make
it through a morning without an early bulletin about the previous night's score of good guys versus bad guys. I didn't think
too much about it, even though it was Sergeant Lee Meredith
on the line.

"Morning, Jen," she said, then added in what sounded to me
like a rather quiet, thoughtful tone of voice, "May I speak to the
lieutenant?"

After calling Geof out of the shower to get the phone, I wandered out of our bedroom and down the hall to search for a

certain blouse in another closet, so I didn't hear his conversation with her.

When he yelled *"Jenny!"* I was really startled.

I'd been lost in sleepy thoughts about rain and teenagers and suicides and easy girls and eager boys and even, once or twice, about my own concerns. On this morning, I was scheduled to see Ginger Culverson—sweet ol' Moneybags herself—to pin down exactly how much money she wanted to contribute up front to the new foundation and how we might use that as seed money to attract other donors.

I ran to the door and nearly collided with Geof, who was charging out of our bedroom and down the hall.

"Get dressed," he said without slowing down. "You're coming with me. Dennis Clemmons got himself killed last night."

"How?" I yelled down the stairs to his retreating back.

Geof stopped long enough to look back up at me. "He fell out of a sliding glass door on the second floor of the place where he lives."

"But there's a landing there and a ramp!"

"Not any more there isn't," Geof called back to me as he raced toward the kitchen. "The support beams gave way."

"Oh, my God . . ."

I felt the bottom fall out of my stomach at the thought of a man falling from that height . . . and in a wheelchair. I grabbed the first clothes that came to hand, threw them on, and raced outside to the garage and was still buttoning my blouse with shaky fingers when I jumped into the Jeep beside him.

"Why do they need you?" I asked him.

"They don't, but when Lee saw who it was who got killed in the accident, she decided it was a coincidence I ought to hear about."

"It *was* an accident?"

"Appears that way, but the paramedics and the officers who got there first had no reason to think it might have been anything else. Understand, I'm not saying it wasn't an accident, Jenny. I just don't know. But if it turns out to be a crime scene, Lee says it's already been compromised by everybody trampling around in it."

"And why do you need me to go with you?"

He roared backward out of our garage and then kicked gravel up in a U-turn in our backyard.

"Because you know where David lives."

"So?"

He shot the Jeep from first into second gear.

"So if this turns out to be something other than an accident, I want to get to him before the cops do."

"Geof, you *are* the cops."

"Yeah, people keep telling me that," he said grimly as we rocketed toward the highway into Port Frederick. I would have given anything for a cup of coffee; it was at moments like these that I almost regretted being addicted to caffeine.

When David failed to answer his door on the third floor of the boarding house, Geof got us into his rooms without the landlady even asking for a search warrant. It was sufficient for Geof to say to her, "I'm his father, and I'm also a cop. We haven't heard from him, and we want to make sure he's all right." To which the landlady said to me with real concern for David in her eyes, "Honey, you don't look old enough to be his mother." When I told her in all seriousness that he was aging me quickly, she smiled with sympathetic understanding and gave us one of her spare keys without another question. As Geof turned it in the lock in David's door, I murmured to his back, "There's nothing like the truth in a pinch."

We walked into a room that was so messy it gave me hope. This, at least, looked like the work of a typical teenage boy.

It was a big square studio that obviously used to be somebody's bedroom when the house was somebody's single-family residence; no kitchen, but he had a small microwave on a kitchen table, and no private bathroom, although somebody had installed a small sink. There was a single bed with a blanket thrown over one sheet, and an armchair and a boom box for music, a small television with a VCR on top of it with a tape sticking partway out of it. Clothes and other belongings were heaped on top of each other in a single tiny closet like leaves stacked up in a compost pile. The whole place smelled strongly of the leftover pizza that lay open in its box on the table beside the microwave.

I strode to the drapes and pulled them open, revealing big old-fashioned windows. "It'd be halfway cheerful in here if he'd open these things." I hooked both of my hands around the handle of one of the windows and tugged, opening it several inches. "Smell better, too, if he'd keep these open." It wasn't air conditioned, but there was a floor fan in one of the corners, although it wasn't turned on.

"Where is he?" Geof said, walking around restlessly, picking things up, laying them back down, as if he were searching for David under the papers, the books, the scattered messes of teenage stuff. "Where the hell is he at this hour?"

It was, by that time, almost seven-thirty A.M.

"Could be working," I suggested. "Jogging, running, staying at a girlfriend's, or maybe he never came home last night. Maybe he went to school early for some extracurricular activity." I caught Geof's sardonic expression and conceded, "Okay, not that. Should we be here? Should we be touching things, Geof?"

"What does *should* mean?"

I shook my head. When he wanted to be obtuse, no one could beat him at it. "Forget it. What do you want to do now?"

He had walked over to the television and was playing with the VCR.

"I want to see what he was watching."

I waited, half expecting to see David's mother show up on the screen again, but what did appear there made me exclaim out loud anyway . . . and step backward as if somebody had tried to touch me with something burning.

It was a man seated in a chair in a doorway with a white wall behind him. Looking straight into the camera, which meant he was also looking straight into my eyes.

Geof turned to stare at me when I cried out, and he opened his mouth to ask me what the matter was when the man on the television screen started to talk. With the man's first words, Geof, too, stepped back from the picture as if he were suddenly afraid of it.

"My name is Dennis V. Clemmons," the face on the screen

151

said, although "snarled" was more like it. He was visibly sweating, and his eyes darted this way and that as if he were looking at a lot of different people. "I confess to coveting another man's wife. I confess to being a thief. I confess to fornication and adultery. I confess to assaulting and grievously injuring another man's wife. I confess to being a man of violence and murderous lusts. I accept my penance commensurate with the depth of my depravity, and I beg the forgiveness of my Lord Jesus Christ."

This time, we heard the other voice more clearly.

"Good," it said, like a kind and loving father, and it was definitely a man's voice, that was also more clear this time. The same voice, the same word, the same soothing, encouraging, approving tone, a voice full of forgiveness and . . . love.

"Jesus Christ," Geof whispered.

"Take the tape," I said before I could think about it.

As a father, he obeyed me on impulse, grabbing the tape out of the machine; as a cop, he turned to me with the plastic box in his hand and said, "What am I doing, Jenny?"

"The right thing," I assured him, adding quietly to myself as we hurried to the door, "I hope."

We walked out with the key, too.

That was the third thing I'd stolen or helped to steal in the last two days, counting the tape of David's mother making her confession and Clemmons making his. Now the key. It was quickly getting difficult to tell the cops from the robbers in our family.

At the front door, the landlady poked her head out.

Geof thrust one of his cards at her. "Call me when he comes home, will you?"

She nodded vigorously, and took the card.

"You notice the priority of sins here?" I demanded furiously as I slammed the door of the Jeep. "If you're a man, the first deadly sin is coveting somebody's wife, and next in line in importance is stealing, and then you get to screwing, and only then do you get around to admitting, oh, yeah, by the way, I beat up a woman and injured her for life."

"And what was *his* penance, I wonder?"

"Not harsh enough," I retorted.

Geof glanced at me as he accelerated away from the curb. "You don't think the death penalty is tough enough?"

"We've got to drive through a McDonald's anyway," Geof said a block away, " 'cause I can't face any more of this without coffee."

I directed him to the one where David worked.

He went in to get our coffee and talk to the manager while I waited in the car.

"Think about that tape," he told me, "and when I get back, tell me everything you can remember about it."

Five minutes later, he was sliding back under his steering wheel and handing over a white cup with a lid to me. "They fired him yesterday after he took off on the cycle with you, and they haven't seen him since. Has it occurred to you that he might have been setting up an alibi with us last night?"

"No, it hadn't." I stared at him.

"Who better to alibi you than a cop and his wife?"

"But not if the cop is also your father."

He shrugged. "Maybe he didn't think that far."

"If he's the kid and we're the grown-ups, how come he's so smart?"

"Tell me your impression of that last tape."

As we sat in the McDonald's parking lot, I recited for him: "He looked younger than he did when Sabrina and I saw him yesterday. On the tape, I thought he looked angry enough to kill somebody, but I also thought he looked really scared, didn't you?"

"Yes. Go on."

"He was wearing a long white-sleeved shirt and white pants and white socks, but no shoes. There was a white wall, like the one in the video of Judy. The phrasing of what he said was similar to what she said, but it sounded insincere when he said it, as if somebody was making him say the words. I thought Judy sounded as if she meant every word of it even though it sounded stilted, like a script. I think she was sitting in a yellow kitchen chair, but I couldn't see the chair he was in. This time, I could see the floor, and it was wood. I can't remember what color."

"White. That kind of whitish wood stain that's popular."

"Oh. That's all I can remember except for the voice at the end. Geof, this time it sounded kind of familiar to me. Did it to you?"

"No, not really."

"Well, maybe it's only because I heard it last night on the other tape, but it wasn't just the voice, it was also that one word, and the way he said it: 'Good.' " I rolled it over on my tongue, tasting for familiarity: " 'Good.' "

"You caught some other things I didn't," Geof said as we turned in the direction of the old fishermen's houses downtown, where Dennis Clemmons had lived. "But I caught one thing you didn't . . ."

"Which was?"

"Did you see the way he moved about halfway through?"

"I don't know, what do you mean, what did he do?"

"He raised his left leg and put that foot on his right knee."

"So?" And then I got it. "He could move his legs! This tape was taken before he went into the wheelchair!"

He nodded. "After Judy. Before the chair."

"My God," I said, appalled at my next thought. "The penance?"

"What?"

"His injury, maybe *that* was the penance he paid. Geof," I said on a sudden inspiration, "did you see white walls like that in Ron's parents' house when you were there yesterday?"

"No, but I only saw a couple of the rooms."

"Didn't we hear that they're religious fanatics?"

"I'll talk to Lee about it."

He was about to get that chance soon, because we were pulling onto Clemmons's street. Geof parked behind a police car—we can't call them "black and whites" anymore, because here in Port Frederick, they're baby blue with navy blue designs on them—and he threw the car into idle and turned to look at me. "I'm staying here. Take my car, go see Ginger, just like you planned on doing, but don't go home until I can go with you. Do me a favor when you get to Ginger's: Call the high school, see if the kid's in school today. I'll drop by when I'm through here, so I'll see you in just a little while, all right?"

"What about the videotape?"

"Put it in the glove compartment." His smile was quick, cynical, unhappy. "Nobody'll ever look there."

"I love you," I said as he got out of the car.

"Great, that'll keep me going when they throw me in jail."

He slammed the car door, and holding his McDonald's coffee cup, he loped off toward Sergeant Lee Meredith, who was waiting for him alone at the scene.

I remained on the block long enough to finish my coffee and to stare at the scene of Clemmons's death until it sent queasy chills throughout my body. The sliding glass door to his second-floor apartment was wide open and the actual ramp was still standing as it had been when Sabrina and I had seen it for the first time the day before. But where there had been a solid-wood first-floor landing then, now there was only a gaping space where a couple of long boards hung down into empty space. It looked to me as if Dennis Clemmons had slid back his door, rolled himself out confidently into the wide space that was the first landing that had been especially built for him by his friends, and instead of a trustworthy wooden floor to support him there had been only empty air, and he had fallen helplessly two tall stories to the ground, riding down all the way in his wheelchair.

It was a horrible way to die.

It made my legs so weak even to think about it that I had to wait a few more minutes before I could get my feet to work properly on the floor pedals of the Jeep.

The gas pedal required even more substantial reinforcement before I drove much further, so I stopped by my Amoco station and pulled into the full-service bay. I just didn't feel like moving from where I sat.

"Morning, Jenny! Got yourself a mouse in this car, too?"

"Oh, hi, Joe. Would you fill it with Silver, please?"

"Drinks gasoline, does it? The mouse?"

I worked up a smile for him.

He laughed as he pulled a nozzle down from a tank. "Check everything?"

"Please, Joe."

I slumped down and leaned the back of my head against the seat and hoped Joe wouldn't think I was being rude because I didn't get out of the car to talk to him. Silly thought: You don't have to get "out" of a Jeep; with the top off, you're already half out of it, and people just naturally carry on conversations with you, especially at stoplights if you look their way. I closed my eyes, thinking how odd it felt to meet a man one day and learn he died the next. I'd have to call Sabrina to let her know.

And who *was* the man, Dennis, who died?

I reviewed the facts and the theories: Juvenile delinquent, adult criminal, married man, divorced man, stepfather, ex-stepfather, laborer, unemployed laborer, convict, ex-convict, able-bodied soldier, disabled veteran, and all-'round bad apple. This was the man that Judy had left her husband to marry? I suddenly wondered: Could Ron Mayer have been even worse? Was there a possibility that he was so awful that even Dennis Clemmons had looked like "up" to her?

Yeah, but his son loved him, so how bad could Ron be?

*Kids will love anybody*, my mind reminded me, *and they'll persist in doing it against all odds.*

When I opened my eyes, Joe was right in front of me, carefully sponging down the windshield. I realized I had to make an effort. After all, Joe always did, whatever the weather, however many customers were waiting to be helped, no matter whether I stopped by to pick up a map or called to ask him to send a kid to recharge a dead battery.

"Why am I so privileged today, Joe?"

"Hmm?" He looked through the glass at me, smiling as always. "What's that?"

"To what do I owe the honor of having the owner himself clean my windshield?"

He laughed and rubbed with his clean red rag at a bug stuck to the glass. "Shorthanded. One of my men got married over the weekend, and he's off honeymooning. Another kid quit, went to work for a car wash, decided rubbing down wet cars was more fun than standing out here in the sun pumping gas, I guess." He grinned at me. "That must be hard for you to imagine, I mean what could be more fun than doing this? There!" He lifted his rag and beamed at the shining clean spot. "Got the little bugger!"

"I know a kid . . ."

*What was I saying! Shut my mouth . . .*

"Yeah?"

"I can't really vouch for him, I don't know anything about his skills or anything like that, but I do know he needs work."

"How old?"

"Seventeen."

"Sure, have him come by, I'll interview him."

*Good, I wish somebody could, and would you please ask him where he was last night when his stepfather was getting killed, and find out if he painted graffiti on his own house, and ask him . . .*

"If I can find him."

"Whatever. I'm always glad to get a kid who'll work. Do you think he knows anything about cars?"

"He's a seventeen-year-old boy, Joe."

He laughed as he wiped his hands. "You'd be surprised."

*Not by anything this kid does, not anymore . . .*

"He has a motorcycle."

"Well, that doesn't make him a bad kid. But it does make it a little more likely that he can tell an oil filter from a spark plug." He smiled at me again. "Be right back with your change, Jenny."

*Change. Just what we needed, more change in our lives . . . So, well, hey . . . maybe David would need a job . . . to earn the money to pay us back for the bail the judge would set when he released the boy into Geof's custody while he awaited trial on charges of killing his . . .*

"Whoa." I sat up, shook my head, grasped the steering wheel to steady myself. "Just . . . whoa."

I accepted my change from Joe's clean hands and drove off under the benediction of his friendly wave. He was a walking commercial, Joe was—a commercial for believing in those angels that my friend and our town's mayor, Mary Eberhardt, believed in. Always willing, infinitely patient, smiling and kind, Joe practically wore a sign that said, I love to help.

*Angels . . . love to help . . .*

Those words were lighting sparks in my brain, but unfortunately it was already so fried that nothing more this morning could light a fire in it or under me. I put eager Amoco angels out of my mind and drove with extreme caution to Ginger's gigantic house in the many-mansioned part of town. I knew I was tired and upset, knew I couldn't have passed a safe driver's test at the moment, knew I'd better pull to full stops at every sign, look both ways—twice—at every opportunity, and give other drivers a wide berth for the sake of their well-being. My slow, careful route took me past the cul-de-sac where Geof had said that David's grandparents lived, and on a whim, I drove slowly around it, taking a covert look at the property, hoping to get a glimpse of them, but all I got was a dirty look from a neighbor.

"What'd you think this is anyway?" I muttered as I left him in my rearview mirror. "Your private street?"

But at least my annoyance shot some adrenaline into my system. I picked up speed to Ginger's.

# 17

GINGER STILL HAD ON HER PAJAMAS—A SHORTIE SET that made her look like some little girl's cuddly doll—when she answered the door bell that I had to ring three times to wake her up. Her hair stuck up in thick clumps all over her head, just like those dolls look after little girls have handled them for a few days. Her cheeks were flushed from sleep and from running down the stairs from her bedroom on the second floor, and her mouth was caught in an O, just like one of those dolls that was always, hopefully, waiting for a bottle. I could just picture her stuck under some little girl's arm, plump legs in the air, head hanging down behind the child's rump. She would have been the treasured one, the favorite. The proof of her affection for me was that she was managing to look pleased as well as surprised to see me standing there so unaccountably early for our appointment.

"What are you doing here?" she blurted, then she found her more mannerly self. Laughing at her own tactlessness, Ginger amended that to, "I mean, hi, Jenny! Did I oversleep? Are you early? What time is it anyway?"

"I'm sorry, Ginger. Could I use your phone? Make some coffee, fix myself some breakfast, use your makeup, borrow your comb. Have you got an extra toothbrush?"

"Sure." She held the door open for me and peered closely at me as I walked past her. "All of the above. Jenny, you're hysterical, aren't you? And you look like shit, unless there's a new fashion in plaid with stripes that nobody told me about, which, God knows, is entirely possible. What's the matter with your hair? Why does it look like mine usually does? What's the matter with you? Why are you here so early? Did you and Geof have a fight or something?"

"We never fight." I kept right on walking—stalking might be a better description—toward her big beautiful new kitchen, the one that Mayer Construction Company had renovated for her when they built her new addition the year before. Eventually, I knew, I'd get there, I'd reach that damned kitchen, even in the endless halls of her enormous home. Eventually, I'd eat something, my blood sugar would return to normal, I'd drink more coffee, my caffeine level would return to normal, I'd smooth down my hair, my clothes, my emotions. Eventually, I'd have a normal life, like a normal woman married to a normal man. Eventually, someday, maybe not this day. "We don't fight. We debate. We discuss. We never fight. Did you know I got a perfect idea for a gag gift for him for his fortieth birthday? I'm going to have one of those glamour photographs made of myself and give it to him like a serious gift that I expect him to put up on his desk at the police station. What a hoot, huh? Toast, do you have any whole wheat toast, maybe a couple of eggs, a quart of orange juice, a pound or two of bacon?"

"Sure," she said from behind me. "Also some Thorazine."

I walked two more steps before I really heard her, and then I started to laugh and stopped and turned around to face her.

"Jenny, what in the world is wrong?"

I put my hands on her shoulders and held her at arm's length from me. "I'm pregnant, Ginger."

"Oh, my God!"

I grinned and dropped my arms to my sides. "Just kidding."

Ginger stared at me, then walked past me into her kitchen.

When I got there, she was already filling a coffee pot with

fresh-ground beans, and she looked up at me, and said, "You can't do this to me so early in the morning unless you tell me everything that's wrong."

"Oh, Ginger." I pulled up a stool to her counter to watch her. "David's stepfather was killed last night."

"David?"

"Geof's new son."

"Oh! How could I forget!"

"Well, we haven't sent out birth announcements . . ."

"Oh, no, Jenny, that poor child . . ."

Bless her sweet heart, Ginger looked truly stricken for him.

I told her as much as the law—meaning, my husband—would allow about the apparent homicide of Dennis Clemmons. I didn't mention the videotapes or my trip to the hospital less than six hours earlier or the mutilated animals on our property or . . .

While Ginger took a few minutes to comb her hair and brush her teeth, I stirred the eggs she'd put in a skillet to scramble and used the portable phone in her kitchen to call Port Frederick High School. By sweet-talking the school secretary, who'd been there when I was a student, I managed to weasel out of her the surprising information that David Mayer was in attendance that morning.

"Uh, Jenny?" The secretary, a formidable woman who had ridden stern herd on tardy students for at least twenty-five years, sounded uncharacteristically hesitant. "You say David Mayer is a relative of yours?"

"Sort of . . ." I hedged. "By marriage . . ."

"Um, and, uh, you're married to that policeman, aren't you? The one who was such a hellion when he was here in school?"

I smiled. "That's the one. Geoffrey Bushfield."

"Hah." A touch of her usual tone returned to her voice. "I haven't forgotten that one, and I still find it hard to believe he's a police officer. But since he is, and since he's related to David, and you are by marriage, I wonder . . ." Her speech became halting again, her voice quieter, as if she didn't want anybody in the school office to overhear her. ". . . if you and he could stop by the school some time today?"

"I imagine so, but is it anything to do with David?"

"Dr. Fellows will talk to you about *that* when you get here."

She sounded just like her old self, terrifying a student with a threatened interview with the principal. I hung up, having added unease to the surprise I felt over the news of David's presence at school that day. I don't know where I expected him to be instead—on the highway, I guess, driving on his motorcycle, putting miles between himself and the latest death in his "family."

Ginger and I were sharing a repast that consisted of the eggs mixed with chopped everything, from bacon to scallions to mushrooms to peppers; a stack of buttered toast; and vast cups of cappuccino made in her own machine when her doorbell rang again.

"Strange morning," she muttered.

"You're tellin' me," I said, seconding the emotion.

This time, when Ginger went to answer it, she returned from the front door with my husband in tow. When I looked at him, he shook his head behind Ginger's back as if to say to me, "Don't ask."

"Have you got any more of that feast?" he said to her.

She turned, patted his arm, and smiled affectionately up at him. "Your wife and I have pretty much gone through the refrigerator like locusts, but we may have left some little bits of food hidden way back in the corners where it was too dark for us to see them."

"That's where the best mold grows." Geof put his arms around her and hugged her, baby doll pajamas and all. The pj's looked enough like a shorts set to pass for regular daytime wear. However, suddenly seeing her through Geof's eyes, I wished for her sake that they didn't accentuate her increasing chubbiness quite so amply.

"Sit down, and finish your breakfast, Ginger," he said to her. "I can cook for myself. Did you make that call I asked you to, Jenny?"

"Yes. He's there."

Geof released Ginger and stared at me. "He *is*?"

"Who is?" Ginger asked. When he didn't answer, looking from one to the other of us, she added, "What's going on, guys?"

"Police business," he growled, making a joke of it. I wanted to tell him about the school secretary's request for us to see the principal that day, but I decided I'd better wait until he and I were alone. Feeling anxious with all the questions and news pent up inside of me, all I could do was sit and watch him loosen his tie, roll up the sleeves of his shirt, and begin to act like a chef. He said, "The Mayers did this kitchen for you, Ginger, right? It looks great. Were you happy with what they did for you?"

"Perfection." Ginger settled down at the counter again and crossed forks with me as we both stabbed at the scrambled eggs at the same time. I retreated my hand from harm's way and let her have them along with the last of the bacon she'd cooked. "They do beautiful work, Geof, and like I told Jenny at lunch the other day, they are totally conscientious. Always showed up on time. Always cleaned up their mess at the end of every day. Never made a decimal more noise than they had to. Always treated me with courtesy and respect. As far as I'm concerned, they were the construction company from heaven."

"Jenny said they weren't real friendly, though."

She paused, fork in mouth, and slowly removed it. Her chin was greasy, so I reached over to dab it with my napkin, and she gave me an affectionate smile of thanks. "Well, I guess that's true, although what I think I said was that they were reserved around me."

"What I inferred," I interrupted, "was that you never got to know them very well in spite of the fact that they were here for months, right under your nose in your own house. I may have jumped to the wrong conclusion, but that didn't sound friendly to me."

"Well." She wasn't agreeing with me. "Maybe not, but it was professional. I don't need to become buddies with my builders. I just want them to do the work for the money. And they did that and more. I didn't require them to become my new best friends. What have you guys got against the Mayers?"

"Not a thing," Geof said as he cracked an egg into a pan. "Did you ever see the kid? Did he ever work over here with them?"

"The kid?" She smiled at him. "Your kid, you mean? No."

"His mother?"

"No."

When he had finished preparing a couple of fried eggs and more bacon along with still more toast for all of us to share, I scooted over to give him room to seat himself beside me at the counter. He looked across at Ginger and said, "So what do you know about this religion they practice?"

"A little," she said carefully and took more toast.

I looked at her, suddenly wondering at her hesitations.

"Would you tell us that 'little'?" he pressed her.

She ate a bite and took a long time draining her coffee before she spoke. "I'm trying to recall. It's about Jesus, but it's not exactly Christianity. I think. I'm real vague on this. They didn't try to convert me, please understand, in fact they hardly mentioned it, except that I guess they felt they had to tell me why they never worked on Tuesdays. It was because they had services on Monday nights, and I guess they always ran late—really late, like three or four in the morning—and then Tuesday was a kind of Sabbath family day when they took it easy."

"Jesus but not Christian?" I asked. "A Tuesday Sabbath?"

She smiled a little. "It sounds kind of simpleminded now that you make me think about it. Jesus was a carpenter, right? And they were carpenters, builders, what have you. So he and they were kind of like in the same building trade, I guess. They felt an affinity, I gather, with what he did to earn a living, with the simplicity of his tools, which were theirs as well. They make a lot of their own tools, they do all of the work themselves if they can, and I mean all of it. They prefer to make pegged hardwood floors, for instance, instead of nailing the boards down."

Geof looked down at her shiny floor and he whistled. "Expensive."

"Oh, they're not cheap," Ginger agreed. "But they're worth it. High standards. Great workmanship. Top quality in everything. They don't take on very many jobs, but then they don't have to, because they charge so much on the jobs they do. It's only people like me"—she made a face at us—"who can afford them, which means they do a lot of their work out of town. They're a self-contained unit, like an air conditioner."

We all smiled at the unlikely analogy.

"They didn't subcontract a thing, which cuts down quite a bit on expenses, really, helps to make up for some of the rest of it. But, yes, it's true, they do charge a torso."

"A torso?" Geof asked.

"More than an arm and a leg," I guessed, and she nodded. "But, Ginger, I don't recall that Jesus only worked for rich folks."

"They may have conveniently overlooked that fact," she observed with a straight face. "I've heard that many do."

Geof asked, "What about the women?"

"Some do carpentry, like I told Jenny on Monday." She shook her head in mock annoyance. "Really, Geof, you ought to come to lunch with us if you're going to make us repeat everything we tell Jenny. And don't try to pretend to me that she doesn't tell you everything we say. As I *told* her, the women did all of the interior painting, some of the exterior, all of the wallpapering, and they were general dogsbodies to the men. I was impressed; I'd never seen women with that kind of expertise before, even if the men did treat them like apprentices sometimes."

I jumped in. "Chauvinists?"

But she shrugged her round shoulders, which made her upper arms quiver. "Hard to say."

"Why? How can that be difficult to determine?"

Ginger looked confused for a moment, and she munched on the last piece of Geof's toast before she answered me. "Because maybe they *were* apprentices, at least compared to the men. The brothers grew up in the business; they probably nailed their own playpens together."

We all laughed.

"But," she added, "the women married into it."

I turned toward Geof and intoned, "With this hammer, I thee wed."

"Do you promise," he said to me, "to drive a straight nail, lay a true plumb line, and pour a solid foundation in sickness and in health, so long as we both shall work?"

"I do. Not."

"I now," said Ginger, "pronounce you man and carpenter's apprentice. You may nail the bride."

We all snickered, and her cheeks got pink.

165

"Do you remember their names?" Geof asked her. "Besides Ron, I mean."

"Sure. Matthew, Mark, Luke, and John."

"Bless the bed that I sleep on," I murmured.

She laughed harder than my joke deserved.

"So Matthew would be the next oldest?" Geof asked. "I guess they really are churchy."

"Churchy?" Ginger's eyebrows rose. "Is the pope Catholic? Are rabbis circumcised? Do Episcopalians know which fork to use with the salad?"

"Ron?" I said. "Matthew, Mark, Luke, and John . . . and Ronald?"

We all three began to laugh again, it sounded so ridiculous.

"Well, he was the oldest," Ginger said. "Maybe they didn't find Jesus until after he was born. Maybe he was such a difficult baby, they *needed* Jesus."

I could feel hilarity rising in me from sheer exhaustion and stress, but then I got a look at my husband's face, which had gone grim and tired on us, as if he'd suddenly recalled himself to the reality of this day. He got up and began to clear our plates for us.

"What a helpful man," Ginger observed to me.

"I'll loan him out," I offered, "for a fee."

"Really?" She brightened. "What's included?"

"All right, ladies! We need to get out of here," Geof told me as he lifted my dirty napkin off my lap.

"Well, heck," Ginger protested. "No more coffee?"

"We do?" I said to him. "I don't. I need to talk to Ginger—"

"Please," he said again just to me. "I'm sorry," he said just for her.

"Oh, all right," I groused.

"Are you going home first?" Ginger asked me.

"I don't know," I said, then turned to him. "Am I?"

"No."

"Then you come with me for just a minute," Ginger instructed me. "I'll give you a T-shirt that doesn't look as if you stopped by the Salvation Army bin on the way over here."

"Why not?" I asked her. "It's probably full of your old clothes anyway."

"I'll meet you outside," Geof said to me, and then he blew Ginger a kiss on his way out of the kitchen. "Thank you for breakfast!"

"Anytime!" she called after him. "I always have hot coffee and a doughnut ready for the local constabulary!"

I traipsed off after my friend, down her long, lush hallways, up her stairs to the landing, and then on down to her opulent bedroom, which the Mayer Construction Company had also renovated, putting in such refinements as a spa/tub, a bidet, and French doors leading to a shaded deck on the back of the house.

She opened a box of fresh dry cleaning and pulled out a pretty purple T-shirt and handed it to me to put on in place of the red and white plaid one I was wearing, which did not, I had to admit, go particularly well with the white shorts with purple pinstripes that I was also wearing.

"I didn't drag you up here just to talk about clothes," she said.

"We were supposed to be meeting this morning to talk about business, weren't we?" I smiled at her as I started to change tops. I was taller and thinner than Ginger, but we both wore large T's. "Did you see what that British rock star did recently? He started his own foundation to help AIDS patients. He thinks more of the money raised by foundations ought to go right to the people who need it instead of into administration and all the rest of that bullshit, and so he's only got a couple of employees and he's paying their salaries himself."

She sat down on the edge of her bed and looked up at me. "That so-called bullshit paid *your* salary for several years, Jenny. And I suspect that when you've only got a couple of employees, they're frequently extremely overworked ones."

"Ah, so you're willing to contribute as much as we need to properly adminster this . . . thing?"

"I think I've just been manipulated by a fund-raising maestro."

"Well, I am supposed to discreetly inquire as to how much money you want to invest in our foundation, Ms. Culverson, and then you're supposed to give me a figure that buys you love."

"Whose?"

"Mine."

"Hell, I've already got that, can't you offer anybody else?"

I laughed, the sound muffled by the shirt I was pulling on.

"I didn't actually drag you up here to talk about the foundation either, Jenny. It's about something else. And since you brought it up, speaking of . . . um . . . love . . . can I tell you something?"

"Well, sure, but don't think it has escaped my notice how smoothly you are attempting to divert my attention from the subject of charitable contributions."

"And you'll tell Geof for me?"

Suddenly I saw how serious her expression had become.

"I can't tell him myself, because I'm too embarrassed . . ."

Really curious now, I asked, "About what, Ginger?"

"Well, Jenny . . ." My friend's face was very pink as if she'd rouged it. "The thing of it is, while they were working on my house, on this room specifically, I had a kind of an affair with Ron Mayer, but it was over so fast—"

I stared at her, then blurted, "You did what?"

"I thought Geof ought to know."

"But, Ginger, I thought he was supposed to be so religious!"

"Oh, Jenny, he wasn't a bad man." Ginger sounded so sympathetic to him that I could have shaken her. "It wasn't his fault that his wife was an invalid, and she couldn't have sex. Did you know that she couldn't?"

I shook my head no.

"What was he supposed to do, be celibate for the rest of his life?"

"I hate it when people expect me to be fair-minded."

She smiled. "He was kind of sweet, Jenny. Not much conversation. Well, I mean he was polite, you know, and he always said thank you." She giggled a little. "We didn't really have anything in common except my room additions." Another embarrassed giggle. "But he said he was lonely, and he was here and ready, and guess who else fit that description?"

"I don't know what to say, Ginger."

"I broke it off," she told me. "Because the sex was all there was, and it wasn't even that great except that he had this great bedroom voice. When he moaned, it was a meaningful experience, let me tell you!"

"Ginger!"

In spite of everything, we were both laughing. Then she said, "But I thought even I could do better than a married man."

"Oh, Ginger, of course you can."

"I've never told anybody else about it."

"Well, don't," I suggested, thinking of what happened to the two people who had already "confessed" to adultery and fornication. "Please don't, ever. How'd you manage it, Ginger, with his whole family around?"

She grinned. "Tuesdays."

"The blessed Sabbath?"

"You said it, baby."

"And you *want* me to tell Geof?"

"If you think it's important, if it adds anything to the picture of Ron's character or their marriage or . . . I don't know."

I didn't know either.

Ginger and I hooked arms together for the long walk back down her steps to her front door. On the way, I said to her even more gently, "When Ron Mayer died . . . were you . . . okay?"

She compressed her lips, and her eyes seemed to deepen as if she were thinking back to those days. "Well, it was over by then, and I hadn't talked to him or even thought much about him for months. So I was shocked, Jenny, I was really surprised. I felt sad for him, for her . . . especially for their kid. Your kid." She smiled, but it was a sweet one. "It seemed like a real tragedy to me all around, no matter how you looked at it."

"Ginger, did he ever talk about David's stepfather?"

"He didn't talk, Jenny, remember?" She laughed a little, remembering it herself. "Except for explaining that his wife couldn't have sex, which was his way of rationalizing the affair, I think. And saying thank you." She laughed again. "So I don't know nothin' 'bout nothin'."

At her front door, she handed me a check already made out with a figure, although the date and the payee and the line for her signature were blank.

I took it and stared, then grabbed her in a bear hug.

169

"Are you really sure you want to give this much, Ginger?"

"Do you think it's enough? When we settle on a name for the foundation and you get the accounts set up, I'll fill in the rest of that check. I thought you might like to have it around to show to other potential donors, maybe inspire them to contribute, too."

"I love you!"

"I know, I know." She pushed me out her door. "Too boring. Go buy me a new lover."

Halfway down Ginger's front walk, I turned back to wave at her. I wondered if she had appeared in pajamas such as those when the Mayer Construction Company showed up for work one morning. I imagined Ron Mayer taking one look and deciding she looked so good—

"Oh, my God," I exclaimed and raced for the Jeep.

"Jenny? What are you doing?" Geof asked me.

I was grabbing for the tape in the glove compartment, that's what.

"I'll be right back!" I promised him and raced back up to Ginger's.

When she opened the door this time, I waved the videotape in her face and said, "I want you to listen to something. Where's your VCR?"

She led me into her family room and showed me how to operate the machine. Hiding the first part of the tape from her vision, I managed to mute it and to fast-forward it to the end.

"Close your eyes," I instructed her as I turned the sound back on. "And tell me who this is . . ."

From the television came the voice of a man tenderly saying "Good."

"It's Ron!" Ginger cried. "I'd know that bedroom voice anywhere!"

And now I knew why it had sounded familiar to me, too: It was the same voice that I and hundreds of other people had heard on the 911 tape the newscasts had played so many times the previous March, when Ron and Judy died. On that tape, Ron Mayer had told the 911 operator that he had just killed his wife, and now he was going to kill himself and would they please send somebody over to see about things? And when the emergency operator, trying desperately to keep him on the line, said, "We'll send help, sir," Ron had responded by saying softly, "Good," and then hanging up.

I grabbed the tape from the VCR, then grabbed Ginger in another hug. "Thank you. I'm sorry to do this to you. I promise I'll explain some day. Right now, all I can say is that you've been a bigger help than you know."

This time I left my friend looking confused and, to my guilty regret, a little forlorn.

# 18

I GOT INTO THE JEEP, WHERE GEOF WAS IMPATIENTLY waiting for me.

"Was it an accident that killed him, Geof?"

"Looks that way. Jenny, what in the world—"

"The voice on the tape belongs to Ron Mayer. I know because Ginger identified it and not just because she heard him when he was working over here. Ginger had an affair with him, Geof. Every Tuesday. Or at least on some Tuesdays. She says he claimed he couldn't have sex with his wife because of Judy's physical problems."

He was staring at me, openmouthed.

"I just love it when I manage to shock a cop."

"You're kidding."

"No, really, it's because you think you've seen everything . . ."

"Jenny!" Geof was shaking his head in wonderment just as I had up in Ginger's bedroom. "Sometimes I think this town is so fucking small you need a microscope to see us."

"An appropriate adjective," I murmured, "considering."

"I thought the guy was supposed to be so religious!"

"That's what I said to Ginger." I shrugged. "He was human. So's Ginger."

He started the car. "I'm not condemning her."

"I know you're not. She wanted me to tell you. She was too embarrassed to confess it to you herself."

"There seems to be a lot of that going around."

"What?"

"Confession." Geof pulled away from the curb in front of Ginger's house. "Let's go see if we can wrest one out of Uncle Matthew . . . like . . . Did he or did he not beat up his own nephew last night?"

"Maybe we ought to go to school first to check up on David?"

I told him about the secretary's request. That news put a nervous twitch into the anxious frown that appeared on his face. But still he said, "All right, but now that we know where he is, there's no hurry. We've got all day and other things we have to do first."

"Well, we have until school gets out," I corrected him. "Geof, don't you have to work for a living?"

"I have to work, but not necessarily for a living."

"I don't think that I understand what that means."

"When I figure it out, I'll let you know."

"Okay, so you're not going in to work. So, where does David's uncle Matthew live?"

"According to the phone book, on the same cul-de-sac where his parents are, and there just happen to be three other Mayers listed next door to one another as well: Mark, Luke, and John."

"Really? They all live together? It's like a compound, isn't it? Geof, can you imagine living so close to your parents and brothers?"

He, who had two brothers himself and even liked them, made a pretense of shuddering. "It's a good thing that you and I live in this century; we'd have had a hard time back when families were expected to stay close together all of their lives."

"I drove by there this morning, and a guy at the house on the southeast corner really glared at me as if I were trespassing."

"What were you doing there?"

"Exercising my curiosity."

"Really? I thought it was already pretty well developed."

"Very funny."

"Good biceps, quads, plenty of aerobic stamina—"

"Will you stop?"

After a couple of blocks of congenial, if highly charged, silence, he suddenly said, "When's Ginger going to lose weight?"

"Why do you care?"

"It's annoying," he said.

"Well, how inconsiderate of her to annoy you with those extra pounds of hers. I'll have to ask her to stop that. Give her a break; she's lonely, Geof."

"Oh, please."

"Oh, please what?"

"You're saying she eats because she doesn't have a man?"

"No, I'm not saying that."

"It's true, though, isn't it? Ginger doesn't consider herself to be good enough company all by herself. So what's she doing about it? Making life more interesting for herself by expanding her knowledge or her experience? Or maybe going into therapy to find out what's wrong with her? Hell, no. Looks to me like she has decided that the only cure for loneliness is having a man and the cure for being without a man is to put on enough extra pounds to equal the entire weight of one. She's turning into two people, each of them weighing about ninety pounds, maybe a hundred."

"I am not going to react to this meanness!"

"Mean? You think I'm being mean?"

After we drove a block in silence, I said, "It would have to be a very small man."

"What?"

"The extra weight that Ginger is adding."

"*I'm* mean?" He smiled a little. "Listen, I'm sorry I picked on your friend. I don't know why I'm taking it out on her."

"She's a big target?"

"Jenny!"

I retorted pointedly, "Just kidding."

He glanced at me. "All right, I get it." And then he patted his own stomach, which was not as flat as it used to be. "And I've got my own."

"Does that mean you're lonely?"

"Will you stop?"

He made a right turn, then stopped the car. Five houses all in a semicircle. All of them big authentic old Colonials, all of them sheltered, nearly hidden, by long setbacks and lush greenery, all of them in beautiful repair, perfectly painted. And each of them inhabited by Mayers.

"Yesterday, didn't you know they were all here?"

"No, I was just looking for his parents."

"So why did Ron and Judy live somewhere else?"

"That, my love, is a damned good question."

"And why was he spending the Sabbath with Ginger instead of home with his family?"

"Another good one."

He pulled the Jeep into one of the driveways and parked us right behind a green truck.

"David over here last night? I wish he was!"

The man who was "Uncle Matthew" had one big foot propped on the running board of his immaculate green pickup truck, the other planted on his gravel driveway. He wasn't the same man I'd seen earlier. This man was bigger, burlier, with a ruddy face with a seemingly permanent smile pressed onto it. He was dressed for going to work in clean white denim overalls, a pressed white T-shirt, and white tennis shoes.

"If I could get my hands on that kid," he said in a mock threatening tone, but all the while he kept smiling.

We had walked up to him, smiled in a friendly way, and Geof had simply said, "Hi, we're looking for David, we heard he was here last night . . ."

"What would you do?" I asked him, smiling back.

"Hold him down!" He laughed, but it had a rueful sound to it. "I'd keep him, sit on him if I had to. We're supposed to be his guardians, my wife and I, but how can you guard somebody who won't have anything to do with you? He's a good kid but stubborn as the day is hot. And the darned thing of it is, legally

175

we can't do anything about it. Well, I mean we *could* 'cause he's still a few months away from being eighteen, but then he'd just escape from us again. He acts like our house is some kind of prison! Like we're wardens forcing him to eat three square meals a day and have his own nice room and give him spending money and help him settle his folks' affairs and give him a real family life. Does that sound like punishment to you?"

"When's the last time you saw him?" Geof asked.

"Oh, heavens." Matthew Mayer took out a white handkerchief and wiped his broad forehead with it. The day was heating up like a blacksmith's anvil. "Weeks, I'm embarrassed to tell you. You must think we're awful, appearing to let that boy loose like this. But you've got to know him to understand how headstrong David is. He will do what he wants to do every time, always has. Takes after both of his parents."

The big man's smile faltered for the first time. He put the handkerchief over his mouth as if he felt sick.

We waited for him to recover, feeling the sun baking the tops of our heads, the tips of our shoulders, our feet, the backs of our hands. I felt a little light-headed and thought about leaning against his truck but then thought about how hot that metal might be.

"I'm sorry." Like an asthmatic, he took several quick breaths as if fighting for air. "I'm sorry . . ."

"So he wasn't here last night, he didn't have a fight with you, you didn't catch him trying to take something from your house, you didn't punch him in the eye . . ."

"Is that what he said?" He didn't try to recover his smile but leaned all his weight against the frame of his truck and closed his eyes. "No. My nephew . . ."

"What?"

He opened his eyes again and stared at his own foot on the running board. "Nothing."

"Is a liar?"

Matthew Mayer pulled himself together, straightened his posture, but wouldn't meet our eyes anymore. "Maybe it was one of my brothers he saw, maybe it was one of their houses. But they'd never fight with him. He's only a boy, for heaven's sake!

And he's ours. Our brother's son. We'd never hurt him, we only wanted to help . . ."

"Mr. Mayer, are you all right?" I asked, feeling concerned for the big man, he looked so pale, so unsteady, so ill. "Why don't you sit down in your truck for a minute?"

"Thank you." He reached for the rim of the driver's door and held on as if he'd fall if it didn't support him. "I've got to get to work. I'm sorry I can't help you. If you find David, if you talk to him, tell him please to come home, will you?"

He was halfway into the truck when Geof said, "Mr. Mayer, did you know that Dennis Clemmons died last night? A handicap ramp outside his apartment came apart, and he fell two stories in his wheelchair to his death."

Mayer turned so quickly to face us that he nearly struck his head on the cab of his truck. "No! That's impossible! That ramp is built so tight it's as solid as concrete. That ramp wouldn't fall down in a million years."

"How do you know, Mr. Mayer?"

"Because my brothers and I built it for him."

"You did what?" We stared at him. "Why . . . ?"

"Because Ron asked us to, because our brother was the nicest guy in the world and the most forgiving, because he felt sorry for that jerk that Judy married after she left Ron, because once he married her, once he had David living with him, he was part of our family whether he liked it or not, and because we always help family, no matter what. Look, that ramp couldn't just fall down, not unless a tornado hit it. I want to look at it, I want to see this supposed accident!"

"I didn't say anything about an accident, Mr. Mayer."

Uncle Matthew looked up, stared, then said, "Then I'll say this: He knew a lot of rotten people, Dennis did, and that's all I've got to say. Just you be clear about two things. One, David is our nephew and we love him and we want him back with us. Two, that ramp didn't fall down through any fault of our design or workmanship. Now I've said all I'm going to say, and I've got to get to work while this weather holds. The sun doesn't wait for any carpenters. Do you mind movin' your car now?"

"What do you know about a videotape that has Dennis Clemmons 'confessing' to coveting another man's wife?"

When he stared at us this time, his knowledge about that tape was absolutely clear in his eyes. He knew just what Geof was talking about, his eyes said. His expression also suggested that he was shocked to hear the question.

"I have to get to work."

"Why would you help out a man who confessed to that sin?" Geof put verbal quotation marks around the word *confessed* and also around *sin*, but maybe I was the only one who heard them.

Matthew Mayer turned his back to us, seemed to have second thoughts, turned back around to face us. "A man who repents, who does proper penance, that man deserves the rewards of heaven."

"What is a just penance for adultery, Mr. Mayer?"

"That's between Dennis Clemmons and God."

"It certainly is now," Geof snapped.

"Will you please move your car?"

"And what was Judy's penance?"

"What?"

"Her penance for the sins that she confessed to, what was it?"

The big man looked angry now, and when he put both of his feet on the ground and faced Geof, I became aware of how much bigger he was than my good-sized husband. If Geof was six feet two inches, then Matthew Mayer had to be at least six feet four inches and probably fifty muscular pounds heavier as well. Geof didn't move back an inch; if anything, he leaned forward. For a slightly hysterical moment, I half expected them to snort and paw the ground, like two overwrought bulls in a pasture. "That's nobody's business either, and I think you could show a little respect for the dead. Judy paid her debts; she doesn't owe any accounting to you." Matthew Mayer reached for his steering wheel to pull himself into his truck. "Neither do I or any of the rest of us." He looked back down at us briefly. "We've paid heavily, already, every one of us."

He slammed his truck door.

Geof and I walked back to the Jeep, and he backed us out of the driveway. Mayer came out behind us, riding so close to Geof's front bumper that I was half afraid he'd run us over if we didn't hurry. Geof, of course, didn't rush. He took his sweet time backing out, pulling back out of the way in the street, pausing to let Mayer get away.

I found that my palms were sweaty as Mayer drove off.

Even after he drove out of the cul-de-sac, Geof didn't drive us away immediately; he seemed to want to sit there for a while in thought with the Jeep idling. Finally, I had to break the silence.

"There are a lot of things you didn't ask him, Geof."

"Only because of what he didn't ask us. I didn't introduce myself, you didn't introduce yourself. He didn't ask who we were, what we were doing there, what business it was of ours to ask about his nephew. I didn't identify myself as a cop. Now why would a man show so little curiosity about two strangers who are being so nosy about him and his family?"

He glanced over at me.

"Right." He smiled slightly. "Because he knew who we were when we walked up there, or at least he knew who I was."

"His parents must have mentioned your visit yesterday."

"You think that's all he knows?"

"What do you mean?"

"I mean, what if they know about David and . . . me?"

"We don't know who's telling the truth around here, do we?"

"Nope. Can't tell the truth tellers from the liars without a scorecard. And, Jenny, I need somebody to tell me the truth about that boy. It's time to find out what kind of kid he is, what kind of parents they were, what kind of life he had with them and with Dennis Clemmons. You want to hear it, too?"

"You know where to go for that information?"

"Yes, I think so."

"Where?"

"Be a detective. Figure it out."

On the way, I said, "So it's not because she's fat."

"What?"

"Ginger. She doesn't annoy you because she's overweight. She annoys you because she's not—your word—autonomous. She

179

says, 'I'm lonely,' and you're suggesting that's a nonautonomous state. Autonomous people don't get lonely?''

''Why should we? We've got ourselves for company.''

''You're a humble bunch, aren't you?''

''I sound arrogant?''

''What's so great about yourselves, you'll pardon my asking?''

''We're not lonely.''

He laughed, and then I did.

''No,'' I said, ''but you're really circular.''

''Actually, Jenny, I'm not so autonomous.''

''I know that.''

''Ack. I thought I had you fooled. How'd you catch on?''

''You're the one who wants a child. Ergo: lonely.''

''I don't agree with that at all!''

''You're also the one who's on his third marriage. Now you tell me: Of the two of us, who thinks he can't make it on his own?'' I probably should have stopped there. ''And you work in a fishbowl. People all around you all of the time.'' Even then, I wouldn't let it drop. ''I'd cope better on my own than you would, Geof.''

''Yeah, you're meaner than I am.''

''Oh, come on! I guess some people can't stand to get the tails of their sacred cows twitched.''

''Who you calling a cow?''

I burst out laughing, and after a second, so did he.

''All the statistics say so.'' Still, I gnawed at this bone, though I lightened my tone of voice. ''Given sufficient income, a middle-aged single woman without any children at home is as happy as a bear in the woods.''

''You're not middle-aged yet.''

''Thank you.'' I waited a beat. ''Unlike some people.''

''Mean!'' he yelled. ''I married a mean woman!''

Actually, I thought he had a point there: For somebody who was supposed to love him I was jabbing him with some awfully sharp needles. If he only knew: I'd put off telling him the truth about my reaction to his new fatherdom for three days now; I wondered how much longer I could delay it.

Forever would have suited me just fine.

"So where are we going now?" I asked him.

"You haven't figured it out yet?"

"All right!" I said, exasperated. "I think I can guess."

"Okay, then, tell me which way to turn to get there."

Sometimes we played very strange games with each other.

Following my directions, we parked at the curb in front of Ron and Judy Mayer's next-door neighbor's house.

"We'll make a detective of you yet," Geof said with a smile. And then he pretended to quiz me as if he were a teacher and I, a pupil. "And why are we here?"

"Because Damon Montgomery told us that Judy Mayer was his best friend." I added, "Sir," and then stuck my tongue out at him. "Let me see that again," he said and leaned over and kissed me.

# 19

"MOTHER WILL BE SORRY SHE MISSED YOU."

Damon Montgomery was all smiles, as he'd been the day before. Dressed in red Bermuda shorts and a white Polo shirt and sandals, he had a ballpoint pen in one hand and a portable telephone in the other when he answered the ring of his doorbell.

"Come on out to the porch, why don't you?"

We followed him into a small but very pleasant screened-in porch that was, happily for us, shaded by a walnut tree.

"Mother left a little while ago to pick up a few things at the grocery store. This is where I work most of the time, actually." He dropped the phone into a cradle and looked rather helplessly at it and then over at us. "I still find myself picking it up, thinking I'll call Judy, and then I remember that I can't anymore."

Overhead, a white ceiling fan was whirling fast enough to blur its blades; it had a repetitive squeak that made it sound like a record stuck in a groove. The noise should have been annoying, but in the heat, it was slightly hypnotizing instead. I sat down in a gliding porch rocker and proceeded to rock myself to the beat of the squeak of the fan into a more relaxed state of mind; Geof stretched his legs out in front of him in a yellow canvas basket chair that made him look so undignified I wanted to giggle; our host sat down on a two-cushion porch glider but only after transferring a laptop computer and some papers onto one of the cushions so that he could sit on the other. It looked as if we had interrupted him at some sort of labor. Nevertheless, he seemed happy, even eager to talk to us.

He leaned forward and rolled the pen between his palms.

"How's David?" he inquired in his soft, gentle voice.

"Not too well," I blurted before I thought to stop myself. I hurried on to cover my blunder. "He got fired from his job at McDonald's." Too late, I realized that wasn't a good conversational gambit either, because I didn't want him asking why. Chattering stupidly on, I added, "But there might be another job for him at the Amoco station on Jefferson if he'd get over there to apply for it . . ."

I appealed to Geof with my eyes, and he jumped in to save me: "Mr. Montgomery—"

"Damon, please. Or Day, that's what Judy called me."

"We were here last night as friends of David's, that's true, but I want you to know that I'm also a police officer."

Our host's eyebrows rose, and the pen stilled in his hands.

"David," Geof continued, "is not satisfied with how the police department handled his parents' deaths, and so I agreed to look into it for him. I want to tell you, too, that I knew Judy in high school. She and Ron and I were in the same graduating class. You described Judy as your best friend. I didn't know either one of them after we got out of school . . . What was she like? Would you mind telling us?"

"Mind?" He smiled sadly at me, then put the pen on a side table, leaned back in the glider, and crossed one leg over the other. "I'd love to talk about her."

Then he paused, looking at the house next door as if to gather his memories about it and about the woman who had lived there.

"There are so many things I could say . . . What exactly would you like to know?"

"I guess I don't know exactly," Geof said with an engaging smile and an air of admitting something to the other man. "I just want to get a feeling for her life and the kind of person she was, so maybe you could start by just talking about her as your friend?"

Montgomery nodded, apparently happy to begin there.

"We spent a lot of time together," he said, turning to me as if he thought I'd be more likely to understand how it was between next-door neighbors. "We talked a lot, you could call it gossip, I guess. We drank a *lot* of coffee together." He laughed a little, a sound of fondness. "It was because we both work . . . she worked . . . at home, you see. I'm a freelance writer." That made sense of the laptop and the papers as well as of his presence in his home during a weekday. It may also, I thought, have gone a long way toward explaining why he lived with his mother; it was my guess that most freelance writers, especially in a city the size of ours, didn't make much money. "Annual reports, training programs, advertising, that sort of thing. And she was stuck beside that phone. Sometimes I'd call her, and we'd just talk on the phone and she'd take her business calls through call waiting. I didn't mind. I could hang around on the phone for hours, anything to keep from going back to my own work." He laughed a little again, and he threw a glance at his computer. "But there are a lot of times when I'm writing and I really need a break, just to get out of the house, you know, so I'd wander over next door and sit with Judy while she worked the phone."

He smiled at me again, a melancholy smile this time.

"We had a great time. We just talked about everything, all the gossip about her clients, I mean, of course it was supposed to be confidential, but she knew I wouldn't tell anybody. And all the latest about Ron's crazy family and her nutty mother and all her problems with poor David, and of course I told her all my woes, too. It's not always easy living with your own mother, as you might imagine!" Again, a little laugh. "I could go complain to Judy whenever my mother really got on my nerves. I miss that! Now I may have to kill the dear old girl, since I can't let off steam with Judy! She knew what it was like to be surrounded by . . . doting . . . parents, like those smothering in-laws of hers." He closed his eyes for a moment, and I saw his mouth tremble. When he opened his eyes again, he said to me, "I really loved her." Then he turned his face toward Geof. "And I really miss her."

Geof let a tactful moment pass, and then he asked, "What sorts of things did she tell you about her clients?"

"Oh, you know, who was cheating on their spouse—she always knew because they'd want her to lie about where they were if their spouse called. Or who was trying to avoid the IRS, that sort of thing. I really couldn't say, not because it's still so confidential—I mean, you are a policeman, so I guess I could tell you—but I really can't remember all the details. I never paid any attention to the names, frankly, I just loved the juicy stories."

"Do you recall the names of any of her clients?"

"Oh, heavens, no, I have enough trouble remembering the names of my own clients!"

"What did you and your mother mean when you talked about that family being . . . helpless . . . Wasn't that the word you used?"

"It was the word Mother used, yes, probably. Mom was always so hard in her opinions of them. Well, first there was Judy years ago, so upset when she had to leave Ron, and I held her hand through all of that, and then I had to wave her off to that terrible marriage to that awful Clemmons person. And then we had Ron just distraught over losing her and worrying about David being raised by that hoodlum, and I was over there next door all the time, trying to make him feel better, poor man. And then Judy came back, all crippled up—oh, that was so terrible, I could have killed Clemmons myself over that—and she needed a lot of help just getting used to her limitations, just making it through the day in the ordinary sorts of ways, you know. That lasted until Ron and his brothers got the house all fixed up for her, that helped her a lot, and then her own attitude improved a little when she got back to work again and as David calmed down. But how much does a teenager ever really calm down? I mean, the two of them came back to Ron just about the time that poor David's hormones kicked in, so things were rough all over, I'll tell you! Well, what can I say? I've just held a lot of hands over in that house, wiped up a lot of tears, and my mother's cooked a good many meals for them during one emergency or another, and she's baby-sat David more times that you could count, and, well, we've just tried to help, that's all."

I could see Geof trying to sort through all the verbiage to find the leads to unanswered questions.

"What sort of kid was David growing up?"

"Quiet, bright, we're very fond of David."

"Was he ever any trouble to his parents?"

"Of course." Montgomery smiled. "What teenager isn't?"

"Anything serious?" Geof put on a half smile to pretend he was joking. "Torture any neighborhood cats, burn down any barns, steal any cars, do any drugs?"

"Don't they all try drugs? And beer?"

To make it seem more like a conversation, less like an interrogation, I chimed in with a question.

"How did Dennis Clemmons get injured, do you know?"

"I understand he got beat up."

I shivered, thinking what a terrible beating it must have been and what poetic justice it was.

"Who did it?" Geof asked.

"A gang of punks was what I heard, but nobody ever got caught."

Geof nodded, but I knew he was recalling the fact that there was no police record of that beating. "Do you know when it happened?"

"Well, it was after Judy left him . . . Let me think about the order of events . . . He got arrested for robbing that house . . . and then he hurt her . . . and then Dennis went to jail, but not for long enough if you ask me, a life sentence wouldn't have been long enough! And as soon as he left, she took David and moved back here . . . and then he got out, and yes, I guess that's when it happened, right after that."

As Damon Montgomery had talked about Dennis Clemmons, his soft voice grew harsher, word by word, and his gentle manner toughened, so that by the time he was finished, he presented the demeanor of quite a different—and angrier—person than he had before.

Geof looked down at the little notebook he was holding in his left palm and referred to something he'd written there. "You said

Judy got *back* to work after she was injured. Do you mean she had that answering service before then? I thought she took that on as a way of finding something useful to do after—"

"No, no, that little business actually started years ago when she took the calls for the Mayer construction business. It just kind of mushroomed into her own little sideline over the years, not that the Mayers liked the idea . . ."

"No?"

"Oh, no!" He feigned disapproval as if he were imitating the reaction of Ron's family to Judy's business. "If you're a Mayer, you're not supposed to do anything for your own advancement, heavens no, you can only contribute to the family."

"Then why did Ron and Judy live here?"

"Instead of over there on the Heavenly Cul-de Sac with Saint Ronald the Elder and Saint Catherine the Martyr?" He snickered, and for a moment, I could picture him with Judy, both of them gossiping to their hearts' content. "Well, Ron built the house for one thing. But the reason he built it is because Judy wasn't a robot like all the other wives. She just plain refused to live there on the same street with her in-laws." Damon smiled in proud memory of his friend. "Judy could be very stubborn when she wanted to be."

I shifted sweatily on the cushion of the rocking chair.

A branch of the walnut tree brushed against the porch, and I looked past the screen, suddenly aware of a new breeze blowing outside. Maybe the weather was going to change, at last, maybe some rain was going to settle in and lower the temperatures.

"How did she meet Dennis Clemmons?" I asked.

"Oh, Judy'd known Dennis forever," our host said with a wave of one hand. "He was a little older, you know, like maybe ten years or so, and he'd known her since she was a kid, because he used to work for her mother, I think, running errands or something, I don't know. Before she married him, Judy used to laugh about this older man who'd always had a crush on her, kind of an obsession, I guess. I thought it was creepy, but she just always laughed about it. Until he made her marry him, that is!"

"He made her marry him?" Geof sounded skeptical.

"She was scared of him," Damon Montgomery said flatly. "Ob-

187

viously, with good reason, as he proved. Do you know that bastard beat her with a *telephone?* Can you imagine?''

"So why marry him?" I persisted.

*"Because* she was scared of what he'd do if she didn't!"

Geof and I exchanged glances that expressed the same thought: What the hell did that mean?''

"But why was she frightened?" Geof insisted.

Montgomery looked toward the house next door. "I don't know."

"I thought you talked to her about everyth—"

"She wouldn't tell me that," he said, looking hurt. I flashed a smug told-you-so glance at my husband. Hadn't I said that Damon might have thought of Judy as his best friend to whom he could say anything, but that didn't necessarily mean she returned the intimacy? Montgomery added as if justifying himself, "And she wouldn't tell Ron either."

"Wait a minute." Geof held up his right hand, palm out, to slow down this so-called explanation we were getting. "Are you saying that Ron Mayer knew that his wife was leaving him and taking his son and marrying another man . . . because she was afraid of that man? Come on!"

"Yes!" Montgomery said, looking annoyed that we'd challenged his veracity. "That's what I'm saying! Ron had to let them go, because he was afraid of what would happen if he didn't!"

"Happen to *who?''* Geof raised his voice in exasperation.

But Montgomery only shrugged, still angry about our skepticism. "I'm telling you I don't know. To Judy, maybe. Or David. Or even to Ron. I just don't know, because she wouldn't tell anybody, including me and including Ron. You think Ron and I didn't agonize over it for weeks, months, years? You think he didn't try to find out? Why do you think he kept such close tabs on Judy and David while they lived with that bastard? Why do you think he gave the bastard employment? To try to protect them in the only ways he could, that's why! And he did keep them safe, at least until the very end. And that's it. That's all I know."

Geof's frustration exploded: "That is the fucking weirdest divorce story I ever heard!"

"Well, I can't help that," the neighbor said with injured dignity.

"Come on, Geof," I urged when I saw that we could only further antagonize our friendly witness. "Let's let Mr. Montgomery get back to his work. And we need to find David before school lets out."

At the front door, Geof said for the first time, "Dennis Clemmons died last night."

"He did?" The other man looked astonished. "How?"

"A handicap ramp came apart, and he fell two stories."

The surprised expression slowly changed into one of open, childlike glee. "I'm delighted to hear it, Lieutenant. That's simply wonderful news. Do you think he would have been scared on the way down?"

"Terrified, probably."

"Good, good! Do you think he died instantly?"

"No. In fact, we know he didn't, because the paramedics said he was nearly unconscious but still aware of being in a lot of pain before he died."

"That's fine," Damon Montgomery said slowly as if he were savoring it. "So there's justice after all." He was smiling to himself as he started to close the door behind us, but Geof stopped him with one more question.

"Mr. Montgomery, did Judy ever mention me to you?"

"You?" A smile flitted across the other man's face before a formal, courteous expression settled back onto it. "No, I don't think so."

This time, he did close the door.

"The things people don't ask!" I exclaimed as we went back down his front walk.

"Such as what?"

"Such as *why* isn't David satisfied with the way the police handled his parents' deaths!"

"Not everybody is as naturally curious as you are."

I couldn't tell whether that was a jibe or he was refuting my point.

"Could you tell if he knows about me, Jenny?"

"Curious, are we?"

189

He smiled but didn't give in.

"Everybody's naturally curious, Geof," I said, still defending myself against what I had taken to be a jibe. "They just get it thumped out of them by adults who say, 'You shouldn't ask things like that.' " Then I answered his question. "I can't tell. He seemed kind of coy about it. So maybe, maybe not."

We stopped on the sidewalk in front and watched as a white van pulled up into the Montgomery driveway. It stopped, and a window on our side rolled down. From inside the van, Sheila Montgomery called out to us. "Everything all right over there?"

"What?" Geof called back to her.

"The house!" she yelled. "Next door!"

"Oh, yes!" He waved at her. "Everything was fine."

She gave him a look that suggested he was an idiot and called back to him in a disgusted way, "Fine! That sounds like something my son would say. Two people die in there, and a boy is left to fend for himself, and some wicked person paints graffiti all over it, and it's . . . fine! I could tell you what it really is, it's tragic and frightening, but why ask me? I'm just the mother, and what do mothers ever know?" With which sarcastic jibe— no mistaking that one—she pulled her car on up the drive and out of our sight.

"You've made a real hit with the neighbors," I observed.

"Expect an invitation to dinner," he predicted.

"That's another question he didn't ask." I stared at Geof. "He didn't ask us what we found when we went in there last night."

My husband nodded. "And he called me Lieutenant."

"You didn't tell him that?"

"I did not."

"Why does everybody but us seem to know everything?" Even with the new breeze, it was still hot, and I felt like whining. "Geof, I'm getting curiouser and curiouser to know more about this strange religion the Mayers practice. Would you care to go with me to find out?"

He looked interested. "How are we going to do that?"

"Know any good ministers in town?"

"Hardy," he said immediately.

Hardy Eberhardt, he meant, the pastor of the First Church of the Risen Christ and the husband of the mayor of Port Frederick and our good friend, as well.

"Do we have time?" He raised his left arm to look at his watch. I felt a lovely and suddenly much cooler breeze flow over my own bare arms.

"We have an eternity," I said, "in the timeless Now."

"It's an hour and fifteen minutes until school gets out," Geof said, giving me a look. "At least that's true in the time zone where I live, I don't know about the strange space that you inhabit."

I thought he was a fine one to talk, this cop who had landed our marriage in a Twilight Zone of violence and death. I wanted this to be a case he kept in a file at his office, not one that came alive right under my nose.

"I wish you wouldn't bring your work home," I muttered as I got into the Jeep beside him once again. It was a totally unfair thing to say, of course, coming from a woman who was ordinarily fascinated by his cases.

He looked over at me. "What did you say?"

"When can we go home?"

"As soon as we can go together."

"You don't think it's safe alone at home?"

"Do you?"

"I don't know."

"Exactly."

I found myself humming "Stormy Weather" on the drive over to Hardy's church. Considering the lyrics, it was hard to know if that was an optimistic or a pessimistic impulse on my part.

# 20

"I WOULDN'T EXACTLY CALL IT A RELIGION."

The Reverend Dr. Hardy Eberhardt and I were seated together in a back pew of the small, empty sanctuary of his First Church of the Risen Christ. I liked the look and smell of the place: dark wood, red pew cushions, sunshine filtering warmly through the stained-glass windows, and a faint, pleasant woody scent that might have been Hardy's shaving lotion or even a hint of perfume left over from one of his Sunday parishioners. I like churches. I don't like to attend them, I don't enjoy their rituals, but I like them as buildings, especially when they're nearly empty: their long, cool corridors; their vast auditoriums; their quiet rooms and silent pews.

Hardy's voice echoed a bit, though he was speaking in a low tone, one that was far removed from the vibrant bombast I'd heard him employ up in his pulpit at the front.

Geof had left us alone while he used a phone in Hardy's office to check in with his own office. God only knew what they thought he was up to that day; I hadn't even asked him what he'd told them, because it didn't matter. One way or another, for the good or ill of his job, he was here, not there.

"Not a religion," I repeated.

"In fact, that's a principle of it, I gather," Hardy told me, sounding tired. "They don't say much about it to anybody as far as I know—they're almost, but not quite, secretive, in fact—but from what little they have said, I think they believe in Christ without being Christians per se."

"How's that?"

"Hardy's smile looked a tad frayed around the edges to me; it wasn't his customary wide grin that hinted at the formidable intelligence and wit behind it. He was a big, good-looking man with a charismatic personality that seemed lately to have lost some of its luster. He and his wife, the mayor, both worked hard enough for four people, and they had a family to raise, to boot.

"Well, think about it, Jenny," he said. "The Christian *religion* didn't exist until Paul essentially created it, and that came long after Christ's death. Paul, of course, didn't even know Christ. But before the religion, there was the man himself—there was Christ wandering around Palestine doing what he did, healing people, offending people, saving people's lives and sanity, breaking rules, saying what he said, with only a small coterie of followers at the time. He was the *cause* of many *effects* during his lifetime, but he was not the center of a religion. He was a practicing Jew, of course, but he was breaking their rules—of diet, for instance— right and left."

"So what are you saying, Hardy, that the Mayers try to live as Christ lived without the trappings of religion?"

"I think that's their idea, which God knows is an attractive one, but it's probably absurd. They've probably got their rituals, just like the rest of us, and they're probably stuck in the concrete of their own version of some sort of creed, just like the rest of us. They're probably just as far away from the actual *experience* of Christ-consciousness as any of us in the mainstream churches are. From what little I can tell you about them, I'd say that all they've done is what everybody does: pick and choose the parts of a holy writ that personally appeal to them, the ones that cause them the least personal discomfort and the ones that appeal to their illusions about themselves and the world, then pretend to form a sort of spiritual life around that."

193

I was startled at the disillusionment his words seemed to imply in regard to his own creed, his own church, and I wondered, *Could this be why Hardy was looking so worried and unhappy?*

He sighed, leaned back against the pew, laid one arm along the top.

"Take that business of wearing all white, for instance, because the New Testament talks about raiments of white. And consider how they seem to concentrate on the worldly family of Jesus, because He came from carpenters and they're home builders."

"Sounds simplistic, Hardy."

"It is simplistic and more than a little silly, and I'm an unforgiving, judgmental son of a gun for saying so."

"Well, then you must have changed," I said in a matter-of-fact way. Something was definitely up with Hardy, something more than mere weariness with his workload. 'Where's their church?"

His tone turned wry. "Probably in their woodworking shop."

"You don't know?"

"I don't know."

"Hardy, is there anything in the New Testament that might suggest that you'd want to videotape confessions of sins?"

He cocked an eyebrow at me. "Are you serious? Do they do that? Sounds like they're more influenced by the television talk shows than they are by Jesus. I don't know, Jenny, it might derive from all of the many references to light that you find in the New Testament. I suppose a twentieth-century person could stretch that into a foretelling of the modern movie camera. Weirder things have been done in the name of God. And we all know you can interpret any holy text to mean anything you want it to. Why not videotapes?"

"What did you mean when you said they were almost, but not quite, secretive about their . . . religion . . . or whatever it is."

"Well, let me think for a minute about what I mean by that." And he proceeded to do just that: sitting and gazing off at the altar thirty rows in front of us. When he was ready, he stirred and said, "You have to understand that I hardly know these people. But now and then they have shown up at theological meetings that Mary and I have attended, meetings that tend to be generalist and nondenominational in character. They always come as a group, they all wear white, they are always polite and pleasant to everyone with whom they come in contact, but they keep absolutely to themselves. The first time I realized they were from Port Frederick, I went up to them, thinking that gave us something in common. Plus, I was curious about these people in white. They were killingly courteous to me, Jenny. I asked them what church they represented, and they said, 'We hold our own services at home.' Or something to that effect. I said, 'Are you Baptists, Methodists, Catholics' . . . and they said . . . no." Hardy smiled a little. "They said 'We're just the Mayers, and we build houses.' That's it and that's all there's ever been. I see them, I smile, they smile. I say hello, they say hello. One time I invited them to attend my services, but they never showed up, and they never returned the invitation, not that I expected them to, but I kind of hoped . . . I was curious." He eyed me. "And now I'm real curious."

"So are we."

"Mary told me about Geof and the boy."

"I expected she would. Would do you think?"

"I think Geoffrey ought to get himself a paternity test."

"He did that yesterday."

"And . . . ?"

A movement behind us made us both turn to look at the doorway.

"Well," said Hardy, turning around and smiling, "the man of the hour."

Geof looked at me with an odd expression on his face; seeing it, my heart turned over in my chest.

"I called the clinic just now," he told us.

"And . . . ?" Hardy asked again.

Geof joined us, sinking down beside me on the red cushion and reaching for my hands. I wanted to drop my head and cry as soon as he did that, but I kept my head held high, my face turned inquisitively toward my husband. He squeezed my hands, smiled nervously, and said, "And I guess it's true."

I squeezed his hands in reply and leaned forward to kiss his cheek softly.

195

"My goodness," Hardy said and suddenly laughed. "My goodness!"

Geof shrugged, fooling none of us. "So, Hardy, did you know a man named Dennis Clemmons?"

"No, who is he?" A hint of the minister's usual vigorous wit showed in his eyes. "Not another long-lost son, I trust?"

"Who *was* he, is the proper question, Reverend Smart-ass. David's former stepfather. He got killed this morning."

"What do you mean," Hardy said, sharp as always, "by the phrase *got killed?*"

"I mean he died."

"You pose a conundrum, Geoffrey."

I noticed that our friend's tone was different with Geof than it was with me, more gentle and serious with me, more bantering with his male, poker-playing crony.

"I do?" Geof retorted. "Sounded like a simple declarative sentence to me."

Hardy stared off at his altar again, but this time he slouched down in the pew to do it. "I'm having trouble with death these days."

"Aren't we all," agreed my husband wryly.

When Hardy didn't reply, Geof pressed him, kidding him.

"Don't tell me . . . Are you having a crisis of faith, Hardy? When Jenny had one of those, she bought a Miata." He smiled at me; I stuck my tongue out at him. I would have mentioned the Jeep, but I wanted to hear where this odd digression between these two long-standing men friends was going. "It seemed to work wonders for her. But of course, she was having a crisis of faith over her hometown, I guess yours would be over your, uh, home god."

Hardy's warm smile appeared momentarily. "Home god. That's good. That's really good. I like that. Like 'homeboy.' Maybe I'll do a sermon on that, about how we try to turn God into a nice little domestic idol that we can cut down to size and carve into a statue and set above the fireplace where he won't bother us."

Geof glanced at me, arching his eyebrows when the minister wasn't looking. "Hardy, let me say it again: What's going on here? It isn't like you to inflict theology on us. No offense. But then you don't much like what I represent as a cop either, so I don't inflict my gun-toting views on you. *Are* you having a crisis of faith?"

"No, I'd call it a crisis of creed. Do you believe in eternal life?"

He included both of us in his questioning glance, but I kept quiet, not wanting to break the rhythm of their communication.

Geof pulled a face. "Hell, Hardy, I don't know."

"Yeah, well, you heathens"—Hardy grinned at us briefly—"what do you know? We Christians say we do, of course, but I preside at funerals where you'd never suspect that was true, and I'm getting to the point where I don't think I can commit that kind of hypocrisy anymore. Christ promised us eternal life, He said spirit can never die, and here we are two thousand years later acting as if we believe just the opposite."

Hardy looked at us, at our concerned, befuddled expressions, and he laughed at himself. "Do you think I'm doing myself out of a job?"

"Then come to work for me, Hardy," I said.

He looked over at me and said, along with Geof, "What?"

"I'm not sure what I mean," I admitted. "The words just came out of my mouth. But now I'm thinking . . . This foundation that your wife is helping me to get started . . . maybe we'll need somebody exactly like you . . ." Full of passion, I meant; somebody who took nothing for granted, who questioned everything, most especially that which was either not "supposed" to be questioned or it didn't occur to anyone else to question. ". . . and maybe that would give you something temporary to do while you figure out what you believe . . ." I trailed off, half wishing I'd never said anything. And yet, I knew it would be so wonderful to have Hardy Eberhardt involved with this nameless entity I was a'borning.

"Somebody like me?" He smiled a little. "And what's that like?"

"Nuts," I said frankly. "Like the rest of us."

"Ah, yes," Hardy said, and he reached over to squeeze first my arm and then Geof's. "Well, then, that's easy. I'm getting better at that all the time, just ask Mary. No, Jenny, you're a dear friend, but . . ."

"Just think about it," I found myself saying. "Besides, the only people I've got involved so far are women, and I've already got a couple of black women—your wife and Sabrina. So I'm going to need a token male, and a black one would be even better . . ."

That made him laugh, a welcome sound.

"Hey," my husband protested, "don't you also need a token white male Anglo-Saxon former Protestant?"

Both men got a kick out of that. Neither of them seemed to notice that Geof's question took me totally by surprise and that it cast me into a most thoughtful frame of mind, which I carried outdoors with me into an afternoon that had gone sultry again.

"Damn, no change in the weather," I observed after we'd left Hardy. "I was hoping it was going to rain some more. When's this heat ever going to break?"

But Geof wasn't interested in my weather commentary. "Where did he take you on that motorcycle ride, Jen?"

"What? A farmhouse, where he said he spent a lot of time as a kid."

"Could you find it again?"

I'd spent a lot of that ride with my eyes closed, either in terror or in bliss, but, "Yes," I said, "I probably can."

"Then let's go there. He wanted you to see it for some reason, maybe so you'd tell me about it, and then I'd go out there to investigate."

"You're not going in to work at all today?"

"I'm calling this work."

"Geof, did you tell Sergeant Meredith or anybody else official about that confession tape of Clemmons?"

"God, I wish it'd rain again." He took off his jacket and draped it over his left arm, undid his tie and put it in one of the pockets in the jacket, then undid the top button on his shirt. Finally, he answered me. "No, I didn't, Jenny."

"What about the fact that the Mayers built that ramp?"

"You've been with me, you know I haven't had time to tell anybody."

"You phoned into the station from Hardy's office, didn't you?"

"Well, yes . . ."

"But you just didn't happen to mention any of this."

"Well, no."

I sighed. "Then maybe you'd better fill out a job application for my foundation. Keep this up, and you're not going to be a cop very much longer, are you?"

"Ah, well," he said in a cynically amused tone. "It's always good to have employment options, isn't it?"

I took hold of his arms and turned him around to face me and to confront the most important new fact we'd been avoiding.

"So. It's a boy, hmm?"

His eyes focused on my forehead. "Looks that way. A hundred and sixty-eight pounds, sixty-three inches long."

"Father doing well?" I asked him, trying for a light tone.

"Um."

Which was more than could be said for either the mother or the "stepmother," I thought but refrained from uttering. I did say, "How positive are they, Geof?"

"Ninety-nine percent positive, based on blood types and blood proteins."

"I guess that's pretty definite, all right." He started to pull away from me, but I put my arms around him and wouldn't release him. "Are you happy about this, Geoffrey?" His body felt restless in my hot, imprisoning embrace. He muttered over my head, "Happy doesn't enter into it, Jenny."

That's what I was afraid of even if I didn't believe for a second that he really felt that way. This was a man who had always wanted to be a father. And now he was.

"Congratulations anyway," I said and kissed the point of his chin, before letting him go. This was not the moment to tell him the truth of what had been tearing me apart ever since David Mayer had walked into our lives: A week before, I had decided that with Geof turning forty, if we were ever going to get pregnant, we'd better do it now. I would tell him—happily, I hoped—that I wanted to stop using birth control so that, with luck, we'd have a child to love for his next birthday or at least one soon after that. Since I'd made that decision, I'd gotten increasingly excited about "giving him" what he seemed to want more than anything else in the world.

And now, out of the blue of an August day, he had a ready-

made child—a distracting, troublesome son whose very real existence had almost instantly dissipated, possibly forever, any desire
I ever had to bear children of my own. So much for my "gift,"
which now seemed like a terrible idea, a mere sentimental notion
born of love and idealism, all too easily thwarted by reality. How
stupid! What had I thought I was going to do? Hand him an
infant and say, "Here, darling, it's all yours!"

I was filled with self-loathing for a moment, until from somewhere inside me came a more gentle voice, one that said, "Hey,
it's all right. The fact that you don't want to have a baby doesn't
make you a bad person. You've got reasons, kiddo, including a
history of mental illness in your family that you don't want to
pass on to an innocent child. It's okay. You can't help it. The
world will keep revolving. Geof knew this was a possibility when
he married you. You haven't lied about anything, not about your
real feelings. So don't start now."

"Yes, ma'am," I murmured in reply to it.

But that moment of acceptance didn't at all keep me from
feeling in the very next moment completely sorry for myself and
guilty toward Geof and furious at the boy who'd changed my
mind.

"No," the gentle voice in my soul quietly corrected me again.
"The boy didn't change anything about you; he is the one who
has given you the gift—by forcing you finally to acknowledge
this one very important part of who you really are."

"What are you thinking?" Geof asked me back in the Jeep.

*Oh, my intuitive love . . . he knew me!*

"Of how to get to where we want to go," I told him truthfully.
"I guess we'd better stop by the school first."

The car was already moving in that direction.

"That's exactly where I'm headed," he agreed.

*I know,* I thought with love. *All of your roads lead to David.*
Maybe I could help him along his journey. Not a bad gift after all.

# 21

AS WE TROD THE HALLS OF OUR ALMA MATER, I SAID, "I love the feel and smell of schools, don't you?"

"No, they make me feel claustrophobic." Geof was looking from one side of the corridor to the other as if searching for a way out. "They make me feel like doing something rude in public. They make me feel like lighting a joint, even though I haven't smoked anything in probably ten years. They make me feel like talking back to somebody, I want to let loose with a stream of profanity, I want to . . ."

"All right!" I laughed and grabbed his left elbow to hold.

He glanced down at me, looking surprised at the firmness of my grip.

"I don't want you cutting school right now," I warned him.

Students looked up at us curiously from inside their classrooms as we walked past. Teachers' voices jarred the air, like different radio stations turned up too loud. Somewhere a couple of locker doors slammed shut, and everywhere there was that smell that only schools have and that echoey sound and that odd slanting light in the halls.

"Let's get this over with quickly," Geof growled.

But me? I could have quietly taken a seat at a desk in one of the classrooms, preferably English Lit, and stayed all semester.

Geof did not explain to the principal, Dr. Nellie Fellows, his actual connection with David and the Mayer family. "We're distantly related," he said. And she didn't press for more, as she appeared much more interested in Geof's function as a cop than in any role he might have as a relative. I wondered later if he'd have been more forthcoming if she had been anything but the principal of a high school and therefore a member of a species of which he was by nature suspicious. "Why did you want to see me, Dr. Fellows? Are you having some problem with him?"

She was a woman in her early forties with very short blond hair and a rather delicately boned face and figure, which was well covered up with a calf-length full cotton skirt and a matching cotton knit sweater—a long-sleeved, thigh-length turtleneck—all in a flattering rust color that brought out the high color in her complexion. Her office was air conditioned, which accounted for all the clothes, but I wondered how she stood it when she walked outside in the rest of the school. An attractive woman, Dr. Fellows also had large blue eyes whose warmth of expression she controlled with an inner thermostat that appeared to be able to go from a heat wave to an ice age in an instant. At the moment, we were still in the temperate zone of her initial response to us.

"We're having a problem *about* him," she said, choosing her words carefully. "Graffiti . . ."

Geof and I "looked at" one another without even turning our heads to do so.

"But before I explain that," Dr. Fellows said, interrupting herself, "I'm afraid we have a more immediate . . . problem . . . and I've called down his teacher for last period to talk to us about it."

It seemed that David had not turned up for his sixth-period class, although he'd been in all of his classes up until then.

"He just went to the bathroom," his teacher exclaimed, looking bewildered when she arrived to explain the student's sudden absence. "And he didn't ever come back."

The teacher's name was Esther Gaines, she was tall and slim, a lively, attractive woman with dark hair and eyes and an intelligent, energetic air about her. Her subject was senior honors math, otherwise known as college calculus.

Both teacher and principal agreed this was not like David. He was a well-behaved kid, they agreed, a student who scored far above average on standardized tests—hence, the honors math—but who didn't work up to his potential in class, a very quiet kid, definitely a loner with no friends they could identify, at least not since his parents' deaths, but he was no problem to the school, never had been.

"Except that he doesn't seem very interested," his teacher said, looking a little embarrassed, a little discouraged. "Sometimes I think we only bore him."

"He had friends before his parents died?" Geof asked.

"He seemed to, but now he's always alone."

Dr. Fellows also told us about the graffiti that had appeared that morning on the blackboards of all of the rooms where David had classes that day. The janitors had caught it early and shown it to the teachers—who called in the principal—before the students arrived.

"In the room in which he had Senior English, it was the title of a book by J. D. Salinger," Dr. Fellows said, and then she named it: *"Raise High the Roof Beams, Carpenters.* In calculus, it was . . ." Tactfully, she looked to Ms. Gaines to say it.

"Three minus two equals one."

In Latin, it was Pater Familias, Mater Familias, which was X'd out.

More meanness, I thought, like the graffiti at his parents' home.

"Did David see any of it?" Geof asked.

"No, but we haven't told you all of it," Dr. Fellows said. "All of those were terribly unkind, of course, but rather tame, I think, at least compared to the last one . . ."

The final piece of graffiti appeared in the room where David had art class: It was a pornographic sketch of the Virgin Mary, an elaborate drawing in several different shades of chalk that covered all three panels of the blackboard.

"Doing what?" Geof asked them.

"Doing *it*," Dr. Fellows explained with a pedantic air.

"With anybody in particular?"

"With just about everybody," the teacher offered, and behind the shock of propriety offended, I thought I saw a hint of amusement in her eyes. I had a feeling she'd be a good teacher, or maybe it's just that I had a bias toward anybody with a sense of humor.

"With all the heavenly hosts, I'd say," the principal affirmed, and then she must have detected a twinkle in her interrogator's eyes, because she turned a quite serious face toward all three of us. "I know it sounds funny in a juvenile kind of way, but it wasn't amusing to those of us who saw it. It wasn't even exactly offensive in the conventional way. It was . . ." She looked over at the teacher, seeking help in expressing her meaning.

"Disturbing?" Ms. Gaines suggested.

"Yes," the principal agreed. "It was very disturbing to see, and I think it can only have been produced from a very sick mind. If it was done by one of our students, we'd better find out who it was and get him or her some counseling at once. If it was somebody from the outside, I want that person caught and kept out of my school." She eyed Geof sternly. "Do you just find this amusing, Lieutenant, or are you able to understand my concern?"

He was too experienced to get snagged by her anger, and so he simply replied in a mild and diplomatically apologetic tone, "I'd probably understand it better if you'd show me the drawing."

"I can't. We erased it." Now it was her turn to sound apologetic. "I'm sorry, but we had to hold class there today, and I didn't want any of the students to see it. And of course I didn't want David to see it or even to hear about it. It would have been terribly upsetting to him, I'm sure, as well as to some of our other students who come from Christian backgrounds. Their parents would certainly raise Holy Ned. Besides that, I hope I'm not exaggerating when I tell you that it was the stuff that nightmares are made of, and our boys and girls are not so sophisticated they can't be scared by things that really *are* frightening."

"Could the art teacher tell us if it was David's work?" I asked.

"What?" Dr. Fellows looked truly shocked. Her glance at me should have turned me into an ice sculpture right there in her air-conditioned office. *"David's?"*

"It's just one possibility," Geof soothed her. "Could she—or he?"

"I suppose. Do you want to know . . . now?"

He did, and so she called her art teacher out of class to ask him if he thought he recognized the handiwork on his blackboard. He didn't want to tell us. But finally, after much persuasion, he said, "David Mayer. But I can't prove it, and we've destroyed them, so we'll never be able to prove it, and I don't believe he'd do that anyway. It's just not like him, it's not like anything David's ever done for class before. I don't want to believe it, and I'm not going to . . ."

We couldn't get any further at the school, though we left on a wave of warm pleading from the principal. "Please, if you're a relative of the boy, please try to help him. Let me know if there's anything we can do. It's up to the rest of us, as adults in his community, to see him through this difficult time, we can't just let him roam loose without any supervision . . ." She paused, taking us both into her serious gaze. "Or love."

Outside the office, back in the long halls again, we mixed with the students who were jostling their way out of their last-period classes. "Bitch," my husband muttered.

"Geof! She's concerned! She's trying to help!"

"She's a self-righteous, lecturing little miss priss who couldn't help a kid like David if he asked her to spell dog."

I stared at him. "You really did hate school, didn't you?"

"There's the last bell. Let's get the hell out."

When we were in the parking lot again, I learned what had him really upset.

"We're being led, Jenny."

"That can't be true, can it?"

"He's still leading us."

"Where?" I asked, feeling cold and bleak as we stood among the noise and bustle of *normal* young women and men. Did we get one of *them* as a potential stepchild? Oh, no . . . *We* got one who specialized in pornographic religious graffiti and confessional videos and, maybe, dead animals.

"All we can do at this point is follow his trail and hope we find out." He must have perceived the upsetting effect he was having on me, because he suddenly laughed and blurted as if to distract me, "Have you ever wondered exactly who Ned was and just why he's so holy?"

"Nancy Drew's boyfriend, you mean? My friends think that's you."

He laughed again, but it was a loud and false sounding amusement. "No, the other Ned, the one people 'raise.' "

"Oh, you mean Holy Ned?" I played along halfheartedly, willing to be distracted. "I'm surprised you don't know. He was, of course, a little known saint . . . Theodore the Forgiven, twelfth century A.D., northern Iberia, founded a monastic order originally called the Holy Brothers of Theodore, whose monks were so greatly loved by the populace that they became familiarly known as the Holy Neds. The order died out in the fourteenth century, though the name was revived in the early 1960s by a rock band in Ohio, later known as the Holy Toledos."

Geof looked puzzled. "How do you know all that?"

I burst out laughing. "Geof, I was joking."

He shook his head and grinned. "You are amazing. You actually had me going there for a second. Why do I give you these openings?" He kissed me before I got out of his car.

Nothing about the rest of the day seemed real after that. We played detectives as if real lives weren't at stake, we joked as if our lives (and our marriage) didn't depend on it. Maybe the weather was partly at fault: The heat that shimmered above the asphalt on the highway and made us feel as if we were continually driving into mirages of shallow pools of silver water; the sun that poured onto us in the open car like hot syrup, sticking our skin to the seats, burning us if we touched metal, sapping our energy, paralyzing our will as if it were stuck in hardening amber. Maybe when nothing seems real, then everything's funny.

So all we could do was laugh.

# 22

A RED AND WHITE FOR SALE SIGN HUNG ON THE fence beside the front gate of the property that David had shown me. It said "10 acres" and listed a phone number that Geof recognized as belonging to the senior Mayers.

"I wouldn't take that sign too seriously," I advised.

"It's too fucking hot to take anything seriously."

We both knew from acquaintances in the building trades that if you were in the real estate or contracting business, everything you had was always "for sale" on the off chance that somebody might happen to drive by and make you an offer.

We couldn't get past the padlocked gate to any of those forty acres, but through the barbed wire I pointed out to Geof the red barn, the one-story house, the outbuildings, which included a garage, a shed, and a metal half-barn stacked with hay. Two brown horses stared at us from over the fence and one cow lowed out of sight in some nearby pasture. It all appeared to be beautifully maintained, ready indeed for sale to some lucky buyers.

"Farmette," I pronounced from where we stood on the wrong side of the fence, sweating under the afternoon broiler.

"What?" Geof batted a slow fly away from my face.

"Thank you. I said, it's a farmette. Farms are what they have in the Midwest, wide open vistas of land. I was on a ranch in Kansas that was ten thousand acres, and I know of one in Texas that's at least twice that big, maybe three or four times as large. Why, they would sneer at this in Iowa. They would consider it a backyard in Nebraska. It would be a median strip along a highway in Oklahoma. This here is a mere farmette."

"So?" He plucked at the barbed wire, lifting the top strand, letting it spring back into place again. "Welcome to Massachusetts. These forty acres probably cost as much as your ten thousand acres back in Kansas. Farmette?" He looked at me and grinned. A bead of sweat dripped off his chin. "I wouldn't go saying that out loud around here."

"No, wouldn't want to hurt the feelings of a farmetter."

"Or his wifette."

"I was actually thinking of a woman farmer."

"Oh, then, her husbandette."

"See? It is not easy to turn words connoting maleness into diminutives. In the English language, it's really only possible to diminish women. Don't ask me to prove this theory."

"I'd never do that."

"But you accept it *ipso facto* as true."

"You bet. Well, I bet. You betette."

He stepped on the bottom wire, then held up the one right above it, patiently waiting for me to finish chortling. "This is why we're still married," I said between snorts. "Even after all this time, you can still make me laugh like a hyena."

"Yes, and that's so attractive, too." He gestured like a gentleman with his free hand, indicating the space between the wires that he was suggesting that I clamber through. "Ladies first?"

"But that's trespassing, and you're a cop."

He feigned a somber mien, still carefully holding the strands of barbed wire apart. "Madam, I am here on official business to question the owners of this property, and there is no other way for me to attempt to find them than to climb through the fence and go looking for them."

"So we're just going to walk up and knock on the door?"

"Right, and if nobody answers, we'll walk around to the back door, just happening to glance in the windows as we do. And if nobody's there in the house, we'll mosey on over to the barn and—"

"Mosey on over?"

"That was for you midwestern girls," he said. "I'm getting real tired of holding this, Jenny. Y'all comin'?"

"Yankee! That was an improper use of y'all. It's always plural, don't you city boys know anything?"

"I meant it plural." He reached out to grab one of my wrists and tug me toward the fence. "I was talking to you and your shadow."

"You are my shadow."

I threaded myself through the prickly hole, then performed the same favor of holding the wires for him from the other side. When we stood together in the field, he grabbed me in a sweaty embrace and said, "Stuck to you."

"It's tempting, isn't it?"

"Right here in the field, under the sun, in front of God and everybody?" He faked an expression of Puritan dismay before turning it into a leer. "What a great idea . . ."

But the word *everybody* inspired a sudden thought that chilled my sun-drenched lust. "Does it occur to you that David might be watching us? If he's leading us . . . ?"

Geof parted from me. We walked sedately, sweaty hand in sweaty hand, over the dirt and grass of the pasture toward the farmhouse. The horses showed no curiosity in us at all.

As no one answered our knocks at any of the doors and as one of the curtains of the house was open, we took the invitation and peered in, our faces to the glass, our hands held up to shade our view from the glare of the sun.

"This is it," was Geof's immediate comment. "We've found it."

"Yes! White walls. White-painted wood floor. This is where they made the confession tapes!"

"Looks like it."

The house was mostly living room: One big room ran almost

the entire length and all the width of it; the remaining portion seemed to be a kitchen with possibly a bathroom.

"Anything else look familiar?" I asked him.

"Yes, the way the furniture's laid out. All the couches and chairs are up against the wall . . ."

"Just like at Ron and Judy's house. It wasn't that way at his parents' house, was it?"

"Not in any room that I saw. But Lee said it was arranged that way at Ron and Judy's house for ease of access for her wheelchair."

"But she could be wrong, Geof, because why would they still have it arranged like this, even after Judy's death?"

"Beats me. Look at that television, Jenny."

"Big sucker," I agreed. "Try to imagine the scene: The whole family, all five brothers, their wives and children, the grandparents, all seated in there against the walls, all watching that television together."

"It's what makes this country great," Geof drawled.

"If they'd known," I said, "do you think they would have bothered?"

"Known? If who had known what?"

"The Founding Fathers. If they'd known about television."

Geof laughed, his face still pressed to the glass, as was mine, too. "Are you kidding? Ben Franklin would have loved 'Star Trek.' "

"I suppose. Did you know he left separate trust funds for the states of Pennsylvania and Massachusetts? Each one was worth a thousand pounds sterling. And now they're worth several million dollars apiece. I'm telling you, if you leave your money to my foundation, you can be another Ben Franklin."

He glanced through his fingers at me. "You'll turn anything into a sales pitch for charity."

I laughed. "What do you think they watch on that monster?"

"How about home videotapes?"

I imagined how it would look: a distraught face—like Judy's or Dennis Clemmons's—projected to giant size on that screen and an emotional confession blasting from the speakers. I backed away from the window and leaned up against the house, my back against it, my arms crossed over my chest. "That's a very sick image."

"These may be very odd people."

"We're not getting anywhere, are we? We're making associations, connections, but we're not proving anything. We're not solving anything. We're not changing anything."

He backed away from the window, too.

"Welcome to most of the work I do, Jen."

The sun was in my eyes as I looked at him. "How can you stand it?"

He strode past me, avoiding my glance, heading in the direction of the outbuildings. "Who says I can?"

I heard that, but it took a moment for it to register, and then I wasn't sure he meant it the way it sounded, so I went trotting after him to find out. "Yo! Geoffrey! What do you mean? I could have sworn that one of the reasons we're staying in Port Frederick is that you enjoy your job. Am I wrong?"

"Some days, I eat the job . . ." he said.

I smiled, having caught up to him. "And some days the job eats you."

The garage was used for machinery storage, which could be seen through its windows.

The shed was locked with no windows to peek in.

"I want to know what's in there," Geof muttered.

"Can you pick a lock?"

"I think you have me confused with the Visiting Team. I'm the Home Team, remember? I do warrants; I don't, as a rule, do burglaries."

"Are you coming back with a warrant?"

"Not without due cause, I'm not." He shook his head, looking as hot, tried, and frustrated as I felt. We seemed to have run out of jokes. "Come on, let's get out of here; I've had enough of country life for one day, haven't you?"

"So what does David want us to see out here?"

Geof shrugged. "Maybe I'm wrong about him leading us."

I certainly hoped so.

This time I held up and pushed down the strands of barbed wire to help him through. We got back into his car, only this time with me behind the wheel, because he was tired of driving. The phrase "turnabout's fair play" popped into my head, and I said, "You're supporting me while I look for new work. Maybe when I find it, when I'm making money again, it should be your turn."

"For what?"

"For taking time off. Thinking about what you want to do—"

"When I grow up?"

"You should do that if you want to."

"Grow up?"

"Oh, stop it. You know what I mean: take a sabbatical."

"Or quit?"

"Or quit. Whatever you want to do, it'll be your turn."

He didn't say anything for the next couple of miles, and I kept quiet, too, not wanting to break in on his thoughts.

"It's a possibility," he said finally.

"Right."

He turned and smiled at me. "You'd do that for me?"

"Of course. I'm insulted that you feel you have to ask."

"Well. Thank you."

"Ah, shucks, what's a wife for anyway if not to help her husband now and then?"

"Wifette."

I swerved the Jeep violently back and forth on the dirt road, throwing him back and forth in his seat by way of reply to *that*.

"Jenny," he said suddenly, and he placed a hand on my right arm. "Stop the car a minute." We were still on the dirt side road that led to the farmhouse, so I could do as he asked without blocking any traffic. Something in his tone and his abrupt movement gave me the shivers, which increased as I saw him turning around in his seat to look over his shoulder. "There's a car parked back there with somebody in it. Back up, will you, Jenny? I want to see who it is."

I put the Jeep in reverse and slowly retraced our tracks.

In my side mirror I finally saw what he meant: a white Lincoln town car parked down another side road, its nose pointed in our direction. As I backed closer to it, I saw a tall white-haired man get out of the driver's side and stand beside it, shading his eyes to stare at us.

"Okay," Geof said when I was perpendicular to that road. "Stop." He put his hand on his door handle. "Why don't you stay here, and I'll go talk to him."

"Do you know who that man is, Geof?"

"Oh, yes." He smiled slightly. "That's Ron's father, David's grandfather."

*No, he's not David's grandfather*, I thought as I watched Geof stride down the road toward the older man. *Your father is.*

Dust kicked up behind Geof's heels, but it stilled when the two men stood face-to-face in the road with the sun shining down a mirage around them: They looked as if they were standing in a pool of shimmering silver water. I heard a movement of leaves, and when I looked up, I saw an oriole flap into the air from the top of a fence post. Whatever the men said to one another only took about five minutes by the count I was keeping on the clock in the Jeep. Soon, Geof gave a little wave to Mr. Mayer, who got back into his white Lincoln. Geof walked out of the mirage and came on back down the road toward me. Behind him, the car started, then rolled carefully past him and then turned into the road I was on in the same direction the Jeep was pointed. I got a glimpse of a handsome, elderly man staring up at me with an intense curiosity that matched my own before he went on by, leaving his own dust trail.

Geof came up to my side of the car.

"Did he ask how we know about this place and what we're doing here?"

"He didn't even ask."

I rolled my eyes; the things these people didn't seem to want to know!

"He did ask me if I had seen the farm, and I told him yes, that you and I had walked up there, looking for anybody who was home. He volunteered that's where they hold their services every week, and he invited us to attend next Monday night."

"He did? Really?"

Geof nodded, looking like the cat that had swallowed the oriole. "I told him I would be happy to but that I couldn't speak for you."

"Oh, go ahead, speak for me."

He raised his voice an octave. "Why, yes, thank you, Mr. Mayer, I'd love to. There are just so many things I could confess if you only knew!"

I batted a hand at him, but he jumped out of my way.

When he got back into the car, I said, "I wonder what they want with us."

"I can tell you that," Geof said as he settled back in. "He said he'd like someone to see they're not some sort of strange cult practicing bizarre rituals out here. He said he'd like to be able to show somebody that David grew up in the bosom of a perfectly normal and healthy family, and that's what they hope he will come home to."

"You believe that?"

"Uh-huh. And rats have wings."

"So I wonder what they *really* want with us."

We were going to have to wait nearly a week to find out.

# 23

WE SLEPT THAT NIGHT WITH THE AIR CONDITIONER on again and the windows and doors locked against . . . we didn't know what or even if such precautions were necessary. The next morning, we awoke, anticipating . . .

"What?" I asked Geof. "What is it we're waiting for?"

"Something else to happen, I suppose, since we can't seem to make it happen."

"Whatever it is."

"Right."

"So what do we do now?"

He shrugged. "I'm going back to work."

"And?"

"And I suppose we'll keep an eye out for David, and you'll stay away from here unless I'm here, too."

"He's not after me, Geof."

"He? *He* may not be after anybody."

"So what are we afraid of?"

"I'm not *afraid* of anything, Jenny. Things are just a little strange, that's all."

The word *denial* came to mind, but for once I buttoned my lip.

"Things" certainly did continue to feel "a little strange" that morning, but at Geof's insistence they kept getting more and more normal as the week wore into Friday. Even the heat wave broke a bit on Friday night, admitting a hint of crisp New England autumn into our evenings, if not yet into our days. No more little corpses appeared on our doorsteps. No one else died who was related to David Mayer, at least not that we heard. It couldn't be proved, thus far, that Dennis Clemmons died any way but accidentally. Even with further searching, nobody found any police record either of the beating he gave or the one he received, which Geof thought odd, but which I didn't have an opinion about at all.

"No opinion?" he exclaimed in jest. "You?"

"I can't hold onto opinions in this heat," I retorted. It was high noon at the time we were having this conversation. "They're too slippery."

While I was working on my foundation business, one mystery was cleared up on Thursday when Geof got into conversation over lunch at the Buoy downtown with an old friend he'd gone to high school with, a man who'd also known Ron and Judy. Not to put too fine a point on it, like Geof, this man had known Ron and "known" Judy, and Geof got him talking about his memory of her. The man laughed and said the irony was, the experience was bad for his ego.

"How could that be?" Geof asked him.

"Because all she talked about, even while we were doing it, was Ron and how much she wanted to marry him and how she hoped someday she could live in a big house like his. Didn't she do that to you?"

"I don't remember," Geof confessed, "I probably had other things on my mind. But maybe that explains something. Remember where Ron's parents live, over on that cul-de-sac? I was at their house the other day, and it felt familiar, but I'm sure I was there only once, maybe twice, when we were kids. You think it felt more familiar because Judy talked about it?"

"Talked about it?" Geof's old friend laughed and shook

216

his head at the memory. "She was obsessed with it! Hell, I could probably still tell you the kind of furniture . . . French Provincial?"

"They've changed it."

"But I was right, wasn't I? That's what it was back then. Judy talked about it, about the house and the Mayers and Ron, incessantly. Don't you remember how the girls used to make fun of her for doing it? Well, they made fun of her for other reasons, too, like we all did . . ." The man, Geof's old friend, had the grace to trail off, to glance at Geof, and to look ashamed. In a more subdued voice, he continued: "I'll swear, she could tell you the name of their silver patterns and their china patterns and what kind of furniture they had and how the drapes hung and what color the rugs were. My wife and I used to joke about it for years"—he'd married a girl from their graduating class—"whenever one of us forgot something around the house, like if I was supposed to get toilet paper, and I got the wrong color to go with our bathrooms, my wife would say, 'Well, if you were Judy Baker, you'd remember!'

"My wife says Judy had one of those—what do you call them?—hope chests! that she talked about all the time, and she had pictures of all the stuff in it and pictures of Ron's house . . ."

"You're kidding."

"No, really, she was always taking photographs, like from way back when we were still in grade school. It was like her hobby. And she had these big albums over at her mom's house that she was always taking out and showing everybody, and we were all in them. Maybe you didn't hang out there?"

Geof shook his head. This man had obviously known Judy better and for a longer time than he had.

"Yeah, well, you lived over with the rich folks." The man, who had parlayed his loquacious nature into becoming a prosperous insurance agent, smiled. "I lived in Judy's neighborhood, just down the block, so I was over there a lot. It was a great place to go when we were kids, 'cause her mom let us get by with anything. We could go in Judy's room and close the door and blast the stereo up loud and do anything we wanted to"—he waggled his eyebrows in an intimidating way—"and Mrs. Baker never said boo about it. She was a number herself." The man paused, shook his head, and grinned. "Annabelle. For a mom, she was a babe. My folks didn't approve of Annabelle, which just made her seem more glamorous to me. You know how that goes. But, anyway, in high school, maybe it was even junior high, Judy started carrying around pictures of Ron—like a lot of girls had pictures of their boyfriends, remember?—but she had pictures of that house, too. I remember looking at them and all I could think about was how was I going to get her to put down the pictures and lift up her skirt? God, poor girl, she could be so boring." His grin held both shame and lasciviousness. "But she was so easy. Back then, I could put up with a lot of dumb chatter if that was the price for some pussy."

His friend's face turned red, Geof told me later, as if saying the word felt vulgar now when said between two grown men than it had between boys "back then."

"When you were at Judy's house," Geof said, "did you ever meet an older guy by the name of Dennis Clemmons?"

"Oh, yeah, Denny. Scruffy guy, about ten years older than us, right? Didn't I read where he just died recently, some terrible accident or other? Didn't surprise me. Denny was a hard-luck kind of guy. You know he went to prison, don't you?" The man suddenly laughed, remembering that Geof was a cop now. "Oh, right, of course you know that. What I remember is that Denny hung out with Judy's mom a lot, so he was over at their house a lot. I think she paid him to do errands for her. She had some kind of little mail-order business, and Denny made the deliveries for her. Or sometimes one of us kids did. It was great; she'd pay us a quarter to run things over to people's houses on our bikes. But we couldn't stand Denny. He was always trying to hang out with us, with Judy's friends, I mean, and he had a crush on her that was kind of disgusting, him being so much older and all.

"Lousy, what happened to Ron and Judy," he ended up saying to Geof before they parted at the Buoy. "Didn't they have a kid?"

When Geof related the story to me that evening, I said, "That helps me understand better about the scrapbook."

"Why?"

"It's more of a piece with her personality, it's . . . I don't know . . . consistent. A woman who'd go on and on like that about a house, so obsessed with it, and who'd keep a hope chest and who'd also keep all those other photo albums, she'd make a scrapbook like that, it would be like her to do something like that."

"Sounds a little intense, doesn't she?"

I raised my eyebrows. "You said it."

"I don't remember that about her."

"Oh, well," I scoffed at him, "you weren't looking at her personality."

David never returned to Port Frederick High School that week, and Geof couldn't find where he'd gone. His relatives said they didn't have him; he wasn't hiding out in his parents' house (Geof checked) and the next-door neighbors said they hadn't seen him; his landlady called to say she was worried—"Where is that boy?"—nobody at McDonald's had seen him since he was fired; Geof even checked the farm a couple of days later but found no trace of boy or motorcycle.

"How worried are you?" I asked frequently enough to annoy him.

"Not very," he said at different times in varying ways. I didn't know whether to believe him or not. "The kid has proved he can take care of himself. He probably heard about his stepfather's death, and it was just one more thing to upset him, even if he hated the guy, and so he took off."

"That's awfully . . . understanding . . . of you."

"What's that crack supposed to mean, Jenny?"

"I'm just thinking about what it would feel like to be David watching that videotape of Clemmons's confession. If I were a kid and I saw that, I'd take off, too, preferably for some other planet where the inhabitants didn't behave that way. Either that . . ." I tried to make my face expressionless as I gazed at my husband. ". . . or I'd kill the son of a bitch."

"It still looks like an accident, Jenny."

"I know, I know."

I was the first to break the stubborn silence that ensued.

219

"So you think he's riding the highways somewhere?"

"Or camped out around here, who knows?"

He seemed nearly to insist by all that he said and did that week that this would, by God, be a period of nearly boring normalcy in our lives, and he bristled when I took exception to that point of view. We locked and unlocked our doors without comment. The air conditioner hummed on without surcease.

The illusion began to work, even for me.

The days began to feel so humdrum that I was half glad to inject some novelty into our lives on Saturday.

# 24

ILLUSIONS, SAID THE SIGN OUTSIDE THE PHOTOGRA-
phy studio.

For Geof's joke birthday portrait of me, I
had settled on this rather discreetly named
business. The single other glamour portrait studio in our town
was listed in our Yellow Pages as Hot Shots.

My choice was located in a strip mall, with a bookstore on one
side of the studio and a shoe store on the other. I parked in
front, then walked right up to the door, boldly going where none
of my friends had ever gone before.

The window display stopped me cold.

It featured framed portraits of several women, all of them looking like movie stars, at least from a distance, an effect that was
encouraged by the fact that their photos had been pasted to great
big glittery gold stars that stuck out from their faces like sun-
beams. Up close, however, they looked like ordinary mortals
made up to look like movie stars.

I stepped up to the window and peered more closely.

A couple of the women in the pictures looked like they were
having fun when their photos were taken; there was a flirty angle

to the way they held their heads, a bold, come-hither look in their eyes, their shoulders thrown back. Those two looked as if they'd really gotten with the program; but when I peered closely at the others, I imagined a wistful, shy glance in their eyes, as if they were a little worried that a certain somebody special might see through their disguise and might even make fun of them.

I quickly glanced away from those.

This was going to be hilarious, I told myself.

And if life kept on traveling down its current path toward delinquent parenthood, it seemed to me that Geof and I might need a few good laughs. Maybe a glamour shot of me would do the trick. For I, Ms. More or Less Yuppie Businesswoman of the Nineties, was here to shed my clothes and my inhibitions, drape satin and fur around me, pose provocatively, and get a mug shot. Mug and gams, perhaps.

"I have an appointment," I said forthrightly to the receptionist inside. "Jenny Cain."

"Jenny Craig?"

"No, that's the diet people. Cain." I was always getting that to the point where I joked to Geof that if all else failed, maybe I could sell diet food.

She seemed to shout my real name: *"Jenny Cain?"*

"Yes," I whispered, cringing. This was, I thought, a little like going to a drug store for the first time to buy condoms. What if somebody saw me?

"Have a seat, Jenny," she said in that same tell-the-world voice.

"Thank you"—I checked her nameplate—"Margie."

While I waited, amidst stacks of *Cosmo, People, Good Housekeeping, McCall's,* and *Woman's World* magazines, I lectured myself. Silently. *Don't be a self-conscious ass. Nobody's looking at you.* Which wasn't actually true. Both of the teenage girls waiting in chairs across from me were definitely staring as if they were trying to figure out what in the world the old broad was doing here. Or maybe it was the way I looked: windblown, no makeup, frazzled. Maybe I symbolized hope to them; maybe they thought that if these people could make me look glamorous, they could make anybody look good. I gazed back at each of them in turn until

222

they looked away, and then I continued my lecture to myself. *Consider this an adventure. Try to remember you're here to have fun, for a joke, to make Geof laugh.*

"Ha," I said under my breath, "ha."

One of the teenagers got called by a young woman who looked about their age and was wearing bouffant hair and a pink smock, and her friend went with her, both of them starting to giggle.

I wished I had thought to bring a friend to giggle with me. God knew, Sabrina would have laughed her ass off.

When it was finally my turn, I followed the bouffant hair and pink smock into a shocking pink room that boasted racks of clothing and fabrics, an array of jewelry boxes, a couple of dressing rooms with curtains dividing them from the rest of the room, and two makeup tables with white frosted lights encircling their mirrors.

"My name's Betsy," the person in the smock told me.

Her smile was nice, friendly, if a little bored.

She waved toward the walls lined with before and after photographs of ordinary women all done up to look glamorous. I would never in a million years have confused most of them with professional models, however, even though that seemed to be the idea. Some of them looked cute in their after photos, others pretty, one or two were naturally beautiful to begin with, but most of them had a self-consciousness about their expressions, a stiffness to their poses, that gave them away as strictly amateurs. It all struck me as a little sad, or maybe it was my mood and not those pictures in particular. These "models" all looked as if they were hoping that somebody seeing their photo might exclaim, "What a beautiful woman!"

Why was this depressing me instead of cheering me up?

"You won't put me up on the wall, will you, Betsy?"

Betsy looked surprised. "Not if you don't want us to."

"No. Please."

"Well, we'll see. You wait. You're gonna love yourself so much when we get through with you that you'll want everybody else to see you like that, too." Her smile was suddenly sweet, genuine. Then she switched into professional high gear; even her voice rose half an octave. "As you can see from these photographs on the walls, you can have practically any kind of picture taken that you prefer, Jenny. You get four poses in four different costumes—"

"Four? I don't want four! Can't I just do one?"

"Well, yes, I guess." Betsy looked surprised but willing to go along with this eccentric customer. "Okay. Well, then, if you want romantic, then I'd suggest a Victorian photograph with lots of pretty lace and maybe a floppy hat with ribbons. Or if you want Foxy Lady, we'll go with satin and a low neckline, very sexy, something like that—" She pointed to a photograph of a plump woman, thirtyish, who had been stuffed into red satin. She was leaning in toward the camera, her lips glistening hopefully, her breasts bulging and powdered, her eyes moist.

"Maybe . . . not," I said.

"One of our other favorites," Betsy continued, not at all dismayed by my lack of enthusiasm for the choices so far, "is Night on the Town, which is all black satin and fur and diamonds. It's really glitzy and glamorous. I think that's the one for you, Jenny."

"Really?" Why did I feel suddenly flattered?

"Really," she assured me.

But why not Foxy Lady? I wondered, plunged into sudden self-doubt. Didn't I look sexy to her? Well, hell. And why not Romantic? Did I look tough, hardboiled? Damn. I let my gaze land on the photos that showed the Night on the Town look and realized she was right. God knows why, but she was right on.

"Yes," I said and started to laugh. "Oh, yes."

"Goodie!" Betsy clapped her hands and bustled into action. "Time for your complete makeover! Wardrobe, jewelry, makeup, hair, lights, camera, action! Oh, this is going to be fun, you're going to love this! Who are you getting it for . . . ?"

And so she chattered and kept me chattering—except when I had to keep my mouth shut while she applied lipstick liner to it—while she draped fabrics and teased hair and dabbed colors onto me. In spite of myself, I was impressed: For as young as she was, her work was quite professional and hygienic, complete with fresh brushes and sponges. When Betsy was finished with her masterpiece, I gawked at the mirror, admiring myself.

"Wow!" said Betsy, bless her sweet heart.

"I'll bet you say that to all the girls." I smiled at her in the mirror.

"Yeah," she admitted with a laugh. "But it's always true."

It was a nice me, smiling there, it was the me the Prince would have returned the glass slipper to, it was the me that somebody would have climbed a rope of hair to reach in order to kiss me in a tower, it was the me that long black limousines would screech to a halt for in front of the Plaza Hotel in New York City, it was the me that was *meant* for diamonds and satin and fur. Or at least the top half of me was. The bottom half was still plain old Jenny in shorts and sandals. But in the mirror I saw shiny black satin draped above my waist to look like an evening gown with a bodice slung low in front; a feathery black boa artfully arranged around my upper arms, soft black gloves to my elbows, the glitter of rhinestones at my collarbones and dangling from my earlobes, my hair piled high and curly on top of my head, my face painted like a movie star.

"Fabulous," Betsy pronounced.

"I'll do one movie," I said, "but I won't sign for two."

She laughed, enjoying my pleasure in my own image.

"And I want a cut of the gross, not the net!" I pivoted on the bench, admiring all my sides, and then I snapped my glove-clad fingers at my image. "Call my agent!" Betsy was giggling, but when she caught me starting to laugh with her, she yelled, "Stop! Don't laugh! You'll ruin your eyes!"

Well, now . . . we couldn't have that, could we?

I swept into the photographer's studio like Greta Garbo onto a cinema sound stage, half expecting somebody to yell respectfully, "Places, everyone! Ms. Cain has arrived on the set!"

"How'd you hear about us?" the photographer inquired.

His name was Ken, which nearly undid me when he said it, because I felt just like Barbie. This was Ken thirty years later, however, with balding scalp, a paunch, and a sweet manner that encouraged his subjects to trust him just enough to make fools of themselves in front of his camera. As I was doing.

"From a woman named Judy Mayer," I said.

225

"Moisten your lips again. Good. Lovely. Say 'seduction.' Perfect. Again." He clicked, clicked, clicked, I licked, licked, licked. "Judy Mayer? That name's familiar . . ." Suddenly he stopped and stared at me over his camera. "Oh, my word, is that the woman who was shot by her husband? It is, isn't it? Do you know she was in here just a week before she died? I'm not kidding, and I want to tell you that it was unforgettable to me even if she hadn't gotten killed later on. Was she a friend of yours, I don't want to offend you . . . ?"

"No, no, I didn't even know her."

"But you heard about us from her?"

"Yes, in a way, because I saw the photo you took of her. What happened when she was here? What did you mean?"

He propped an elbow over his camera and we both forgot our task. "Well. I've never had anything like this happen before or since. I was taking her pictures just like normal, everything seemed to be going along okay. She had the white fur, didn't she? And the red satin? Right, I remember. And some physical problem, what was it? She was in a wheelchair, I remember, and we had some trouble getting her in place for the shots, she just couldn't get comfortable. But that's no big deal, it's not that unusual. What was unusual was her emotional response to the whole thing. At first, I didn't notice anything except that she was a little nervous, so I was trying real hard to put her at ease. Telling little jokes, complimenting her, just trying to get her to relax and feel good. And then I got behind my camera, and before I know it, what I'm looking at through my camera lens is that her eyes look real moist, which is good, you know, for pictures. So I get some real quick, 'cause I'm seeing real emotion in her face. It's good, I like it. But then I'm looking through my camera and I see tears! Little by little, they're starting to come down her cheeks. Just ruined her makeup, I'll tell you. So I stop. Naturally. And I ask her what's the matter. And she says she doesn't know! And I bring Betsy in here to try to fix the damage, but the poor woman can't stop crying! Before I know it, she's just downright sobbing, and of course the photo opportunities are ruined, and her makeup's ruined, and Betsy and I are scared to death the fur is going to get ruined, and this woman . . . Mrs. Mayer . . . she's apologizing all over the place and saying she doesn't know what's come over her."

"Did she ever say?"

"Well." He thought it over. "Yes and no. I mean you can bet I thought about it later after I saw in the paper what happened to her, which was like maybe only a couple of days after I brought her pictures to her 'cause she said it was too hard for her to come in to pick them up. She didn't want to look at the video of them, she said I should pick the best one and do it up and bring it over to her and even pick out a frame for her. So that's what I did. And then when I saw the news, I had this little paranoia, it sounds dumb, but for a minute I almost worried that it was my photograph that put her over the edge! But I knew that was crazy. She was plenty unhappy before I ever delivered it to her. But it upset me enough I almost called the police about it, but I thought, well, no, it only goes to show that maybe her husband did the merciful thing, I mean if you believe in mercy killing and all that. I'm not sure I do. But . . . she really was that miserable, I guess, and she really did want to die, I guess."

"But what did she say to you . . . about why she was crying?"

He shook his head, frowning. "Just that she was remembering things she hadn't thought about in years. That what we were doing here—her posing, me taking her picture—that it was bringing back terrible memories."

"She said 'terrible'?"

"Bad. Terrible. Horrible. Something like that."

"Did she say anything else?"

"Yeah. She said she wished she'd never been born." He looked at me challengingly, as if he felt I wouldn't believe him. "She really did. She sat right there where you are, she sobbed like a baby, and she as much as said she wished she was dead." He shrugged, but there was nothing callous about it. "And then she was."

My surprise was ruined; I was going to have to tell Geof about this.

After a moment's silence, I said, "I thought the picture you took of her was very nice."

"Thank you. I selected one of those where her eyes were moist.

227

It made her look real, she looked nice and genuine and kind of pretty, I thought." He glanced kind of shyly at me. "What did you think?"

The truth was, I could hardly remember it, I'd been so swept up in the idea that it had inspired, of doing something similar for Geof's birthday. But I told Ken the photographer what he wanted to hear: "I thought so, too."

His smile looked gratified, and my compliment seemed to lift his spirits enough to speed up our photography session again. I had a feeling it would be one of these later pictures that I would choose for myself, too; they would be the ones that showed some moisture, some genuine emotion, in the eyes of Ken's subject.

Afterward, when we were all finished, I didn't want to remove my glamorous finery. I knew my photos wouldn't look any more like a professional model's or a movie star's than anybody else's did, but for a few moments there, the magic had even worked on me, transforming my cynicism into something almost approaching innocence. I halfway wished I could leave my hair up and leave the makeup on my face. The only trouble with the birthday joke now was that if he laughed when I gave him the picture, I'd kill him!

I'd felt svelte, sexy, powerfully seductive.

An aphrodisiac, the whole experience was, charged, erotic.

I could hardly wait to get home to my husband, whom I would probably find puttering about the house in his old red shorts and nothing else . . .

When I walked out, I turned back to look at the sign in the window.

Illusions indeed!

Maybe partly because of that experience, on Sunday night, I had an extraordinary dream.

Just before I woke up on Monday, I dreamed that Geof and I were making love: I was lying on my back on our bed, he was seated, facing me. Suddenly, my consciousness, invisible, rose and entered his body so that I was looking out of his eyes, seeing myself, feeling what it was like for him to love me. I sensed his excitement, his sheer physicality and strength, his energy, and I felt how moved my husband was when he looked into my eyes. And then, suddenly, his consciousness was slipping into my body and turning around and looking out of my eyes, so that now he could see himself and experience what it felt like to me to love him and to be loved by him. I felt his sense of wonder as he saw through my eyes how beautiful he was and as he felt through my heart the power of my thankfulness for his very existence. And then our consciousnesses separated again, only to intertwine, lacing softly, rising above but remaining connected to the two loving, moving bodies on the bed.

I woke up with tears in my eyes, feeling stunned, not even sure at that moment if I had dreamed it or if maybe it had really happened.

"Jenny?" Geof was staring at me. "What's the matter, sweetie?"

To his surprise and mine, my lips were trembling, and the only words I could get out were a rather choked "I love you."

He brushed my hair softly away from my forehead. "Well, my goodness," he said in a surprised and gentle voice.

With the appearance of that dream everything mundane began to flee from our lives like birds hurrying south, starting that very morning with the news from the police lab that the ramp from which Dennis Clemmons had plunged to his death had been sabotaged and that what had looked for almost a week like accidental death was, in fact, homicide.

Geof left hurriedly for work that day, which was perfectly understandable, appropriate, even normal, under the circumstances.

There wasn't anything that I, however, could do about the news, and because I was unaware that it presaged a quantum shift from the ordinary to the extraordinary in our lives, I just went on with my day as if it were like any other.

# 25

 Even the weather changed dramatically. That morning, Monday, the temperature outside dropped twenty degrees in three hours, from eighty-five to sixty-five, just like that, accompanied by a thirty-second hail storm and then driving rain that started about ten in the morning and hadn't let up by noon, the time when I had to be in town for my weekly luncheon meeting with my friends.

Driving rain seemed a highly unlikely concept to me as I navigated the highway with my windshield wipers on high.

"Nobody should drive in rain like this," I muttered.

My headlights sliced a narrow path in front of me.

Even with the bad weather, however, I was early to the coffee shop at the Holiday Inn just to show I could do it. Ginger Culverson, Mary Eberhardt, Sabrina Johnson, and Marsha Sandy trailed in one at a time, greeting me and each other with little kisses and friendly pats.

"It's official," I told them as soon as we were all seated in our regular semicircular booth. "We are with child. If you like, but only if you all want me to, I'll give you a quick rundown of what has transpired since last we met . . ."

Which I then did at their unanimous command.

". . . but I *promise* that's not all we'll talk about today. Mary said something the other day that gave me an idea for a name for our foundation. How about the Angel Foundation?"

"Perfect!" exclaimed Mary, looking pleased.

"Brack," said Marsha, sticking a finger in her mouth.

I was wounded. "You don't like it?"

"How about calling it the Angel Food Cake Foundation?" said Sabrina. "That would be *really* sweet."

"Ginger?" I appealed.

"I like it," she said to the obvious astonishment of the two who hated it. "Because since I'm giving so much money to it, we can call it by its full name: The Ginger-Bread . . . and Angel Food Cake Foundation."

That crack combined with Sabrina's raucous snort of laughter put us all into hysterics.

"We're off to a great start," Marsha finally said as she wiped her eyes on her napkin. When she looked at the napkin she saw streaks of black mascara on it. "Hell." She threw down the paper, then reached down to the floor, while we wondered what she was doing. We watched her bring up her briefcase, open it, and dig through it until she came up with a couple of stapled sheets of paper, which she thrust across the table at me. "Here, Jenny. Since we're not paying any attention to business anyway, take this."

"This" turned out to be a list of names, personal and businesses; phone numbers; and addresses.

"Those are the names of Judy Mayer's answering service clients," Marsha informed me. "When I was calling around for you, just checking up on her business . . . uh, practices . . . I ran into another doctor who was using her right up almost until the time she died. He told me that she sold her list to another service . . . and they're the service I use now . . . and they gave me this list."

There were many unlikely things about that explanation of Marsha's—for instance, that she just happened to know another doctor who just happened to, et cetera, and also that her own answering service would hand over to her a supposedly confidential listing of customers. But that's the thing about living in the same town all of your life: You know a lot of people or their children and they either know you or your parents, and if they know you well enough, they trust you . . . I mean *really* trust you, no questions asked . . . and connections just get made that way that might not for people whose lives and paths never cross. I didn't even have to quiz Marsha, and neither did anybody else at the table; some things were just understood by the natives.

But not everything.

"When did she sell her service?" I asked.

"About a week before she died, was what my friend told me."

"Hey," said Sabrina, "it's almost like she knew she was going to die!"

"You think so?" I asked our shrink.

Marsha was cautiously noncommittal. "I'd need more facts to support that hypothesis; I wouldn't want to guess."

I thanked her, although I doubted that the list she'd gone to so much trouble to obtain for us would prove to be of much help. But my best friend wasn't through offering help, it seemed.

"Jenny," she said thoughtfully, "has this boy of yours . . ." She stopped and grinned. ". . . of Geof's had any counseling since his parents died? If he hasn't, Geof might want to encourage him to get some; they might even consider getting counseling together."

"Marsha, I don't think he wants a relationship with Geof."

"I'd say he's already got one, wouldn't you?"

Reluctantly I said, "I guess so. But he'd never listen to us."

Marsha, who knew a "yes, but" syndrome when she heard one, tactfully let the subject drop. I suspected she was satisfied, however, because she'd also let the idea drop into my brain where it might eventually root and grow into something nourishing. That was *her* hope. Personally, I doubted it.

"I thought we weren't going to talk about this," I complained.

"Oh, shut up," Sabrina instructed me. "We can discuss foundations any old day, but it isn't every day that I get to bring you a clue in a murder mystery. Nancy."

Snickers traveled around the table, jumping over me.

"You asked me how in the world a middle-class wife like Judy could ever go live in a dump like that with a man like Dennis Clemmons, and I got to wondering about that myself. So just out of curiosity I went back to our real old files and I looked her up by her maiden name. And what I found out is that Judy's own mother—Mrs. Baker—got state aid for years when Judy was still grade-school age." Sabrina sat back, looking pleased with herself. "So my theory is that the reason she could do it is that she'd done it before. The thing of it is . . . and this will be news to you, Ginger"—Sabrina made a face at her—"but if you've been poor once, you may not ever want to be poor again, but at least you know it won't kill you."

"I've been broke," Ginger protested. "I'll have you know I lived on a commune in Idaho, and we had to grow our own food, and I waited tables in town just to make money to help buy tools and toilet paper. I've been poor!"

But Sabrina only snorted. "You still had a rich daddy back home."

"Yes, but when I dropped out of college, he said he disowned me!"

Sabrina grinned maddeningly. "I guess not."

Ginger, realizing she was arguing a point she couldn't win, suddenly relaxed back against the booth and laughed. "It's just so sad how we poor rich folks don't get any respect." Then she turned to me. "I had an idea for naming this foundation, Jen. Let's call it the Concrete Foundation."

The rest of us groaned as one.

Ginger smiled placidly. "Because it's something solid to build on."

Mary patted her hand kindly. "We get it, dear."

"All right then." Ginger faked a pout. "If you don't like that idea, I've had another brilliant one."

Sabrina exchanged glances with me: We couldn't wait for this one.

"Instead of calling it a foundation," Ginger said with an air of perky brightness as phony as her pout, "let's call it a religion. We'd get better tax breaks, wouldn't we, Jenny?"

"I don't know, Ginger," I said, laughing, "but we could sure think of some great names for it. The Church of Holy Charity . . ."

"St. Philanthropist," Marsha chimed in.

"The Give Unto Others Cathedral," Mary said.

Ginger beamed. "I just knew you'd love it."

"Church of the Helping Hand," said Sabrina. "Run by the Holy Down and Outers . . ."

"Stop!" I held up my hands to keep it from going on all day.

"But seriously," Ginger said, "that's what your stepson's family did, and look how they avoided paying lots of taxes."

"He's not exactly my stepson. Excuse me for being picky. What do you mean, that's what his family did?"

"I think he is your stepson," Mary corrected.

"Mayer Construction Company," Ginger said, answering my question. She looked at us as if amazed at our denseness. "That's only what I call them because it's so embarrassing to tell people my kitchen was remodeled by Jesus's Carpenters."

Three of us, the heathens, stared at her.

This was the sometimes infuriating thing about Ginger Culverson, whether she was aware of it or not, she kind of liked to spring surprises on people, as witness her bombshell on me about her little affair with Ron Mayer. If we'd said to her, accusingly, "Ginger! Why didn't you tell us?" she'd have looked surprised, and she'd have said, "I'm sorry, I thought everybody knew that."

But Mary, the minister's wife, was nodding her head as if this wasn't any surprise to her.

"Mary," I said, "is that true?"

"Um-hmm," she said as if agreeing that yes, it was raining outside.

"But it's very hard to qualify with the IRS as a bona fide church!"

"Not if you're a bona fide church," she said equably.

"Are you telling me," I said to Ginger, "that they called their construction work a . . . a religious . . . service?"

"Well, yes," she said. "I thought you knew."

"And what do they call those big homes on their cul-de-sac?" I fumed. "Synagogues?"

"Jenny, I think they're sincere," Mary defended them.

"Madam, you think everybody's sincere," Sabrina jibed her.

"That is not true," said our mayor with dignity. "I am, after all, a politician. I should think I can spot hypocrisy when I see it; and I certainly do see it—both at town council meetings and church on Sundays."

"Whew!" Sabrina grinned. "Beg your pardon, Madam."

"Well, those rascals!" I exclaimed. "Can you imagine . . . ?"

"Jenny, really," protested Ginger, "Mary's right, I think you are being entirely too cynical here. These people are truly religious, real believers. They work very hard, very ethically, and it just happens to be one of the tenets of their faith that a person who does that . . ." She couldn't help it, she was starting to laugh. ". . . a person who does that gets his reward a little early."

"Doesn't have to wait for heaven?" Marsha suggested.

"No, I think you get a little heaven on earth," Ginger said, then gave it up and laughed out loud. "What a racket, you're absolutely right, and we're paying for it with *our* taxes. Why, I'm going to report them to the IRS. I want my money back! For the work they did on my house! And then we can start our church and call it the . . ."

"Don't . . . start," I advised her sternly.

But Mary wasn't happy with us. "I'm not sure you're being fair," she insisted in her diplomatic way. "If we only accepted the traditional, mainstream churches, we wouldn't have freedom of religion, now would we? Some people just don't believe in the regular way . . ." She trailed off, her words having grown uncharacteristically vague, and I had the distinct feeling she was thinking of someone she knew rather better than she'd ever known any of the strange Mayers: her own husband, Hardy, the doubting minister. We all got kind of quiet, watching Mary, and when her attention came back to us, she had changed the subject a bit. "You never know what'll set people off down an eccentric spiritual path . . ." We lost her again, as Mary was seemingly distracted by watching other diners walking by.

I tried to rescue her. "Some event that catalyzes them, maybe."

"Or traumatizes them," Sabrina said.

"And transforms them," Marsha offered, and we looked at her,

235

figuring that as a shrink she knew more about such changes in the psyche than we did. "I'd be curious to know why the Mayers stepped off the traditional religious path onto this odd little trail of their own."

"And why Judy left Ron for Dennis and took David with her," I said, "speaking of catalyzing events. What was *that* one all about?"

"And why did Dennis Clemmons turn violent all of a sudden and beat her up," Sabrina added, "when he apparently didn't have a history of domestic violence," and then quickly amended, "schmuck though he may have been in every other way."

"And why did David wait as long as he did to come to Geof?" I threw in. "What catalyzed *him* at that moment?"

"And most of all," said Marsha dramatically enough to swivel our attention back to her end of the table, "why did they die at the precise moment in time that they did?"

We were all silent a moment, considering.

"All right," I said finally. "I give up. Why did they?"

But we didn't have the answers to those questions, so we settled into our desserts and another quarter hour of discussing business, namely, exactly what kind of foundation was ours going to be? Private or community or a private fund within a larger community foundation or . . . what?

"It's a good thing we're not in a hurry," I remarked as we paid up.

It was Sabrina who brought me up short on that opinion. "Maybe we are, Jenny," she corrected me in a tone of voice so uncharacteristically serious, so stripped of her usual joking or cynicism, that the rest of us stopped everything we were doing and gave her our full attention. "Maybe what we're going to do with this foundation will somehow help to prevent deaths like Ron and Judy's . . ."

"Or childhoods like David's," Mary added.

I glanced down at my credit card so Sabrina couldn't see how touched I was by her words; this was one time I didn't want to let her make fun of any of us or of herself.

"Maybe so," I said lightly and got up to go.

"Did we eat?" asked Ginger, sounding plaintive as she stared at her now-empty plate. "We've been so busy talking, I can't remember."

On the way out, I maneuvered so that once again I was walking alone with Mary Eberhardt. She gave me a sweet smile. "Find that treasure yet, Jenny?"

I tried to be tactful. "I think it's still hidden several fathoms deep, Mary, or stuck way back in the cave. I'm sure we'll recognize it, though, by the big angel sitting on top of it. I understand they put out quite a glow." I smiled back at her. "Did Hardy tell you that Geof and I dropped by the church last week?"

She reached for my right hand to squeeze and hold. "Yes, and I was so glad you both did. Maybe you could tell that he needs his friends right now."

"How 'bout you? You need your friends right now?"

That earned me another warm squeeze. "Yes, ma'am. I'll tell you the truth, my dear, for all that I am considered in some circles to be something of a radical, I am also something of a traditionalist, did you know that?"

"I may have guessed," I teased gently.

"I may be the first woman to be mayor of this city, and I may be the first black person to do it, too, but Hardy is also the first and only man I've ever known, isn't that something in this day and age? My marriage, my family, my church, they're my rock and my security." She looked at me out of her deeply intelligent and expressive brown eyes. "They make everything else possible, they make the world safe for me. I don't know what I'd do without them exactly as they are."

"You'll still have them, Mary, won't you?"

She sighed. "Yes, of course, I will, you're right."

"But if Hardy leaves the ministry . . ."

"And our church."

"It'll be hard for you."

"For all of us."

"I'm sorry," I said and squeezed back. "But you know, a very wise woman once told me that wherever there are trials and perplexities, there are angels . . ."

Mary's eyes widened, and then she began to laugh softly.

". . . sitting on top of a treasure," I finished.

She let go of my hand, only to put an arm around my waist. "What a cross it is for me to bear," Mary said with an exaggerated sigh, "to have such smart friends."

"Smart aleck, I think you mean," I suggested as we walked with matching strides back out to our cars.

Mine needed fuel, I decided, after I got in, even though the gauge was only at the halfway mark. But I didn't know which of our cars we'd be using to drive out to the Mayer farm that evening to check out their Monday night church services. I decided that I'd better be fully gassed, just in case.

"Thanks for sending the kid in," Joe said to me as I paid my bill at the Amoco station.

"I beg your pardon?"

"David, the kid, he's working out so far."

"You hired David Mayer, Joe?"

He looked up from his cash register. "Yeah, that's what I'm saying. Thanks to you."

"Uh, when does he work?"

"Last shift, seven to ten, weekdays, all day Sundays."

"I'll be damned," I said, feeling completely at a loss.

Joe looked surprised, then grinned. "You will? Why so?"

"It's just so surprising," I stammered, "when things work out like this."

"No, it isn't," he said pleasantly. "This is the way the world works, Jenny."

"You're an optimist, Joe."

"No, I'm not, I'm a Knight of Columbus."

I left his station laughing as usual and feeling a little better about things in general. Joe had a definite knack for filling his customers' "tanks" with a kind of fuel that was richer and ran longer than mere petroleum.

# 26

THE RAIN WAS THRUMMING AGAINST THE SLATE ROOF above our heads and pinging against the closed windows in our bedroom as we dressed to go to "church" that night. Our invitation, issued by Ron's father, had been for nine o'clock, but Geof wanted us to arrive a little early. This meeting would, he hoped, be a good opportunity to ask some questions about Dennis Clemmons, about their relationship to him, and about the ramp they had so nobly constructed for him—the one from which crucial bolts had been removed and supports half sawed away.

"Who told David about the job?" he asked me as he unbuckled the trousers he'd worn to work that day and let them fall to the floor.

"Did you mention it to anybody, Geof?"

"No, who did you tell?"

"Only one other person heard about it from me besides you."

"And that is . . . ?"

"Don't you remember?"

"Jenny," he said, sounding annoyed. "It's been a long day, so just tell me, okay?"

"Try to figure it out," I suggested as I sashayed into my closet. "We'll make a detective of you yet."

I heard him grunt and mutter, "Fucking touché."

"What, dear?" I called out sweetly.

"Damon Montgomery!" he yelled.

"Good thinking," I said in my most patronizing tone as I emerged from the closet in only my underwear. "Now think about what we ought to wear to this thing."

"All white, like they do?"

"A little blatant," I said doubtfully. "They might even think we're making fun of them. Besides, it's already September."

"What's that got to do with it?"

"Why, everybody knows you can't wear white after Labor Day."

"Who makes up these stupid rules?"

"The same ones who decreed for years that women weren't supposed to wear blue eye shadow. The queen bees of the hive."

So we settled on neutral colors with a bit of white: a beautiful, light gray suit with a white dress shirt and a muted necktie for Geof; a bland beige silk fitted dress for me with low beige heels. I pulled back my hair at the nape of my neck with a big fluffy beigeish bow attached to a barrette.

"You look . . . nice," Geof observed.

"Ah. Damned with faint praise."

He hadn't actually dressed yet but stood nude in front of me, a pair of fresh undershorts in one hand.

"You," I said, "look *awfully* nice."

"Why, thank you," he said, and his tired face lit up with a grin.

I looked down from his face. "Maybe you'd better get dressed quickly, or we won't get out of here at all."

He made a laughing grab for me as I left the room, but I managed to escape his clutches, unfortunately.

There was an unreal, comfortable, almost voluptuous feeling about our drive to the Mayer farm. Because it was raining and there might be mud, we took the Jeep and drove along feeling cocooned within it. Normally, with sunset still so late in the day, our way would have been illuminated by daylight, but the clouds extended across the sky, horizon to horizon, like a black canvas cover without so much as a rip to admit some light.

Motorists were driving with their headlights on.

In town, the streetlamps were already on, but we passed through them and out of reach of their glow as we drove on to the other side where the country began again.

We played a cassette tape, a soft flute and guitar accompaniment to our quiet, steady conversation about this and that and the other. I would have been happy for Geof to just keep driving on through the state, for us to stop someplace late that night and get a motel room, to sleep for a few hours, and then get up and drive through the rain some more. When we slowed down beside the fence with the For Sale sign on it, the time was still only eight-thirty, a half hour before our invitation, and I felt reluctant to disembark so soon.

They'd left the gate open for us.

Geof turned his headlights off.

"What are you doing?" I asked him.

He drove the Jeep into the darkness under the trees beyond the gate.

"Being careful," he said without explaining further. It seemed to me that far from increasing our safety, driving without lights considerably boosted our chances of going into a ditch or hitting a tree.

I clutched the front edge of my seat and said, "Why?"

There were several pickup trucks and a couple of cars parked near the house. The draperies in the house were pulled tightly shut so that we could not see in nor could anyone in there see us.

There was no one about in the yard.

Geof backed up, then pulled off to the side among the trees and parked. I hadn't been particularly nervous up until the moment he turned the headlights out; it had all sounded so straightforward when we talked about it at home: just walk up to their door and ask to sing their hymns. Now that it was turning into a prowl in the dark, I was already beyond jittery and clear into scared. This seemed to me to be an excellent way to get shot at by big men in pickup trucks, who would hear rustling in the wet grass on their property and confuse us with prowlers.

"What do we think we're doing?" I repeated.

"I've got rain gear back here," Geof said as if that were an answer. He tossed a blue Gor-Tex jacket at me, his size, which meant it would cover most of my beigey silkness. I gazed sadly down at my shoes, which were about to be ruined, and thought, *Well, the hell with it, this is what happens to women who dare to scorn the rules of fashion*. "You can stay here," he told me as he slipped a black parka over his own head and settled it down over his shoulders. "In fact, I wish you would. I just want to look around and see what's going on before we go in there."

"If you think I should stay here, why give me this?"

I indicated the blue pile of water-repellent material in my lap.

"Because I don't think you'll do it," he said with a slight smile for me. "Will you?"

"No, I'd rather go with you, okay?"

"I gave you the rain gear, didn't I?"

"But Geof, why, exactly, are we doing it this way?"

"Because we'd like to know what's really going on in there as opposed to what they want us to observe."

Okay, that made sense to me.

He reached under the driver's seat and came up with a gun—a .45, I think—and then he reached over me to open his glove compartment, came out with a couple of small flashlights, and held them both out to me. I said prissily, "I believe I'll have the blue this time," leaving the red one for him. I grasped his hand before he could get out of the Jeep, and I looked seriously into his eyes. "Do we have to do this? Couldn't we just have regular foreplay next time?"

"No," he said, smiling in the dark, "the danger excites me."

*Too true*, I thought as I climbed down from the car. My own heart was palpitating rather rapidly, too.

We slogged through the rain, over the muddy grass, without speaking for the quarter mile or so up to the one-story house. It appeared to float in darkness, giving off a cozy golden aura because of the light seeping around and glowing through its closed draperies. There were no other lights on the property, nothing to spotlight our presence outside in the storm. Nor did the storm itself betray us: It was a quiet, gray, and steady rain and had been now for the last couple of hours, the lightning and thunder having moved on past us. Geof and I moved easily under natural cover, as it were, shielded by the rain and by the sheer blackness of countryside at night.

I followed Geof right up to the house, where he evidently hoped to be able to get a look inside by locating an open seam, a crack, in the drapes, but they were well and tightly closed, admitting no Peeping Toms or Tomasinas, for that matter.

Geof grasped my left wrist and led me around back, looking for other windows to spy through, and we finally found a small one, a quarter pane of glass in the rear door that was not entirely protected by the curtain pulled over it. He peeked through first, then gently shoved me forward for a look.

I nearly drew back in alarm, because there was someone so close to the door, just on the other side of it. Then she moved, clearing the way for me to view the length of the house from the back of it. It was like looking down a lighted tunnel. Right on the other side of the door was a small kitchen, where a woman was working at a table, pulling cellophane wrapping off the tops of various desserts; I couldn't tell what each of them was, but I definitely identified a meringue pie of some sort. My mouth watered, thinking of lemon. Past the kitchen was the long living room Geof and I had seen the first time we had come out, but now it was filled with people, big men, women, lots of children, a few older people, and every single one of them dressed entirely in white from their shoes to the tops of their heads. The women wore mantillas or scarves or even what looked like white doilies pinned to their hair; the men wore white skullcaps, although a couple of them had white baseball-type caps on. The children's attire mimicked their elders in every detail. All the chairs and sofas around the room were taken by the grown-ups; the kids, even the older ones, teenagers, sat or played on the floor at the feet of the adults.

Except for the littlest children and the woman right in front of me in the kitchen, the attention of every person was focused— no, riveted—toward the other end of the living room. There I saw what we had thought, in the videotapes we had seen, was a wide doorway leading to a white room. Now I could see that it wasn't a doorway so much as it was a frame of sorts made of woodwork, painted white, arcing over the floor and over the woman seated under it in a yellow kitchen chair.

She had her hands folded calmly in her lap, and she was talking.

David's Uncle Matthew was standing just in front and to the side of her, taping her "performance" with a hand-held camera, and she was talking directly toward him.

The woman in the kitchen suddenly turned toward our window.

I jerked back, landing softly against Geof's chest.

We waited a silent count of ten, then backed away from the door. Geof took hold of one of my wrists again, and this time he led me toward the outbuildings.

First the garage, but it was open and full of unmysterious farm equipment. And then, the shed.

# 27

THIS TIME, THE SHED DOOR WAS UNLOCKED, THE padlock that had fastened it was now hanging open, its clasp only loosely attaching the door to the structure.

"They're not very security conscious," I whispered.

"Maybe they should be," Geof whispered back. "You never know who'll take advantage of an unlocked door." With which remark, he slid out the padlock, looped it over the door handle, and opened the shed to let us into it.

"Welcome to Hollywood," Geof breathed in my ear.

Even in the darkness, we could see that the shed was a video-tape library. Tape box upon dark tape box lined the inside walls on shelving that was floor to ceiling in a couple of places and various other heights in others. There was also room against the walls for a small built-in desk, on which a small television sat, and an alcove for videotaping equipment, including a camera case and a tripod. Although the shed was only about eight by ten feet in size, there was still room enough for the two of us to step in and to move around. Geof silently closed the door behind us.

Then both of us wordlessly perused the labels on the shelved videotapes by the light of our pocket flashlights.

A lot of it looked totally innocuous, typical American family stuff: Matthew and Dinah's Wedding, Bryan's First Birthday Party, Mom & Dad's 40th Anniversary, that kind of thing. But besides the birthday parties and Christmas dinners, there was also Uncle Raymond's Visitation, Uncle Raymond's Funeral, Uncle Raymond's Graveside Service, all of which sat on a long shelf with other tapes all similarly labeled with other people's names, of course. And there was another short row given over apparently to tapes of the births of babies in the family.

"These people tape everything!" I whispered. "I suppose what we saw tonight in the house will wind up in here, too. The woman who was sitting in that chair must be one of the wives ... I wonder what she was confessing to?"

"Look at this, Jen."

I turned, put my hands on Geof's shoulders, and peered around him to see what row of tapes he was looking at. His flashlight played on the title: Mark, Confessions, 89, and the next one after that, Mark, Confessions, 90, and then he showed me how Mark's confessions were recorded year after year and also those of every other member of the Mayer family, including Grandma and Grandpa and all the kids.

"Find Ron and Judy and David," I suggested.

And he did, all together on a top shelf near the roof of the shed. As he ran the light down David's row, we counted seven tapes, starting from when the boy was two years old and ending when he was nine, which might have been just before he left with his mother to go live with Dennis Clemmons.

"What does a two-year-old have to confess?" I asked.

"That he was born into a family of goddamn voyeurs and sadists," Geof retorted, his voice strained and angry. "Bastards! Look at this, for Christ's sake!"

"Shh," I warned, glancing at the door, "take it easy, get mad later."

But I was plenty incensed myself at what we'd seen thus far, and then especially at the new shelf Geof's light revealed, for it was row after row of tapes with labels, like Ryan, Penances, 86.

Before Geof could object, I took that one off the shelf, opened it, and stuck it into the open maw of the VCR that sat beside the little TV on the desk, but I left it to Geof to turn it on.

There was a flash of startling light in the dark shed, and the tape began to roll, but silently, because Geof had found and hit a mute button on the controls.

We watched, holding hands with my fingernails digging into his palm as on the television a man struck a very small boy ten times on the boy's palms, which he held out like tender little gifts to the man. The child's mouth was trembling with the first slap, and with every subsequent slap, it opened a little more, until we could imagine the cry coming out of it.

As he hit the child, the man gazed lovingly into the boy's face. At the end, the man grabbed the child in an embrace.

"No more," I said and reached for the controls to find the off button, but Geof beat me to it.

"Find an adult penance tape," he whispered.

After watching that child being punished, my hands were shaking as I did as he asked. Behind me, he with his calmer hands that were more accustomed to unpleasant tasks rewound the tape, folded it back into its plastic carton, and replaced it on its shelf.

"Here." I had picked a more recent one labeled Luke, Confessions, 93.

That tape amounted to recordings of a grown man being beaten across his bare back with a device that looked downright medieval: There was a long handle to which thin leather straps were attached. They came down across the man's back as if to flay him alive. The device was wielded by the same man who'd slapped the little boy's hands. Midway into the beating, the man's back began to bleed. Geof fastforwarded to another penance segment in which the same man—evidently the brother named Luke—was being whipped again. Now we noticed that his back was heavily scarred from previous punishments. But when Geof started to turn that off, too, I stopped him.

"The end," I whispered. "Let's watch what they do at the end."

When that beating finished, a woman appeared on the tape

with a bowl of what looked like water in her hands, and then another woman appeared with a cloth and they gently dabbed the man's wounds. Meanwhile, the man I had come to think of as the Executioner walked around to the front of Luke and grasped his elbows, and the two men embraced as much as they could, considering one of them was in agony and bleeding.

"They're both crying," I pointed out to Geof.

"Fuck!" he said suddenly, sounding so shocked and disgusted that I turned to stare at him. But it wasn't the men's tears that had elicited that reaction from him. "Look at the man with the whip, Jenny. The same one who hit the kid. It's Ron."

"Oh, no," I said, the words coming out like a low moan; they were carried away by the sound of the rain falling even harder outside the shed. I heard a loud crack that at first I thought was lightning; half a second later, I realized it was the more frightening sound of a door slamming at the house.

"Geof . . . !"

"Shh." He shoved me back into the corner behind the shed door. My spine slammed against wood, causing me to gasp and the rain jacket I had on to rustle noisily. I reached back with my hands to touch bare wood and to keep my balance, and I froze in place, willing the fabric and my breathing to be quiet. The rainy air smelled so fresh at that moment, and it released the heavy sweet scent of the wood in the shed walls; I felt embraced by invisible fragrances that surrounded but couldn't hide us.

Cautiously, Geof risked a look outside but then quickly stepped back.

I said nothing, swallowing the *"What?"* that was in my mouth. Someone must be right outside, I thought, or else Geof would be trying to close the door, or—better yet—he'd be leading the way back to our car. My heart began thwapping like loose film on a projector.

*"Who's in there?"* I heard a man's voice shout. And then a yell: *"Luke! John! Somebody's hiding in the shed!"*

Silently, Geof reached out a hand to me, and I took it.

There was another slamming of doors back at the house, bam, bam, bam, then a loud movement of people near us, and Geof withdrew his hand from mine. In another moment, I felt something heavy fall onto my right foot, something that made a slight metallic clang when it landed, then my husband stepped forward and around the shed door, revealing his presence there.

But not mine.

I looked down. His car keys lay on my right shoe.

There was the sound of people moving around outside the shed, but very few words reached me over the racket the rain made as it coursed onto the roof and down the drain spouts. I thought I heard Geof identify himself by name and then, very clearly, as a policeman. I heard grunting, and somebody slammed up against the outside wall of the shed. Then there was silence or, rather, only the rain. I could only guess that the men of the Mayer clan had taken my husband with them, presumably back to the house, leaving the shed door wide open and me cowering behind it.

While I waited, afraid to move too soon, heavy footsteps pounded back to the shed. I saw a man's hand, a flash of a white-covered arm, and I pressed further into the corner as the fingers of the hand grabbed hold of the edge of the door, pulling it shut. Next, I heard metal going through metal.

*Please*, I prayed, *don't lock it.*

There was no sound of the padlock snapping shut, and with that realization came a great wave of relief that weakened my knees. I pushed my shoulders against the wood, so that my legs couldn't fail me, and I listened to footfalls running away from the shed, their noise disappearing into the rain. And then came a muffled slamming of a door.

I made myself take ten breaths before I moved again, and the first move was to snatch Geof's keys and hold onto them like a weapon. Then I inched forward until I could see out the crack where the edge of the door met the edge of the building. All was a rainy black outside, no light except from the house, no people in sight, nothing to stop me.

Except, possibly, the padlock, which was once again attached to the door but hanging open.

I pushed the door slightly, just enough to reach my fingers through, and then I jiggled the padlock until the clasp moved up and through the hole. On my first try it fell with a sodden thud onto the ground, and once again I experienced relief so intense it felt like an ocean wave swelling over me.

I pushed open the door just enough to slip through, then refastened the lock, now muddy as well as wet, just as they had left it. Wiping my hands on the rain jacket Geof had lent me, I considered my best course of action.

Run to the car phone in the Jeep?

But my husband was inside that glowing house.

I crept up to the back door again, drawn to it by the magnet that was Geof. Again, I peered through the crack in the curtain. This time, there was nobody in the kitchen, so I looked past it into the living room where all of the clan were gathered, all of them staring intently at the far end of the room.

This time the person in the yellow chair was my husband.

He'd removed his parka and his suit coat, or they'd been removed from him.

One of the big men in white had my husband's own gun pointed at him.

Geof was talking, looking the way he did at home when he wanted to persuade me to believe something that went against my natural instincts. What kind of story was he giving them, I wondered, to rationalize his presence in that shed with its treasure trove of evidence against these people?

The man with the gun lowered it.

I touched the window pane with my fingers and nearly wept with relief when I saw him actually lay the gun aside on a small table. Then the old man, Ronald Mayer, Sr., the white-haired man we had seen on the country road, stepped into my view, dressed all in white, and started talking to Geof.

Geof's face was turned up, listening.

Then he looked down at the white flooring. I watched as he put his face in his hands and then raised it, looking suddenly wretched and talking fast, from the looks of him.

And all the while, through all of it, David's Uncle Matthew was standing to one side, videotaping the whole scene.

I crept away from the door although I wanted desperately to batter it in, to ram my way into that damned house and to scatter men, women, and children as I dived for my husband, freeing him, grabbing his gun, saving him. If he needed saving. Maybe he didn't, that's what I couldn't know. My intelligence overrode my desire, and I left him there, feeling as if it was abandonment. I thought—hoped—that the best way to help him was to get to the car phone as fast as possible.

That short run through the rain was the loneliest I had ever made. The trees I was running toward appeared to be taller and darker than any trees ever had before, and the rain—the same rain that had been falling all day—felt suddenly as cold as the sides of knives pressed against my skin. I was terrified for myself and desperately afraid for the man in the yellow kitchen chair.

These were people who didn't forgive trespasses; they punished them! These people beat children and made the children believe it was only because the grown-ups loved them. And these people had my husband!

I flung myself at the Jeep as if it were an old friend, and once inside it again, I grabbed for the car phone, knowing the person I most wanted to reach for advice and for help was Sergeant Lee Meredith. But it was a useless effort. After a few increasingly despairing tries, I slammed the receiver back down in its cradle. Because of the interference of the storm or the distance from town or I didn't know what problems, I couldn't make the telephone connection to Port Frederick!

*Now what?* Wait for him to come out of that house?

Barely able to see through the rain coming down the windshield, I sat and waited for five minutes, ten, fifteen, until I got too frantic with worry to be able to bear it any longer. I started the Jeep and would have driven off and rocketed back down the highway for help, but I thought, *Wait. I'll try the phone one more time.*

"Information. What city, please?"

"Oh, my God! Oh, thank you! Port Frederick. Meredith, Lee."

I memorized the number the computer gave me.

"Blessed modern conveniences!" I babbled while I dialed again. Water was dripping from my hair, my jacket, from everywhere on me onto everything that I touched. "Oh, wonderful twentieth-century satellite telecommunications system, I love you!"

"This is Lee Meredith. Hello?"

"Oh, Lee, thank God! It's Jenny. Can you hear me? Let me talk, so I make sure you hear all this in case we lose our connection. Geof may be in trouble, Lee, and I need you to tell me what to do . . ."

I described the situation to her.

"Sit tight," she told me. "I'm coming, and I'm bringing reinforcements with me. But it may take me at least an hour to get it together and then to find you. You stay the hell away from those people, all right?"

"Yes."

She hung up even before I did.

And then I had nothing to do but worry again.

Five more minutes, another ten, fifteen . . .

I picked up the phone again on a whim of an idea.

"Information, what city, please?"

"I don't know, operator, but it's right outside Port Frederick, and the name is Mayer, Ronald, Sr."

"Would that be a city street or a rural route?"

"Rural route! Oh, yes!"

When the computer gave me that number, I memorized it, then dialed it before I could forget it and before I could stop and think, perhaps more wisely.

Somebody in the farmhouse picked up the phone.

"Mayer Farm," a woman said.

"Hello!" I said brightly, trying to cover the tremor in my voice. "This is Jennifer Cain. My husband was invited to your church service tonight, and I'm terribly sorry to disturb you, but I have an emergency here at home, and I just really need to talk to him. Could you ask him to come to the phone, please?"

There was a very long pause while I held my breath.

"Yes," she said finally, courteously. "I'll get him."

The next voice I heard was the only one I wanted to hear.

"Jenny?"

"Oh, my God, is that really you? Are you all right? Can you talk, can you listen?"

"Where are you?"

"In the car. Tell them I'm having an emergency appendectomy, tell them something, but tell them you have to leave and come home right away."

"I'll be right there!" he exclaimed, faking it. "Will you be okay until I get there? Tell them to take good care of you!"

And then he hung up the phone inside the house.

I didn't want to let him go; I felt he was only safe while I held on to him via the telephone line.

Now, I thought, I prayed, they have to let him go.

Because now they knew that other people knew he was there.

Again, I waited . . . five minutes . . . almost ten . . . and I was ready to call the farmhouse again when their front door opened. I held my breath, then released it when I saw my husband come out alone, moving slowly, wearing his parka again.

Geof continued to walk away from the farmhouse unimpeded.

No one followed him, though I thought I saw a beam of quick light as if somebody sneaked a peek by drawing a curtain back but then let it fall into place again.

My heart tugged him toward me, willing him to move faster, but he didn't. He walked slowly, head down, back slightly bent, one step at a time, carefully, as if he were not sure of his footing in the muddy darkness. Once, he turned and looked back at the glowing house as if he'd heard something, but then he turned slowly back around and resumed his long, wet walk.

"Here," I softly called to him through a window when he was close, and then I couldn't stand sitting there a moment longer, so I opened the door and ran out into the rain to meet him. He held out his arms, robotlike, and I hurried toward him. He caught me by my hands before I could embrace him.

"Get us out of here, Jenny."

I didn't stop to say a word but ran back to the car and started the engine while he climbed in slowly—oh, so slowly, I thought he'd never get in!—on the passenger's side. As I rapidly pulled us out onto the road leading to the highway, I told him, "I called the Mounties, Geof. Lee's rounding up some reinforcements and bringing them out here."

"Stop them," he said. "Call her back."

Using one hand to dial and the other to drive, I did as he asked and handed him the phone.

"False alarm, Lee," he told her. "They thought I was a prowler." He smiled, and only I could see how false it was. "We agreed to let each other go with only a warning this time."

"But Geof," I started to say, "what—"

He reached over and squeezed my right hand until it hurt enough to shut me up.

*What about the way they manhandled you?* I'd been going to protest. *What about the way they videotaped you, what about the gun they took off you and held up to you?*

After a little more quiet consultation with his would-be rescuer, he quietly replaced the receiver, and then I could say it. "Geof, what about—"

"Thanks for calling out the troops," he interrupted, his voice sounding odd, thin, strained. "You did just what I hoped you would do when I threw my keys at you. I'm sorry about all this, I know it probably scared the hell out of you."

I could only nod my head.

"Yeah, well, me, too."

In the darkness of the front seat, he looked at me out of the face of a stranger—someone older, haggard, hurting. I moved instinctively to touch him, but again, he fended me off.

"Geof . . ."

"You mind driving?"

"Of course not."

"Thanks. I'd rather not talk either."

All the way back, he leaned forward, his head in his hands as if he was thinking deeply or was too tired even to lean back.

"Geof, are you all right?"

"Apart from being embarrassed, you mean? Jenny, just drive straight on home, will you?"

"Don't we have to go to the station? Make a report? Get in deep trouble? Take our medicine?"

"Yes." He was still talking into his hands, not lifting his face. "But we won't, all right?"

I looked over at him, reached out, and started to touch his shoulder, but he moved a little just at that moment, and my hand fell on thin air. "Okay," I said. "Whatever you want to do."

"Let's just go home, Jenny."

"You really don't want to talk to me, do you?"

"No," he said, his face in his hands.

I drove my husband home, both of us silent, and the only noise coming from the rain and the traffic.

Geof groaned when he saw our driveway. "Damn!"

The Reverend Hardy Eberhardt's car, his old Pontiac sedan, was parked in front of our house. When I stopped our car in the driveway rather than going on into the garage, my husband moved, his hand angling for the door handle, and I thought I heard him make a sound like a hiss indrawn through his teeth. In a voice so tight and strained it frightened me, he said, "Ministers have a code of confidentiality, like shrinks, right? So if Hardy sees some secrets tonight, he's damned well got to keep them."

"Secrets . . . ?"

Again, I reached out to him, this time intending only to stroke his face, still damp from the rain. But he moved away from me again, and this time he said, breaking my heart, "Don't touch me, Jenny."

# 28

 HE WALKED ALONE TOWARD OUR FRONT DOOR, where Hardy was sitting on our stoop under our porch light, gazing out at the rain and at our arrival. He had on a brown suit with a pale red shirt, undone at the neck. When the minister stood up and started down the steps toward us, I saw a necktie stuffed in his coat pocket.

" 'Bout time," he joked. "It's hell to drop in on people without any warning and then discover they're not even home."

As we neared him, I brought up the rear, hovering over the progress of the man in front of me. Geof took a step on the gravel with his right foot, but when he stepped onto his left again, it buckled, and he lurched forward.

"Hardy, help him!" I cried.

"No!" Geof took another step, faltered again, and swayed where he stood, like a drunk trying to get his balance.

Hardy ran the rest of the way over the gravel toward us and reached out to support Geof, who stopped him by commanding again, "No! I'll lean on you, Hardy, just let me lean on you!"

"What's the matter with you, boy?" Hardy's voice was

brusque. "Somebody shoot you? You finally forget to duck?"
I heard Geof's strained laughter as the two big men slowly
made it to the door, the one leaning heavily on the other.
"I've been paying for my sins, Hardy. They finally caught up
with me."

" 'Bout time," the minister retorted, echoing his greeting to
us. The gruff, macho persona he was feigning was just the shot
of vigor Geof needed; I could practically see my husband draw
strength from the tone of his friend's deep voice and the touch
of his beefy shoulder. *This is why cops have partners*, I thought
irrelevantly. And more relevantly, *This is why people have
friends*. But when our friend looked back at me, over Geof's
shoulder, I saw in his eyes the apprehension I was feeling in
my heart. I scurried past them with my keys to get the doors
unlocked, then we all made it inside as I turned on lights ahead
of them.

"Couple of drowned rats," Hardy observed of us.

Geof headed straight for our kitchen, walking like Franken-
stein's monster, staggering a bit, waving off Hardy and me as
we fluttered around him like useless moths around a burning
lamp.

"Please," he instructed us through clenched jaw, "do not fucking touch me."

"I'll kill them," I promised him, nearly hissing it.

He smiled coldly at me. "Fine with me, sweetheart."

When he reached our kitchen sink, he put one hand on it
for support and with the other he began to try to pull off his
rain parka.

"What's he doing?" Hardy asked me.

"He can't do it by himself," I said. "Geof, stop. We'll do it.
We'll be careful, I promise. Hardy, help me get this off of him,
but for God's sake be careful! Don't let anything touch him if
you can help it."

"It's my back," Geof told me in a low voice. "Just don't let it
touch my back, Jenny. Please."

"I'll kill them! I'll kill them!" I swore.

"I suppose," Hardy said as he jumped to assist me, "that one
of you is eventually going to tell me what kind of emergency we

have going on here. Fine thing," he added as we slipped the last of the parka over Geof's head, "a man comes out to drink a beer with his friends and tell them *his* troubles, and they go and steal his thunder by having problems of their own."

I smiled thinly at him. "Inconsiderate of us."

His return smile was a worried one. "Terribly."

"Stop that," I said again to Geof, whose right hand had strayed to his shirt buttons. "I'll do it, it'll be faster and hurt less." While Hardy went to lay the parka on the counter behind the sink, I undid Geof's buttons one by one. Then Hardy turned around, and he got his first glimpse of Geof's back.

"Sweet Jesus," he breathed. "What is this?"

I finished unbuttoning, so that I could walk around and look. At the sight of Geof's shirt, I just stood there and started to cry. Hardy put his arms around me as much to comfort himself, I think, as to offer solace to me, since neither of us dared to lay a hand on Geof.

"It's not that bad, is it?" Geof asked us.

My husband's shirt was red with blood that had soaked through from his back. And when we worked up the courage— all three of us—to gently strip the cloth from his skin, with me having to control my sobs so that my fingers wouldn't shake so hard that they slipped and hurt him, we discovered that his back was striped by shallow, diagonal cuts. Pinstripes. There were so many of them, laid across him one by one, that his bare skin appeared pinstriped.

It was then that Sergeant Lee Meredith walked into the kitchen. We hadn't even heard the front door open; I couldn't even remember if we'd closed it.

"No problem out there, huh?" she said, pausing in the doorway. In trousers, shirt, and jacket, she looked dressed for work. "Am I taking you to a hospital, or do we call an ambulance?"

"You stay the hell out of this, Lee," Geof commanded her.

The sergeant stared at him. "Stay out—?"

"These cuts need stitches," Hardy said.

But Geof shook his head. "I doubt it, Hardy. They're not that deep, are they? They've got flogging down to a fine science out there, so they can tend to their own wounds."

Reluctantly, feeling deeply hurt myself, I examined the pinstripes more closely. "He's right. If he doesn't get infected, I think
they'll close by themselves. But what about scarring? If you don't
get the right medicine on them?"

"No hospital!" he snapped. "No doctors! No talking about this
outside of this room."

"Why not, Lieutenant?" Lee sounded furious with him.

"Geof." I came around in front of him, touching his face lightly
with my fingertips, moving my fingers to my lips, returning them
to his face, unable to stop touching him, comforting him, wanting
to heal him. "This is what they did to you for trespassing?"

"No." He looked into my eyes. "This is not the penance for
trespassing. I don't know what that would be, only a couple of
whops with the belt, maybe." He tried to laugh but failed at the
effort. "This, my love, is the penance for impregnating a teenage
girl out of wedlock."

My fingers went to my mouth again. "They knew!"

He nodded, sighed. "They know now because I told them. They
wanted me to confess to something little, like trespassing? I decided to give them something big, like Judy and me and their
grandson."

"Lieutenant!"

All three of us snapped our attention to the woman standing
in the doorway with her hands on her hips. "What the hell was
the matter with you out there? Why'd you tell us to go away,
why'd you say everything was under control? They've assaulted
a police officer, for Christ's sake, excuse me, Reverend. We
should have busted those people, right then, but we can sure as
hell still do it."

Geof didn't answer her but said plaintively, like a man who
didn't think he could take much more, "Can't somebody clean
me up?"

I turned on the faucet. "Hardy, look two drawers down for
clean towels. Lee, look in the bathroom upstairs for antiseptics,
painkillers, gauze, anything you can find that you think will do
the job." I looked squarely at my husband as I held a clean white
towel under the cool water. "This is not going to hurt me more
than it hurts you. Grit your teeth, my darling."

259

"Hardy?" Geof asked, and his friend came around front so that the two men were looking at one another. "Distract me, Hardy. Talk to me about something, tell me about all your problems, better yet, preach me a sermon."

Hardy smiled, although his eyes looked closer to tears.

"That's a new one," he said. "A Novocaine sermon. I've had people tell me my sermons put them to sleep, but you're the first person to actually call them narcotics." I touched the first damp towel to Geof's back. His whole body contracted with the pain. "Okay," Hardy said quickly, "okay," and he began to pace the kitchen, drawing Geof's attention to him, making like an evangelist preacher, talking bombastically, gesticulating, in other words, putting on a bravura performance to distract his audience of one from his agony, while the sergeant served as nurse's aide to my ministrations to Geof's devastated flesh.

"You see the problem?" Hardy began, widening his eyes dramatically, pointing like a preacher at Geof's wounds. "This is what I've been talking about, the problem of believing in sin! Brothers and sisters, if you believe in sin, then by definition you have to believe in vengeance, and if you believe in that, you must also believe in punishment."

I smiled at him over Geof's shoulder, egging him on.

"And that concept works backward, too! You may think yourself a modern person, you may think you laugh at the very idea of such an old-fashioned notion as sin, but if you ever punish anybody for anything, if you ever want anybody to suffer in any way for any cause, then, trust me, you do believe in sin!"

Hardy paced the kitchen like a small stage and worked the kitchen table like a pulpit, banging on it, but gently, not wanting to arouse another and unnecessary flinch in his audience.

He took off his suit coat to free his arms.

"But you see, my friends, the problem with vengeance is that it's insane, because it never ends! And that's because it never punishes only the one who is accused of sinning. It goes on forever, like the pebble dropped in a pool, creating widening circles of pain that hurt everybody they touch. Just look at what happened in the wake of Ron and Judy's deaths. They believed they

260

sinned; they believed they deserved punishment, but it didn't end with their deaths. It reached out to corrupt his brothers, their son, their neighbor . . . and look what it is doing to this very household!"

Hardy paused, his attention caught by the suffering we all heard in Geof's low moans and intermittent gasps. But then our friend pressed bravely on, making an absolute, eye-catching ministerial spectacle of himself in our kitchen. I loved Hardy very much at that moment.

"Punishment is a voracious bastard!" he preached to us. "You can never satisfy it. It eats everything in its path, reaching out for new victims, going on and on; until, at last, somebody in the long chain of retribution stops believing in it. By that time it has left a wake of such devastation that the original sin and its original punishment look positively puny by comparison."

"But what's the answer, Hardy?" Geof whispered.

"Mercy," the minister said simply, and for a moment his arms fell to his sides, and he stood still, just looking at the tableau in front of him. Hardy stuck his hands in his pockets and said in a normal tone of voice, "Let us be easier on ourselves from the beginnings of our lives. How about that for a revolutionary idea? Let us begin by being merciful to the children from the moment of their births. Let us consider their little errors to be only that, mistakes to be gently corrected and then forgotten rather than sins to be punished."

I wiped away a bit of clotted blood, only to have the cut begin to bleed anew. Geof's breath was coming fast and shallow, he was panting like a woman in labor. Hardy noticed that our patient's capacity to endure the torment was reaching its outer limit, and so he picked up his preaching pace again.

"Parents claim that we only punish our children because we love them, but that is a lie, brothers and sisters! We only punish whom we hate. And whom we hate we would kill."

I stopped, my hands stilled, and stared at him. "My God, Hardy—"

We were all silent for a moment, until Geof made a sound deep in his chest, like an animal suffering.

261

"And the children of people who don't believe in sin?" I asked quickly over the sob caught in my own throat.

"They have a chance to grow up to be merciful to one another," Hardy said, coming closer to us, speaking eagerly, sincerely, "and to be free of the desire to punish each other and themselves."

"We're finished," I announced in another few minutes.

"Thank you," Geof whispered.

"I'm going to the bathroom to wash off," Lee said, since I was using the kitchen sink to do that for my own hands. Geof still clung to the edge of the sink, like a man stunned into immobility. His back looked pink now, raw, like a steak that a cook has lightly scored with a serrated knife; a little blood still seeped from some of the cuts, but others were closing because of swelling. It seemed to me that his whole back was puffing up. We had already given him two capsules of the strongest painkillers we had in the house, pills left over from treatment for a root canal. He closed his eyes. I decided to let him remain like that, recovering, until he was ready to speak or to move again.

Abruptly, Hardy sat down in a kitchen chair.

"What happened to you tonight?" I asked him.

"Church meeting. I made those same points in my sermon on Sunday." He smiled at me, and his own pain was there on his handsome face for me to witness. "It seems to have upset a few people, although I tried to do it gently. I guess I don't have much practice at being a loving parent of a congregation; I've been a bit of a fire and brimstone man myself."

"No kidding," Geof murmured dryly, barely getting the words out.

"So tonight I had to take my punishment, too."

"Not impressed," Geof whispered.

Hardy nodded and smiled sympathetically up at him.

"You unregenerate sinner, you," I said to our friend fondly.

"Hang in there," Geof encouraged him.

When Hardy heard that, his eyes got moist again.

"Fine one to talk," he said and cleared his throat.

"If you need a job, Hardy . . ." I left it hanging.

"Thank you, Jenny Lynn. I may be calling you."

"Okay," I said. There was now a pile of bloody towels in the sink, and the sergeant had come back into the kitchen. "We're putting you to bed, buster."

After the other two helped me to get our patient up the stairs, Geof said privately to me, "You didn't believe any of that silly bullshit of Hardy's, did you?"

I had undressed him down to his skivies and laid him on his stomach, turned off the air conditioner, turned on the heat, and pulled the sheet and summer blanket up to his waist. He lay now with his face toward the left side on his pillow, facing where I would lie, with his arms at his sides, about an inch away from his body.

"Every word," I told him as I leaned down to give him a kiss on his left temple. He laughed into the pillow. "Every word," I repeated, kissing his forehead, his hair, and the side of his mouth. "Geof, I'm sorry, but I have to spray antiseptic on you."

No answer. And then a crisp, "Get it over with."

I did it, covering every inch of his raw back, feeling like a torturer the whole time, knowing how that "little sting" must be magnified a thousand times by the extent of his wounds. I hadn't wanted to do it downstairs; I'd wanted to lay him gently down up here in our bedroom, give him privacy and the comfort of our bed for this last assault on him.

Afterward, I sat on the floor, giving him time to recover again.

When he took a deep breath and moved slightly, I decided it was probably okay to try to talk to him. I walked around the bed and crouched down beside the other side of the mattress, so that I could see his face. "Geof. Tell me that you don't want to keep this a secret because you think you deserve this punishment."

"Christ, is that what you think?"

"Take it easy. I want to be reassured, that's all."

"The reason I want this kept quiet, Jenny, is that they threatened David. They told me that if I report this, they'll get him. Their words. Get him. Sometime, somewhere, some one of them will make him pay my penance for turning them in. They're patient, Jenny, they're patient and they're deadly. It's not just a matter of putting the men in jail even if we could manage to

263

lock them all up. There are the women to consider, and I don't know how violent they are; and someday, the men would get out of prison if I even managed to get them convicted of something. Look how long they waited to pay Clemmons back for hurting Judy. They'll wait. And then they'll get David, some time or some place that I can't help him."

"We have to let them get away with this?"

"Until I think of a better idea."

*Or I do*, I thought but didn't say.

I kissed him good night again, hiding from him the rage that felt like a time bomb in my heart.

# 29

"GET HIM INTO BED ALL RIGHT?" LEE ASKED, BACK in the kitchen.

I blinked, then rubbed my eyes. The lights seemed too bright after the dark stairway. "Yes. I knocked him out with a billy club, and that put him right to sleep. I hoped it might bash some sense into him, too, but don't count on it. Where's Hardy?"

"Home. Said he heard his wife calling to him."

"He's a love, isn't he?"

"Um." She was seated in one of our kitchen chairs, and now she pulled out a second one for me. She'd put her jacket back on, and I realized it was still cool in the house; the central heating hadn't kicked in quite enough to take the chill out of the storm yet. I could see the gun at Lee's waist, where her jacket fell back. She looked tense, unhappy, explosive. "Sit down. Why have you come downstairs looking as if you want to kill somebody? What's going on with *your* love?"

"He's lost his mind over this kid, Lee." I sat, put my palms together, pressed them between my thighs for warmth. "You want some coffee?"

"No."

"Me either. I'm already on hyperalert. I can't thank you enough for all the help you tried to give him tonight, even if he wouldn't take it."

"How could this happen?" she burst out. "Geof let himself get whipped? They had to have held guns on him. I *know* him. He'd *never* let anyone do this to him, not without a hell of a fight—"

I had to stop Lee from pursuing her anger and her very logical questions. Geof wanted to protect David.

David . . .

And then I had it: a tiny hint of a plan. "Lee, can you wait here for a couple of hours? No, never mind, that's asking way too much, how about this: You go on home, and I'll come by your house—"

"Why do you want me to wait here?"

"I think I know where the kid is. I could try to talk to him."

"What will that accomplish?"

"I don't know," I said in utter truth. "But it's the only thing I can think of at the moment, and I'm about ready to try anything."

She thought about that and then said, as I'd hoped she would, "I'd better wait here. In case he wakes up, I can help him. If he asks for you, I'll tell him I'm letting you sleep for a few hours."

"Perfect. I'll try to be back within a couple of hours."

"Where is the kid, Jen?"

I looked at the clock over the refrigerator. Eleven-thirty. David would have already left his new job at the filling station, since his shift ended at ten. "I think he might be staying at the next-door neighbors' house, remember them?"

"A mother and her son, right? Montgomery, Damon, Sheila."

"Very good, Sergeant." I tried to grin at her. I felt guilty, knowing she would never be so sanguine about waving me off on my own to find David if she knew everything: about the animal corpses, the graffiti, the confession tapes. I should have been ashamed of myself for fooling her into thinking she was sticking around just for the sake of being a good friend, when all I really wanted her there for was her gun and her badge to protect the man upstairs in case he needed it and for her authority in case I returned with a reason to use it.

"Don't let that man out of this house," I warned her.

Lee patted the very item at her hip that was endearing her to me at that moment. "If he moves, I'll shoot him," she promised me.

"Just not any vital organs, please."

As I exited through the back door, she called out, "What do you consider 'vital'?"

I barely registered the drive back into town.

It had stopped raining, but I didn't know that until I got out of the car again; I hadn't even noticed that driving was easier, safer. All the way in, I was formulating what I wanted to ask David, all the things we needed to know.

I walked up to a completely dark house and rang the bell several times without hesitation. Damn all these secretive people. Somebody was going to tell me something on this night, in this house.

"David?" asked Damon Montgomery to my query. He made a show of rubbing his eyes, avoiding my gaze. "He's not here, I thought you knew where he was."

"Mr. Montgomery, do not give me any shit. Somebody told David about that job at the Amoco station, and you're the only person it could have been. He's not anyplace else we have looked, but he's here in town working every night. So that means he's staying with you."

It didn't necessarily, but luckily, that didn't occur to me. I was stuck on the idea that they had baby-sat David all those times, and that convinced me they were doing the same thing now.

"Has something happened?" he hedged.

"My husband has been nearly killed by those maniacs that David calls family," I exaggerated. "And I want to talk to him. Now."

"Oh, my God," Damon Montgomery said on an indrawn breath. "You'd better come in. I'll get him."

But a voice behind him said, "I'm already here, Day."

"The porch," Montgomery urged. "We'll go there, so we don't wake up Mother."

"Wake up Mother?" questioned a clear, derisive voice from the stairway to the second floor. I looked up and saw her there in a bathrobe. She said sarcastically, "Mother has already been disturbed, Mother will join you on the porch if you don't mind."

"No," the kid said to both of them, but he was looking at me from out of the shadows of the hallway where he stood. "Just her and me."

"Please," I urged, for once agreeing with him.

"I don't know . . ." Damon hesitated.

"Fine," his mother said.

# 30

IT WAS ONLY ONCE I WAS SEATED ON THAT PORCH with David that I realized I was still wearing that damn beige dress, now spotted with blood, and my ruined shoes. I'd even slipped Geof's blue rain jacket on again when I left the house, so I was wearing exactly the same clothes, down to the no-longer fluffy bow tying back my hair. It and my hair were stringy and plastered down now. *What a sight I am*, I thought.

The kid had on blue jeans, nothing else.

"Aren't you cold?"

"I am cool," he said sardonically, making a joke of it.

"Let me tell you what happened tonight, David."

He shrugged, but I didn't let that discourage me. At some point in my recital, he stopped looking me in the eye and began to gaze off into the distance beyond the screens that encircled us on the porch. And his posture changed, his spine curving out of its usual straight rigidity into something more hunched, making him look as if he were hiding something. When I finished, he said after a few beats of silence, "So?"

I had nearly talked all of the emotion out of me. All I had left by then was exhausted, desperate sincerity, but at least it didn't sound like pleading.

"David, none of this makes any sense without your memory of it. Nobody else remembers everything. Or, if they do, they're not saying the truth. Do you really want your father cleared? If you do, answer my questions."

He stared coldly at me from the couch where Damon had sat.

"How old were you when your mother divorced your father?"

For a moment, I didn't think he was going to cooperate, even now. And then he muttered, "Eight."

"Why did they split up, David?"

"*Mom* split," he said bitterly. "Dad never deserted us."

"All right, why did she leave him?"

He gave me an ugly grin. "Love!"

"Really?"

"How would I know? I was just a kid."

"Did you and she go to live with Dennis Clemmons immediately?"

"Yes."

"Did he have a job then?"

"Dennis the Menacing? Yes."

"What was it?"

"Construction, working day labor for my dad's company."

"Your father kept Clemmons on? The man who stole his wife and his son? Why did he do that?"

"Because Mom wouldn't take any money from Dad, no child support or alimony, no settlement, nothing. And Dad knew we had to have money to live somehow, so he let Dennis keep his job."

That bespoke a generous spirit that surprised me; no, it shocked me, because it bore no resemblance to the man in the videotapes, the one I thought of still as the Executioner.

"Why wouldn't your mother take any money from him?"

David shrugged. "Pride, I guess. Stubborn. I don't know."

Pride? Judy Baker Mayer hadn't been a woman with a whole lot of "pride" to spare, it seemed to me. Stubborn? What for? Although maybe some unexplainable stubbornness helped to account for why Judy had applied to Sabrina's office for state financial aid—to keep from taking any help from Ron Mayer, even indirectly through Dennis's job.

"How do you know that about your father, David?"

The expression in his eyes was unreadable. "Mom told me so."

That statement stalled me again; I was once again completely baffled by this family's strange intertwinings of apparent love and apparent hate. Then I doggedly pressed on; if I couldn't figure it all out yet, maybe I just didn't have all the facts yet.

"Okay, so how old were you when Dennis lost that job?"

"Uh, ten."

*Two years, for two years Ron Mayer had provided a job and a salary to the man who was his wife's second husband and his son's stepfather.*

"Why'd he get fired?"

"He beat Mom up."

"Your father knew about that?"

He sarcastically replied, "I think he figured it out."

"So he fired Dennis."

"Well, yeah, but that's not why he said he did it, I mean he didn't want to humiliate Mom by telling people what Dennis did to her. So what he told people, what the public excuse was, was that Dennis was a lousy employee, which was true, and that he was a criminal, because of being caught burglarizing those houses."

"Why'd your parents say your mom had Parkinson's disease? Why not something else, like a car accident?"

He shrugged again. "It was the first thing that came out of Mom's mouth the first time somebody asked her what happened to her. Then she had to stick to that story." The bitterness piled up in his voice again. "We all did, Dad and me, too."

"Were you there when Dennis did it?"

"I'm not going to talk about that," he said quickly. "Ever."

I waited, but he remained absolutely silent.

"I understand—"

"I fucking doubt it."

"Have it your way. So . . . Dennis got caught, then he beat up your mom, and then he got fired, is that the way things happened?"

He nodded almost imperceptibly.

271

"And she suffered the nerve damage that put her into the wheelchair, and *then* she applied for state financial assistance, and then . . ."

"Dennis went to prison."

"And your mom went back to your dad?"

"Yeah, and she divorced Dennis and married Dad again, and we all lived happily ever after."

I felt myself near tears and fought them back.

"So when did Dennis suffer his injury?"

"You mean when did he get the shit beat out of him as he so richly deserved? Right after he got out of prison."

"Do you know who did it to him?"

"Yeah, my dad's brothers."

I wanted to take a deep breath, to react, but I knew I couldn't, that I had to disguise my responses.

"Do you know why?"

"The fact that he beat up my mother isn't enough for you?"

"I don't know, David, was that the only reason why?"

He let out a deep, angry, impatient breath. "He said he was coming back for her. And me. My uncles made sure he didn't."

"Did your dad want them to?"

"No!" He was angry suddenly, defensive for his father. "He wasn't like that, he wasn't like them." David looked down at the ground between his feet and then up at me, directly into my eyes. "Like me."

Again, I tried to hide my reaction; I didn't dare let him see how much he frightened me by doing that, looking like that, saying that.

"Whose idea was it to build the ramp for Dennis?"

"My dad's."

Again, he had shocked me. "Why?"

He shrugged and turned slightly away from me. "Because that's how he was."

I wanted to embrace him suddenly in spite of everything, I wanted to reach out and grab him and take him into a tight hug and comfort him as I told him, "No, that wasn't how he was." But I couldn't comfort this boy, I couldn't touch him. I was afraid of him.

I sat back, pushing my palms into my thighs to still the visible trembling of my hands.

"David, those videos, those confessions . . ."

I saw him tense, and I was frightened again.

"There were penances, too . . ." I said.

I waited, but he didn't say anything.

"Beatings. Who did the beatings, David?"

"My uncles," he said quickly, too quickly.

"What about your father?"

"Sometimes." Defensively, he added, "He had to. All the men did, I would have had to do it, too, if I'd stuck around, but that was one good thing about Mom leaving Dad, it broke our ties to the Carpenters, and there's no way I'm ever going back to that now, no way, not even if they nail me to a fucking cross."

How was I to reconcile the paradox of a father who made sure his divorced wife was taken care of on the one hand but who could punish the tiny child in the film so cruelly on the other?

It was then that I thought of the embrace—the warm, loving embrace—at the end of that video. And I remembered the warm, loving voice at the close of the videos of Judy and of Dennis and how that voice said so forgivingly, "Good."

That was Ron, too.

"Did somebody make them do the beatings, David?"

"Yeah, sure, Granddad. He's the"—he snorted with sardonic amusement—"patriarch."

"He's in charge?"

"Fuck, yes. It's all his ideas, everything."

The patriarch with a sword that cut two ways: with punishment, he controlled them; with forgiveness, he controlled them.

"Anything else?" David asked, his voice less guarded now.

"Who killed Dennis Clemmons?"

His head came up, his dark eyes blazing; instantly, he was all tension. "My uncles."

"You know that?"

"I don't have proof if that's what you mean!"

"Do you think they killed your parents?"

He shot to his feet. "That's what you're supposed to goddamn

273

prove, damn you! What do I have to do, give it to you on a fucking platter?''

*Yes, please!* I thought. *Serve it to us!*

I opened my mouth to ask another question, but he walked across the porch floor and then passed through the doorway. Pushing myself out of the rocking chair, I hurried after him.

''David, wait, please.''

He was heading for the stairs.

''Why did you come see us when you did? Why then?''

He had his hand on the banister, but he turned to face me, his face as hard as his voice, nothing young, nothing innocent about him, except perhaps his faith in his father. ''Because I found the scrapbook, Mom left it for me, and she left me those tapes of her confession and Dennis's.''

''Is that what you meant when you said your mother told you so, about Geof?''

He nodded yes.

''Where'd you find those things after she died?''

''Here.'' His voice was a little softer, holding what sounded like a touch of gratitude to the only friends he had. ''Damon kept a box of stuff for my mom here, personal stuff that she didn't want anybody in Dad's family to see, because they'd make her confess for it and do penance. You can't keep anything personal around those people.''

A gentle voice came down to us from the top step. ''I didn't know what was in it—''

''Day?''

'It's okay, David, I'll tell this part.'' Damon Montgomery, dressed in pajamas and bathrobe, looked down on us, talking softly. ''She kept a box here, like David said, and after she died, I was too heartbroken to dig into it for a while. When I got into it, I saw it was for David, she'd even put his name on it, so I knew she wanted David to have everything that was in it. I think she put that tape and that scrapbook there the very morning she died, because she came over that day—Mother told me—asking for me, but I was at a client's.'' His voice caught in regret. ''Mother told me that Judy had a videotape with her and a big pink book. Mom said Judy told her that she was going out to the Mayer farm that afternoon with Ron."

"Wait a minute," I said. "Just one tape?" I turned to David. "Where'd you find the other one?"

"In my parents' VCR," he said. "Like you did."

"And all of that made you come out to find Geof, because—"

"Because then I knew my uncles had done a penance on my stepfather." His voice had turned cold and old again. "They waited until he got out of prison, then they beat him up. They could do it then, because Mom and I had already gone back to live with Dad. If they could do that, I figured they killed Mom and Dad, too."

"Why would they do that, David?"

But that was a question that threatened his view of the world, and his only response was anger. He jabbed his right hand in the air at me. "That's that fucking cop's job to find out!"

"David," gently cautioned the voice on the top step.

"You've been helping him all along, haven't you, Day?" I moved closer to the banister to see him better. "You've been helping David to lead us around by the nose. You turned the air-conditioning on next door, didn't you? He must have called you to tell you we were on the way. And you gave us that cocka-mamy story, so we wouldn't suspect that you'd been in there right before we were."

I looked at both of them. "Who did the graffiti?"

"I did," David said challengingly.

"Only at the school," Damon gently corrected him. "I did it next door."

"And the dead animals?" I heard my voice rise in my distress. "Did you do that?"

"Big deal," David said. "They were already dead. Road kill, for God's sake."

"I'm sorry if that upset you." Damon Montgomery sounded embarrassed. "I thought David was getting a little carried away, but we only wanted to get your attention, you see. And keep it. Can you please understand? It was so important, and we didn't know anything else to do. Who would pay attention to a teenager with no evidence? Or to me? I'm such an authoritative kind of person!" He laughed a little in self-mockery. "So David kept watch on your activities until we were pretty certain we'd hooked your husband into investigating the case again."

"Just a couple of boy scouts," I said.

"You've got to clear my dad," the boy said, and for a moment, I thought he sounded like a boy, and I was tempted to believe that's all he was and to look at what they had done as escapades, mere pranks. But then I remembered the high school principal's description of the chalk drawing in the art room, and I thought of what it would be like to lift road kill from the highway and carry it to our door, and I thought of this "boy" lingering around our property, spying on us. And the "man" at the top of the stairs? Maybe, I thought, he was the only child here.

"I'm tired, and I'm going home," I told them.

Nobody stopped me, but only Damon said good night.

Nobody stopped me in the house, that is. Somebody was waiting for me near my car, however, crouching in the shadows of an oak tree: Damon's mother, Sheila.

"Please," she whispered, and I was so tired I didn't even flinch. "Let me talk to you."

I walked into the darkness under the tree and looked down at her.

"They told me what they've been doing," I said.

She let out a sigh. "Thank God. I wanted to myself, but he's my son, I was afraid he'd go to jail. He won't, will he?"

"I don't know." But I crouched down beside her then, because finally I realized that what I had taken for coldness in her, for a kind of snooty matriarchal anger, had only been fear all along. Fear for her child and, as I was about to learn, for herself. I said, wondering why she felt she had to approach me like this in such an odd, furtive way, "Are you all right, Mrs. Montgomery?"

"I baby-sat him," she whispered. "So many times. I loved him. But you know, cruel families beget monsters. I don't know any longer what sort of child he is. If he's his mother's son, then he is sad and lonely. But if he is his father's child, then I'm afraid of him, of our own dear David. I'm afraid of his influence on my son. I'm afraid to sleep at night. I'm just so afraid . . ."

She touched my jacket sleeve, and I took her hand to hold.

"May I take you somewhere else to sleep tonight?" I asked her.

"No, I have to go back in there."

I realized she was afraid to leave her son alone with . . . Geof's son.

"Please," she said to me, "find out what kind of boy he is."

She shooed me away then, so that no one would become too suspicious of the time it had taken me to start my car and to drive away. I hated to leave her. I suspected she had chosen to sit on the ground and wait for me because she was so frightened that her legs wouldn't hold her up until I came back out of her house alive again.

# 31

 "TELL ME AGAIN, JENNY, SLOWLY."

I was so tired, but I forced myself to recite the whole thing one more time for Lee Meredith. "Judy went to live with Dennis when David was eight years old," I began.

This time through, I told the sergeant everything. Everything. I handed everything over to her as well—the scrapbook, the list of Judy's telephone answering service clients that Marsha Sandy had obtained for me, the videotaped confessions, even Lee's own files that she had brought over for us to study. As I talked, she wrote down the chronology, and when we were finished, she studied it for a few moments, then looked up.

"You asked the right questions, Jenny."

"Thank you, but then why don't we have all the answers?"

"Because this raises still more questions." And she ticked them off on her fingers. "Was this the first time Clemmons was violent with Judy?"

"Yes, I think it was."

"Okay, then what made him go off like that?"

"The stress of losing his job?"

"No, no, he hurt her first and *then* he got fired."

"Right." Wearily, I put my confused head in my hands. "Right."

"Why did she leave Ron in the first place?" Lee asked, pointing to a third of her fingers, going down her list, "we still don't know that, and why did she go back to him in the second place?"

"Financial security? She needed a home, food, a father for David?"

"Could be any of those, yes."

"What else?"

"I don't know." Suddenly she was moving on her feet, looking down at me. "I'm going back down to the station to check Clemmons's arrest and conviction record one more time, you want to come with me? No, what am I thinking of, you have to stay with him." She pointed to the ceiling where Geof had slept all the time I'd been gone.

"I'm exhausted anyway."

Lee smiled sympathetically at me. "I know. You did great. I'm sorry, this is all my fault, all of it, if I'd done a better job with the first investigation, you wouldn't be in this mess now."

I shook my head but didn't have the oomph to argue with her.

"You'll be all right alone?" she asked me.

"Lee, if he was going to hurt me, he would have hurt me."

David, I meant, because that's who she suspected now.

She nodded, looking momentarily valiant. "Nobody's going to hurt either of you."

*Too late*, I thought but refrained from saying.

An hour and a half later, she woke me up, calling from the station, sounding jubilant. Beside me, Geof slept through the ringing of the telephone.

"Jenny, I've got it. Listen to this! Dennis Clemmons attacked Judy after he was arrested. Jenny, it was his first arrest for burglary. I think that's the stress that put him over the edge. But why pick on her? I asked myself. Just because the wife is the usual target? Maybe or maybe not . . . and so I got to thinking about what that neighbor said to you and Geof, how Clemmons beat her with the telephone, remember that?"

"Yes . . ."

"Why a phone, Jenny? Pretty weird weapon when he could have used his fists or a dozen other things. But a *phone?* What did a phone have to do with it?"

"Her answering service . . ."

"Bingo. Yes. I checked the address of the house where Clemmons was arrested against the list of Judy's clients, and guess what, Jenny? The house where Dennis Clemmons was picked up for burglary that night was owned by one of Judy's telephone answering service clients."

"And so . . . she was supplying him with his targets?"

"Yes, whether she was aware of it or not—"

"In her taped confession, Lee! She called herself a thief!"

"Ah. She'd always know when her clients were going to be away, wouldn't she, because she was taking their messages for them?"

"That's no reason to beat her, though."

"She turned him in, Jenny."

"Oh, my God."

"And he knew it or guessed it, or she confessed it, and he beat her up with the frigging symbolic telephone, no less."

"Is that in your files, that she turned him in?"

"No." I heard a sad, satisfied note in the sergeant's voice. "It only says, 'Anonymous tip, woman caller.' The anonymous woman caller gave us the exact address of a burglary in progress."

"Lee, do you think that Dennis Clemmons killed Ron and Judy Mayer?"

I could feel my heart beating in dreadful anticipation of the solution of the murder of David's parents. I waited for Lee to say the word *yes.*

"No . . ."

"No!"

"He was alibied, Jenny . . . you're forgetting."

"But . . ."

"He *didn't* do it, he couldn't have."

"Well, why not?" I yelled and nearly threw my own phone across the room in my frustration and disappointment. If it wasn't him, it had to be David, which was horrible, or David's uncles, which was nearly as horrible because it would put Geof back in their path again. "I want him to have done it, Lee! He was a monster! Why can't he have been the one?"

"Jenny, we're getting there."

"We're not, we're not!"

"We are. Listen to me. We are closer now."

But I didn't want to be any closer to the darkness. *Please,* I thought despairingly as I hung up. *Please, no closer.*

I wanted to slide closer in bed to my husband, though, to slip into his embrace, to get our arms protectively around each other. But I couldn't. I didn't dare touch him.

I fell asleep about the time the sun was coming up. When I awoke again, it was eventually to discover that I was closer than I knew, both to the darkness and to the answer.

# 32

For the next three days, Geof stayed home from work, barely moving on Tuesday except to pop painkillers, getting gingerly out of bed on Wednesday, and almost back to normal movement by Thursday. He would have gone into the station then, except that he was still terrified of somebody slapping him on his back or grabbing one of his shoulders in a lock grip, as his own police chief was famous for doing when he wanted somebody's full attention. He could picture himself going to his knees if that happened. So we told them he was ill with a flu virus, and I collected his messages for him.

He rested, he healed, we talked and talked.

Among those telephone messages from his office on Monday was a call from Mrs. Ronald Mayer, Sr. I did not pass it on to my husband, although I knew I probably should have. But for that first day I couldn't bear it, not any more contact between him and any of them. On Tuesday, when the same woman called the station and left a similar message for him, I felt honor bound to inform him.

He was as surprised as I was.

"Did she leave her number?"

"The message is, she'll call back."

"Then I won't call her." He yawned, started to stretch, then quickly changed his mind. "I'll play hard to get."

"I would like it better if you played impossible to get."

"Can't do that."

"Can."

"Won't."

"Will you come get this soup, or do I throw it at you?"

On Friday, he went back to work, with a new sheepskin pad against his back on the driver's side of the Jeep and an unlikely story of getting sunburned the day before, a lie meant to discourage anyone who might be so inclined from throwing an arm around his shoulders or giving him a friendly pat. Fortunately, the clouds had broken long enough the day before to make the story just barely possible if not very plausible. He was going to tell them he'd been recuperating from the flu on a chaise longue in the yard, and he'd fallen asleep on his stomach.

"Yeah, right," I said, always the supportive spouse.

"I'm very convincing when I lie," he claimed, a boast to which I should have paid more attention.

When she called the police station again on Friday and learned that Lieutenant Bushfield was there, she asked to speak to him

"I hope you are feeling well," she had the gall to say to him. He said nothing.

"I would like to make an appointment with you," she said, all chilly formality and reserve. And so they set it up for that afternoon. "She doesn't sound like she's in any hurry to see me," he told me when he called home to satisfy my curiosity, "but there's something very set and determined about the way she talks to me. The word *implacable* comes to mind."

"Great," I said, suppressing a shudder. I really hated these people now; Hardy's sermons about vengeance notwithstanding, I wanted them punished for what they did to Geof. Hanging by their thumbs in hell for eternity would not have seemed gratuitous to me at that point. Implacable? Yeah, me, too. "What great news, honey."

He responded by telling me he'd seen an article in the newspaper that morning about a woman in New Hampshire who had choked to death on her own sarcasm.

"The story said they tried CPR, but they couldn't dislodge the snide comments from her throat. Really tragic, huh?"

"You're right," I snapped, "you are a great liar."

Sergeant Meredith—Lee—told me later that she saw Mrs. Ronald Mayer, Sr., enter Geof's office dressed all in white or tones that were nearly that light: a long-sleeved white silk shirtdress with a nubby white silk jacket, pale hose, bone-colored shoes. Lee didn't know what happened next, until she listened to the tape recording of it, because Geof shut the door. But through the glass, Lee watched Geof offer Mrs. Mayer a seat in a steel-gray armless chair. She observed as David's grandmother slowly sat down, crossed her legs at her ankles, folded her hands in her lap, while Geof walked around to the other side of his desk and sat down, facing her with an unreadable expression. Lee told me afterward that it was fascinating, like being deaf and watching a scene in a play unfold and trying to guess only from the faces and the body language of the actors what was going on. She fervently wished she could overhear the dialogue, though, because both players were all too experienced at keeping their faces frozen, their bodies immobile, giving nothing away, no hints or clues to their curious audience.

Outside Geof's office, Lee watched as Mrs. Mayer began to speak, but it was only afterward that any of the rest of us learned from the tape and from his memory what it was they said to each other:

"Lieutenant Bushfield." Her first words sounded formal, even memorized. "I am here to do something very difficult. I hope you will comprehend how difficult it is and that I am convinced that I have to do it. I will not waste your time, but I will get right to the truth. Which is that my son Matthew, my second eldest child, is responsible for the death of Mr. Dennis Clemmons."

(At this point, almost everyone who has heard this interview stops breathing for an instant. Including Geof, he claims, at that moment in his office.)

She seemed to be, as he had intuited, implacable in her need to get the words said. She continued without stopping and, at least at first, without any sign of the deep emotion she had revealed during Geof's first visit to her home.

"Let me be clear: I am saying that Matthew killed the man on purpose, murdered him with malice aforethought, whatever the legal parlance is. I will tell you how this happened and how he did it. On Tuesday evening, two weeks ago, my grandson David went to Matthew's home. David was very angry, and he demanded that Matthew give to him all videotapes of confessions or penances related to Ron and Judy and Dennis. When Matthew asked why, David said it was because he wanted to turn them over to a policeman. We assume he meant you.

"Of course, Matthew refused. David attacked Matthew then, no doubt out of frustration, and Matthew was forced to strike back in self-defense."

For the first time, she paused as if she had run out of script.

Or maybe it was the scene she was replaying in her mind that actually gave her pause: her son hitting her grandson and the implausibility of a huge grown man feeling forced to defend himself against a skinny kid and with sufficient violence to blacken the kid's eye. She took a breath—you can hear it on the tape—and suddenly emotion was seeping into her voice. Geof found himself watching with a rather cold and detached fascination as the elderly woman disintegrated right in front of him. The quality of his mercy, as he coolly observed her, felt decidedly . . . strained. Every time he moved, every twinge of his healing back, reminded him of her family and especially of Matthew, who had wielded the strap.

"You see," she said next, sounding tremulous, old, "Matthew realized that if David brought police attention to his stepfather, eventually you would be bound to find out that it was my sons who exacted that first terrible penance on Dennis."

Geof's voice, efficient, unemotional: "Your boys crippled him?"

285

"When he was released from prison. They took Dennis out to the farm. They beat him until he was . . . permanently injured."

"And Matthew didn't want anyone to know about that . . ."

"Of course, he didn't! It would have been terrible, you would have investigated us, you would have pried into all of our . . . lives."

"And so you're saying he killed Dennis so that . . . ?"

"So that . . . he could never tell you who . . . beat him."

Geof said nothing.

She said, "Matthew was protecting us, you see?"

"The beating. Was that your sons' idea, Mrs. Mayer?"

"No, they only did what their father told them to do. It is their father who decides penances. The boys merely exact them."

"Merely," Geof echoed after a moment. Quickly he added, "Why did they wait until he was out of prison?"

"So it wouldn't appear to be related to Judy's injuries."

Sergeant Meredith says that through the glass she could see Mrs. Mayer begin to cry, but on the tape, all you can hear is a voice that curiously combines qualities of imperiousness and pleading, rather like an empress begging for understanding from her enemies: "Matthew killed Dennis the night that David came to see him."

No response from Geof, just a waiting silence.

"He climbed the ramp that he and his brothers had made, and he sabotaged it as only one of them could do."

With that simple declaration, she sounded finished, her task completed.

"Mrs. Mayer, will you sign a statement to that effect, and will you agree to testify to what you know in court?"

"Yes." It was a whisper, but then in a stronger, more determined-sounding voice, she added, "Yes, I will."

"Does your husband know you came here?"

"Of course. They all know, Lieutenant."

You can't hear Geof's indrawn breath on the tape, but he swears he sucked it in. Would these people, he wondered, never lose their ability to shock him?

"They allowed you to come and tell me this?"

"It is his penance," she whispered.

"What? I didn't hear what you said."

She looked at him out of brimming eyes that he would never forget. He wondered, as he stared into her eyes, if they taped her confessions; he wondered if they beat her, her own sons. He thought of her thin bare back under the delicate silk, but his mind skittered away from the image. She said, "Matthew made his confession of killing one of God's children. That is the one sin for which we do not feel delegated by God either to punish or to forgive. The family decided that his earthly penance must be exacted in the way that Dennis Clemmons paid for the illegal acts he committed."

"By going to prison?"

"Yes."

"But why did they make you the messenger, his own mother?"

"I volunteered," she said, her voice a dying fall.

Geof stared at her and thought, *Penance.*

"Why did you volunteer?" he asked point-blank.

There is the sound of sniffing, then her voice grows stronger, nearly passionate. "I want you to see for yourself that I tell the truth about my sons! If I confess this terrible truth to you about Matthew, then you simply have to believe that I am also telling you the truth about Ron when I tell you that he didn't kill Judy and himself! He didn't, he couldn't, no matter what my husband or anyone else says! My grandson"—she emphasized the word—"is right!"

"I still don't understand why, Mrs. Mayer."

"But you knew him!"

"Not that well, we were just guys passing in the halls."

A lesser woman might have made a bitter crack about how much better Geof had known Judy than he had known Ron, but Mrs. Mayer didn't. Instead, her voice softened again, and a deep sadness crept into it. "Then let me tell you about him."

*Yes,* Geof thought, *tell me about this man who was capable of looking a child in its eyes and striking it while it cried in pain, tell me about this man who could then hug that child as if he loved it. Please do explain that monster to me.*

"Ronnie was the dearest of my children," she began. "Or maybe it only seemed that way to me because he was my first, and he was also my only child for a long time. I suppose as a result, he was more sheltered than my other sons, he stayed a little boy much longer than any of them did . . .

"Do you remember what a sweet boy he was, Lieutenant?"

"He seemed like a nice guy, I guess."

"There was something innocent about Ronnie," she asserted. "He always had a little boy's willingness to take people exactly as they presented themselves to him. Just look at how he accepted Judy! After all the ways she betrayed him!"

"Did he know . . . What did he know about her?"

"That she was a whore? Do you think she would ever confess that to him? Of course not. Any other man would have guessed the truth, but not—" her voice trembled—"not my son. But then, that's what I'm telling you—that's the sweet, accepting person he was. He was . . . susceptible. He was . . . naive. When people were friendly to him, he liked them; if they weren't, he avoided them. He was such a good child, always obedient to his father and to me, and he remained that way, always respectful—" Her voice tightened as if some prick of conscience had prompted a moment's pain. "And that is why I know he could never have done what you think he did, because it would have defied his father, both his earthly father and his Father in Heaven."

Geof thought then of Ginger. Their affair, no matter how brief or superficial, suggested that Ron Mayer—when pressed hard enough by circumstances or by his own unhappiness—could defy the faith of both of those fathers.

"Matthew defied them, didn't he, Mrs. Mayer?"

That made her pause, perhaps even shocked her. But she recovered well enough to say, "Matthew is not Ron. They were different sons entirely."

What Geof did not say in response was, *But they had the same horrifying mother and father.* He found her astonishing, this woman who would sacrifice the freedom, maybe even the life, of one son to try to salvage the memory of the one she loved better.

"Mrs. Mayer, why didn't they live on the cul-de-sac with the rest of you?"

She was silent for a moment, and Geof thought maybe she was trying to recall old memories. Finally she said, "Ron and

Judy were married when they were very young. Matthew was only a junior in high school, and the other boys were even younger. We weren't even thinking then about houses for so many families."

"Why did your family start your own religion?"

"It isn't our religion, it's God's."

"Then I'll put it this way: Why did you feel called to worship God in the way you do?"

"Ours was a family in need of cleansing," she said tightly. "I'm very tired, Lieutenant. What must I do next?"

When she and Geof emerged from his office, Lee Meredith thought that Mrs. Mayer looked a century older than when she'd first gone in.

# 33

 ON A RAINY, COOL FRIDAY MORNING IN SEPTEMBER, Matthew Mayer turned himself in and was arraigned and imprisoned to await sentencing for the first-degree murder of Dennis Clemmons. He came to the courthouse dressed in a white suit. He was accompanied by his mother and father and his brothers, also all in white, and three attorneys. The attorneys didn't wear white. One of them carried the videotape of Matthew's "confession" of his "sins."

Geof and I attended the preliminary hearing.

David Mayer was there, with Damon Montgomery on one side of him and Sheila Montgomery on the other side, at the rear of the courtroom. When we entered through the double doors at the rear and walked past the aisle where they sat, I looked down and saw that they were holding David's hands. The two adults acknowledged us with nods and smiles; David glanced at Geof only once, then looked away.

Geof paused there for a moment, as if he were wondering if

he should say anything, even if it was only hello. The moment disappeared with the turn of David's face away from him, so Geof merely nodded back to the Montgomerys, and we walked on toward the front.

But when it was over, and everyone was standing up, getting ready to leave, David stopped Geof in the aisle to ask him about the investigation into his parents' deaths.

"We can't prove it happened any other way," Geof told him.

The boy's response was "Screw you, cop."

David ran out of the courtroom then, before the grandparents and the uncles had reached the door at the rear. The Montgomerys, mother and son, quickly followed him out. While I hung back, staring at Mrs. Mayer, Geof stepped toward the family of the accused, or, as he thought of them, the accusing family.

"I'm coming after you next," he told the elder Mayers in a clear voice. Then he stared at the sons in turn: "And each of you."

"Don't talk to him," one of the lawyers advised his clients, while the other two attorneys shepherded the Mayer men out the door.

"Like a flock of white sheep," Geof said on our way out.

It took only a few calls to Port Frederick High for us to learn that David returned to school the next week. They made no mention to him of the graffiti, they slid him smoothly back into his classes, they delicately suggested that he visit the school counselor.

His response to them was, essentially, "Screw you, too."

But he stayed in class. We knew, because we checked.

His landlady called to report that David had moved back "home."

I avoided the Amoco station during his shift, but Joe gave me good reports on him when I pulled in at other times during the day. He was showing up, he was catching on to the job, he was, it appeared, getting on with his life.

During that period, Geof got on with what he seemed to believe was his life's work at that time, too—dismantling the Mayer

291

family and Jesus's Carpenters, down to their last tack and nail. With search warrants, he went after their videotapes without success, because the tapes had already disappeared from the shed; with arrest warrants, he went after the adults, attempting to prove they had beaten the children, but without the tapes, it was going to be difficult; with the IRS, he went after their tax-exempt status. He developed infections in his back and had to see a doctor after all. But that pain only seemed to drive him harder for his vengeance.

*Penance* was the password at our house during those days.

He could think of nothing but the Mayers. If he couldn't stop them, he would at least make their lives miserable and expensive for as long as he could stand to concentrate on them. "For David," he said, like a vow.

And me? I found myself thinking mostly of Judy. It felt as if she'd gotten lost in all that had happened. She who started it all had disappeared from the story as if she were too short to be seen among all the tall men who were so loudly and violently mixing it up in every direction. It seemed as if she had vanished, along with the other women of the Mayer family, those invisible sisters-in-law and the grandmother, whose first name I didn't know. She was still Mrs. Mayer to me, until I finally recalled that Damon Montgomery had referred to her as St. Catherine the Martyr.

When I had glimpsed some of the women through the crack in the kitchen curtain at their farm, they hadn't been individuals to me; they had been only figures clothed in white, a group of pale faces with no distinguishing features, the female members of the hive.

It was true, even the other sons in the family were unknown to me as individuals. I wouldn't have recognized Mark or John if I'd passed them on a street, and there was only a slim possibility that I'd recognize Luke from the videotapes I had seen. They, too, seemed to exist only as part of the group, the malevolent organism, that was their family.

But it was the women who puzzled me the most. The women who'd given their children over for penance. If only I could understand even one of them . . .

# CONFESSION

Finally, after stewing about it for a week, I realized that what I really wanted to understand was ... Judy. Easy lay. Pregnant girl. Thief. Snitch. Liar.

A line from William Blake's poetry ran through my mind: *"Little lamb ... who made thee?"*

# 34

ANNABELLE BAKER TOLD ME OVER THE PHONE THAT she still lived in the "little house" where Judy had grown up. She sounded pleased to hear from me a second time and delighted that I had known Judy even a little bit in high school. She seemed grateful that I wanted to pay my condolences to her, and she gave me the impression of being eager for a visitor.

"You just drop by any time," she said warmly. "I was just so busy before—"

"I understand," I assured her.

Over the phone, she sounded more girlish than elderly.

When, on an impulse the next day, I dressed up and drove to her house, I expected to meet a lonely white-haired woman, rouged and lipsticked to look younger.

"Jenny!" she greeted me as if she'd always known me.

The woman who opened the door to the slovenly little house was probably no more than twenty years older than I was, which would have made her only about sixteen when her daughter was born.

"I've got whiskey and I've got beer, honey."

# CONFESSION

My telephone impressions of her went straight to hell.

Rouged, she was; lonely, she wasn't, to judge by the number of people inside her house. She squeezed me into her crowded living room, shouting at me to make herself heard over the blast of jazz music.

"Come on in, it's just a little ol' Tupperware party!"

"Tupperware?" I shouted back at her as I goggled a bit.

"Kinda like that." She giggled.

"I'm sorry!" I yelled at her. "Are you the hostess? I'm interrupting. I could come back another time—"

"Don't be silly!" she screamed in my ear. "Think maybe you could use some nice little storage boxes?" She giggled loudly, as if she'd told a dirty joke. "Stick around! Got a brand new line! You might see something you want to buy!"

I was not dressed for this: There I was in my nice pay-your-respects kind of shirtwaist dress and flat black shoes, with my hair all sweetly curled around my shoulders. And here she was: pink miniskirt, off-the-shoulder gypsy blouse, sling-back heels, and dangling earrings. It was three o'clock on a Tuesday afternoon, and there was definitely a party of some kind going on at Judy's mother's house, but if it was Tupperware, I'd eat my plastic lettuce bowl. I began to feel a little queasy, wondering just what exactly she was selling, like maybe this was one of those sexy lingerie sales parties.

And then I smiled to myself behind her back. I'd almost forgotten: I *like* sexy lingerie.

I followed her trim pink behind through the mob.

"A babe," Geof's old high school friend had called her.

No wonder the neighborhood boys had liked making bicycle deliveries for her as he'd told Geof. Now I began to wonder what they had delivered . . .

Annabelle guided me past a small portable bar where several men and women stood talking, laughing, and pouring drinks.

"Who's this pretty doll?" one of the men asked, eyeing me.

I had an impulse to draw myself up, purse my lips, and demand, "Are you referring to me, sir?"

"This is Jenny," Annabelle said brightly, with a wink for me. "She's an old friend of my daughter's, isn't that nice?"

She took me by my hand to a tiny bedroom with a single bed, a dresser, and a desk, all painted bright pink.

"Remember this, Judy's room?"

"I'm sorry, I was never here, I really didn't know—"

"Ya'll shoo!" She laughed at a smiling man and woman who appeared to want to come into the room and join us. The people at her party were middle-aged and older, frayed around the edges of their clothes and their smiles, a good many of them already very drunk. So far, however, the party seemed to be in the jovial phase. I decided I'd like to get out of there before that changed. Annabelle laughed again and kicked a shapely leg up. "And close the damn door on your way out!"

She sat perkily down on the little bed and patted its cover.

I took the invitation and eased down beside her.

"This is so nice!" She touched my arm. "You're the only one of Judy's old friends to even call me. Can you imagine? And her with all those friends she had in high school! Why we had boys running in and out of this house day and night, it was so much fun!"

The picture of Judy's life was getting clearer to me by the second, coming into focus like a camera lens.

"Really," I said, leaning away from her beer breath.

"I miss my baby girl, I really do," Mrs. Baker confided. "We were never like mother and daughter, we were more like sisters!" She fluffed her strawberry hair. " 'Cause I was so young when I had her, of course. She had her boyfriends and I had mine, and we just told each other *everything*. Well, until she married Ron, that is, and his parents put the kabosh on everything Judy did that was fun." A malicious amusement came into her face. "But I guess they're having fun now, aren't they?"

"Not much," I agreed.

She laughed in a burst of raucous pleasure.

"Sure you don't want a drink, Jenny, honey?"

"Thanks, no. Mrs. Baker—"

"Oh, honey," she drawled, patting me, "I'm not Missus anything, I'm just Annabelle. That's what Judy called me, I wouldn't ever let her call me mom." She made a face. "I'll never look old enough to be anybody's mother, now will I?"

"No." I so wanted to add "ma'am," but I bit my lip instead.

The door opened suddenly, and a man poked his face in. "You comin', Belle? We going to get this thing started or not?"

"Oh, hold your own, Percy," she said, laughing at him. "I'll be there. You don't need me. You can start passing the albums around, Percy, and you know where the order blanks are."

He withdrew, but he left the door ajar, so the little bedroom where we sat was awash in loud music. I could feel the drums vibrating into me, up from the floor, through the mattress, into my hips.

I heard him yell above the party noise, "Annabelle says we can start this without her! Everybody sit down, and I'll show you some pretty little things!"

"Tupperware?" I said to her.

Suddenly Judy's mother's eyes got a guarded look in them, a sly expression, like somebody waiting to see how somebody else would react. "It's a little party for some of my customers, Jenny."

"What do you sell really?"

She licked her lower lip as she gazed appraisingly at me. "Videotapes. Magazines. Personal pleasure equipment. It's what some people might call pornography, Jenny."

I swallowed.

"Honey, all people are sexual beings." She reached over and patted my hand. "Especially children." She began to lightly stroke my forearm with her fingers. I kept my arm very still, although I felt the hairs rise as well as a cringing inside of me. "Why, Jenny, honey, we need to be touched and loved, especially when we're little. Little children just naturally love their sexual feelings and their sexual organs, and they want to express those natural ... uh, feelings. And people who say otherwise, why they've just got dirty minds, don't you think so?"

Carefully, I slid my arm away from her fingers, masking the movement as a need to scratch my shoulder. I disciplined my eyes, my mouth, my body, my voice, to express only a neutral kind of interest.

"You're holding a party to sell child pornography?"

I smiled, or tried to, attempting to look intrigued.

"Oh, no, honey! I'd never do anything to hurt a child! I sell

297

things to *educate* people, how there's really no such thing as pornography, why it's all in the eye of the beholder, isn't it? A picture of a naked child is a beautiful portrait, only a pervert would find anything evil in it! We want to *educate* people to the truth, to *protect* the little children."

"I see what you mean," I said, slowly feeling my way over this strange, upside-down terrain I had walked into. It was hot in her house, and there was a crowd of people just outside the door of the bedroom, and I was bigger than she was, but I felt chilled and frightened in her presence. I wanted my anger to kick in, and soon, to protect me from this vulnerable feeling I was having. I stared at her while she was talking, and I kept thinking, *Judy grew up here, Judy grew up here,* even as her mother was saying, "A really loving parent encourages his child to pleasure himself and to be pleasured, and a photograph of that can be as sweet as a picture of a baby playing with a kitten."

"Oh," I said and swallowed again.

She touched me again. I had to force myself not to flinch. "So you see, we are meeting here as concerned adults. We need to abolish legal penalties against the perfectly decent people who are now being railroaded for their private enjoyment that doesn't hurt *anybody*. We need to legalize all expressions of sexual pleasure and beauty for the sake of our children."

I thought of Judy in the studio of the glamour photographer.

Judy, who was so sexually promiscuous, who married a man whose family would punish her for her sins, over and over, and who used a camera as a tool of their vengeance. She had wept, the photographer said, and she had told him the session brought back early, painful memories. She wished she had never been born, she had said to him. The following week she had sold her business, and she had left two tapes and a pink scrapbook in a box for her son to find.

"Mrs. . . . Annabelle . . . do you remember Dennis Clemmons?"

"Oh, Dennis!" She dismissively waved a hand at me. "Worthless little fucker. Only good for running errands. I've known Dennis forever. He had a crush on Judy practically from the time she was born. I hated it when they got married, but I imagine he thought he'd died and gone to heaven."

"Why'd she marry him?"

"Oh, 'cause he knew, honey."

I took a deep breath. "Knew. What?"

"That David wasn't really Ron's son." She laughed as if that was a good one; hah, what a joke on the Mayer family.

"Was it like blackmail, you mean?"

"Yeah, I guess so, sort of like that. He'd been using it against her for years to get her to tell him which houses to break into and rob. Then he finally got smart and realized he might as well use it to get what he really wanted—her. He always told her he'd hurt Ron or David if she didn't do what he wanted."

"I don't understand how you can sound so calm about—"

"He never would have!" she protested. "I always told her that! Besides, she oughtn't to have felt so ashamed of what she did. I don't believe in shame. I always told her, don't be ashamed! I'm certainly not ashamed of anything I've ever done."

"Geof Bushfield . . ." I started to say.

"Who?" she said. "Oh, yeah, that kid in high school she had a crush on for a while, the one who became a cop? He was a cute, wild thing—I could have gone for him myself. Just a crush, though, that's all he was for Judy. None of those crushes ever lasted, 'cause she was really always crazy about Ron. She'd make these scrapbooks, you know? Crazy girl! I'll swear she had scrapbooks about practically every boy she ever knew."

Annabelle smiled, a parody of parental fondness.

"It was just so cute. She started putting together little albums when she was tiny, maybe only four or five years old. She was just doing it to imitate me and my work! I'd have my pictures, she'd have hers, I'd make my little albums for my customers, and she'd make a little album for herself to play with. So cute!

"She kept 'em up, too, those scrapbooks, a long time after she was all graduated and all that. You know, if she'd see their picture in the paper, she'd get out the old scrapbooks and paste it in. I threw a lot of 'em away when she married Ron, and I threw a whole bunch more away after she died. It was fun, though, going through them one more time, seeing all those cute boys again, like it used to be."

"Do you have a scrapbook of her . . . baby pictures?"

"Sure, I do." And then she finally caught something, maybe in my tone or in my eyes. "You mean *those* kind of pictures? I hope you know I would never do anything immoral to a child, you do understand that, don't you? Especially not to my own baby girl. I only did what she liked. Babies enjoy that kind of attention! And besides." She looked down and examined her fingernails. "They're way too young to remember anything."

"Judy remembered," I said.

"No, she didn't. Not that."

"Yes, she did. Before she died, she told someone."

"I don't believe you!"

Judy's mother flounced off the bed and started to walk out of the room, but I called her back by saying, "Annabelle . . . who was David's father?"

She looked back and laughed at me. "You think it's only crummy people who like pictures of children, don't you? You think it's only people like me and my friends. You think we're slimeballs and that nobody rich or respectable ever does anything like that. Well, you'd be surprised, sweetheart. Dennis used to make my deliveries for me, and Judy would, too, and some of the other kids on their bicycles. It was a real private service, I never even used the mails, so nobody could ever get me in trouble that way." She gave me a challenging glare. "Dennis or those kids could walk right up to the front door of any of my customers with a nice white envelope full of photographs.

"That's how Judy met Ron and got into that gorgeous house the first time. Delivering my pictures to his father. Before he got religious, Ron's dad was one of my best clients. Judy met him first, Ron's father, while she was delivering pictures for me." Her eyes glinted when she smiled. "Is that what you wanted to know?"

She went laughing off to her meeting in progress.

*"Why did you start your . . . religion?"* Geof asked Ron's mother.

*"Our family needed cleansing . . ."* she replied.

I found my way out through a back door, but not before the

man named Percy stopped me, standing between me and fresh air by propping his arm against the screen door, blocking my exit. "This is a private party," he said, staring down at me under lowered eyelids. "It's nobody's business but the people who were invited. Were you invited?"

"Not exactly. I just dropped by."

"What did you see inside?"

"Nothing," I said truthfully.

"That's right," he said, nodding. "That's exactly right. And who are you going to mention to that you didn't see nothin' here?"

"Nobody," I told him.

"That's right, because you have a family, don't you? A nice little suburban wife and mother, like you, I'll bet that's what you are, am I right? Annabelle will know. She knows who you are. And you care about children, I know you do, just like we care about children, and you especially care about your own kids, don't you?"

I nodded.

"That's good. It'll help you to forget us if you remember them."

And with that threat to my nonexistent offspring, he raised his arm high enough to allow me to slip through into the backyard. Once there, I just kept walking to the street, not looking back. I was, indeed, thinking of my family just as he'd advised: of how my own family needed cleansing.

On my way home, I stopped at a pay phone to call a cop I knew on the vice squad, and another on the crimes against children. I invited them to move quickly to sweep some dirt out of Port Frederick.

# 35

THE CHANGE HAD COME, FROM SUMMER TO THE BE-ginning of autumn, from hot to cool, from sultry to crisp, from dry to increasingly wet. It wouldn't be long until we had the furnace going on all the time, snow tires on our cars, smoke in our chimneys, and ice on our windowpanes. Winter was a cozy season at our house, a season of blankets and cuddling, hot chocolate and cinnamon toast served by one of us to the other one late in the evenings.

After I fled from Annabelle Baker's house, I drove home, parked the Miata, went inside the house, and made two more phone calls. Then I moved from room to room, unlocking windows and doors, letting the chill, fresh air into the house.

That accomplished, I went and stood by a living room window, staring out at the leaves trickling down from the trees, watching for Geof to drive up, and longing for another winter just like the ones before.

As I stood there, I thought about how I had quite a bit of experience with betrayal—not to be self-pitying—but never before by him. I felt as if I had been shoved down a well by the hands that I trusted most in the world, the hands in which I would have placed my life for safekeeping. I was looking up from the bottom of the well now, waiting for the one who'd pushed me to appear, hoping he could explain, but knowing there probably was no explanation good enough to excuse him ever.

"What will we do about this monstrous lie of yours?" I murmured to the glass. "David isn't your son. Either the tests lied or you did. Why would they lie? Why did you?"

When I tired of standing and watching, when my own obsessive thought hurt too much, I went looking for Judy's pink scrapbook, because Lee had returned it to us on her last visit. I found it on the dining room table and carried it into the living room with me, where I slipped down onto the same couch where I had sat with Geof when David first stormed into our lives.

I stroked the pink cover. "David didn't lie to us."

Now I viewed the scrapbook as an even more loving gift from Judy to her son than we had ever known: *For David: Take these videotapes and this scrapbook, and jump to the conclusion that this man is your father. In this way, I will divert your attention from the truth, so you'll never look any further* . . .

She had loved her son, and she had underestimated him.

I heard a car's tires crunching on gravel, and I looked up but didn't otherwise move. What could I do, but set the trap and wait? I listened as he put the Jeep into the garage, closed its door. I had left the back door open, so now I heard his feet on our back walk, rustling through leaves, and the sound of the kitchen screen door opening, closing.

"Honey!" I could hear the good mood, the joking in his voice. "Jenny, were you born in a barn? Why did you leave the back door open? Hey, honey! I'm home!" And then a couple of minutes later, "Jenny? Where are you?"

"Geof!" I called.

And then he appeared quickly in the entrance to the living room off the hall. He looked in at me, his expression puzzled and concerned, just as I had felt the day I had stared in at him and David.

"What's the matter, honey?" he asked.

"I never can hide anything from you, can I?" I said, feeling frightened and sad and angry, suddenly so angry! I hadn't meant to do it like this, so bitterly, but the words kept coming out of me. "I only sometimes fool myself into thinking I can. But you can fool me, can't you?"

His mouth opened, but no words came out. He edged further into the room, and the expression in his eyes had changed from concern to wariness.

"I think I know what happened, Geoffrey."

"What happened?" he said carefully.

"To Judy and Ron." I waved at the couch where the boy had sat. "Sit down. Let me tell you about my visit to Judy's mother's house today. I learned that when Judy was a very small child, maybe even a baby, her mother used her for pornographic pictures, which she sold. I think she had a little porno business, a little distribution center, you might say, in her house. It seems to me that abuse alone could be enough to account for Judy's behavior in high school, because children who have been sexually abused tend to act out sexually later in life. I know this, you see, because I have a best friend who's a shrink and who tells me such things."

I never took my eyes off him.

"Before she died, Judy went to that glamour photograph studio to get her picture taken. The photographer said she came apart at the seams, said it brought back terrible old memories, and she wished that she had never been born. I think Judy decided at that moment to kill herself. Right before she died, she acted like a woman who is going to commit suicide: She sold her business, she arranged things for David. I think she took Ron out to the farm that day to tape her confession, and then they went home and she killed herself . . ."

"There was no sign that she handled the gun, Jenny."

"She killed herself," I continued inexorably as if he hadn't even spoken, "by making one more confession to her husband and thereby so enraging and overwhelming him that he killed her, just as she wanted him to do. Her last confession; her final penance. And then, realizing all the truths he didn't want to face, Ron killed himself."

"What confession could be that bad?"

"Oh, you mean besides the fact that she'd starred in pornography when she was a child? Or that she had slept around on him every chance she got when they were younger? Or the fact that she had helped Dennis Clemmons burglarize houses?" I took a breath and then plunged in. "Then how about the one that his son wasn't really his son? How about that one, Geof?"

"Jenny!" he said, looking hurt.

"Yes, how about the truth, which was that the grandfather begat the grandson—"

Geof shot to his feet. "What!"

"The truth is that Ron's father was also David's father. She didn't put that on the tape because she left the tape in the VCR for David to find. I think she told her last secret to her husband, alone, so nobody else would know. That's why she was in the doorway; she was confessing one more thing. One last time."

He didn't say anything; he was clearly too shocked.

"Stay there, please," I said when he started to come toward me. "Why did you lie about it, Geof?"

He found the nearest chair and sank into it. For a long time, he didn't speak, and I was afraid there was nothing he could ever say that would give me a good enough reason to forgive him for this monstrous lie.

"Oh, Jenny, I wanted it to be true," he said.

"Not good enough!" I shot back furiously.

"I don't mean I wanted it to be true for me," Geof said quickly. "I meant for David. Jenny, I couldn't take another father away from him."

"Oh, please!"

"But I was already so deeply involved in his life, I felt as if I couldn't back off!"

I hated this excuse, the sentimentality of it.

"The truth is . . ." Suddenly there was something different in his tone, as if he'd only just discovered an important truth himself. ". . . I thought the truth was that David could never know who his father was. If it wasn't specifically me—and that scrapbook suggested that even Judy thought it was me—then that meant it was just one of the guys . . ."

He sounded desperate to make me understand the un-

understandable. And surprisingly, I was beginning to. A feeling of hope, of warm relief was beginning to flood through me. *Please*, I prayed, *make this good!*

"I was ashamed of us, of all of us, I felt bad for her . . . and for the boy . . . I thought, we were all his father."

I caught my breath, felt tears come to my eyes.

*Good man*, I thought happily. *Oh, you good man!*

"I thought I could redeem us, Jenny, all of us teenage boys, with this one boy we had helped to create. We were father to that boy, all of us men, we're all fathers to all the boys, I guess, or we should be, we could be. I thought . . . I guess I didn't have time to think . . . I just stood there when you and Hardy looked at me and I felt . . . responsible. So I claimed the responsibility. I was willing. I still am."

We sat there for a few moments, with Geof looking over at me now and then, but not pleading with me, not asking my forgiveness, not making any move to influence me. I thought of Hardy and the ever-widening circles of punishment and how somebody had to stop them, sometime, somewhere, by forgiving.

"What are we going to tell David now?" I asked him.

"We? Did I hear the beautiful sound of the word *we?*" He got up from the chair then and started slowly toward me as if afraid that I'd bolt or tell him to. "I don't know what to tell him. Why don't we talk about it?"

"We are still pretty upset," I warned him.

"We know." He slipped onto the couch beside me.

He put his arms around me, and I put mine around him.

"Happy birthday," I murmured, though it had already passed. "Your real gift is outside."

He looked up at the sound we were both hearing: a motorcycle pulling into our driveway. Through the window, we watched David get off the cycle, remove his helmet, and attach it by its straps to the handlebars.

"I called him," I said, "because one way or another, we have to tell him the truth."

"Not all of it!"

"At least the part where you're not his father anymore." I looked up at my husband. "Don't we?"

"Yes. I suppose we'll figure out the rest of it later."

Our doorbell rang.

"He actually came," Geof said, sounding pleased.

"Well, I said it had to do with his parents' deaths."

"That's okay. It does . . ."

"And it doesn't."

We saw the boy stare at our windows as if he could see us watching him. I knew he couldn't, because the light was too low where we stood. But the sunshine was still bright enough outside for both Geof and me to see clearly the open vulnerability on David's face before he had a chance to hide it from us again. I felt suddenly as if I'd given Geof a child for his birthday, after all, because I sensed that in some important internal way, we would never be "just us two" again. We'd never see the last of this boy; we would have to rearrange our molecules to accommodate his powerful presence. For good or ill, in some deep way, he was going to be "ours" from now on.

I knew Geof's heart was large enough to hold him.

But was mine?

"You were going to tell me, weren't you?" I challenged him.

"Of course, I was!"

"Yeah, so you say—"

"I was!" He dared to laugh a little. "I promise."

On our front stoop, David Mayer pushed the doorbell again.

"Well, are we going to let him in?"

Geof kissed the top of my head and said gratefully, "Let's do it together."